THE
OWNER
&
THE
WIFE

A NOVEL

THE
OWNER
&
THE
WIFE

❖ A NOVEL ❖

SARAH ARCURI

SELVATICA
BOOKS

Palm Beach Gardens, Florida

For information about this title or to order books and/or electronic media, contact the publisher:

Selvatica Books
P.O. Box 32841
Palm Beach Gardens, FL 33420

Cover and interior design by The Book Cover Whisperer:
OpenBookDesign.biz

Library of Congress Control Number: 2023936200

979-8-9875613-1-7 Hardcover
979-8-9875613-2-4 Paperback
979-8-9875613-8-6 eBook

Printed in the United States of America

FIRST EDITION

SELVATICA
BOOKS

For my mother, Liz, and my grandmother, Carmela. My greatest encouragers, very best friends, and the two halves of my heart. There is no me without you.

For all the versions of me it took to get me here—thank you for never giving up on us and our dream. We did it!

"Vano è l'amorese non c'è fortuna!"

"Love is in vain if Luck isn't there."

— **GIACOMO PUCCINI, PUCCINI'S *TURANDOT*: LIBRETTO**

"Your soulmate will be the stranger you recognize."

— **R.H. SIN**

"It's always been yours, I cannot find another this heart will beat for."

— **S.L. GRAY**

CHAPTER

ONE

LITTLE ITALY, NEW YORK

The scent of sweet tomatoes and lemon-drenched veal filled the room, wafting above the constant hum of dinner chatter and clanking silverware, the rise and fall of laughter, and faces flushed with the contentment that comes with a good meal shared with people you love. Though breaking bread together is a simple sentiment, the work that went into this show of hospitality was nothing short of grueling. Scarlett Valenti knew this better than anyone.

She was The Owner.

Having owned the place just shy of a quarter century, both Scarlett and her restaurant fell squarely in the category of *legendary*. She could feel the stares like hands on her body as she made her way through the dining room, greeting each patron with a nod, a dazzling smile, a quick word. She doled out her attention as if it were a gift, stealing glances at the family photographs papering the walls. Her son, Emilio, clad in a tiny suit, perched on the marble bar top for his first New Year's Eve celebration; her baby girl, Pia, in her father's arms – both photos taken in this very dining room two decades ago. While Emilio and Pia had yet to join in the family business, unbeknownst to them, they were already involved.

One day, this place would be theirs. Scarlett yearned to have her adult children remain close to her; she blamed this on her Italian genes. Her innate need to cling to the things, and people, she treasured most was precisely the reason why Scarlett worked to keep the doors open, no matter how tough it became.

Tonight almost felt like the old days. She buzzed with the excitement of a busy night – a rarity in recent years. How easily the past wrapped its arms around Scarlett, tricking her into thinking she was twenty-something again, still searching for the set of eyes that made her feel secure yet thrilled all at once. The heart of this place: her husband.

A patron pulled out their cell phone – one of those high-tech types with a camera on the back to which Scarlett had an aversion – and snapped a photo of the artful spread of food, bringing Scarlett back to the present. Her husband was not here, or anywhere. This place was a body with no pulse. He had taken the past with him.

This was all she had left of the man she loved most.

Gold bangles decorated her wrists, all gifts he had given her, each one representing a holiday, a celebration, a moment in time. They jangled, cascading down her arm as she waved to a few regulars despite not being in the mood to socialize. With silky wefts of hair pinned high atop her head in her signature French twist, her trim figure draped in a designer dress, Scarlett oozed the confidence of a movie star. But tonight, her usual display of hospitality was only a mask for her jittering nerves.

"Dirty martini?" Christian, the bartender, asked as Scarlett approached the bar. A bottle of Grey Goose in hand, he already knew the answer.

Scarlett felt a hand on her arm. She turned, expecting a regular saying goodbye, but instead, it was the woman she had been waiting for all night. Lucia Gentile was a highly acclaimed filmmaker famous for creating captivating documentaries uncovering the history of nuanced groups and underground organizations. Lucia's latest venture was a documentary centering on the history and people behind New York's most iconic dining establishments. But for Scarlett, this was not a shot at fame; in Lucia's bright hazel eyes, Scarlett saw her chance to save her failing business. Lucia was nothing but an attractive, five-foot-nine reminder that Scarlett was on the brink of losing everything that mattered to her.

"Lucia. So nice to finally meet you in person." Scarlett flashed a blinding smile and made her eyes turn warm and soft. No matter the concerns plaguing her mind, she could turn on her charm as easily as flicking on a light switch.

She lifted the martini to her lips, careful, as always, not to spill, and took a sip. As the ice-cold drink trickled down the back of her throat, the familiar flavors were like wrapping herself in an old knit blanket. She recognized the redundancy of the drink, always the same few ingredients to create the same blend. But she craved familiarity. Comfort came from knowing what to expect. Once you get accustomed to a taste, why change? Change, frankly, wasn't something Scarlett was particularly good at. Even when it came to something as simple as a cocktail.

Lucia stepped back, taller than Scarlett even in her heels – though it wasn't hard to be – and gave the restaurant a quick survey. "The place looks amazing. Hasn't changed since the last time I came here," Lucia said.

"And when was that?"

"Had to be at least ten years ago."

Scarlett drew in a jagged breath. "Ten years too long."

"You're not kidding. It's so nostalgic. I kind of love that you haven't remodeled the place."

Scarlett refrained from telling Lucia that the reason she had chosen not to paint over the outdated stucco walls or replace the aging artwork was because doing so would be like painting over her past. She couldn't pick and choose which pieces to remember or erase; one swipe, and it was all gone.

"It certainly is part of the charm," Scarlett managed to muster.

"My team should be pulling up any minute now," Lucia said. "Where should I have them set up the lights and camera?"

While outwardly she was a showstopper, Scarlett was private woman by nature, and the thought of divulging the most intimate details of her past made her shudder. Her hands instinctively flew to the Miraculous Medal around her neck. It wasn't too late to come up with an excuse and end this before it began. But when the image of her latest profit and loss statement flashed in her mind – in particular, the six-figure number printed at the bottom in red – she released her religious accoutrement. Scarlett was a woman with secrets she could no longer afford to keep.

"Upstairs," Scarlett said. "I have a big private dining room." She drained her martini in one gulp and set her glass back down on the marble bar top. With her tenure in the restaurant business, her tolerance was unmatched. "Come with me."

Lucia came to a stop before she reached the staircase to examine the photographs on the wall. "Are these your children?"

Scarlett's heels clacked against the marble tiles as she joined Lucia. *The four of us*, she thought. Her heart twisted with pride. "My babies. My Emilio, and my Pia." Then, eyes focused on a family photograph, the deep, familiar ache. "And my husband."

"Beautiful family."

We were. "Thank you."

As they climbed the stairs, Lucia paused, her eyes moving like a camera lens as she scanned the dining room. Scarlett wondered what Lucia saw as she followed her gaze. Maybe Lucia noticed how the ceilings were low and the carpet was matted and how from this vantage point, the chandeliers needed a good dusting. But Scarlett saw something that wasn't visible to the naked eye. What once was.

Before she was the owner. Before she was the wife.

CHAPTER

TWO

Tucked behind the battlement of an L-shaped bar and the rowdy crowd surrounding it, Scarlett reached for her compact mirror and crouched down out of view, though she didn't have a hard time when it came to being invisible. As the lead bartender, Heather, moved around her, Scarlett rushed to apply a heavy coating of a pink Max Factor lipstick, pinched her cheeks with her fingertips, and fluffed her golden hair. Satisfied, she stood and faced the bar crowd, made up almost entirely of men. Though they were focused on the Yankees game flashing on the grainy television, it was Scarlett's job to be more interesting than America's favorite sport.

"Who's ready for another round?" Scarlett called out to her small section. She breathed in, letting the gazes of these strange men fill her up.

When Scarlett was only a girl, her mother had taught her that beauty was a powerful tool. On countless occasions, Scarlett had watched her mother's bright wefts of blonde hair break necks. Swipes of crimson across her lips gave her a certain unattainable allure. Those wispy eyelashes drew people in. Long, lacquered fingernails on hands decorated with bracelets and rings denoted femininity. As far back as she could remember, Scarlett had witnessed beauty in action, and tonight, it was her turn to wield the most powerful weapon in a woman's arsenal.

In her line of work, beauty was not only a tool; it was a currency.

A man slid two empty glasses towards her, glancing her way before turning back to the game. "Two gin and tonics."

She gave the man a smile as she took his empty glasses. While mixing his drink, Scarlett tried to swallow her envy as she watched Heather, a beautiful, all-American, *natural* blonde with bright blue eyes that could appear bubbly and warm with one customer, sultry with the next, interact with their patrons. Heather didn't just know how to use beauty; she had mastered it, as was evident by the large sum of tips she earned each night and the amount of phone numbers written on bar napkins that were left behind. Though Scarlett got a cut of Heather's earnings, it wasn't the money Scarlett was hungry for.

Scarlett longed to be noticed. Though her stage at this corner dive bar in Hell's Kitchen was small, it was a stage nonetheless. She just needed her chance in the spotlight that Heather enjoyed six nights a week, and she knew she would shine.

"Two gin and tonics," Scarlett said as she set the fresh cocktails down.

"One more round over here," another man said, raising his arm to gain Scarlett's attention. He was closer to Scarlett's age and let his gaze linger on her a while longer. Seizing his interest, she expertly opened six bottles of Budweiser. "You taking over Heather's spot?" he asked.

"Just helping out tonight. It's always crazy when the Yankees play."

"You're a hell of a lot more interesting to look at than the Yanks," the man said with a shake of his head. He gestured towards his group of friends. "Have a drink with us."

As Scarlett took a breath, eager to exhale *yes,* her smile deflated at the sight of the one person who could take the wind from her sails: her mother, Lana. At once, all eyes landed on the older, sexier version of Scarlett.

"She can't drink while she's on the clock," Lana said. Though her expression was stone cold as she scolded her daughter with just a glance, within a second, Lana's features turned alluring when she faced the young man who had shown interest in Scarlett. Lana puffed out her chest and gave her best bedroom eyes. "How are you doing?"

When Scarlett took in the way her mother had managed to make the man's cheeks go pink and how he struggled to get the word *good* out, she retreated. Maybe it was better this way. Lana was happiest when she was the center of attention, particularly that of the male species.

Once finished with her meaningless flirtation, Lana found her usual spot at the far end of the bar. "Care to explain?"

"Heather was drowning," Scarlett said, catching peripheral glances of Heather expertly making small talk with her customers while she mixed one of her most popular cocktails – an amaretto sour. "She told me I could help."

"I own this bar. Not Heather. You're not ready to bartend."

"But she needs me."

Lana's eyes moved past Scarlett. "And who is going to wash all those dirty glasses? Hm? Polish them? Restock the bottles?" She found her daughter's dark eyes again. "You're barback, Scar. Fix my drink and get back to work. And wipe off that lipstick. You look ridiculous."

Hot tears stung Scarlett's eyes. She was too hurt to speak. Instead of attempting to change Lana's mind, she busied herself with gathering the necessary ingredients for her mother's drink of choice. The irony was never lost on Scarlett that the very vice that divided the two of them was the one she always fed. As Lana's daughter, Scarlett longed to cut her mother off; as her employee, she couldn't. She began to pour. Ice. Gin. Vermouth. Olive juice. Shaken, not stirred, and strained into a dainty glass until the cloudy liquid reached the tippy top. She stabbed a skewer through three green olives and dropped it into the center of the glass. She slid the martini towards Lana, careful not to spill any of its precious contents.

But before the drink reached Lana, a big, tanned hand landed smack in the middle of the glossy counter. It was Dustin, Lana's latest boyfriend, not that Scarlett was all too sure they were even really a couple. Scarlett didn't understand how her mother always managed to move on so fast when her many relationships came to abrupt endings. She often wondered what Lana's trail of men saw in her. She highly doubted her mother's drinking habit was a calling card. Perhaps it was her mother's beauty, or maybe it was something else entirely. Something intangible – a quality invisible to the naked eye, something her mother and Heather and all the other women whom men fell all over innately had and Scarlett clearly lacked.

Where Lana was loose and carefree, Scarlett was severe and sharp. While Scarlett's blonde locks were artificial, Lana wore her naturally golden mane long and straight as if it were still the seventies. Though Scarlett's father was a Sicilian, she hadn't gotten any of the genes to prove her ancestry, save for her deep brown eyes that served as her shield, and dark brows that gave away her every emotion no matter how hard she tried to conceal them. With origins tracing back to everywhere from Poland, Croatia, and nameless places in between, Lana was a mutt, which meant Scarlett was one, too. Lana found freedom in not belonging to anyone or knowing where she came from, whereas Scarlett felt its shackles. She couldn't rest until she belonged, though it was hard to find belonging when she didn't know where she fit.

Lana ran manicured fingers through her hair as she fixed her gaze on Dustin. He whispered something in Lana's ear that made her lean her head back and giggle. Scarlett's eyes glossed over. Would she ever have this effect on men? Could she someday reduce a man to a mere puddle with the heat of her eyes? She dismissed the thought. Her mother always stole what little attention Scarlett received, and no matter what efforts she made, Scarlett didn't foresee that changing anytime soon.

Keeping her hand firmly planted on the base of the martini glass, Scarlett waited patiently for Dustin to finish sweet-talking her mother like she didn't have a bar full of customers to take care of. Finally, Lana acknowledged her daughter's existence again, though the feeling of being invisible wouldn't leave Scarlett.

"Scar, baby, we're going to get out of here soon." Still wearing a radiant smile from Dustin's sweet nothings, Lana slid a pair of keys towards her only child. "You'll close up, won't you?"

⁓

AFTER THE YANKEES LOST to the Astros, the bar cleared out fast. Scarlett began her closing tasks, clearing dirty glasses and racking clean ones. Gathering paid tabs and stabbing them over the check spindle. Wiping down every conceivable surface, a seemingly unending task. Though one lone man remained at the bar, Heather gathered her things to leave.

"You look tired," Heather said.

"I am." Scarlett ran her hands under the tap, trying to rid herself of the lingering scents of vodka and vermouth.

"I'm sorry about tonight. I didn't think your mother would mind," Heather offered. She peeled some bills off her wad of cash. "Here. There's a little extra in there for you, but don't tell Lana. She's strict about tip outs."

Scarlett gave a meek smile. "It's okay. You tried. But listen, I was watching you tonight. That amaretto sour everyone orders, how do you get the froth on top?"

"I'd love to teach you," Heather said, although, judging from how fast she worked to get her jacket on, Scarlett knew it was simply a pleasantry. "But I have to get home. My mom is watching Ryan, and he refuses to go to sleep unless I tuck him in."

"I get it. That's okay. I'll see you on Monday." After the bell above the door chimed, announcing Heather's departure, Scarlett counted the bills. For her back aches and the dark circles that would hang like half-moons under her eyes in the morning, she'd earned fifty bucks.

"For some reason," the sole customer said to Scarlett, "I don't think that's fair."

Scarlett blinked a few times as bars of a Bryan Adams song filled the smoky air between them. "Which part?"

The man laughed. "The part where you do all the work, and she keeps all the cash."

"I know," Scarlett said with an eye roll. She leaned her forearms on the bar. Finally, someone who understood. "But that's the way things work around here. And it's definitely not fair." Butterflies swarmed her stomach, not because the man was particularly handsome or charming, but because he was looking at her. "I don't think I've ever seen you in here before. I'm Scarlett."

"Ronnie. Good to meet you, Scarlett." He took the last few sips of his drink and reached into his worn leather jacket for his wallet. "What do I owe you?"

Scarlett turned to the counter behind her to find his tab. When she turned back around and set it in front of Ronnie, her eyes fell to the bar napkin that lay between them with a phone number scribbled in black pen. Scarlett's heart began to race as one side of her mouth curved into a smile. "I guess we're exchanging, then?"

"The blonde that was down at the other end of the bar," Ronnie said as he pointed, "you two kind of look alike. She your sister?"

Scarlett didn't need to swivel her head to see where his finger was pointed. No, she knew his gaze was fixed on her mother's permanent seat. Her smile fell. "My mother."

"She looks young."

"She is young."

Ronnie slid the napkin and some cash towards Scarlett. "Give her my number for me, will you?"

Scarlett's body went hot with humiliation as she locked the door behind the stranger, tossed the napkin into the trash, and hung her waist apron on the hook behind the bar. Alone now, realization fell over her shoulders like a gentle snow.

So long as she lived under the shadow of someone who didn't want her to find the spotlight, Scarlett would never be noticed.

CHAPTER

THREE

LITTLE ITALY, NEW YORK
SPRING, 1985

All his life, Enzo Valenti believed he had a sixth sense. When it came to luck, he could feel it in his bones. He knew which horse would win the Kentucky Derby, which number would pop up next on the roulette wheel, whether to bet or fold in a game of poker. But this extra sense extended far past games. Enzo was also lucky in life.

Today, he had bet heavy on the Yankees, more out of his loyalty to his team and city than instinct, but as the whitewall tires of his sparkling white Cadillac De Ville rolled down Mulberry Street, he couldn't ignore the sinking feeling in his gut. The Yankees were playing at home in the Bronx, but he could feel it. They were going to lose.

He was eager to see the game with his own two eyes. As it did on the weekends, Little Italy had a certain energy. Above the packed streets and sidewalks, archways were illuminated in green, white, and red, casting a glow on the people enjoying gelato and cannoli, taking in the charm of the neighborhood. Enzo enjoyed the familiarity of these streets. Countless bakeries and restaurants lined Mulberry, with their managers proudly standing out front, doing their best to convince the many passersby to dine with them. Above the businesses, those who were lucky enough to live in the neighborhood were out on their fire escapes, enjoying the early spring breeze with their boomboxes perched on the metal steps. No matter how the game went, Enzo reveled in the promise of an exciting Saturday night. At his place, his restaurant that bore a neon sign with his last name overhead, every night was exciting. He made it that way.

A few blocks down from his restaurant, Enzo pulled into a lot, careful not to scratch or scuff the car. He took his time getting out, surveying his surroundings as he shrugged on his sport coat and lit a cigarette, letting it dangle from his full lips as he tossed his keys to a parking attendant. As he turned the corner and walked down Mulberry, his gait long and sure, he shook hands with the neighborhood bodega owner and winked at a woman walking by, breaking his neck to give her a good once-over. Around Enzo, there was never a shortage of women.

Valenti's Ristorante lived at the corner of Mulberry and Grand. Spanning three storefronts with a cozy outdoor patio and a grand dining room inside, Valenti's was by far the busiest, buzziest establishment in Little Italy. It was a special place, the kind where everyone wanted to see and be seen. Enzo liked to believe it was all thanks to his charm and warm hospitality, but he had to give credit where credit was due. The culinary magic of his younger brother Francesco had much to do with their success. As long as the two of them remained in their roles, it would stay that way. Enzo would take them to even greater heights, so long as he was the one calling the shots.

As soon as Enzo walked through the double-doored entrance to his restaurant, it was like parting a sea. He was aware that when he entered his place, he filled it with a presence with no effort at all.

"Good to see you, boss." Fausto, the restaurant's maître d', nodded at Enzo as he breezed into the entryway, shifting the gravity the second his Ferragamo loafers hit the carpeted ground.

"My God. Look at this place." Enzo smiled, satisfied at the loud hum of dinner chatter. "It's nuts in here."

"I won't even tell you how many people I had to turn away."

"I need a bigger restaurant." He scanned the dining room. It was packed and the energy was high, both figuratively and quite possibly literally – just the way he liked it.

"Enzo!" Enzo's friend John made his way over to Enzo, grabbing him by the shoulder and steering him towards the bar. "Thought you were gonna skip out on us."

"Come on, you know I wouldn't do that." Enzo followed John and found a spot at the center of the bar crowd, right where he belonged. Though everyone looked his way, he focused his attention on the TV behind the bar. "I want to see the game."

Enzo didn't need to order. The bartender slid him a whiskey neat, his usual drink. As he took his first sip that trickled down his throat with a slight burn, he caught the eyes of a group of women at the end of the marble stretch of the bar. He graced them with a wink as the whiskey warmed his body, enjoying the looks on their faces as they nearly melted.

"You made it just in time," Enzo's friend Michael said to him as he pointed to the TV. "Bottom of the ninth."

"They're gonna lose," Enzo said without taking his eyes off the screen.

"Come on, man. Don't jinx us."

Smalley was up. He was their last shot at winning the game. But Enzo could feel it. His deep brown eyes focused on the screen, but he didn't see Smalley strike out. He saw the money he'd just lost.

"Shit." Michael sighed. "How much did that cost you?"

Enzo drained his glass. "About six grand. What are you gonna do? I'll get 'em next time."

Enzo tried to shrug off his loss, but he was already calculating in his head how he could win the money back. It wasn't that money itself mattered to him. Precisely the opposite. It was the thrill, the adrenaline rush he got from knowing his instincts were right. That was all Enzo was after anyway. Rushes and highs, they were his addiction.

He was a man with, admittedly, many vices – gambling, women, and whiskies neat – and he made no bones about living his life in excess. After all, why did he work so hard if he couldn't enjoy the fruits of his labor? Why shouldn't he savor his success? Coming from nothing but a set of working-class parents back in the ghettos of Naples, his appetite for the finer things in life was insatiable. He liked to indulge. He didn't like to consider the consequences, nor did he need to. When you're on top, you don't have to answer to anyone.

The thing was, Enzo had been on top for so long, he was beginning to look up. Beginning to wonder what else he could chase. *More.* Enzo wanted more of all the things that teetered on the line of being dangerous.

Enzo raised his empty glass to the bartender. "Another."

"Enz, you're late."

Enzo turned around in the plush velvet barstool to find his younger brother, Francesco, standing there. He was dressed in a crisp set of whites that had suffered a few stains over the course of the evening, the true uniform of any chef. They didn't much look like brothers. Where Enzo's features were dark, his hair an even hue of blue-black and his eyes nearly the same color, Francesco was golden. A mop of warm chestnut curls topped his head, and his eyes were the shade of caramel. Though the temperature had not yet hit seventy in Manhattan, his skin was permanently a golden tawny.

"Look at you. Sweating over a gas stove all night and you still look handsome, you son of a bitch," Enzo said. He reached for his brother's shoulder and rocked him back and forth. "Have a drink with me."

Francesco shook his head. "I'm good."

"That means you're drunk already."

"It's Saturday night. I'm drowning back there. The wine helps."

"Hey, Fran," John said, greeting Francesco with a handshake. "Come sit with us."

"Thanks, but I can't."

"Come on, don't disrespect me," John half-joked. John looked to Enzo, his groomed brows furrowed. "He's shy, this kid."

Enzo watched as Francesco's broad shoulders tensed up. Enzo stood. Though he was shorter than Francesco, Enzo loomed larger. "You try doing what he does all night. Then you tell me if you wanna come out here and have a drink at the bar." Enzo jutted out his chin, knocking John off his high horse with his words alone.

"Alright, *calmati, calmati*. Sorry, Fran." John put his palms up as he backed away.

Enzo scanned the bar as he downed some more of his cocktail, his eyes landing on the group of women he had winked at earlier. The women stared straight at the pair of handsome brothers. "I know something else that might help you. Those girls are checking you out," Enzo said with a discreet jerk of his head to the side.

"Please." Francesco rolled his eyes. "I'm sure it's you they're after."

Enzo laughed as he put his hand to his chest. "I'm a 'one woman at a time' kind of guy."

"Yeah, and I dance like Michael Jackson."

"Lighten up, kid, will you? The women want you. Indulge them a little. It's fun, trust me."

"Did you forget you're married?"

"Did you forget how lucky you are not to be? I'm married. That don't make me a saint," Enzo said with a shrug.

"No, it sure doesn't." Francesco put his hands on his hips. "Listen, you hungry?"

"Starved. The Yanks lost. Bring me out some veal, would you?"

"Yeah. How much did you lose?"

"None of your business." Enzo looked away, still mentally cursing himself for his loss.

"I won't judge you."

"You won't because I'm not telling you. Veal. Now."

Francesco tossed his hands up. "You're a pain in the ass, you know that? You gotta pick the one dish that takes the longest to make."

"I'll stop being a pain in your ass when I die," Enzo said with defiance.

"Give me a half hour. It's slammed."

"Take your time, kid. And hey—" Enzo stopped Francesco before he could turn away— "say hi to those girls on your way back to the kitchen. It'll make you feel good."

<hr />

FRANCESCO WANDERED TOWARDS THE kitchen doors. It was where he belonged, just like Enzo belonged among the people. He preferred to be behind the line in the heat of the stoves, enveloped in the intensity of managing eight frying pans and six boilers at one time. Food was his life; cooking, his gift. He regarded both with seriousness. The fast, rushing pace of the kitchen ran through his veins. Francesco wasn't good at small talk like Enzo. In fact, the thought of talking about meaningless subjects with strangers he might never encounter again filled him with a sense of dread. He was a man who felt things deeply, even when he didn't want to.

He considered Enzo's words. Sure, the women would make him feel good. Maybe entertain him for a few minutes. He might even take one home later that night to his apartment two floors above the restaurant.

And then what? After he'd have her, he'd send her home and on her way. She'd come back to the restaurant time and time again, vying for his attention, wanting to do it all over again, hoping it would turn into more. It had happened so many times to Francesco, that vicious cycle, he did his best to avoid it. In theory, he would have liked to have a girlfriend, someone to call after a long night on the line, someone to spend his days with during the slower lulls of the week. But the women always wanted more than he was willing to give. They wanted a future Francesco didn't see in them.

Some time ago, Francesco had wished he could be like the others. Like the gruff men who surrounded him who searched for amusement rather than love. The ones who were entertained by lengthy card games and whose ears perked up at the sounds of crooners rather than swells of operatic bars and vibrato. But he had learned that wishing you were someone else didn't lend itself to becoming someone else. No, Francesco had a need to find beauty in places where others wouldn't dare to look.

Enzo wasn't much better. He was a terrible excuse for a husband. If it weren't for his affairs and his penchant for gambling, Enzo would have been bored and miserable. Perhaps this was the origin of Francesco's aversion to commitment. He didn't want to make an empty promise to be faithful to someone only to spend all his time breaking that vow. So his string of old lovers was as long as the stretch of the West Side Highway. He could hardly walk through downtown without running into an ex. He could have his pick of women as easily as he went to the butcher and picked out cuts of meat. But that wasn't what he wanted. He wouldn't commit to just anyone. He wanted *the one*. The one who could make him feel something other than temporary satisfaction, the one who could take his heart and give it the home he always longed for.

Even still, as he passed by the end of the bar, he gave the girls a smile and a wink. Predictably, they swooned. He leaned against the wall as he asked them how they were enjoying everything and took in the way they gushed over him. He wished he could be like Enzo. He wished he could soak it all in and let their words and awe of him be enough to fill him. But as Francesco looked into their expectant eyes, he felt nothing.

And he felt it deeply.

CHAPTER

FOUR

With her freshly washed hair wrapped in a towel, Scarlett tightened the terrycloth belt of her robe over a pair of mismatched pajamas and turned on the kitchen lights. To drown out the silence, she flipped channels until she reached MTV, where scenes of a Madonna music video lit up the screen. Scarlett hummed along to "Crazy For You" as she poured herself a bowl of sugary cereal – the kind her father had never let her have as a kid, with the tiger on the front – and sat down at the Formica kitchen table. Food was nothing more than a means of survival for her; she took the fastest route possible to fullness without concern for quality.

Scarlett turned her attention to the front door where Lana struggled to remove the key from the knob. She made out Dustin's shape just beyond her mother, though he remained outside. Her mother let out a chorus of girlish laughter as she reluctantly bade Dustin farewell. As Lana approached the kitchen, Scarlett took in her mother's flushed cheeks, wild hair, and the smile that seemed to be permanently fixed on her face.

"Hi," Scarlett said as she chewed her cereal.

Lana jumped, evidently not expecting to find her daughter up so late. "God, you scared me." She opened the fridge and pulled out a beer, opening it with the back of a spoon. From the counter, Lana swiped the banker's bag filled with the night's cash and sank into the chair opposite Scarlett. As she took a sip and set the bottle down with a thud, Lana sifted through the tall stack of green bills. With a smile, she shook her head. "Heather is *good*. Before she came around, the only time we did numbers like this was on New Year's Eve."

Scarlett set her spoon down. "You know, I helped earn some of that. And I would've brought in even more if you would've let me keep bartending."

Lana sighed as she zipped the bag shut. "I told you, Scar. You're not ready."

"You promised me if I worked barback long enough and earned my way up, you'd let me bartend."

"*If* you were ready. But you're not."

"What else do I have to do?"

"God, Scarlett, give it a rest," Lana hissed as she stood. "I come home from a fun night, I want to relax, and you start with this? Listen, you think you can bartend just because you can mix a drink? That's not what it's about."

"Then tell me what it is about."

"I can't. That's just it, Scar. You either get it or you don't, and you don't get it. Heather doesn't bring in this kind of money because she makes good drinks. It's because she knows how to work a man. She can look in their eyes and know what's wrong with them. She gets how to manipulate them. She wears the right amount of makeup to catch their eye, but not too much to turn them off. She can lead a guy on so he'll sit at the bar all night and keep drinking. You don't know how to do any of that."

Scarlett pushed back her chair and stood. "Maybe I would if you would've taught me."

"Look, I don't have time for this. I have a business to run. The minute you and I walk through those doors, I'm not your mother anymore."

"You're not a mother at home, either."

"Oh, poor you," Lana scoffed. "Trust me, if there's anyone who wishes you were more like Heather, it's me."

Scarlett took a deep breath to calm herself. "All I'm saying is, how do you expect me to take over the bar one day if you won't let me bartend?"

"Take over the bar?" Lana removed one of her fingers wrapped around the neck of her beer bottle to point at Scarlett. "You are like your father's people. Emotional. Dramatic. Weak. You'll be like the women in his family. A wife that cooks and cleans and pops out babies like it's nothing. A girl like you—" Lana sat back down— "you're not made to be a boss, baby doll. Instead of worrying about work so much, you should be out trying to find a husband. Would be a better use of your time. You can bleach your hair all you want so you'll look like me, Scar. But you're not like me."

"So I've been wasting my time?" Scarlett searched her mother's cold green eyes. "You lied to me. You said I had a future there. I'm twenty-three years old. I've been working at that disgusting, run-down bar all these years waiting to make something of myself because I'm too scared of what'll happen to you if I leave."

"Scared of what?"

"That you'll drink yourself to death."

Lana laughed and took a long gulp of beer. "If I were going to drink myself to death, I'd have done it by now. Your father is the one who left the bar to me. He must've thought I could handle it."

Scarlett's chest heaved up and down. Though Scarlett had rendered her father almost saint-like after he had passed more than a decade ago, in truth, she burned with resentment. Hadn't he considered that a bar wouldn't be the ideal place of employment for a woman like Lana? Did he have no concern for what would become of his wife and daughter? "I just wish you'd give me a chance," Scarlett said, her voice laced with longing for something her mother could never give her. Lana stumbled around the kitchen, dropping her empty beer bottle in the recycling bin. "You don't think I'm good enough, do you?" Scarlett said, barely audible.

"No, I don't," Lana said with conviction. "And if you're so miserable, then leave. I'm tired of having to explain my decisions to you."

Scarlett felt the sting of her mother's words in her chest. She blinked back the tears that pressed against the back of her eyes. "If you don't think I'm good enough, then maybe I should go work somewhere else."

"Scarlett," Lana said with a smirk, planting her palms on the top of the kitchen table. "I'm your *mother*. If I don't think you're good enough, you think someone else will?"

"I don't know." Scarlett considered the possibilities. Despite her jadedness about certain things, there were other areas of life where Scarlett still held a certain degree of naiveté. Her real-world experience was limited to her interactions at the bar. Perhaps Lana's sheltering of her wasn't done out of protection, but to keep Scarlett from building the skills necessary to break free from the bubble Lana built for them. To keep Scarlett trapped where she could control her. Maybe she would venture out only to discover her mother was right. It was a risk. But if Lana wouldn't give her a chance, she would give herself one. She owed that to herself. "But I guess we'll find out."

⁓

"I DON'T BELIEVE IN *the one*," Scarlett said to her best friend, Helen. Lying on her stomach with her heels kicked up behind her, she flipped through the *Times* while Helen opened her bedroom window, the warm spring breeze causing the curtains to dance.

"Trust me, you will. You'll just *feel* it," Helen said, plunking herself down on her bed next to Scarlett. Though her gaze was fixed on the ceiling, she wore a dreamy expression.

Scarlett arched a brow at Helen. "And what did you *feel* when you went out with Andrew last night?"

"Excited." Helen sat up and crisscrossed her legs. "I mean, he's practically perfect. He's in his last year of law school at Columbia. Graduates in a couple months. His family lives in Chicago – that's where he's from. Oh, and get this, he spends his summers on Cape Cod. The Cape! We're going to be like the Kennedys. And I'm bringing you with me."

"So the Cape Cod summers are really what sealed the deal here?"

"No." Helen laughed. "Do you always have to be so cynical?"

"Yes."

"We clicked. I can't explain it. Haven't you ever, I don't know, connected with someone? And you didn't even know why?" Helen's brows were raised so high, they nearly slipped past her hairline.

"And again, a resounding no." Scarlett's words dripped in sarcasm – a poor attempt to conceal her yearning.

Helen smirked. "What's it like to be you?" She raised her index finger in the air. "Oh wait, I know. Jaded, tired, and sometimes downright miserable."

Scarlett swatted Helen's arm as they fell into laughter. "I hate you."

But the truth was, Scarlett loved Helen, probably more than Helen even knew. Helen was the opposite of Scarlett in every way, and her stability and certainty were what Scarlett appreciated most about her. Helen came from a traditional, Irish-Catholic family with two parents, two brothers, and a dog. They even went to mass every Sunday. She was an academic, graduating *magna cum laude* from Fordham. Though they had little in common on the surface, they had formed their bond in Sister Conti's second grade math class at Our Lady of Pompeii. Even at the tender age of seven, one made up for what the other lacked. Helen had a knack for numbers, whereas Scarlett shined in the arts. Scarlett's cardinal sin was vanity, but every so often, Helen would serve her a slice of humble pie and remind her that intelligence was equal, if not paramount to physical appearance. But like the start of every great friendship, they disliked the same classmates, and from then on, they were a duo.

Scarlett had worried that once high school ended and Helen shipped off to the Bronx for college to study economics, they would lose their way completely. But Helen, always steady, made sure their friendship remained intact with monthly visits and almost daily phone calls. She was the closest thing to family Scarlett had.

Helen was back in the city now, living with her parents. With her education, it had taken Helen all of three days to land a job on Wall Street. Scarlett loved having her best friend back in town. But hearing about Helen's date, Scarlett knew this reunion wouldn't last long. Soon, Helen would be rubbing elbows with the Manhattan elites, with a diamond engagement ring on her hand and a sprawling apartment overlooking all of Tribeca. Scarlett was sure of it.

"Enough criticizing me. Can we get back to what's important?" Scarlett gestured to the *Times*. She had finally reached the classifieds page. "I need to find another job to show Lana I'm serious."

Helen lay next to Scarlett and rested her chin in her palms. "Serious about what exactly?"

"Becoming head bartender and taking over the bar."

"So you think if you get a job somewhere else, Lana will beg you to come back?"

Scarlett stared at Helen, unable to decipher if there was any irony in Helen's words. "I mean, that's what I'm hoping."

"It might be good to work somewhere else for a while. You probably wouldn't even want to go back to work at the bar. Get some other experience. Meet new people, make new friends. Just don't replace me."

Scarlett leaned her head against Helen's fiery red ringlets. "Never."

"You don't want to work somewhere else though, do you?"

Scarlett squirmed under Helen's stare. "I'd love to work somewhere else and figure out who the hell I am without Lana deciding my every move. I worry about her, that's all." Worried that, if she wasn't around to look after her mother, Lana might slip from her grasp completely. And despite it all, underneath the hard veneer she put up, there was still a piece of Scarlett that needed her mother.

"Seriously?" Helen rolled her blue eyes. "That's what you're worried about? She's the mother. Not you."

Scarlett glanced around Helen's bedroom. The décor had changed only once, when Helen had made the transition from middle to high school. A wooden jewelry box and a radio topped her pink vinyl dresser, along with framed photographs of Helen's many family vacations. Though Helen had what few would consider much, she had everything Scarlett ached for. "Only people with real mothers say that."

"It's not your job to take care of her, Scar. It's the other way around."

Scarlett sighed and met Helen's eye again. "Look, I have to try this. Once my mother sees that other places want to hire me, she'll want me back. It'll all be fine."

Though Helen's sympathetic look said she wasn't convinced, she put a supportive hand on Scarlett's shoulder. "I love your delusion."

"I'm optimistic, not delusional."

"I beg to differ," Helen said as they sat up.

"Whatever I am, let's just get me out of Hell's Kitchen, alright?"

"Yeah, we seriously need to do that."

As they scanned over the job listings together, circling ones of interest,

Scarlett's throat constricted at the prospect of starting from scratch. But a warmth enveloped her knowing that, wherever she landed, she'd always have her best friend in her corner.

CHAPTER

FIVE

LITTLE ITALY, NEW YORK

SPRING, 1985

"I can't believe this," Scarlett said with a frustrated sigh. She opened the *Times* again, her fingers black from the ink, and drew yet another *x* through one of the job listings. "Not *one* bar in this city wants to hire me?"

"There's always New Jersey," Helen said seriously, though her lips curved into a smile.

Scarlett's eyes turned to slits. Helen was a relentless tease. "Skid Row sounds more appealing."

"Oh, give me that." Helen reached for the paper and began to scan it. "There have to be some places you missed."

"I read those listings the way you Catholics read the Bible." Scarlett tapped her foot against the concrete.

"Here's one," Helen said, flipping the paper to face Scarlett. "They have the biggest ad on the page. Probably means they pay well."

Scarlett glanced at the ad, featuring a large black-and-white photo of a restaurant with a tall neon sign. "That's a restaurant."

"Restaurants have bars."

"This place looks fancy. They'll never hire me. I don't have that kind of experience."

Helen grabbed Scarlett's arm. "Where's your delusion when you need it?"

"I told you, I'm optimistic, not delusional. I'm also realistic."

"Well right now, I want you to get delusional. We're going to Little Italy."

Clocks weren't necessary in Little Italy. Time was told by bells ringing from the Church of the Most Precious Blood. The Melody of "Salve Regina" swirled through the air, and even though Scarlett wasn't all too religious these days, there were some things Catholic School had ingrained in her so deep, she never forgot them. She hummed along to the ancient hymn as she and Helen walked deeper into the neighborhood.

With the sun shining bright, Mulberry Street was crowded. Street vendors were selling assorted fruits and flowers, tourists admiring the green, white, and red flags billowing in the spring breeze, and groups of fedora-wearing men were convened around a shiny black Cadillac, trailing smoke with their cigars as they talked with their hands. In the distance, sirens wailed, and taxi horns honked, but it all felt a million miles away. Instead, Little Italy was filled with the song of the Italian language and a mandolin being played outside a café nearby. Scarlett and Helen stopped to marvel at the restaurant that bore a tall neon sign that read "Valenti's." The sheer size of it was impressive; the grainy black-and-white photo in the paper did it no justice. It was flashy in a way that said *look at me.*

Though Scarlett tried to fight it, she could feel it right away. There was something about this place. Something exciting.

"I don't know," Scarlett said, backing away from the curb onto the sidewalk, though her gaze remained fixated on the sprawling restaurant.

"We're not leaving until you go in," Helen commanded. "What have you got to lose?"

Scarlett looked down at her blouse and pleated skirt, her very best outfit. She had set her hair earlier that morning and taken her time applying makeup. "Do I look okay?"

"You kidding me? Princess Diana would be jealous."

Scarlett dropped her arms to her side. "Seriously? How am I supposed to believe anything you say?"

"Too much?"

"Way too much."

"Fine. You look beautiful, and I'm not lying. Stand up straight, look confident, and ask if they still have any openings. You got this," Helen said.

Scarlett straightened her posture before striding across the street to the other side of Mulberry. Though she had been plagued with nerves the entire day, now, her body vibrated with intimidation as she clutched the brass door handle and pulled it open. Inside, she was met with the familiar scent of vermouth, soft jazz music, and an unnerving sensation that she was home.

"*Ciao signorina.* May I help you?" A man with the most piercing blue eyes Scarlett had ever seen greeted her from behind a marble host podium. His bright, blond hair was flecked with a few streaks of gray, but his tanned skin was free from any creases. Standing tall with an air of ease and clad in a fitted white jacket, Scarlett figured he was just the person she was in search of.

"Hi. I'm actually here about a job," she started, her voice sounding small. "I saw your ad in the paper. Is that something you can help me with?"

"I'm sorry. We actually filled all the positions already."

Though the day had already been filled with disappointment, she couldn't help her shoulders from falling even further. She turned towards the door. "Well, thanks anyway."

"Hold on."

Scarlett stopped and turned back around to find another man coming into the entryway. At the sight of the raven-haired man clad in a pinstripe suit, her heart hammered against her chest. She had seen thousands of faces in her lifetime and in her line of work, but never one that struck her the way his did. His black hair was slicked away from his face, putting his features on display, and his eyes were so dark, she could barely make out the pupils.

"Who made you the head of Human Resources?" he joked to the blue-eyed host. "What's your name, sweetheart?"

"Scarlett," she said, barely able to get her name out. She wondered where her breath had gone.

"You got any experience, Scarlett?" He rocked back and forth on his heels, a stiff drink and a half-smoked cigar in hand.

"I was a bartender," Scarlett lied, hoping this slight twist on the truth would help land her employment. "At a place in Hell's Kitchen." She took in the rest of him. He wasn't all that tall, but he seemed big, like he was larger than life itself. His loafers were so shiny, she could almost see her reflection in them.

"Well, Fausto was right." He patted the marble podium, referencing the host who had since disappeared into the dining room. Not that Scarlett noticed. She didn't notice anything except for this man. It was as if there were a spotlight on him, like she couldn't look away. "I can't make you a bartender, but we still need bussers."

"What's the pay?"

"Six bucks an hour, plus twenty-five percent of the pool tips. That something you'd be interested in?"

Scarlett tried to calculate the pay in her head, but no numbers would come. She knew it was her turn to speak. It was her turn to either accept a job that seemed to be a regression rather than a promotion, or to politely decline it. But she couldn't find the words. Her polyester blouse felt as thick and hot as wool. Scarlett watched as he took a sip of whiskey, the way his jaw clenched as he swallowed it. She wasn't thinking clearly. She wasn't concerned with how she could use this job offer to leverage a promotion at the bar, or how this place might open a whole new world for herself. All she could think about was how she might like to run her fingers along his angular jawline and kiss his full lips that glistened with traces of whiskey. When his dark eyes locked with hers, she wanted to hide. The way he was looking at her, it was as if he could see all of Scarlett, down to her very thoughts.

"Yeah. I'd be interested in that."

"And you're free on nights and weekends? We're never not busy."

"I can be here whenever you need me." Scarlett rolled her shoulders back, becoming surer of her decision with each passing second.

The man scanned her up and down. "Alright. If you don't have any-where to be, Fausto can start training you today."

Scarlett exhaled into a smile. At once, the air felt energetic. The sun peeking through the front windows seemed to brighten. She had her *yes*. "I don't have anywhere to be."

"Good. Fausto," the man yelled over his shoulder, summoning the host to the entryway. "Start training her, would you?"

"Absolutely." Fausto flashed a warm smile in Scarlett's direction.

The dark-haired man had already turned back towards the bar, but Scarlett's eyes followed him. She realized she didn't even get his name.

"Wait," she called out. "What's your name?"

He turned around on his heel, his eyes sparkling as he looked at her. "Enzo." His lips parted, revealing a dazzling, bright smile that knocked the wind out of her. "I'm the owner."

"LET'S PUT THAT IN here and then we'll get started," Fausto said. He took Scarlett's purse off her shoulder and led her over to the coat closet. Through the window, Scarlett tried to catch a glimpse of the street to look for Helen, but she didn't find her. Later, she would call her and provide every detail. But for now, Scarlett wanted to discover every inch of Valenti's. "This is the coat closet, but it's also the junk drawer of the restaurant. All the odds and ends are in here."

Scarlett studied the contents of the closet. Old coats that were never reclaimed from the winter months, a silver boom box, orange traffic cones, and a poster of an old Sophia Loren movie all lived in this little space.

"What's with the pencil sharpener?" Scarlett twirled the handle of the old-school device attached to the wall.

"It came with the place and Enzo refuses to take it down. Plus, the hosts use pencils for the reservation books, you know, on the rare occasion someone cancels." Fausto flicked the light off and they were onto the next. "Now, the bar." Fausto led the way with Scarlett trailing closely behind him, matching his fast pace of a true New Yorker.

The bar was a far cry from her mother's corner dive. The top of it was a long stretch of onyx lined with black velvet barstools. Everything about it was rich and luxurious, like only the most beautiful people in New York ate and drank there. Though it was empty at that odd four o'clock hour when nearly every restaurant felt a lull, she could clearly picture the bar at night, packed with people dressed in expensive, glamorous clothes, chatting about important topics while the dim lights glistened off the bar top like a Broadway marquis.

"This is the famous Valenti's bar." Fausto slapped the marble. "It's the hottest place south of 38th Street. Anyone who's anyone will be found here, especially on the weekends. Now onto the kitchen. Back of house. As a busser, you'll be back here a lot."

They reached a pair of stainless-steel doors, each with a circular window and scuff marks covering the bottom no doubt from being kicked open too many times. But before they entered, Fausto stopped and faced Scarlett.

"Scarlett," he lowered his voice, "think of the kitchen like a church. Only speak when you're spoken to, and always remain quiet. And when in doubt, just say *chef. Tu capisci?*"

Scarlett wasn't sure she understood exactly what he meant, but nonetheless, she followed him into the kitchen. Her senses went into overdrive. The lights were bright, and the kitchen was bustling, gleaming. Gas stoves were ablaze as sous chefs in white jackets chopped, sautéed, and stirred. Identical stainless-steel frying pans lined the span of the stove tops, hanging from the ceiling. She took in the sounds of clinking plates and silverware dropping into the wash pit. A half-empty bottle of Pinot Grigio sat on the counter, still chilled.

"Now, this is the pickup station," Fausto explained. He started showing Scarlett the innermost workings of the kitchen. "Here are the trays, right underneath here. When an order is ready, chef rings the bell, puts the dishes in the window, and you pull a tray. Line up the plates and make sure they match the pink ticket. Whoever's on expo will help you with this. And don't worry, we'll practice."

Though Fausto was speaking English, the new restaurant terms felt like a foreign language. She didn't know what an *expo* was or what he meant by *window,* but she did her best to infer their meanings by Fausto's hand motions. But Scarlett always had a hard time concealing her emotions.

"Am I going too fast?" Fausto asked, reading her confused expression. "If I am, you can tell me. I can take it. I'm a New Yorker."

"So am I," Scarlett said with a proud smile. "There's no such thing as too fast."

CHAPTER

SIX

Francesco was well versed in the area of nursing hangovers. There were two cures: sleep it off, or keep drinking. Today, he opted for the latter. With over two hundred covers on the books, reveling in slumber wasn't an option. So, there he was on a Thursday afternoon, half-deep into a bottle of Pinot Grigio. He stopped by the pickup station and took a swig straight from the bottle. The crisp, dry notes invigorated him, reviving his senses. But it wasn't only the wine that snapped him out of his trance. As soon as he caught sight of the pretty blonde girl, his senses were heightened. Though her dark eyes lent her a veil of mystery, as she moved about the kitchen with tense shoulders and hands clasped together, she wore an earnest expression that made him want to help her. She looked like she couldn't quite make sense of everything going on around her.

He watched her through the window, the way her eyes followed Fausto's every move, the way her brows furrowed in concentration. The way she tried hard. Francesco left his post at the stove and went around to the service side of the line.

"Don't tell me they put you in charge of training," Francesco said to Fausto as he took another swig of wine.

"Hey, your brother told me to." Fausto put his hands up in defense. "Scarlett, this is Francesco Valenti, Enzo's brother. Co-owner and head chef."

"Scarlett," Francesco said, testing out the way it felt to say it. The way the wine and her name mingled on his lips him smile. "Welcome to the family."

"Hello, chef," Scarlett said. She looked scared to even greet him.

Francesco laughed as a curl flopped into his eyes. He swatted it away. "You can call me Francesco."

"Oh." Scarlett's cheeks flushed the color of the San Marzano tomatoes Francesco had simmering on the stove. "Sorry."

"He seems nice right now, doesn't he? Don't go near him on a Saturday night," Fausto half-joked. Fausto and Francesco shared a laugh, and after a beat, Scarlett joined in too.

"Come on, am I that bad?" Francesco put a hand on his hip and leaned against the stainless-steel counter.

"Why don't we let Scarlett be the judge?" Fausto turned to Scarlett.

Scarlett shook her head. "I'm here to work, not get on the boss's bad side."

Francesco's chest tightened at the way her smile seeped into her eyes and how her nose scrunched up on the sides. There was something familiar about her. It was like he had seen her before. Known her before. Though she was a stranger, he had a burgeoning sense that this was one of those serendipitous moments when one soul recognized another.

But he was positive that if he had crossed paths with her, he would have remembered. She didn't look like any of his exes; she didn't feel like any of them either. He wanted to talk to her, but he didn't want to make her more nervous than she already was.

"Busser?" Francesco asked and Scarlett nodded. "Good. Everybody should start out like that, so you know how to do everything by the time you work your way up. Fausto over here walked in here like he owned the place, and now he thinks we can't function without him." Francesco winked at Fausto before letting his eyes fall back to Scarlett. "He's the best. You do everything he says, you'll be the best too."

"Listen to you, buttering me up," Fausto teased.

"Thanks for the advice," Scarlett said. Francesco watched as her eyes fell to the bottle of Pinot Grigio he was holding. "It was nice to meet you. I'm sure I'll see you around."

"I'll be seeing you," Francesco said, surprised at the sudden rise in his heart rate. As he watched Fausto and Scarlett exit the kitchen, he finally caught his breath.

"What's up?" Enzo waltzed into the kitchen, craning his neck to get one last look at Scarlett before she was fully out of view.

"Just met the new girl," Francesco said, shaking himself out of his trance.

"She's cute, isn't she?"

Francesco glanced down at his brother. "Is that why you hired her?"

"Mm hmm." Enzo smiled as he took a piece of semolina bread from the counter and popped it into his mouth.

"You're shameless."

"Hey, she did have experience. And like I said, she's hot."

"You said she's cute, not hot."

"Cute, hot, what's the difference?"

"She seems nice. Which is exactly why you should stay away from her."

"If she's nice, she won't want anything to do with me. But that won't stop me from trying."

Francesco tossed a bar rag over his shoulder. "Are there any women left in this town that you don't want to sleep with?"

"Sure." Enzo reached for Francesco's bottle of wine and took a few long gulps. "Claudia, for starters."

"You're sick in the head, you know that? Claudia's your *wife*. You need help."

"One day, you'll be just like me, kid. Then you'll understand."

"Look, just try to cool it, okay? Cheating is one thing. Cheating with a member of the staff is another."

Enzo looked like he wanted to slap Francesco. "You want a go at her?"

"What? No." Francesco swatted the air. "I'm just looking out for you."

"Drink your wine and cook. Leave the women to me."

And as he usually did, Francesco listened to his brother. He figured by the time he got to talk to Scarlett again, she would already be halfway in love with Enzo anyway. Once Enzo put his mind to something, he always won. That was just the way it went.

SEVEN

LITTLE ITALY, NEW YORK

SPRING, 1985

"Bowls are not your friend. Bowls are the enemy. Bowls want you to break plates and drop things, and they want to make your life miserable. Remember this," Fausto said with the same level of seriousness as if he were preparing soldiers for battle. He paced in front of a large round table scattered with various-sized plates, bowls, glassware, and flatware, one hand behind his back, the other clutching a bowl.

"What the hell are you talking about?" Scarlett giggled.

"Trust me, it will all make sense in no time. Now, I heard you had some experience. So go on. Show me how you'd clear this setting."

Fausto stepped aside, giving way for Scarlett to survey the mess of dishes on the table. She scanned it over, plotting her next move. On a nearby table, she spotted a tray and reached for it. She was reserved, somewhat hesitant as she approached the table; her so-called "experience" hadn't prepared her for such a task. Fausto watched her closely, but his eyes and expression held no judgement. Scarlett began clearing, stacking up plate after plate, careful when placing the bowl on top, and she made a small pile of silverware next to the dishes.

"How's this?" She looked to Fausto for his approval but all she saw was a stifled laugh.

"Great, if you were working at a diner in Hoboken."

"Tell me how you really feel."

"I should've warned you sooner. I can be a bit blunt."

"Can be?"

"I know, I know. Now listen, this is *fine* dining. I want you to forget everything you know and remember everything I teach you." His light-heartedness was gone, his work mode back in full force. "How many people do you think it takes to clear this table?"

Scarlett surveyed the table surrounded by six chairs. "I have no idea. Four?"

"One. One really good busser."

"How?" Scarlett asked with hands on her hips as she tried to conjure up a plan of action.

"I'll teach you."

Learning this set of skills felt like a big undertaking, and Scarlett remembered how teaching had been a burden on Heather. She didn't want to have the same effect on Fausto. "Maybe I can learn how to do this on my own. I don't want you to take all this time to teach me if you're busy."

"We do things a certain way here, and if you're going to stick around, my time is a worthy investment."

Though the man was a mere stranger, Scarlett had an immediate appreciation for his kindness. For his willingness to see her as something other than a waste of time. "Alright, then. Teach me."

"Now, you might think it's best to go for the biggest plate first, but that's wrong. *Allora*, salad plates first." Fausto demonstrated the proper way to clear a place setting, contorting his fingers into a grip Scarlett had never seen before. "This is the proper grip, the tri-pod grip. Three fingers underneath the plate, resting on the ridge, and your pinky and thumb on the edges. No matter how hot the plate is, if you use this grip, you won't burn yourself. Then, place the entrée plate on your forearm like so. Ready to try it?"

Scarlett picked up an entrée plate and rested it on her forearm. It wobbled left and right until Fausto stabilized it.

"I know it feels awkward, but this is going to become second nature. Now, with your free arm, pick up another entrée plate," Fausto instructed her.

She remained quiet, her concentration sharp as she layered another plate on top of the first.

"Great. Now place the silverware on your salad plate, horizontally."

Scarlett followed his every instruction as beads of sweat formed on her forehead. Her arms shook, but adrenaline gave her strength to keep going. "I think that's all I can carry, Fausto," she said after a while.

He relieved her by taking the stack of dishes off her arm that was indented with red marks. "This job is more about mental strength than physical," he said as he scattered the dishes and flatware all over the table again. "Unused muscles, that's all it is. This is the easy stuff. Wait until I teach you how to carry a tray. Let's keep practicing this until you get more comfortable."

Like an athlete preparing for the Olympics, they trained. Over and over again, going through the routine. Her arms and fingers were decorated with dents and lines, her skin red from the plates placed on top of them, but despite her imbalance, her insecurities about not being up for the job began to melt away. She messed up; she got it right. They kept going until she started to get the hang of it. It felt like nothing else existed outside of this moment, outside of this restaurant. The task in front of her was all she could think about and for that, she loved the job already.

Enzo took a seat nearby, his intense eyes following her every move. As she felt his stare on her, her heart began to pound again, though she didn't understand why. Perhaps because he was her boss and she wanted to impress him; perhaps it was due to the fact that he was quite literally the most handsome man she had ever seen outside of a silver screen. She worked quicker, harder as the two men judged her progress.

"You're getting it," Fausto cheered her on. "Now, don't forget the bowl."

Her limbs shook as she leaned down, her eyes becoming mere slits as she reached for the bowl. And then, it was game over. The plates slid off her arm in one sweeping motion and the flatware crashed to the ground. Forks and knives bounced up and down as if they were alive. The nearby waitstaff and the few patrons in her line of vision turned to see what the commotion was as she felt her cheeks flush the color of her name.

"Oh my God." She jumped back in horror. "I'm so sorry."

"See what I mean?" Fausto held up the bowl. "The enemy."

Scarlett scowled at the bowl, mentally cursing the piece of tableware as she retrieved pieces of a broken bread plate and as many forks and knives as she could.

"Alright." Enzo joined the training chaos, bending down to retrieve a stray butterknife on his way over. "That's enough for one day. I think it's time for a drink. What do you say?"

"Couldn't agree more, boss," Fausto said with a wink.

"Not you, *cucuzza*. You're still on the clock." Enzo punched Fausto in the shoulder. When he turned to Scarlett and looked into her eyes, all traces of sarcasm were gone. "Come with me."

She didn't know the man nor where they were going, but she understood one thing for certain. Enzo? She would follow him anywhere.

CHAPTER

EIGHT

Enzo took his time as he shrugged off his sport coat, draped it over the back of his bar stool, rolled up the sleeves of his button-down revealing his Rolex and a gold chain link bracelet, and settled into the seat next to Scarlett. With her back as stiff as a board and uncertainty written on her face, Enzo fished out a lighter and a pack of cigarettes from his jacket.

"You smoke?" he asked.

"Yeah."

While he lit her cigarette, her eyes darted around the room. "You alright?"

Finally, Scarlett's face relaxed. "Sorry. It's just, at my old job, I never actually *sat down* at the bar for a drink."

Enzo handed her the cigarette. "We do things differently around here. I like to get to know everybody that works for me. We're like a family, you know?"

"A family," she repeated. She held up her cigarette before taking a drag. "That's nice."

Enzo turned to Antonio, the bartender, and ordered two glasses of Chianti. "Antonio, meet Scarlett." Enzo paused and looked at Scarlett. "Sorry, I didn't get your last name earlier."

"Ciccone," she told him.

His eyes lit up. "You're Italian."

"Sicilian." She drew on her cigarette and exhaled a cloud of smoke. "But only half."

"Half is better than none," Enzo said. "You're from Hell's Kitchen?"

"Terrible place to call home, isn't it?"

Enzo laughed. "It is." He took hold of one of the two glasses of wine Antonio set in front of them. When they clinked glasses, he adjusted in his chair to get comfortable. "So, Scarlett. Beautiful, half-Sicilian girl from Hell's Kitchen. What else do I need to know about you?"

"I don't know. I'm not that interesting."

Enzo tilted his head as he leaned in, resting his elbows on his thighs. "I'll help you out. I'll ask the questions. How old are you again?"

"Twenty-three."

"And what's a twenty-something like you doing in this city? You in between jobs or something?"

"What do you mean?"

"I mean, what are you doing working here? Nobody's in this business because they want to be. People end up here because they're shit at everything else. Or they work here before they do something else. It's a man's business. For most girls, this kind of work is temporary."

Scarlett set her glass down on the bar and rested her hands in her lap. "I guess I'm not most girls, then. I like hospitality."

"That's because you don't know how tough it is," Enzo said, like it was a dare.

"I don't look tough to you?"

Enzo waved his index finger at her. "You know what I think it is? I think you like a challenge."

"I think *you* like a challenge," she countered.

Out of quick comebacks, Enzo let her have this one. His eyes wrinkled at the sides as he laughed, and he felt a pang of satisfaction when she did the same. Chemistry was a subject Enzo was an expert in, attraction a force he knew how to wield, but even he, always with the upper hand, felt unsteady. He had met her just hours ago, this pretty young stranger, and yet he felt connected to her. His gaze fixated on her as if nothing else around them existed.

"You know what I did before this?"

Scarlett leaned in, her dark eyes finding light that lent them a warmth Enzo hadn't noticed earlier. "Tell me."

"I was a builder in Naples," he said, taking a long sip of wine before setting it down again. "We lived by the water, but fishing wasn't my thing. Too fuckin' smelly. So I built. I worked with my hands. And let me tell you, I hated it. But I knew there was a whole world out there. I knew I had to get out of Naples and be something. I saved every dime, and as soon as I was old enough, I left home, and I came here, right here to this neighborhood. And I never looked back."

"Why would you? There's no place better than this city."

"You know, everybody is so in love with this city. They think it's like magic or something. But you know what I think it really is? I think people like who New York makes them. Everybody wants to come to

New York to be something, be somebody. A singer, an actor, a chef. This is the one place everybody comes to chase something." He took a drag on his cigarette, his cheeks going concave.

Scarlett looked at him in a way that was neither judgmental nor flirtatious, but rather in a way that suggested she could see right through his shell and into his heart. "What are you chasing?"

He paused, his eyes searching her face. "Success."

She looked around at the grand restaurant they were sitting in. "You don't call this success?"

"There are different versions of it. Personal success. Money. Notoriety. What makes me happy might not make you happy. It's different for everybody. Me? I want more. But you? No." He shook his head and pointed at her with his cigarette. "A woman like you shouldn't get sucked into this thing. Once you're in, you can't get out."

"What should a woman like me do, then?"

"Take this city by the horns. Break a few hearts before you fall in love and make some man the luckiest guy this town's ever seen."

At the mention of love, she stiffened. "I don't want to fall in love," she said, though her intonation suggested it was a lie.

"Oh? And why is that?"

"Love does terrible things to people." This sounded true.

With a smile, Enzo hung his head, considering maybe he had her pegged all wrong. Maybe she wasn't just a pretty face like all the other girls he met who showered him with praise and yessed him to death. He was reeled in by the way she wasn't afraid to speak her mind. To scratch deeper than the surface. He had a growing sense that Scarlett's greatest desires weren't diamonds and a fat bank account. No, she was a woman who wanted something else, and he wanted to find out what that something else was. She had a roughness about her, yes. Perhaps a bit jaded, though she still had room for hope that her cynicism would be proven wrong. Enzo knew women better than he knew a deck of cards. He knew she wouldn't be easy, but that only made him want her more. To have her. To know all the layers to her. Maybe she would even be the type to drive him crazy and make him chase her, but wouldn't that be all the more thrilling? Enzo never backed away from a challenge. He thrived on them. Sought them out. The bigger the challenge, the bigger the high.

Confusion resting between her brows, she blinked a few times. "What?"

"You're already more interesting than you think."

Scarlett's smile fell, and Enzo attributed it to the fact that maybe she felt it too. She was beautiful, but Enzo knew she had no idea. She wasn't trying to capture his attention with flashy makeup or by pursing her full lips, which only made her more alluring. But Enzo could feel something else, too. He had women around him all the time, but what existed between him and Scarlett was something he hadn't felt in years. Not since he was a young man off the coast of Naples who had been struck by the lightning bolt of first love, only to trade that love for the promise of a better life in New York. A chemistry so tangible he felt like he could reach out and take hold of it with his own two hands.

Enzo caught sight of Francesco out of the corner of his eye, and all at once, their moment was over. Francesco held a bowl of pasta that billowed with steam.

"Fran," Enzo jutted his chin out towards his brother, "what's up?"

"Thought Scarlett might like to try the food," Francesco said as he placed a bowl of *cacio e pepe* in front of Scarlett.

"Oh, wow." Scarlett came to. "Thank you. That's so sweet."

Enzo and Francesco watched her as she twirled her fork in the creamy spaghetti decorated with black pepper and Pecorino Romano and took a bite, then another, and another. She closed her eyes, enjoying the blend of flavors Francesco had created. A grin of satisfaction took over Francesco's face.

"Oh my *God*," Scarlett moaned as her eyes rolled back into her head. "This is amazing! I've never had food like this in my life."

"I'm glad you like it," Francesco beamed, clearly proud of himself.

Enzo had to stop himself short from smacking his brother upside the head. If he hadn't made it clear to his younger brother that he had dibs on Scarlett earlier, he would have to make it known another way. Enzo put a firm grip on Francesco's shoulder and squeezed it. "How you doing kid? You good? Need a drink?"

"I'm good, I'm good. Going to finish up. I'll be back in a bit," Francesco said.

"Do me a favor. Relax, will you?"

"Thank you again," Scarlett said with a smile before Francesco was out of earshot.

Enzo's eyes found Scarlett once again. They wouldn't leave her for the rest of the night.

"You like working with your brother?" Scarlett asked.

"I'd die for that kid, you know that? He's a pain in my ass sometimes, but I love him. What about you?" Enzo leaned in once again and she did too, as if pulled together by magnetic force. "You got anybody you'd die for?"

"Nope." She drained the last of her wine and set the glass down with force. "Never have."

As it always did, his sixth sense went off. He could feel it, in his bones, in his gut, in his heart. "Someday, you will."

CHAPTER

NINE

S carlett's body thrummed with the satisfying ache of the day's work and the slight wooziness of drinking too much wine. Her forearms tingled with soreness as she launched her messenger bag overhead and across her shoulder. After she thanked Francesco for dinner and Fausto for the training masterclass, she found herself on Mulberry again, except tonight, everything looked and felt different. It was late and the air had a chill to it. Though her eyes were heavy with fatigue, she lit up when she found Enzo outside, pacing the stretch of windows as he puffed on a cigarette.

"Thank you. For everything," she offered.

"You're welcome." Enzo held up a cigarette. "You want one?"

"No, I should be going." In all honesty, all Scarlett wanted to do was go home and digest the day. Landing a new job was one thing, but the evening spent with Enzo was another. He had made it sound like this welcoming ritual was his ordinary practice, but still, Scarlett couldn't help but appreciate the evening he had shown her. As for her attraction to him, she attributed it to the fact that he was, objectively speaking, as charming as a movie star. Which gave her even more of a thrill that a man like Enzo had not only noticed her, but paid attention to her. Listened to her when she spoke. *Looked* at her in a way that made her feel like she was the only woman who existed. She assumed a man of his stature received this kind of reaction from every woman he crossed paths with, but then again, Scarlett had been wrong before.

Enzo looked up and down Mulberry. "I'll get you a cab."

"That's okay. I'll catch the train over on Spring Street."

"The hell you will."

"Excuse me?"

Enzo dropped his cigarette to the ground and put it out with the sole of his loafer. "Better yet, I'll drive you."

"I'm okay, really."

Enzo shot his arm out of his sport coat and read his watch. "When's the last time you took the train alone at eleven-thirty at night?"

Scarlett swallowed. "I can't recall."

"Exactly." Enzo walked in the opposite direction. Without turning around, he called after her. "You coming, or not?"

As if an automatic response, Scarlett put one foot in front of the other, quickening her pace until they were walking side by side. He lit another cigarette before they reached an outdoor parking lot. After the attendant tossed him his keys, Enzo unlocked the car and held the door open for Scarlett. "Get in."

She slid into the buttery red leather passenger seat of his Cadillac. It was roomy and smelled just like he did – delicious, like warm citrus and moody musk. Once in the driver's seat, Enzo fired up the engine and took off down Mulberry in one swift motion.

In the shadow of the darkness, she studied him. His profile was like a painting. His nose sharp and straight, his jaw strong and angular, his eyes the shape of almonds. Every move he made was intense, intentional, like the way he drew on his cigarettes as though for dear life. When they came to a red light, he popped in a cassette tape and Italian music filled the car. He sang in unison to the Italian lyrics and his voice was as smooth as olive oil.

"You know any Italian?" he asked over the music.

"A few of the bad words. None of the good ones."

"I have to teach you," he said, glancing over at her before turning his eyes back to the road.

She caught a glimmer of the gold chain dangling around his neck and the mound of charms at the base of it. Before she could think through what she was doing or stop herself from moving towards him, she leaned over and took hold of the necklace. When her skin brushed his and their eyes met, she felt a rush through her veins.

"What are all of these?" she asked.

"The saints. I got all the good ones on here. Michael, Joseph, and Anthony. Anthony's everybody's favorite. Then this…" he reached underneath to reveal another more delicate, thin chain, with a gold charm resembling a pepper. "This is *il corno*. The Italian horn. Wards off the bad luck – the *malocchio*."

"You believe in that stuff?"

"Not really, but I'm supposed to wear this shit. You know me, I do as I'm told. I follow the rules."

"Why do I think that's complete bullshit?" Though the instant connection she felt with Enzo only seemed to be growing, she fell back into her seat and her eyes went wide. "Sorry. You're my boss. I shouldn't be talking to you like that."

Enzo's face danced with amusement. "You can talk to me any way you like, alright?" His eyes found the road ahead again. "You live alone?"

"With my mother."

"And what does she do?"

"She owns the bar where I used to work."

Surprise washed over Enzo's face. "Breaking free from the family business?"

"I guess that's what you'd call it."

"Can't say I haven't thought about doing the same. Everything gets old after a while. It's important to keep things fresh and exciting. Keeps us alive."

Scarlett hadn't thought about things in this way before; that perhaps, prior to this day, she hadn't been living, but merely existing. Her mundane life was in need of reinvigoration. A change of surroundings could mean a shift in her perspective.

After a short while, the car came to a stop. Enzo lowered his head to get a better view of the block. "This the place?"

"This is it." Scarlett felt embarrassed of her street, which was a mix of commercial buildings and businesses topped with modest apartments. Judging from the way Enzo was dressed and how luxurious his car was, she had to imagine he lived in a version of a New York City palace. "Thank you again. You didn't have to do this."

"I wanted to."

She inhaled, trembling under his sure, steady gaze. "Okay, well, I'll see you tomorrow then."

For however comfortable she had grown in his presence over the course of the night, she was riddled with nerves, breathless with anticipation.

She leaned down to grab her bag, but she could feel his stare on her back. When she sat upright again, Enzo leaned over the armrest between them and craned his neck to press his lips against her cheek.

"*Buonanotte,* Scarlett," he said, his voice raspy and low.

However fast Scarlett's heart had been racing before, now it multiplied tenfold. She fought with herself not to smile, but it was a losing battle. How, and why, was a man of Enzo's status paying such a great deal of attention to her? "Goodnight, Enzo," she said as she let herself out of the car. She floated, from the curb, to the staircase, to the front door of her apartment.

She could feel it, from the top of her head to the tips of her toes. Because of this chance meeting, a line had been drawn in the sand. There was life before Enzo. And there would be life after him.

<hr />

"Let me guess," Lana said as soon as Scarlett closed the door behind her. "New job?" She had one hand on her hip, a martini in the other, as she stared at her daughter with raised brows that wouldn't fall until she had answers.

Though Scarlett was proud to have secured a job, she felt torn in half about how her mother would respond. Part of her still held onto hope that Lana would realize her worth and ask her to return to the bar. The other half of her feared Lana's reaction. Sometimes, especially when martinis were in the mix, Lana's temper rivaled Scarlett's late father's. Screaming matches between the two of them weren't uncommon, and not yet able to read her mother's mood, Scarlett stood tall and braced herself. "Yes. New job."

"Where at?"

"A restaurant," Scarlett said, trying to hide the fact that the extent to which she was excited about her new job surprised even her.

Lana made her way closer to Scarlett, standing taller than Scarlett as she took a long sip of her drink. "Where?"

Scarlett swallowed. She wasn't sure why she wanted to keep this information from her mother, but she felt as if the job were only hers. She wanted to protect it. Still, under the constant of her mother's heated gaze, she caved. "Little Italy."

Dressed in a silk kimono, Lana's head fell back as she laughed and began to pace. "Nice. Nice. You went to work for some wops? For gangsters?"

"They're not gangsters," Scarlett started, but Lana was quick to cut her off.

"Let me guess. A couple of guys own the place. And they saw you coming in a mile away. All sweet and innocent and looking for something better than you got. I told you, baby doll, you're a pretty face. That'll get you some places in life, but not everywhere."

"They hired me because I have experience," Scarlett defended herself.

"Let me tell you how this is gonna go down, sweetheart." Lana drained her drink. "They'll let you believe that. But then one of them is gonna charm the pants off you. Use you like a cheap suit and put you back out on the street. You'll see. And then you'll come crawling back to me with your tail between your legs."

Scarlett felt the familiar pit of disappointment open wide in her stomach. "Why do you want to see me fail so bad?"

"I want you to wake up, Scar. Smarten up. You want to know the truth? I'm happy you got a job somewhere else."

"You're *happy*?"

"What'd you think? I'd beg you to come back?" When Scarlett remained silent, Lana walked up to her so their faces were almost touching. "I'll never beg. When you realize how good you had it, you'll be the one begging *me*."

"How good I had it?" Scarlett yelled, surprised that between the two of them, she was the one to snap first. "You're my own mother and you're hoping I'll fall flat on my face. And you know what the worst part is, Mom? I probably will, because you've made me believe that's all that'll ever happen to me. That I'm not good enough or capable to do anything other than wash dishes and mop floors. And I want to," Scarlett cried. "I want to believe that I can. That I can do something else and be good at it. That I can be someone other than who you've told me I am. But it's so hard to fight something you've believed your whole life."

For a moment, Scarlett wondered if she had gotten through to her mother. Lana's face gave way to no emotions. Instead, she remained silent and stoic. Scarlett thought maybe behind her mother's blank stare, her mind was reeling. "I was exactly like you," Lana said, her voice soft yet cold. "Thought because I was young and cute, the world would roll out the red carpet for me. Everything was going to magically work out. That's what I thought."

"That's not what I think."

Lana's arms dangled at her side, droplets falling from her now empty martini glass. "Then what the hell are you thinking, Scarlett?"

Years of frustration bubbled up in Scarlett's chest until everything erupted. "That I don't want to end up a drunken tramp like you! Mark, Andrew, Dustin — and that's just in the last six months. Who's next?"

Scarlett didn't have time to regret her outburst. As fast as Lana let out an audible gasp, in the same breath, she wound up her arm and hurled the martini glass straight at Scarlett. Scarlett ducked as it shattered against the wall, shards decorating the carpet. Everything went silent, but a piercing sound buzzed through Scarlett. Her veins pulsed at the very thought that her own mother had tried to hurt her.

"How. Dare. You," Lana said. "You ungrateful little brat. Do you have any idea what the hell I've been through? I'm the one who had to bury my husband. I'm the one who had to keep a roof over your head all these years. You think it's been easy? And you have the nerve to go around treating me like I'm some shit mother. You wait, Scarlett. You wait. One day, you're gonna be in my shoes. Then you'll see."

"I will never be anything like you."

"You say that now."

Scarlett's vision went blurry, and she felt like her chest was breaking open as it rose and fell with each shallow breath. Of course Scarlett knew what her mother had been through. Lana reminded her every chance she got. What Scarlett didn't understand was why her mother had to drink herself nearly to death just to get by.

"Go," Lana demanded.

Scarlett's legs shook beneath her. She raced to her room, collapsing on her bed after locking the door behind her. She tried to catch her breath as she replayed the night in her head. The shattered martini glass. Calling her own mother a tramp. The new job. The kiss on the cheek. Enzo.

The slower her breath became, the more her reality crushed her, the more Valenti's felt like an escape rather than a plan to win her mother over.

The more Enzo felt like a dream, the more she realized he'd never want anything to do with her if he knew who she really was.

A broken girl, in desperate search of someone to put the pieces back together and make her whole again.

CHAPTER

TEN

LITTLE ITALY, NEW YORK
SPRING, 1985

The only thing Enzo loved more than the act of playing poker was playing it with three of his closest friends, John, Angelo, and Michael. They were all older than Enzo, but he had no qualms about keeping up with them. Enzo liked that he was the youngest one. He figured he could learn something from them. After all, these guys? They had it all. Everything Enzo wanted. Sure, he wanted the custom-made pin-stripe suits and the mansions out on Long Island, but it was the invincibility he craved the most. These guys were untouchable. Every good gangster was.

They convened at Valenti's every week on the same day at the same time for their ritual. Cigars, cards, and cash. Enzo passed around a heavy jug of homemade wine as they each refilled their glasses. It was the middle of the day, and the dining room was empty. Sunlight flooded in, illuminating even the back of the restaurant where they were seated, out of sight from anyone passing by.

"One more hand," Angelo said as he shuffled the deck.

Enzo fiddled with his chips between his fingers, the clacking noise satisfying him as he watched the cards being dealt. He looked around at his friends, but he couldn't decipher anything. The thing about this crew was that all three of them had incredible poker faces. Their lives depended on it.

"All in." Enzo shoved his chips to the center as everyone else followed suit.

"You lucky son of a bitch," Michael said. He shook his head as he took in Enzo's hand, a royal flush.

John squeezed Enzo's shoulder. "Kid's got the golden touch."

"Let him collect." Angelo rolled his eyes as they watched Enzo collect the four grand he had won, smiling as he organized and folded the bills. "You know, maybe if we play on our turf, one of us will start winning."

"Tradition is tradition," Michael protested. "Besides, we don't have food like this at our club."

"We love coming here, Enz," John assured him. "This is the one place in the neighborhood where we really feel like family. It feels safe."

"I appreciate that," Enzo said with a nod.

"Listen," John started as he shifted in his seat. Ordinarily, their afternoons consisted of shooting the shit and busting one another's chops. But Enzo could tell John's tone was different. Everything suddenly felt very business-like. "We have a proposition for you."

Enzo adjusted in his seat to sit up straighter. "Go on."

"We've been playing cards with you here for what," John said, looking around at the other men, "three, four years now?"

"Something like that," Enzo said, resting his cigar on the edge of the ashtray.

"You've proven to us that this place is safe. We can trust you, and your staff. Nobody's ever come up to us and asked any questions," Michael chimed in.

"I treat them with respect, and they respect me," Enzo said.

Angelo nodded. "Respect is important."

"Enzo," John said, taking the reins of the conversation, "we want you to host games here a few nights a week. During off hours, so it won't disrupt your dinner service. The house," John pointed at Enzo, "cuts thirty percent of the pot. We'll split the pot seventy thirty to start. Now the guys that come in here will start off slow until they know they can trust you and everybody else in this building. But once they know they can, business should be booming. The games will get bigger, as will the bets. When that happens, we'll increase your shares."

"How does this all sound?" Angelo asked.

Now it was Enzo's turn to put on a poker face. Adrenaline coursed through his veins, though not out of nervousness. Out of an eagerness to accept the offer. He had been waiting for a day like this for what felt like his whole life. Now, Enzo wasn't just the guy selling pasta or the overzealous gambler placing bets on his favorite teams. He was accepted. Respected. Needed. It was success on a different level than anything he had ever known before, the kind that couldn't be measured by money alone. And *God*, it felt good. It was the very *more* he was so desperate to obtain.

"John, it's not even a question," Enzo said. "Anything for you guys. You're like brothers to me."

Everyone relaxed at Enzo's agreement. But Enzo? He wasn't relaxed in the least. He felt like he was on top of the world, like he could hold all of New York City right in the palm of his hand.

"Thank you, Enz." John patted Enzo's tanned hand. His veins were budding out. "We'll send over a couple of dealers later in the week to meet with you. You all can organize the days and times, and we'll all spread the word."

"Of course." Enzo did his best to look calm, but he was nothing of the sort. He had made a name for himself in the restaurant business. But now? Now Enzo had the chance to make a name for himself in all of New York, among the circles who were power personified.

———

FRANCESCO ALWAYS KNEW HE and his brother were different. He had felt it from the time he was a child. They were three years apart, and even when they were kids in a small, humble home in Naples, Enzo was the one putting on shows and talking to anyone who would listen to him, while Francesco waited in the background for his brother to include him. Enzo was the leader. He was born that way. Power ran through his veins. But as Francesco watched, unnoticed from the bar, doing his best to catch pieces and glimpses of their conversation in the nearby dining room, he knew he couldn't let Enzo take the lead any longer. He couldn't let Enzo go through with the arrangement. Francesco knew enough to know that when it came to the life of a gangster, it ended in one of two ways: jail or death.

Francesco sipped on his wine as he watched John, Michael, and Angelo leave, but the minute Enzo went upstairs to his office on the second floor, Francesco abandoned his drink and jogged up the steps. He had to put an end to it before it was too late. By the time he reached the second level, the door was already closed. Despite Enzo's cardinal rule of not allowing anyone into the office unannounced, Francesco went in anyway.

"No fucking way," Francesco said. He was taller than Enzo by a good four inches and as Enzo remained seated at his desk, Francesco's shadow enveloped him.

Enzo didn't look up. "What?"

"It's one thing that you insist on being friends with these gangsters, but now you want to host *illegal* card games for them? In our place?"

Enzo finally looked him in the eye. "Yeah. And?"

"I won't allow it."

"Come on, Fran." Enzo laughed, leaning back into his chair, amused by his younger brother's sudden bravado. "It's a game; it's not a big deal."

"I'm serious. I want to keep our business legitimate. If it were up to me, I wouldn't even let those guys eat here."

"Well that's why everything in this business is up to me, otherwise we wouldn't have one."

Francesco took his dig to the chest. Did his cooking account for nothing to his brother? Were his endless hours over the hot stoves done in vain? "That's bullshit. I mean it, Enz. I let everything slide. Your gambling, your affairs, the drinking. I don't want to end up in jail. I mean, what are you doing, Enz? You're thirty-three years old and all of a sudden you wanna start a new career? An illegal one at that."

Enzo leapt up from his chair. "Do you need me to remind you how you got here? How you have a place to live and cook and how everyone in New York City knows your name? You're looking at him. I brought you here."

Francesco stood there, his broad, muscular chest rising and falling at a rapid pace. He was desperate to knock some sense into his brother, enough to make him see that he was getting himself into a mess, one there wasn't a way out of. But he didn't have it in him. Not yet, at least.

"You'll do as I say," Enzo commanded. "I own this building, but they own the block. If they ask me to do something, then we're gonna do it. You got that?"

"Yeah." Francesco stared at Enzo. Storming out, he slammed the door behind him. Francesco remembered how he used to see his brother.

He used to wish he could be as confident and brazen as Enzo, brazen enough to leave his native country on his own merit and start a new life without looking back. But in times like these, Francesco wanted to be nothing like him.

CHAPTER

ELEVEN

LITTLE ITALY, NEW YORK

SPRING, 1985

"Now, first things first. You've got to learn the table numbers," Fausto said. Though dinner service was in full swing, Fausto was still training Scarlett, and they stood in front of the kitchen doors facing the dining room. "Picture it like columns." He held his hands out in front of him and directed her vision. "That's table twenty, and then it moves up as you walk towards the other side of the restaurant. Twenty-one, twenty-two, and so on. Those are the two tops. The two rows of round tables, those are the thirties and forties. Those are probably the hardest to learn since they're not in perfect rows. The two sides of banquettes, those are the fifties and sixties. That's where we put most of the four tops."

Scarlett gave the room a onceover. There must have been ten tables in each row, making for somewhere in the ballpark of sixty tables. She tried to not feel overwhelmed at the prospect of learning each of their numbers.

"Then, seating positions. This is important for when you run food. It moves clockwise," Fausto said, moving his pointer finger in a clockwise motion. "Whichever server you're paired with will write the positions on the ticket, and their order next to it. If they forget on a busy night, they'll tell you verbally. Table sixty-one, seat four, the *spaghetti vongole*. Something like that. You understand?"

"I understand." To her pleasant surprise, it clicked.

"Alright. So you'll work on memorizing the table numbers. Now, I'm going to teach you the skills that aren't technical." Fausto directed Scarlett's attention to the host stand. He put his hands on her shoulders. "The most important thing about working in a restaurant is having your eyes open at all times. Always be aware of your surroundings."

"I'm from New York. I was born aware of my surroundings."

"Then this should be easy for you. I want you to look around the restaurant. From the front door to the back of the dining room. Tell me what you see."

Scarlett scanned the dining room, starting from the top. "I see the hostess."

"Giovanna," Fausto provided her name.

Scarlett's eyes followed the svelte, sultry Giovanna as she led a pair of couples through the dining room. She radiated the confidence of a woman who had not only seen the world but owned it. "She's seating a four top."

"Correct. Where?"

Scarlett waited for Giovanna to seat them. She remembered the columns and counted. "Forty-four?"

"Close. Fifty-four. Not bad. Now, look closely. Look at the tables. Think about the details," Fausto said. "Think about what you would do if you were bussing this section."

There were four tables in full swing in the banquette section. Fausto trailed behind Scarlett as she inched her way closer to the dining room. She started with what she knew. "That table," she said, pointing discreetly, "is halfway through their cocktails."

"They are. And?"

"And their breadbasket is empty. There are crumbs all over the table." Scarlett looked to Fausto for his approval. He wore a proud smile.

"I'm listening."

"And," Scarlett said, confidence growing, "their water glasses are low. And the silverware is all over the place."

"You see it. Now tell me what you'd do about it," Fausto said.

She thought about what she had learned the day before. "I'd clear the table. Get rid of those small bread plates, clear off the silverware. I'd clean off the table with one of those things."

"A crumber." He reached into the pocket of his sport coat and presented it to her.

"A crumber. I'd refill their water glasses. And I'd ask them if they want another round of cocktails."

"You wouldn't. Their server would."

"Oh. Right." She had to remember her place. In hospitality, there was a chain of command. Scarlett was at the bottom of it.

Fausto put his hands on Scarlett's shoulders again. He bent his head down so their eyes met. "You've got it, kid."

"Got what?"

"The instinct. I try to teach it all the time, but God, it's so much easier when it comes naturally. You're still green, but this is good."

"Seriously?" Scarlett let herself smile, reveling in his compliment. "So what now?"

"Now," he turned her around, "go do what you said you'd do."

Scarlett glanced down at the crumber in her hand. She figured she would start with that. As she did when working barback, she gave a meek smile to the customers as she approached the table, though she mostly went unnoticed as she ran the crumber along the tablecloth and scooped up the fallen pieces of bread. She took one of the bread plates and used it as a catcher. Then, she gathered up the rest of the dishes, and returned to Fausto.

"How was that?"

"You did okay. But that's easily a one-person clear. Use the tri-pod grip, even on those small plates," Fausto explained.

"Got it."

"And you would hold the silverware in your hand. Like this." Fausto reached for her left hand. He instructed her to hold the bread plate with the tri-pod grip, and then, he placed the silverware in her open palm. "Know what we do next?"

Scarlett shook her head. "*Mise en place*. And that's the only French phrase you'll hear around here."

"Which means?"

"You take this, and you reset the table for the next course." Fausto presented Scarlett with an organized tray holding all variations of forks, knives, and spoons.

"I swear, it's like you all have your own language," Scarlett marveled.

"We do. And now that you're around it, you'll pick it up in no time."

Giovanna breezed past them again, leaving a trail of her floral perfume in her wake. From the service station, she retrieved a stack of menus. Fausto stopped her on her way back.

"Giovanna." Fausto put his arm around her waist.

"*Ciao, amore*," Giovanna said. Her exotic accent matched her appearance. She wore peep-toe, patent leather heels that gave her several inches on Scarlett. Her hair was the color of chestnuts, her eyes not much lighter. She stared down her sharp, narrow nose at Scarlett.

"Meet our newest hire, Scarlett," Fausto said.

"Hi," Scarlett said with a smile. "Nice to meet you."

"Oh," Giovanna purred, "aren't you adorable." Then, she muttered something in rapid Italian to Fausto.

As Scarlett and Fausto watched Giovanna's leopard-clad backside sashay back to the host podium, Scarlett turned to him. "You're not going to tell me what she said, are you?"

"No shot in hell, kid. She'll warm up to you eventually. You just keep your eye on the prize."

She didn't know what *prize* Fausto was referring to, but maybe it had nothing to do with work at all. Maybe it was the raven-haired man who graced her with a smile and a wink whenever he passed her, the man who she couldn't stop thinking about since the moment she had laid eyes on him.

<hr>

"You called her a tramp? To her face?" Helen's eyes looked like they might bug out.

Though Scarlett had called Helen to tell her what had happened with Lana, it was the kind of story that deserved a retelling in person. They sat across from each other in a booth by the window at the local diner, sipping on hot cups of coffee before Scarlett had to head to work.

"I can't believe it," Helen said as she set her mug down on the paper placemat covered in local advertisements.

"Neither can I, and I'm the one who said it."

"You know what? Good for you. You were just standing up for yourself," Helen said. "Has she spoken to you since?"

"Only to let me know when Dustin's coming over so I'm not home." Scarlett's face twisted in disgust.

"So, was I right? Is this new job so amazing that you have zero interest in going back to the bar?"

At the mention of her job, Scarlett's mouth curved. "I love it. I mean, the work itself is hard, you know? My arms have never been so sore in my life. But I love it. Fausto is the most amazing teacher."

"Fausto? That's a funny name."

"He's a funny guy. He's the maître d'. And get this, we have three hundred covers on the books tonight. Three hundred! Do you know what kind of tips I'm looking at?"

"That's amazing. See? By the time Lana wants you to come back, you'll be rolling in the dough."

"Yeah." Scarlett's gaze fell to the table. "There's something else that happened at work. Well, after work I guess."

"What is it? You look so secretive."

Scarlett couldn't suppress her excitement any longer. She had been dying to talk about Enzo with someone. "Enzo kissed me. I mean only on the cheek, but I swear, I think he likes me. Which is insane. If you saw him, you'd never believe a guy like him would even *look* at me."

"And Enzo is?"

"The owner."

"Wait." Helen leaned her elbows on the table. "The owner of the restaurant kissed you? How did this even happen?"

"Just on the cheek," Scarlett reiterated. "It was probably nothing." She tried to diminish her enthusiasm as she recounted the night's events to Helen.

"And how did you *feel* when Enzo kissed you? On the cheek," Helen added with an eyeroll.

"I like him, Helen," Scarlett gushed.

Helen took a sip of her coffee, searching Scarlett's face. "How old is he?"

"I don't know. Thirty-something? He doesn't seem that much older."

"Does he live in Little Italy?"

"I don't know." Scarlett's voice went up an octave.

"What *do* you know?"

"We clicked, Helen! We clicked. Just like you talked about." Scarlett shook her head as heat rose to her cheeks at the thought of her night with Enzo. "He looked at me like I was the most important person in the world."

"Oh Lord." Helen covered her face with her palm. "You're a goner."

"And so were you with Andrew. I don't get why you're reacting this way."

"You know how restaurant guys are. I can't believe you're being so naïve."

"I don't think I do know, actually."

"They're cheaters. Drunks. Drug addicts. I wouldn't be surprised if he's got a wife he runs around on. Italians are notorious for cheating. My mother told me and my brothers if we brought home an Italian, she'd disown us," Helen said with wide eyes. "No offense."

"No. There's no way." Scarlett did her best to tune out everything Helen was saying. "He wasn't wearing a ring."

"Scarlett, come on. You're the toughest chick I know, and you think a wedding band is a surefire way to tell if someone's married or not?"

"I would've known if he was married. I would have been able to tell."

"How?"

"I just would have!" Scarlett's shoulders almost reached her ears.

"Okay, for someone who said they don't believe in *the one*, you sure fell for this guy pretty fast. And honestly, I'm surprised."

"I don't get it. I thought you'd be happy for me."

Helen leaned in and put her hand on top of Scarlett's. "I'm worried about you, that's all. I just want you to be careful. You've been at this job for five minutes and you just met this guy."

"You're not my mother. I don't want you to worry about me. I want to talk to you about how amazing it felt that a guy like Enzo paid me attention and I don't want you to judge me for it," Scarlett said. She could feel a lump forming in her throat, but she swallowed it down. She wouldn't let Helen know how hurt she was by her reaction. "What?" Scarlett asked at Helen's non-responsiveness.

"If Lana's not going to worry about you, who will?"

"Me. Don't you get it by now? I'm on my own. I always have been."

"You've always had me. And you know I'll always be here for you, no matter what happens."

"I know that." Scarlett crossed her arms and looked out the window. Sure, Helen might have said she was there for Scarlett, but it didn't feel like it. Wasn't a friendship like theirs supposed to be a place of safety? Free from judgement? And where was Helen getting these wild ideas about restaurant workers and Italians anyway? Scarlett had known Helen's mother long enough to know that her world consisted of the ancient church on their block and the fresh market on the corner where she purchased her ingredients for things like casseroles and homemade pies. What could Mrs. O'Connor possibly know about the world? You have to be in the world to know it.

"Scarlett?"

"What?" Scarlett snapped.

"Come on. I don't want to argue with you. I was just trying to look out for you, but now that I know how you feel, I won't do it again. Okay?"

"Yeah." Scarlett glanced at her watch, disinterested in Helen's sudden change of heart. "I have to catch the train. My shift starts at three."

"Okay. Call me if you need anything, okay? I'll be out tonight with Andrew, but if it's an emergency, you can always call my parents."

"Thanks. I'll be fine."

Scarlett breathed in the crisp spring air as she found her way to the subway station and became aware of how alone she felt. If she didn't have Helen to share things with, who did she have? The harder Helen tried to get her away from Enzo, the more Helen was pushing her towards him.

Her pace quickened. She couldn't wait to get to work.

CHAPTER

TWELVE

"**M**ore bread on twenty-four."

"Do you not hear the bell ringing?"

"I need you to clear fifty-two, ASAP!"

"Eighty-six ossobucco."

"Thirty-eight wants their cappuccinos hot. Piping hot."

Scarlett's head whipped back and forth at every request as her face was washed with panic. Charged with energy, the kitchen buzzed with waiters and waitresses rushing by. Francesco and the sous chefs rang the bell incessantly as steaming hot, glistening plates were slid into the window, which Scarlett learned was a stainless-steel countertop between the chefs and waiters, covered by heaters to keep the dishes warm. It was like a symphony. A crazy, rushed, chaotic symphony. Despite the chaos, Scarlett was exhilarated by the adrenaline pumping through her. She learned right away that working in a restaurant was all consuming. When she was in uniform, a tray on her arm and an apron around her hips, she was engulfed in the bubble of Valenti's with no room for thoughts about her life outside of it. Time didn't exist. Everything was a rush. She was a part of something larger than herself.

Finally, she latched onto a task. She grabbed a tray from underneath the service station and looked for the pink ticket like Fausto had taught her to do. But when she looked up at the window, she had trouble deciphering which dish was which.

"Hey." A waitress around the same age as Scarlett materia-lized next to her. Her curly black hair was twirled into a tight French twist and her lips were swiped with crimson. "You need help?"

"That would be great."

The waitress scanned the pink ticket over and matched each dish with little effort. "This is going to table fifty-four. Do you know where that is?"

"I think so?" Scarlett said more as a question as she hiked the tray above her shoulder.

"Come with me."

"What's your name?" Scarlett asked as she kicked open the swinging doors.

"I'm Julie. You're Scarlett, right?"

"That's me," she said, already feeling the weight of the tray on her shoulder as she followed Julie to table fifty-four. As it turned out, Scarlett did know where it was, but it was nice having Julie lead the way.

Julie worked with ease and expertise. She pulled a tray stand from a nearby service station and opened it. Slow and steady, Scarlett bent down and placed the tray on top. Julie picked up each dish and placed them in front of the proper guests, working with speed and delicacy. Scarlett admired how warm Julie was as she spoke to the patrons, making them feel at home.

"You're really good," Scarlett said as they headed back towards the kitchen.

"Thanks." Julie smiled in a way that expressed she knew just how *good* she was. "I started out as a busser like you. They promoted me to waitress in three months. Wanna know a secret?"

"Of course."

"They like to see you go out of your way to do things. Like, you see that empty water glass over there?" Julie pointed to a nearby table as Scarlett's eyes followed. "Even though it's not in your section, you see it, right? So if you were to go out of your way to refill their glass, Enzo and Fran see that as a sign that you really care about this place and what you're doing here."

"I'll be right back," Scarlett said, putting Julie's advice into practice. She grabbed a water pitcher on her way to the table.

"Thank you," the woman said to Scarlett as she refilled her glass.

"You're welcome. Can I get you anything else?" Scarlett asked.

"Could you get our waiter? We're ready to order dessert."

"Of course," Scarlett said, bowing out. She found Julie again and relayed the message. It was like a game of telephone as Julie passed along the message until it reached someone who was working in that section.

"Nice," Julie said.

"Thanks for the advice."

"Come on, you can shadow me for the rest of the night. Weekends are absolute shitshows." Scarlett continued on in a daze, guided by Julie's help as she refilled glasses, cleared tables, and ran expensive entrées to important guests. But as she made her way to the bar to drop off freshly polished wine glasses, the gravity of the room had shifted.

Scarlett went on her tiptoes. The attention had moved to the bar and the dinner chatter went quiet. Scarlett followed everyone's gaze, trying to make sense of the way the energy had changed, to the small crowd forming around the bar. At the center of it all was Enzo and a mesmerizing woman with big, permed hair the color of ink and legs like a gazelle.

"Cher." Fausto said as he joined Scarlett. "God, she's gorgeous. What a voice."

"I love her music," Scarlett marveled, starstruck at seeing a celebrity like Cher in real life.

"She is so beautiful." Julie chimed in, standing on the other side of Scarlett. She didn't try to busy herself. None of them did. Everyone went still, taking in the fact that a star was in *their* place. It was the most exciting thing Scarlett had ever witnessed with her own two eyes.

"What's she doing *here*?" Scarlett asked.

"Told you, Scar," Fausto said. "It's the place to be seen."

<hr />

"YOU'RE GOING TO SEE a lot of celebrities in this place. Politicians, movie stars, gangsters, they all come here. You'll get used to it," Fausto said as he puffed on a cigarette.

With dinner service over, he sat on the counter while Scarlett polished silverware. On the other side of the line, Francesco cooked. Scarlett wondered who he was cooking for, since the restaurant had already closed.

"I've never gotten used to it. I still get starstruck like a babbling fool," Julie said as she breezed through the kitchen.

"I've never seen anything like that," Scarlett said, adding a polished butter knife to her clean stack and picking up a cloudy fork to work on next. "It was like she was the only person in the whole restaurant that mattered."

"That's because she was. They're not famous for no reason. They're a special breed. In comparison, the rest of us might as well be invisible."

Scarlett couldn't help herself. She let out a snort at Fausto's dramatic flair and from the stove, Francesco did the same. Francesco turned around to face them. He had since changed out of his chef's coat and into a Henley, the thin fabric clinging to his large, defined arms.

"Don't let Fausto and his life theories get to you," Francesco told Scarlett as he pulled some plates down from an overhead shelf. He set them in the window and began plating dish after dish of some sort of pasta. The air smelled like the sea.

"Who are you cooking for?" Scarlett asked.

"Family meal," Francesco said. "Staff's gotta eat too."

Scarlett became aware of how ravenous she was. "Oh. What did you make?"

"Spaghetti *alla Luciana*." He plated the last dish and tapped his tongs on the side of the frying pan.

"Which is?"

"Octopus," Fausto said as he took a dish from the window. He handed it to Scarlett.

Scarlett's insides churned. How could she eat this when she could barely stomach the sight of it? Pieces of deep purple octopus with the suckers covered in a light tomato sauce stared back at her. "I'm actually not hungry," she lied.

Fausto narrowed his blue eyes at her. "Come on, try a tentacle." He held one up and waved it in front of her face.

She laughed and jerked her head back. "I'm good."

Francesco rang the bell a few times, and the remaining staff swarmed in and picked up their plates from the window, taking clean silverware from Scarlett's pile and heading back out to the dining room. Instead of joining them, Fausto sat back down on the counter next to Scarlett's polishing station.

"You sure you don't want some?" he asked.

Scarlett gestured towards the pile of flatware. "I'm going to finish up."

Fausto looked to Francesco. "She's dedicated, this one."

Francesco pulled down a clean frying pan from the hanger. "So no octopus. What *do* you like?"

Scarlett looked around, but no one answered. "Me?"

"You're not actually invisible, Scarlett," Fausto teased.

"Very funny," Scarlett said to Fausto before meeting Francesco's gaze. "You don't have to cook something for me. I'm fine."

"I have to feed you. It's my job."

"Really, I'm not hungry. You've been cooking all night."

"I'm a chef. I can't rest until every stomach in this house is full." He rested the palms of his hands on the edge of the counter and blinked a few times, waiting.

"No seafood. Anything else is fine."

He opened the latch to his row of ingredients. "You good with olives?"

"Yes."

"Good." He turned away from Scarlett and got to work.

Scarlett polished forks, knives, and spoons until her hands went numb. But all the while, she studied Francesco, fascinated. He drizzled olive oil all over the base of a pan, then he tossed in a few handfuls of olives and capers. A loud sizzling noise emerged as he added in the tomatoes that bubbled as soon as they hit the heat. He swayed the pan back and forth over the open flame of the gas stove and the ingredients danced through the air. Off to the side, he dropped some fresh pasta into the boiler. Scarlett's eyes followed his every move.

"*Ti piaci formaggi?*" he asked, his back to Scarlett as he faced the wall of stoves.

"No, thank you," Scarlett said, pleased with herself for understanding his Italian.

"Somehow I knew." Swirls of steam rose from the bowls to the ceiling but instead of putting the plates in the window, he carried them around to the other side of the line and handed one to her. "*Spaghetti alla puttanesca.*"

"Do you know what that translates to?" Fausto raised his brows at Scarlett.

"I've had this before. I didn't know it meant anything," Scarlett said as she picked up a fork.

"It means *the whore's pasta*," Fausto told her.

"*Stai zitto!*" Francesco laughed, telling Fausto to shut up. "It's a quick sauce, from Naples, where I'm from. You'll like it."

Scarlett took the plate from Francesco. "Thank you, chef."

"Please," he said as he waited for their eyes to meet, "call me Francesco. Fran. Anything but 'Chef'."

"Okay." But before she could dig her fork into the pasta, the kitchen doors swung open. It was Enzo, carrying a bottle of wine.

"Can't have pasta without the wine." Enzo burst through the doors, his presence filling up the room to the brim. "If these two won't teach you the proper way to enjoy Italian cuisine, then I will," he said, looking directly at Scarlett. He took four glasses off a nearby tray and poured everyone a glass of red. "I bet you worked up an appetite on a night like tonight," Enzo said as he handed the final glass to Scarlett. Despite his brother and Fausto in the room, his eyes never left her. "*Cin cin* everybody."

Scarlett's pulse began to race under Enzo's attention. She took a long sip of wine, and it soared through her body, warming her from the inside out. Finally, she broke their gaze and swirled her fork around, loading it up with thick bands of spaghetti. Flavors of salty capers and sweet tomatoes and nutty olives exploded in her mouth. She thought of her steady diet of sugary cereal and shuddered. "I don't care what it's called. This is my new favorite dish." Scarlett caught the smile on Francesco's face. He didn't try to busy himself with eating or drinking, but instead, he remained still as he took her in, looking pleased with himself that he had impressed her with his food again.

"Let me taste." Enzo jumped in. He took hold of Scarlett's fork and swirled a quick bite for himself, but he froze mid-chew. "*Puttanesca?*"

"She doesn't like octopus," Francesco explained.

Enzo looked at Scarlett. "Come on. You have to try it."

"No," she said in between bites, her lips curving into a smile as she chewed.

Enzo took Fausto's plate and stabbed his fork through a small piece of octopus. He held it out. "For me."

Scarlett set her bowl down and crossed her arms in front of her chest. How could she say no, with all of them staring at her? "Get me a napkin."

"Why?"

"In case I need to spit it out."

"Thanks a lot," Francesco joked as he set his dish down and got her a bar rag.

Scarlett stared down her nose at the piece of octopus as Enzo moved the fork closer and closer to her mouth. Finally, she closed her eyes. She chewed, momentarily disgusted with the rubbery texture, but then, it melted in her mouth, and she swallowed the flavors of what she imagined to be a summer spent on the southern coast of Italy. She blushed as the three of them laughed.

Francesco held up the bar rag. "Not needed?"

"Not needed. Sorry," Scarlett said.

"No, no. I'm glad you got to try something new," Francesco said, holding her gaze longer than he should have. She wiped the corners of her mouth, wondering if maybe her face was dirty.

"See what happens when you listen to me?" Enzo interjected. Then, he picked up Francesco's plate and shoved it back in his brother's hands. He shot Francesco a look full of intensity that Scarlett didn't quite understand. "Eat yours, kid. Pasta's getting cold."

CHAPTER

THIRTEEN

LITTLE ITALY, NEW YORK

SPRING, 1985

Cigarette smoke clouded the Cadillac as Enzo steered the car towards Brooklyn. He had one hand on the steering wheel, the other dangling over the passenger seat that had become Scarlett's regular spot over the last couple of weeks. He rolled down the windows to let the breeze wash through the car, glancing over at her. She was clueless of the effect she had on him. He felt like he was twenty-three himself again, young, reckless, and carefree, driving away from reality, no destination in mind. Finally, he parallel parked in a spot close to the park beneath the Brooklyn Bridge.

"What are we doing here?" Scarlett asked.

"This is one of my favorite spots," Enzo explained as they found a vacant bench. "I wanted to show it to you."

The two of them were quiet as they took in the sounds of cars whisking by overhead and how from this vintage point, Manhattan seemed to be dripping in glitter.

"This is beautiful," Scarlett said, crossing one leg over the other.

"I like to come here and think."

"You have to come all the way to Brooklyn just to think?" she teased.

"I don't get a lot of peace and quiet in Manhattan." Though Enzo could feel her stare on him, the sight of the city before him never lost its luster on him. In fact, it looked prettier from this side of the island. From this vantage point, Manhattan looked like a dazzling place where dreams lived, rather than a mass of grit and grime and concrete.

"Can I ask you something?" Scarlett said, breaking him out of his thoughts. "The other night, when Cher was in the restaurant, how do you do what you did?"

He turned to her. "What did I do?"

"A *celebrity* was in the restaurant, but everyone was paying attention to you. Everyone wanted *your* attention."

Scarlett's flattery made Enzo smile. "It's simple. You gotta know what people want, and all you have to do is give it to them."

"How do you mean?"

"People don't go out just for a good meal. That's what you gotta understand. When they come into my place, it's the whole experience. People want to feel special and important, right? Like they're valued. It's in the little things – remembering their names, their kids' names, making them feel like family. So that's what I give them. I give them something they can't get anywhere else, and that's why they come back. I know Fran's a good cook, but there are a lot of good cooks in this city. What keeps them coming back is the combination of both. The food and the magic. And the magic, it's as simple as knowing what people want."

Scarlett leaned in closer towards him. "Alright. Work your magic on me. What do I want?"

Enzo thought for a moment. "The world. You want Versace clothes hanging in your closet, diamonds around your neck, a gold watch on your wrist. You want a big house with a nice car parked in the driveway. A husband who's gonna treat you like a gem, and a little girl who's as pretty as you."

"You know what's funny, Enzo? I never thought about any of that stuff before."

"I bet you will now."

She fiddled with her fingernails and let her gaze fall to the ground. "I bet I will."

"And what about me?" Enzo scooted closer to her. "Tell me what I want." But as Scarlett's face froze and uncertainty clouded her eyes, Enzo sensed he had said the wrong thing. He put his hand on her face. "What is that?"

"What is what?"

"That look. Like you're doubting yourself."

"I am. I don't know what you want."

"Try," he whispered, even though no one else was around.

She hesitated before speaking. "You said you think things should be kept fresh and exciting," she started, and he nodded, encouraging her to go on. "Maybe you want to travel to all kinds of different places. Start another business. Buy a new house, maybe one by the beach. A pretty wife who will always change her hairstyle, so you won't get bored with her. And maybe a little boy who's as handsome as you. I think all of that would make you pretty happy."

Enzo thought about his wife at home who hadn't changed her hair once in the ten years he had known her, the little boy who was named after him, and the two little girls who bore all his facial features. With a few blinks and a laborious swallow, he pushed the thoughts of his family away and smiled so big, all his bright teeth showed.

"Did I get it right?" she asked.

"Pretty close."

"What did I miss?" She searched his face, as if the answers were written right on his skin.

There it was again, their chemistry that Enzo couldn't put into words. He wasn't sure he had ever felt this odd, familiar connection with anyone before. It was like he had known her always, known what she wanted while she understood parts of him he was too afraid to share with anyone else.

"You," he said, though his voice was barely audible.

Her jaw clenched and released, but she didn't dare move her eyes away from his. He was sure she wanted him, wasn't he? The time had come. In this game of theirs, he was going all in.

He pulled her tiny frame towards him, and she wrapped her arms around his neck as their lips locked. The chemistry exploded. Enzo's heart felt like it was bursting. He was alive again, like he had been woken up from a long, deep slumber. His flame had been relit. She kissed him back at full force as she held onto his neck. Their kisses were messy and mad as he ran his fingers through her long hair, all the way to the ends until they finally landed on her waist. They didn't come up for air. They couldn't. They couldn't get enough of each other.

She finally collapsed into his neck and kissed him there a few times, trailing down to his chest. He was surprised at her sudden boldness, her ability to get over her nerves and go after what she wanted. And Enzo, he was surprised at himself, too. Enzo never got his heart intertwined in his affairs. But as he held her in his arms, her petite frame resting on him, he didn't want to let her go. He would keep her safe, so long as she kept him alive.

Happy. Maybe Scarlett equaled happiness. Maybe she held the key to unlock that intangible entity everyone so desperately desired. Or maybe he hoped she did so he wouldn't have to go around searching for it anymore.

The guilt, it would catch up with him later when he passed by his children's rooms and climbed into bed next to his wife, when he wouldn't touch her, when he would replay the images of Scarlett in his head until he fell asleep. He was obsessed with her by her kiss alone. But as it always was with Enzo, he was insatiable. He wanted more. Kissing her wasn't enough.

Enzo wanted all of her.

CHAPTER

FOURTEEN

HELL'S KITCHEN, NEW YORK

SPRING, 1985

"**E**ven though you don't work for me anymore, I still expect you to pay your share of the rent."

Scarlett recognized the voice right away, even in her sleep. It was Lana, the most familiar voice she knew. Scarlett listened to the sound of her mother ripping her drapes open as sunlight flooded her bedroom. As soon as Scarlett opened her eyes, she rammed them shut again. It felt like an earthquake was going on inside of her head. She cringed as she opened one eye, then the other. Lana was leaning over her, examining her.

"Did you really have to wake me up like this? I was still asleep," Scarlett complained as she surrendered to the sun and sat up. She felt the blood rush to her head that pounded with a massive headache. A hand flew to her nauseous stomach.

"It's two o'clock in the afternoon."

"I have a headache." Scarlett fell back into the softness of her pillows and closed her eyes.

"You're hungover."

"You're one to talk."

"Scarlett Marie, you better watch how you speak to me. What time did you get home last night anyway?"

"I don't know. Two-thirty? I don't remember."

"Are you gonna be working that late every night?"

"Why do I have a feeling you didn't wake me up to talk about my work schedule?" She finally opened her eyes again. "What is it?"

"I'm going away for a few days," Lana admitted.

"Where?"

"Long Island. With Dustin. I'll be back by the weekend."

"And I need to know this because?"

"Because I don't want to have to worry about you taking the subway home at two in the morning," she said. Sometimes Scarlett was surprised by her mother's concern. It wasn't in the way of a doting parent, but more of the bare minimum of motherhood, of making sure her kid came home in one piece. "I don't remember you ever coming home that late."

"Well you don't have to worry about me." Scarlett hugged her knees to her chest. "I don't take the subway home."

Lana sat on the edge of Scarlett's bed. Their eyes met. "Then how do you get home?"

"One of the owners drove me. Enzo," Scarlett said, her heart pounding at just the mention of his name.

Lana arched a brow. "Does he drive everybody home?"

"Not that I know of."

"Well how old is this Enzo?"

"Thirty something? Why does it matter?"

"Because a man doesn't drive a girl home at two-thirty in the morning unless he wants something from her," Lana said, her voice rising louder.

Scarlett felt her cheeks go hot. She was sure she looked a wreck, too. She wanted to hide, but there was nowhere to run. Lana had her under a microscope.

"Did you sleep with him?" Lana asked, her tone accusatory.

"Ew, Mom, please!" She stood up. The last thing she wanted to talk to her mother about was sex. But before she could move past her, Lana grabbed her arm.

"I'm talking to you. Don't walk away from me."

"What, Mom?"

"Your cheeks are red. I know when my own daughter is lying to me. You like him, don't you? Didn't I tell you this would happen?"

Scarlett felt like she might pass out. Liked him? If Lana only knew. If Lana could only understand how utterly consumed with Enzo she had become. Scarlett wasn't sure she thought about anything else besides Enzo anymore.

"He's my boss. And like you, he didn't want me taking the train by myself at two in the morning, so he offered to drive me home. That's all it was."

"So he cares about you."

"Okay, I'm done talking about this. I need coffee." Scarlett put her hands up, pleading with her mother to stop.

"Scarlett! I don't need you going and making the same mistake I did."

"And what mistake is that? Getting pregnant with a child you didn't want?"

They went silent. Scarlett knew she had taken things too far again, but it was as if she couldn't control the things that came out of her mouth anymore. If she didn't get the way she felt off her chest sooner or later, she was going to explode.

"Scarlett," Lana said, her shoulders slumping, "it's not that I didn't want you. I couldn't take care of you."

"Because you don't love me enough to stop drinking. Right? Isn't that it?" Her throat constricted. Scarlett hated talking about Lana's drinking, but it was always the elephant in the room. It was the one thing that had stolen so much from her, from them. Lana's martinis and gin and tonics had robbed Scarlett of having childhood friends over, of being a carefree teenager, of knowing what it was like to be able to think about a future that didn't involve worrying about whether or not her mother would wake up in the morning.

"You wanna talk about how much I love you?" Lana's voice went quiet. "I was younger than you when I got pregnant. You think I knew anything about being a mother? About being a wife? I didn't want to marry your father, if you want to know the truth, but I did it for you. Because I wanted you to have a real family. I knew I couldn't do it on my own. I gave up everything for you. Everything I could've been, for you." Lana's voice broke as her green eyes glossed over with tears.

Scarlett's face twisted with hurt and confusion. At learning that her parents' marriage was nothing but a farce, something done out of obligation, at now having to carry a sense of guilt for ruining her mother's life. There were things in life Scarlett wished she didn't have to know, these few facts now topping that list. "A lot of good it did me."

Lana stood. "Come home at two in the morning, Scarlett. Go sleep with your boss. I don't give a shit. Just don't come home pregnant. Do you understand me?"

Lana moved past Scarlett and left her, the scent of her cheap rose perfume trailing behind her. Scarlett's eyes clouded with tears because the truth was, deep down, that was what she'd believed all along. That her mother didn't care. And even though it was something she'd always known, it still felt like a knife in her heart to hear her mother say it.

CHAPTER

FIFTEEN

Scarlett wasn't sure why Julie and Fausto were working at a restaurant. Not only did she look up to them when it came to their work, but she was beginning to grow closer to them as friends. But the two of them had another talent besides their hospitality skills. They could sing like nobody's business. As the three of them polished and racked glasses behind the bar, prepping the restaurant for dinner service, Fausto and Julie sang a number from *West Side Story*, taking turns in what was a colorful duet. Scarlett was in awe of them, but seeing them act alongside each other, bar rags in hand, she couldn't contain her laughter. Working with Fausto and Julie barely felt like work at all.

As their musical number came to an end, Francesco approached the bar, amused by their scene. "You two better not leave us for Broadway,"

Francesco said as he took a seat. "I need this type of entertainment around here to keep me going."

"You know I'm too loyal for my own good." Fausto placed a coaster in front of him. "It's Julie you have to worry about."

"Hey!" Julie slapped him with her bar rag.

"What's the word?" Fausto asked Francesco.

Francesco let out a long, stress-filled exhale. "Have to drink before family occasions. You know how that goes."

"Come on now. It's a kid's party. Play nice." Fausto gave him a daring look. "Scar, grab me a bottle of Pinot?"

Scarlett didn't need to question of he meant pinot noir or Pinot Grigio because she had seen enough of Francesco to know he drank exclusively white wine. She bent down and grabbed a chilled bottle of his favorite label. Fausto poured a generous glass and slid it across the bar.

"Look, I'd do anything for Little Enzo. It's all the other people I can't stand. People from Puglia are different. They're assholes," Francesco explained.

Scarlett didn't hear a word after *Little Enzo*. She froze. Her body went cold and simultaneously, she broke out in a sweat. Her breathing became shallow, but she worried if she didn't keep working, everyone around her would notice that she was wearing a look of panic. And then they'd wonder why she cared so much about Enzo being a father.

"Little Enzo?" Scarlett asked.

"Enzo's son." With cheeks now flushed, Francesco sipped on his wine. "Turns seven today. Great kid. He's a clone of my brother. My sister-in-law's family is a bit tough, that's all."

Scarlett wondered if she was imagining the trembling behind Francesco's voice. She gave a polite smile, but rushed to turn around. Resting her palms against the countertop, she let out an exhale and slammed her eyes shut. Every fiber of her being was riddled with anxiety.

Her heart thudded, deep and fast, as a pit grew in her stomach.

She put all the pieces together. Enzo was a father. Enzo was married. *Married.* Her ears rang as everything else went silent. All she could think about was that Helen had been right, from the very beginning. If she had listened to Helen from the start, she wouldn't have had to feel like disappointment was bleeding into every crevice of her body.

"Nothing like in-laws." Mary, another waitress, joined in the conversation, dropping off a rack of rocks glasses in need of polishing. "Why do you think I'm divorced?"

"Why do you think I never married?" Francesco said with a playful tone, though Scarlett suspected he wasn't joking around.

"Scarlett," Fausto said, quiet and low. "Come with me."

Grateful for Fausto's intuitive nature, she followed him to the back of the restaurant.

"You okay, kid?" Fausto shook her out of her trance.

"Yeah," she forced out, eyes darting around the room.

"I say this with love, but I hope you don't have aspirations to become an actress. You're a terrible liar."

"I swear, Faus, I didn't know," Scarlett said. She sat down at a table stacked with a pile of unfolded napkins.

"Of course, you didn't." He leaned against the table and folded his arms across his chest. "And now that you do?"

"I don't know. I guess now that I know, that's it, right?"

"Sweetheart, I know I don't know the details," Fausto said and put a supportive hand on her shoulder, "but from what I've seen, you fell pretty hard for him. I don't see you standing up on your own two feet again just yet, unscathed."

"It's that obvious?" Scarlett looked up at him. He nodded. She dropped her face to her palm. "God. I don't know what to do. I'm mortified. Everyone must think I'm some clueless idiot." A shiver trailed down her spine at the thought that her mother's impression of her might not have been an impression at all, but a true reading of who she really was. She didn't know how to work a man and this time, it wasn't just affecting how many tips she brought home or whether or not she got promoted. It was affecting her heart.

"Listen, don't be so hard on yourself. Enzo's a charmer. There's just something about him. But talk to him. Tell him the truth, and all you can do is hope he does the same. He's got some funny ways, but deep down, underneath all of that, he's got a good heart."

Scarlett began folding napkins one by one, and soon, her stack grew tall. As she worked, she didn't hear anything. She was lost in her own mind, wondering what she had gotten herself into, and if there was a way out. She wondered what it all meant. The drives home, the kisses, the attention, was it all a lie? Why could she feel the way she felt about Enzo when she couldn't even have him? Though she had little relationship experience herself, she wasn't totally naïve to the fact that people cheated on each other. She had learned a lot from her bartending days, listening to the woes of strangers. Cheating was bad. Wasn't that a fact of life? If that were true, how could something so bad feel so good?

She had never mattered to anyone before. Why would this time be any different?

<hr />

ENZO WAS ON EDGE. He usually kept his extracurricular relationships outside of his restaurant. Sure, he would meet women there, but the affairs always took place where no one would find out, where none of them would risk running into his wife. But this time? This time was different. There Scarlett was, front and center, working herself to the bone. He admired her for that. She was hungry for more, just like him. She wasn't afraid to work hard and get her hands dirty. He liked to be around someone like her, someone who still thought the world had something to offer them.

He couldn't let her go before he'd even had her. Which was why he had to get her out of the restaurant before his wife arrived.

"How's my girl?" Enzo pulled out a chair and straddled it. Scarlett was seated, folding napkins at a rapid pace.

"I heard today's a special day," Scarlett said, not meeting his gaze.

"Yeah?" Enzo raised his brows and waited. Surely she didn't know. How could she?

"A birthday." She finally looked at him. Her eyes were filled with intensity, with an edge. "Little Enzo."

Her tone was like a razorblade, sharp and cutting. Enzo's lips thinned to form a line, but he tried not to let her see him sweat. His immediate concern was not that she knew, but how she found out. His eyes scanned the restaurant and landed at the bar where he saw his brother halfway through a bottle of wine. He didn't have to wonder much longer who the source was. But he couldn't lie to Scarlett. She would never believe him, for one, but also, he didn't want to lie to her.

"Yeah. My son. Seven years old, he's so handsome," he said evenly, resting his arms on the back of the chair. Enzo watched her, the way her gaze fell, the way her shoulders caved in. He had to get her out of there before things got even worse. "Listen, you've been putting in a lot of hours. It's not too busy tonight. Why don't you take the night off, rest up for the weekend?"

"Could it be," she said and leaned in, her voice low, "that you don't want me to meet your wife?"

"You know for a minute, I forgot how tough you can be."

"What's her name?"

Enzo smoothed back his already immaculate hair. "Claudia."

"And you were going to tell me when?"

"Scarlett, it's not what it seems," he said, growing flustered. If she only knew what it was like, what went on inside of his home, she'd know it wasn't a real marriage at all.

"It seems to me like you're married. Are you not?"

"It's an arrangement," he pleaded with her, trying to explain as she let out a scoff. He wished he could make her understand. "It's not like I'm in love with her, Scarlett. We have kids together. That's all it is. It's something I'm stuck in."

"How many kids do you have?"

"Three. Little Enzo, and the girls. Maria and Antonella."

Scarlett blinked a few times before her face contorted in sarcasm. "And what are you gonna tell me next? She doesn't understand you?"

"She doesn't. But I think you might."

He knew he had her, even if just for a moment. She looked like she might even believe him. But there was still a fire in her he couldn't put out.

"I can't believe you've been lying to me this whole time. You let me…" she trailed off, shaking her head.

"I let you what? *Dimmi.*"

"Nothing."

"Do you know how lucky you are?"

"For some strange reason I'm having a hard time seeing my luck in all of this."

"You're young. You can be anyone you want; do anything you want. You have all the freedom in the world. You've got your whole life in front of you. I've done everything a man is supposed to do. The family, the business. And yet, you're the one I envy. It's just…" Enzo looked out the window. "You're lucky."

"Yeah, well, you've got it all wrong. I've never been lucky."

"Take it from me, Scar. Luck can change."

Scarlett wore a look of confusion. He was sure there was a part of her that hated him. But while his own face was etched with lines of stress, hers softened. Maybe the part of her that cared for him was bigger than the part that held disdain. He hoped so. God, he hoped so.

"Go," she told him. "Go get ready for your son's party."

"Scar, please go home."

"I can't. I need the money."

"I'll pay you for your shift anyway."

"I can handle meeting your wife and kids, Enzo."

They looked at each other, their connection intensifying. It was as though they were exchanging thoughts. They both knew she was lying. It would nearly break her to meet Claudia. And it would break him to watch it happen.

———

FRANCESCO WASN'T ALL TOO surprised when he saw Scarlett leave out the back door without saying goodbye. He had been drinking himself into a stupor, beating himself up for mentioning Claudia and Little Enzo. If he thought Scarlett was so nice, why did he tell her something that would hurt her? He hadn't meant to, but sometimes intentions weren't enough. The damage was done. But then, he reconsidered. Maybe he had done her a favor. Maybe if she knew the truth, she would stay away from Enzo. It would only be for her own good.

"I need a drink." Enzo fell into the barstool next to him as the bartender immediately began pouring a whiskey neat.

"You okay?" Francesco asked. He could feel the angst radiating off Enzo's body.

"You've got a *big* mouth, you know that?"

"Oh, God." Francesco stiffened. He knew his brother. He knew Enzo was just getting started.

Enzo leaned in, his voice as low as a whisper. "You told her I'm *married?*"

"I didn't mean to."

"I should crack you."

"She deserved to know. I told you, she's nice."

"Yeah, she's not that nice."

"What?" Francesco tried to decipher his brother's expression. "Something happen between you two?"

"Not yet, and now it probably won't because you screwed it all up."

"Enz, it was an accident. I've been drinking all day."

"Hey, Ant," Enzo turned to the bartender as he clutched onto his drink, "cut my brother off. Understand me?"

"You can't do that," Francesco protested. "I own the place."

"Not another sip." Enzo moved the near empty bottle away from him. "And I want you to stop cooking for her."

"Excuse me?" Francesco's face burned as if someone had taken a match to it. Cooking was his life. It was all he did. "She has to eat, just like everybody else."

"What do you think, I'm stupid? You cook special things for her. You try to impress her."

Francesco smirked. "Well, if you want me to stop, then it must be working."

"Don't get cute. She doesn't want you. She doesn't even notice you."

Francesco let out a laugh. He knew his brother had affairs more often than not, but he hadn't seen him like this in years. "You got it bad."

"You think this is funny?"

"Yeah, actually, I do," he said, failing to stifle his laughter. Between the wine swirling around in his head and the way Scarlett had Enzo wrapped around her little finger, Francesco's laughter became uncontrollable.

"Yeah, keep laughing." Enzo shook his head. "Cook her one more bowl of pasta and see what I do to you."

"I look forward to it, Enz."

In the entryway, Enzo's family poured through the front doors. "My boy is here." Enzo stood up, shoving away his drink. He smoothed down his tie and buttoned his sport coat. It was time for him to be a father. "Get your shit together. I don't need you acting all sloppy around my kids."

"You got a lot of nerve, Enz," Francesco called after his brother as he walked away. "A lot of damn nerve."

SIXTEEN

HELL'S KITCHEN, NEW YORK

SPRING, 1985

S carlett had made it a point not to see Enzo one-on-one anymore. Though she threw herself into work, she couldn't help but notice how dull her days were starting to feel without him. But no matter what, she couldn't forget the way she felt when she had learned the truth. How foolish she felt for believing their connection was a rarity. That the feeling she got when she was with him, the electric current that seemed to move between them with zero effort, was genuine. Still, something ached inside of her. Enzo's attention had become like an addictive drug, not so much due to the attention itself; by Enzo putting her on a pedestal, she had begun to see herself in a different light. She had started to believe that neither her job nor Enzo's interest in her was due to the reasons Helen and Lana provided, but instead, because Scarlett genuinely deserved those things. Maybe she had something to offer Enzo, to the world.

It didn't matter. It didn't matter how much she missed him, and how she wondered if he missed her, too. Enzo was unavailable, and whatever she felt for him, she would have to live with it until she didn't feel it anymore. Her work would have to be enough. Her work wouldn't let her down.

After setting her section of the dining room, going over each detail with painstaking precision, kneeling on the ground to ensure that every piece of flatware and glasses were aligned, Scarlett immersed herself in dinner service. Her training sessions with Fausto had concluded weeks ago, but she could still hear his voice in her head. Her eyes served as the lens to her instinct, leading her to clear and reset tables without being told to do so, picking up cues from customers, and lending a helping hand wherever she was needed.

In the kitchen, Scarlett plucked out a tray and began to examine the dishes in the window. She scanned over the pink ticket in her hand as she began to load her tray with hot plates of chicken piccata, veal scallopini, *zuppa di pesce* and *spaghetti vongole.*

"We're missing the lobster *fra diavolo* on this order," Scarlett called through the window as she held up the ticket.

Francesco turned around and tapped a set of tongs on the side of his frying pan. In the pan, strings of linguine were topped with plum tomatoes and fresh lobster meat. "Two seconds," he said with a smile as he married the ingredients with wrist action.

"Bossing around the chef," Julie said as she joined Scarlett, stabbing a completed ticket over the spindle. "Never a good idea."

"I don't think he minds," Scarlett laughed.

Francesco slid the plate into the window. "Somebody has to keep me in check," he said to the girls.

"Yeah, I'll leave that to her," Julie said as she cocked her head towards Scarlett.

After successfully serving the entrées, Scarlett stopped by the bar to pick up a round of espressos for another table. She walked them over to a table of men who, judging from their light washed denim and casual windbreakers, had to be tourists.

She turned the corner, holding her breath and walking with an even pace so not to spill the hot liquid, her dark eyes focused on the drinks. One of the men at the table spoke animatedly, his arms gesticulating wildly, so wildly that his arm knocked her silver tray upside down. Hot, sticky brown liquid covered Scarlett's chest and stained her white blouse. She, along with the four men at the table, went quiet.

"Watch where you're going next time," one of them said. Then, they erupted into laughter.

Scarlett slunk down, vibrating with embarrassment and frustration, as she began to gather the now empty demitasse cups. Rushing back to the kitchen, she disposed of the glassware into the dishwashing pit and glanced down at her chest. It had gone beet red.

"Hey," Fausto said. He reached for her arm and turned her around. "What did those *strunzi* say to you?"

"Nothing," Scarlett said, determined not to let the men get the best of her. "I just need some burn cream. And a new shirt."

"There are some spare shirts up in the office. You go up, and I'll have someone else finish your section, alright?"

Scarlett's heart was in her throat, not because of the embarrassment that had just occurred, nor due to the fact that her skin felt like it was on fire. No, instead, anticipation boiled in her stomach as she climbed the stairs to see the one man she desperately wanted to avoid and couldn't wait to see.

ENZO LOVED THE SMELL of cash. To him, it was a finer scent than any luxury perfume. His hands felt raw from counting, but finally, he deposited the final stack into his safe. The first poker night had been a minimal success as John had predicted, but a success nonetheless. A step in the right direction. Enzo didn't shy away from having to prove himself; sometimes, it felt like his entire life thus far had been one long stretch of wanting something just out of his reach and having to prove why he deserved it. It certainly was the case in his new business arrangement.

And so it was with Scarlett.

He couldn't blame her for avoiding him. Maybe she thought less of him, or maybe she was only trying to protect herself. From what, he couldn't quite understand. Even when Enzo hurt someone, it was never done with the intention to do so. He lit a cigarette and turned the radio up, considering his next play. Either he would put in the work to prove himself to her, or he would replace her. The latter would be the easier of the two options, though the less intriguing. Enzo's affairs weren't merely fun and games; they were a distraction, lest his mind lay dormant enough to think about the reality of his life.

Over the music, Enzo heard knocking at his door. When he found Scarlett standing there, they stared at each other for a few moments before either of them said anything. Though they went to speak at the same time, he let her have her turn.

Her eyes fell to her shirt. "I need a new blouse. Fausto said you have some extras."

Enzo opened the door wider to let her in. "You okay? What happened?"

"This guy was talking with his hands and knocked over my tray. I'm fine." Scarlett looked around the office. "Where are the shirts?"

Enzo closed the door behind her. "Look, can I please talk to you?" Though she darted her eyes away from him, he placed his fingers on her chin and guided her back to him. "I've missed you."

Scarlett glared up at him, though he could see beneath her façade that the feeling was mutual. "You lied to me."

He brightened at her response, not because he liked what she was saying, but because she was talking to him at all. "I know I did. And I'm sorry. But I told you the truth. Might have taken me too long, but I told you the God's honest truth. I'm married. I don't love Claudia, but we've got the kids."

"And that's fine, Enzo. I'm glad I found out before anything happened. But I can't do this with you."

"You were doing just fine before."

"Exactly. Before. But now I know, and I can't pretend I don't. No matter—" she started, but stopped herself short.

"No matter what?" When she didn't respond, he lowered his head so their eyes were level. "Why you hiding from me?"

Scarlett swallowed. "Before I started working here, my mother told me that I don't understand men. And I don't understand you. I don't understand why you want this with me."

"You know what my life felt like before? Black-and-white," Enzo said no louder than a whisper. "You brought the colors. Bright colors I've never seen before. Does that make sense?"

When Scarlett nodded, he continued. "These last few days without you, everything started to fade again."

"I know," she whispered. "I felt it too."

"You understand perfectly, Scar," he said. "Why would I want to live my life in black-and-white when the colors are right here in front of me?"

Sounds of their heavy, anticipatory breathing filled the room. Her eyes opened wider, earnest and uncertain, yet filled with fire. "This is a bad idea, Enzo."

"My whole life is built on bad ideas." Though their bodies moved ever closer to each other, he didn't want to push her. A woman like Scarlett had to make her own decisions. "I'll do whatever you want, Scar."

Their breathing was heavy and fast. Enzo waited for Scarlett, searching her face for any indication that she wanted him as badly as he wanted her. He would wait however long he had to.

"I want you." Her voice sounded shaky, but he knew she was sure. "You have no idea how bad I want you, Enzo."

She grabbed him by his collar and pulled him towards her until their lips met with force and passion, his lips pressing hard against hers. They devoured each other, and neither one of them could help it. She was crazy about him. And he was crazy about the way she made him feel. She wanted him, but he knew Scarlett wasn't a woman who operated on desire alone. She had a need for Enzo, a need for what he could give her, what he could mean to her, how he could save her. That was the greatest power of all, wasn't it? To have a woman who needs you.

They stumbled back until Scarlett fell onto the desk. He held her tight against him as she wrapped her arms around the entirety of his broad shoulders, holding nothing back as she kissed him. He knew she would give him everything she had; be his completely. He buried his face in her neck and trailed the length of it with soft, slow kisses as he unbuttoned her blouse, leaving his scent of citrus and musk on her skin. It felt better than he even imagined. The high of his other vices wore off quickly, but the feeling he got as he ran his strong hands up her thighs and wrapped her legs around him, the rush he got when she yelled out his name in the most excruciating euphoria, that would last for weeks.

CHAPTER

SEVENTEEN

LITTLE ITALY, NEW YORK

SPRING, 1985

Scarlett wore a little black dress Enzo had bought for her. Made of fine, expensive silk, it fit her small figure like a glove. She spritzed her neck with some fresh, floral perfume and swiped her lips with crimson before making her way towards him. She paused, letting him drink her in. Judging from the mischievous grin on his face, he liked the way she looked. Didn't he always? He took her in by her waist and gave her a long, delicious kiss before they made their way through the Valenti's dining room. It was packed. All eyes were on them. Two stars, two people who shifted the gravity when they entered a room, and together, that shift was all the more powerful. Enzo flashed his perfect, disarming smile as they weaved their way through the tables. They made one hell of a couple, and Enzo was enjoying every second showing her off as his girl. Enzo's girl.

She beamed at the thought of it. God, she loved the way that sounded.

She felt someone shaking her. They were calling her name.

"Scar."

She heard Enzo's voice. And then, she woke up. It was just a dream. A delicious, perfect dream. "What time is it?" Scarlett blinked a few times. She didn't immediately recognize her surroundings, but then the pieces fell back into place. They were in a glamorous hotel suite on a high floor overlooking all of downtown New York. This was not a dream. She had spent the night with Enzo and now she was waking up in his arms. She looked up at him, his face still sleepy and his chest bare save for the gold chains that he never took off.

"Ten, honey. We've gotta be out of here by eleven," Enzo said as he rolled onto his side and studied her.

Though by now she knew the expression on his face meant he wanted her, she laughed and sat up. "Wait, wait, wait. I just woke up."

She got out of bed, pulled the sheets around her, and made her way to the bathroom. Locking the door behind her, she let the sheets fall to the ground as she met her reflection in the mirror.

She was the whore's pasta personified.

Her hair was a disaster, she had a bruise on her neck, and her lips were swollen from too much kissing. She leaned in closer, looking herself in the eye. And that was the precise moment when the guilt started to creep in. The guilt for sleeping with someone who belonged to someone else, for calling her mother a tramp when she was no better. In the absence of the delirium of late nights and liquor, she was left to face reality. The sprawling suite suddenly felt claustrophobic, and the only thing she wanted was a long, hot shower and a few gallons of water to wash away the sins of last night. A sinking feeling settled in her stomach. Why did she want something, someone, if it was wrong?

Scarlett began to consider that perhaps it wasn't only Enzo that she wanted. It was what he could mean for her. Enzo, a man with so much — for him to risk it all for her would mean her value was greater than everything Enzo had combined. Visions of their life together clouded her mind, though the image in front of her looked nothing like the origin story of the life she dreamt of. Their reality was a love affair meant to be hidden and concealed. The shame of it all enveloped her, as did the fact that, despite those feelings, she was utterly and completely in love with him.

Enzo knocked on the door. "Sweetheart?"

Jolted out of her thoughts, she wrapped a robe around her and opened the door. "Hi."

"You okay?"

"Yeah."

"You sure?"

She leaned her hip against the counter of the vanity. "You ever do this before?"

"Do what?" he asked as he reached for a towel and tied it around his hips.

"See somebody else. While you're with Claudia."

Enzo took a seat on the edge of the bathtub and Scarlett went to sit next to him. "Will you think less of me if the answer is *yes*?"

Scarlett pursed her lips though her eyes were warm. "I'll think less of you if you lie to me."

"Then yeah. I have."

Scarlett hugged her knees to her chest. "I don't get it. Why not just leave if you're not happy?"

"You're Italian."

"Only half."

"Still. You know what we're about, don't you? Family. It's everything. I'd die for my brother, and I'd die for my kids. If I leave, that means I'm a selfish bastard. Not putting my kids first. I know I'm no saint, Scar, but this way, they have a home. They don't have to go back and forth, or even worse, be raised by only one of us. This way, I get to live my life the way I want to and do the things that make me happy without hurting them."

"What about your wife? Does she…" Scarlett paused, unsure if she wanted the answer, "know?"

Enzo bounced his knee up and down. "She's not a stupid woman. I'll give her that."

"Do you love her?"

He ran his fingers through his hair, slices of sharp black hair peeking through them. "She gave me my kids. I know I'm not around for them as much as I should be, but it's only because I'm working to give them the best life I can. I love those three little critters. She's their mother."

"A simple *yes* would've sufficed."

"I'm not in love with her. I'm not sure I ever was."

"What's the difference?"

He cupped Scarlett's face in his hands. "You know that thing we have? This feeling we get when we're together, like we're on a drug or something?"

Scarlett had never done a drug in her life, but being with Enzo felt like what she imagined it was to be high on ecstasy. She knew exactly what he meant.

"I never had that with her. Not even in the beginning," Enzo said.

"So what are you saying?"

"That you don't need to waste your time thinking about Claudia, or anybody else. You're the only person I wanna be with."

As Scarlett stood and wrapped her arms around his waist, he drew her in close and kissed her forehead. All her life, Scarlett had believed men to be complicated creatures. Puzzles that could never be solved. Maybe it was nothing more than an illusion she had created for herself to avoid the heartbreak and disappointments her mother experienced on numerous occasions. But with each layer of Enzo she uncovered, the more she understood him, she didn't find him all that complicated in the least.

"But Enzo," she said, looking up at him, "nobody can know about this."

To her surprise, he smiled. "It's nice not being the only one who has to keep secrets."

"Mom?" Scarlett called out. Stacks of brown boxes and piles of clothes lined the entryway. Though Scarlett now spent several nights a week sleeping in luxury hotels, seeing her apartment turned upside down left her with an unsettled feeling.

"Scar, baby, is that you?" Lana's voice traveled down the hallway until she appeared in the entryway. "There you are." Lana scanned her daughter up and down. "You haven't been home much lately."

"I know." Scarlett put her hand on her neck, but it was of no use. It was written all over her where she had been. "Are you going on vacation?" Scarlett motioned to the suitcases, hoping her change of subject would work. To her surprise, it did.

"Oh, Scarlett, sweetie." Lana put her hands on Scarlett's shoulders and steered her towards the sofa. They sat side by side. "It's Dustin. He's bought this amazing house out on Long Island, and he's invited me to go live with him," she gushed, breaking into a Cheshire grin.

"And you said yes?" Scarlett searched her mother's face. She looked for the usual signs of tired eyes and the scent of liquor, but her mother showed none of the usual symptoms. Had it been so long since Scarlett had experienced her mother's happiness that she'd forgotten what it was like?

"Yes!" Lana beamed as Scarlett's face fell. "With you being away so much and me staying with Dustin, it didn't make sense to keep the apartment."

Though Scarlett and Lana had moved three times since her father passed, Scarlett couldn't shake her sense of disorientation. "When are you, we, moving out?"

"In a couple of days. Landlord has to get the place cleaned up before the first."

"A couple of days," Scarlett said under her breath. Panic began to rise in her. Had this all been her doing? She had left under the guise of returning, only for it to result in tearing the two of them apart, further than they ever had been before.

Lana settled back into the sofa and brushed her fingers through her hair. They were quiet for a few minutes, Lana's earlier exuberance replaced by her usual disposition. "You been staying with friends?"

"Yeah. Friends."

"That Enzo guy, right? He's your friend?"

Scarlett focused her gaze on her lap where she fiddled with her peeling manicure. "I didn't mean for any of this to happen, Mom. I was just trying to get you to see me, and—"

"And exactly what I said would happen, happened. Didn't it?"

"Not exactly."

Lana leaned towards Scarlett. "You left because you wanted me to understand you better, right? To see your *potential.*" She stood up and pulled a business card out of the pocket of her jeans. "Maybe now that I'm gone, you'll understand *me* better. That I wasn't such a shit mother after all. Here," she said, handing Scarlett the card. "You can call me if you need me, although I'm sure Enzo is taking great care of you."

Scarlett scanned the card with Dustin's name, business address, and phone number. She tucked it into her bag with care, as if it were the last shred of her mother she'd ever have. She didn't want to need her mother, but she had an innate sense she would. "Will you answer? If I call you?"

"I've always been here, Scar, when you wanted me, and even when you didn't." The phone rang from the kitchen and Lana turned to answer it. "Start packing, kid."

EIGHTEEN

UPPER WEST SIDE, NEW YORK

SPRING, 1985

With duffel bags at her feet, Scarlett pressed the buzzer for Helen's apartment and a few moments later, Mrs. O'Connor appeared behind the door.

"Scarlett," Mrs. O'Connor said as bright and welcoming as she always was. She wore a frilly apron over an otherwise drab outfit. Her eyes fell to the bags at Scarlett's feet. "Are you going on a trip? Helen didn't mention anything."

"Not exactly. Is she here? I need to talk to her."

Helen appeared behind her mother. "Hey, Scar." She glanced down at the bags, then back up at Scarlett. "Leave them here. We'll get them later. Come on, I want to hear everything."

Once inside Helen's bedroom, Scarlett relayed the story. "She made me feel like it was all my fault that she was leaving. Like she's always been some great mother and I never appreciated her. And the worst part, Helen, is that it worked. She made me feel like I'm some..." Scarlett paused, searching for the right words, "ungrateful monster. And you know how she used to be, Hel."

"Oh, I do. Her drinking got so bad in high school, you practically lived here."

"I know."

"So don't take the blame. It's not your fault. You know, I always thought you'd be happy to get away from her, but I don't know. You don't look like it."

"All I ever wanted from her is what you have. To hug me and smell like laundry detergent instead of Jean Naté and hairspray. To ask me if I'm hungry after I come home from being out all night. To believe that I'm good at something and encourage me to get out in the world the way your mother does. That's all I want, and she won't give it to me."

"She can't," Helen said, reaching for Scarlett's hand. "She's sick, Scarlett. And you can't fix her."

"She drinks. That's not the same as being sick. She chooses to drink."

"It's an addiction. She probably wants to stop but doesn't know how."

"I wish she would try. Do you know how much better I would feel if she just *tried*?"

"Let's give her some time. You two have never lived apart. Maybe once she's away, she'll start to feel differently." Helen's forehead wrinkled in confusion. "I just don't understand how she could leave you with nowhere to live. I mean, even for Lana, that's pretty bad."

Scarlett's heart began to race, something that didn't typically happen when she was with her best friend. Helen had always been Scarlett's sense of safety, but now Scarlett was keeping the truth even from her. "I've been staying over at my co-workers' apartments a lot. Fausto, and Julie. They live closer to the restaurant, so it's been easier. I guess my mom figured I didn't need our apartment anyway."

A strange expression of disbelief moved through Helen's eyes. "You know what's always been your telltale sign that you're lying?" Helen pointed to Scarlett's chest. "Your neck and your chest get real red."

Scarlett looked at Helen. Her best friend. She had always been the one person Scarlett could tell anything. But the longer she stared at Helen, the more space she felt between them. They weren't the same at all anymore. The little similarities they did have had vanished. Scarlett had changed, and Helen would either love the new her or hate her, but either way, Scarlett was about to find out. She took in a jagged breath. "I've been staying with Enzo."

Helen let out a sarcastic, dry laugh. "I'm sorry. What?" Helen's mouth hung open. "The last time you and I spoke, you said you were going to end things with him."

"Well, I didn't."

"So let me get this straight. You found out he's married, you found out he has *children,* and you're still seeing him?" Her disappointment turned to disgust. "You're sleeping with a married man, Scarlett. Do you know how low that is?"

"Can you lower your voice, please?" Scarlett pleaded, her throat burning and her palms going clammy. "I knew you'd never get it."

"No." She shook her head. "I could never *get* this. What do you even get out of it? A few meaningless compliments?"

"I love him, Helen."

"Like you even know what that means." Helen's laughter pierced through Scarlett – her mockery, a different kind of heartbreak.

Scarlett stood. "I came here because I needed you, Helen. You say you're always there for me, and now when I really need you, you're not."

"I have been there for you every step of the way. I was there for you every time Lana got too drunk to pick you up from school. I was there for you when her boyfriends slept over and I let you stay at my place, so don't say I haven't been there for you. But this? How could you expect me to be okay with this? You know what kind of person I am, Scarlett. You know, I don't even know why you bothered to come here and tell me all of this. It's not like we have anything in common anymore."

Helen was red, from her chest up to her forehead. Her face looked twisted with disdain and hurt and frustration. But all Scarlett felt was this deep pit of disappointment that another person in her life was slipping through her fingers. She had lost Lana. Was she about to lose Helen too?

"I'm sorry. I can't be friends with someone who lives like this, let alone let them stay in my home," Helen said, her tone definitive.

"Helen, it's me," Scarlett yelled, pleading with Helen to see her again. Ironic, she thought, that the more she tried to get people to see her, the more invisible she became. "It's me."

"You're not *you* anymore."

"I never knew you were so perfect, Helen."

"I'm not perfect." Helen stood in a huff. "But I know who I am. You don't have any idea who you are. That's why you fell for the first man who paid any attention to you. I've been right about everything so far, haven't I? Well here's my next prediction. He's going to break your heart. And when he does, I'm not going to be there for you to help you pick up the pieces."

"Screw you!" Scarlett yelled. Her hands curled into fists by her side and her knuckles went white. "You're just jealous."

"What am I jealous of, exactly, Scarlett?"

"That my life is more exciting than yours. That my future doesn't follow some predictable script that fits into a neat little box like yours does."

"Maybe that's what you think. Maybe to you, your life is more exciting than mine. But I think it's pretty sad that you think all you deserve is a man who belongs to someone else. You can only blame your mother for so much. At some point, you have to take responsibility for your own choices."

Mrs. O'Connor swung the door open. "Girls, what's going on in here?"

Tangible tension ignited between the girls. As angry as Scarlett was, as boiling hot as she felt with frustration, it was the hurt she felt the deepest. Helen's betrayal cut her in different ways than Lana. Helen and Scarlett had chosen to be friends throughout their lives, and all it took was one misstep for Helen to stop that choice. Scarlett backed away, leaving Helen, who, in her eyes, looked high and mighty, like she thought she was better than Scarlett. Out on the sidewalk, alone, Scarlett cried. She cried for her losses, for her father, for Lana, for Helen, for the fact that if Helen was right and she lost Enzo, too, she'd have nothing left at all.

She had lost everything over Enzo, and only time would tell if he would do the same for her.

NINETEEN

LITTLE ITALY, NEW YORK
SPRING, 1985

It was only mid-morning, but as Francesco made his way into Enzo's office, it was already clouded with smoke. Enzo sat behind his desk, enjoying his usual breakfast of a fine cigar and several shots of espresso, a silver moka pot sitting atop Enzo's desk. Francesco took a seat opposite of his older brother, taking in the way Enzo moved energetically through his administrative tasks. A pang of jealousy hit Francesco. They worked the same hours, but Francesco was the one who went through his mornings feeling sluggish and exhausted.

"Morning," Francesco said with a raspy voice.

Enzo gave his brother a good onceover. "You look like shit."

"Thanks, asshole," Francesco deadpanned. But then, he caught sight of the seemingly permanent smile on his brother's face. "Where were you last night?"

"Here," Enzo said, keeping his gaze on the checks he was writing. "Were you so gone that you don't remember me being here last night?"

"After," he clarified. But as Enzo finally looked up and let his smile expand to show all his pearly white teeth, Francesco didn't need him to explain. He already knew. "You were with her."

"Yeah."

Francesco considered that if he were a normal man, one who lived by physicality alone, he would be making jokes with his brother, commending him for being able to get with a younger, beautiful woman like Scarlett. But he wasn't wired that way. He couldn't ignore the pang in his chest as he thought about the two of them together. "You sure look pleased with yourself," he finally said. He rested his elbows on his knees and his back hunched over.

"You would too. She's amazing."

"Please spare me the details." He avoided his brother's eyes and his head hung low.

Enzo laughed. "What's going on with you, kid? You okay? You still seeing that Maria chick?"

"That ended at least a month ago. Been seeing Lisa, the one with the blue eyes."

"I can't keep track. You've had more girlfriends than me."

Francesco studied his brother, the way he looked carefree, like he was high on nothing but Scarlett herself. Francesco wasn't sure he'd ever had that feeling. But as he thought back to his girlfriends, one blended into the other. Maria, Karen, Lisa, what was one from the next? What made one different from the other when they all felt the same? "How do you do it, Enz?"

"Do what?"

"Have all these girlfriends. Don't you ever feel guilty?"

"I can't believe you just asked me that." Enzo finally stopped writing. "You'll see. When you get married, you'll see."

"That'll never happen." Francesco scoffed like Enzo had made the most ridiculous statement ever.

"What's that supposed to mean?"

"I've never dated a girl for more than a couple of months. You've been married for what, ten years? I don't think I could do it. Longevity wise."

"It's a job, Fran." Enzo looked down at his desk, scanning over an invoice. "You've been cooking your whole life. But you like to do other things too, right? During the week, on your days off, you do things that make you happy besides cooking. Being married is no different." Enzo reached over and picked up the ringing phone. "Yeah, hello?"

Francesco stayed quiet as he watched his brother on the phone. He could faintly hear a woman's voice on the other end, though he couldn't make out any of the words. Judging from the look on Enzo's face, he was positive it wasn't Claudia. He wondered if it was Scarlett. He didn't know why, but he hoped it wasn't.

"Listen to me, you wait there. You wait there, and I'm coming to get you now." Enzo stood as he hung up the phone.

"Who was that?" Francesco asked as soon as the phone hit the receiver.

"Scarlett. Her mother ran off with some fella and now she's got nowhere to go."

Francesco's heart dropped to his stomach. "You're kidding me."

"We gotta know someone with an extra room." Enzo ran his palm over his face as he stood up and pulled on his sport coat.

"What about," Francesco paused, reconsidering what he was about to say, "what about my place?"

Enzo arched a brow. "Your place?"

"Yeah." Francesco kept his cool, but his pulse quickened.

"You got something for her?" Enzo put his hands on his hips and narrowed his eyes.

"Yeah." Francesco rolled his eyes. "A spare bedroom."

Enzo paused, thinking things over. "Alright. But you make a move on her, you're dead."

"You should know by now that I don't involve myself in your affairs."

"I'm going now. I'll be back in an hour. Make sure the place is cleaned up, you hear me?"

"I hear you." Francesco sighed. It was his idea, but Enzo would take all the credit. He was sure of it.

THE CADILLAC CAME TO a screeching halt in front of Scarlett. Heavy, gray clouds were rolling in as she stood up from the bench in front of the phone booth. Enzo emerged from the driver's side and lugged her bags into the trunk.

"Get in." He opened the door for her and closed it behind her once she was in safely. He put the car in drive and pulled away. "You okay?"

"I don't know, Enzo."

"What kind of mother leaves her kid to run off with some fella? I don't understand."

Though Scarlett hadn't wanted to share this part of her life with Enzo, she was left with no choice. She had called him in her time of need, and he was owed an explanation. "She drinks too much, Enz." Scarlett's gaze fell to her lap. She could feel his stare on her. "She drinks too much and she sleeps around. That's what kind of mother she is. She's been with this guy all of four, five months and she's already moving away with him. And that's my mother taking things slow."

"Scarlett. I'm sorry." He took a breath, hesitating before continuing. "Why didn't you ever tell me about her before?"

Scarlett caught a glimpse of herself in the passenger side mirror as they headed downtown. Enzo knew so much of Scarlett, the most intimate details of her, yet she had left a gaping hole. "I didn't want you to know about her."

"Why? Scar," he glanced over at her, "I've been honest with you, haven't I? You can tell me anything." He reached out his hand and interlaced his fingers with Scarlett's. "Tell me."

"I lied to you. The day I came in looking for a job, I told you I was a bartender. But I had only ever worked as a barback."

"A little white lie. No big deal."

"My mother didn't think I was good enough to do anything else. She made me think I was useless. All I had going for me was a pretty face, that's what she used to tell me. And I believed it." Scarlett tightened her grip on Enzo's hand. "I didn't want you to know what she thought of me, because I was afraid you'd think the same thing. But ever since I started working at your restaurant," Scarlett said and looked over at him, "and ever since I started spending time with you, I don't believe it anymore."

"Sometimes, people make us feel like we're nothing. Like we're real small. Like we're not the kind of people that matter in this world. And sometimes, they do it on purpose. Some sort of motivation tactic. And believe it or not, it works sometimes. But when it's your own mother..." Enzo trailed off, tsking tongue against his teeth. "I don't think that's what a mother is supposed to do to her kid."

"You've felt like this before?"

"For as long as I can remember. I came from nothing. When you come from nothing, sometimes you feel like you are nothing. But I took all that frustration and anger and I turned it into fuel. My family, including my brother, they didn't want me to come to New York. They thought it was too dangerous, and that I'd fail and have to go back. But I had to try. I had to prove them wrong."

"And you did."

"And you will too. But you gotta do what I did. Don't let her hold you back. Make it motivate you. You like what you do, right? What's the top of the ladder in our business?"

Scarlett sat up straighter. "What you do. Owning the place."

"Exactly. How would you feel going back to your mother, telling her you own your own place when she didn't even think you were capable of being a bartender? Hmm?"

For the first time all day, Scarlett smiled. Excitement danced up and down her spine. "I think that would feel pretty amazing. But the only place I ever thought I'd own was my mother's bar."

Enzo poked Scarlett's head. "Think bigger." They shared a laugh. "You can do anything you set your mind to, so set it to something big, Scar. People like us can't let people like them win." As Enzo pulled into the parking lot, he stole a long glance at Scarlett. "There's that smile. Now come on," Enzo said as he unbuckled his seatbelt. "You've got a new home now."

<hr />

"This is temporary," Scarlett protested. Francesco had made her too generous of an offer, opening his place to her rent free. As Enzo lugged the rest of Scarlett's bags up the stairs and set them down with a heavy thud, Francesco lit a cigarette. Both brothers shrugged at her suggestion, and though Scarlett had always noticed how dissimilar they looked, their nuanced movements took her by surprise. "I'll start looking for a place right away."

"Relax," Enzo brushed her off. "You've got a nice setup here. Enjoy it."

Scarlett looked at Francesco. "I'm going to pay you rent."

"No," the brothers said in unison.

"Yes," she insisted.

"Scarlett, I'm not taking your money. I have to get downstairs and prep. Enzo can show you to your room. And make yourself comfortable. You have as much free rein of the place as I do," Francesco said before jogging down the steps two by two.

Once he closed the door behind him, Scarlett moved about the space. The apartment was immaculate, everything in its proper place. In the small living room was a television set, a silver boombox, and a record player with an impressive vinyl collection underneath. Her bedroom was next to Francesco's, similar in its eclectic style but a bit smaller. She surveyed the small, cozy kitchen, the long stretch of a closet in the hallway, and the way there was an ashtray on every surface. She expected to feel like an outsider, crashing in someone else's sacred space, but as she did in his restaurant, she felt at ease in Francesco's home.

"You like it?" Enzo asked her.

"It's so nice."

"Good."

"Enzo, I can't believe you two did this for me. This is crazy."

"Have you not yet noticed that I'm a little bit crazy?" His smile traveled all the way to his eyes as he took her face in his hands.

She held up two fingers close to each other. "Just a tad. But like I said, this is temporary."

"Don't be in such a rush. Fran doesn't mind."

"I do. Living with your brother? I mean, come on. It's kind of weird."

"Kid's never home," Enzo explained. "When he's not working, he's out with women. When he's not with women, he's here, but all he does is sleep."

"Sounds like he dates a lot."

"Sleeps around a lot," Enzo corrected her. "He tries to have a girlfriend, you know? Kid can't commit. They all fall in love with him, but he never wants to settle down. I don't know what's wrong with him. That's not how *Mamma* raised us."

"Maybe he just hasn't found the right person yet."

"Broads come in our place and throw themselves at him. Women make him crazy."

"I think you two have that in common."

"Know what I told him before I came and got you?" Enzo asked. "If he makes a move on you, he's dead."

"You don't trust your brother?"

"When it comes to a girl like you? Not at all."

A smile crept up on her face. "Somebody's jealous."

"You think that's funny?" He laughed as he wrapped his arms around her. "I'm not jealous. Know why? Because I care about you. And I know you care about me too."

Her smile began to fade, not because of a lack of appreciation for what he had said, but in awe of it. He began to kiss her, but she pulled back. "Enzo, can I tell you something?"

"You can tell me anything. Anything at all."

"I don't just care about you." She took a deep breath, preparing to say the one thing that scared and thrilled her all the same. "I love you."

He didn't say it back. Maybe he didn't need to. Maybe Enzo showed Scarlett he loved her through the things he did for her and the way he treated her. Or maybe she only had a piece of him, and that was why it was so easy to love him in the first place. She didn't have all of him, and in turn, he didn't have all of her.

It's easier to love someone when you don't have to lose yourself to them.

TWENTY

LITTLE ITALY, NEW YORK

SUMMER, 1985

"Now hold on," Julie leaned in. She, Fausto, and Scarlett were enjoying cigarettes and a bottle of vodka in the back alley behind Valenti's. "You're *living* with Fran?"

"It's temporary," Scarlett reconciled, for her sake and Julie's. Even still, she couldn't help but cringe. "God, it really is kind of weird. I mean, we don't know each other like that."

Julie moved her brows up and down and shimmied her shoulders against Scarlett's. "You could *get* to know him like *that*."

"I don't think Enzo would like that," Fausto sing-songed as he lay on the ground and adjusted his arm behind his head.

While Julie shot him a look, Scarlett did her best to adopt a poker face despite having never played the game. "What's that supposed to mean?" Julie said to Fausto.

"I don't know." Fausto's blue eyes traveled to Scarlett. "Why don't you tell us?"

Scarlett stuttered for a few moments, trying to hide from their stares, but soon, the three of them erupted into laughter. Scarlett looked between Julie and Fausto. They were her friends, weren't they? They had to know. They had to feel the chemistry that seemed to take over every room Scarlett and Enzo were in, and they had to notice the way they looked at each other. Scarlett had wanted to keep their thing a secret as much as Enzo did, but she needed someone in her corner. "Can I trust you guys?"

Julie put her cigarette out. "Look at me." She put her hand on Scarlett's shoulder and pulled her close. "When you walked through those doors, we became your family. That's how this thing works. You understand?"

Scarlett nodded, more thrilled at the prospect of calling her two friends *family* than she was about sharing the news of her relationship with Enzo. "Family."

"Alright." Fausto sat up. "Let's hear it from the horse's mouth. Who's the lucky guy who has the pleasure of keeping that smile planted on your face?"

Scarlett reached for the bottle of vodka between them and took a shot. Her nose wrinkled as it scorched her throat. "I'm in love with Enzo."

<hr/>

FRANCESCO STARED AT THE ceiling. He lay flat on the couch, smoking his way through a pack of Lucky Strikes as a Puccini record spun in the background. His favorite — *Turandot,* about the beautiful yet icy princess who would only marry a suitor should he be able to solve three riddles. Should one try and fail, their fate was death. Tonight, Francesco felt a kinship with the fictional princess of the opera. How many women had tried to solve the enigmas of his heart? How many of them hadn't succeeded, leading to yet another failed relationship—its own kind of death?

His night hadn't gone according to plan at all. He had been seeing Lisa for the past three weeks, and though he wasn't planning on ending things tonight, all it took was the mention of marriage to make Francesco flee the West Village as if it were on fire. He was waiting. Waiting to feel something, like a stab of regret or maybe even a pang of sadness. But they wouldn't come. Instead, his perpetual loneliness disappeared when he heard Scarlett walking up the staircase.

"Hello?" she called out.

"I'm up here," he yelled back. "Hi, Scarlett."

"Hi. Sorry," she said, creeping her way into the living room. "I didn't mean to wake you."

"You didn't."

"I didn't think you'd be home, and I was hanging out with Fausto and Julie and lost track of time, but then I heard the music," Scarlett rambled. "Sorry."

"I told you, you don't have to tiptoe around me. You can come home whenever you want." He smiled at her, hoping to make her feel more comfortable in what was her new home.

"I know." She dug her hands into the pockets of her high-waisted jeans.

Francesco began to laugh as he put his cigarette out in the ashtray on the coffee table. "What the hell did my brother tell you about me?"

"What?"

He had a rocks glass and a bottle of whiskey on the coffee table. He sat up and poured himself a shot. "You didn't think I was coming home, so I can only imagine he told you I'd be somewhere?" He took a sip, waiting for Scarlett's answer.

"He said you're out a lot."

"With?"

"Women." Scarlett cringed. "But look, you don't need to explain nothing to me. It's none of my business."

Francesco took the rest of his shot and fell back into the sofa. "I want to ask you something."

"Okay?" she answered, her voice gone high-pitched.

"Why are you women so obsessed with getting married?"

Scarlett's shoulders fell in relief. "I'm sorry but you're asking the wrong girl. I'm not obsessed with getting married."

"You're not?" He sat up. Now, she had his full attention.

"Not really."

"Why?"

"What does marriage even mean? Two people wear nice rings, they have a piece of paper. But that doesn't mean anything. My mother thinks the men she dates are going to fix her, but she still drinks. People cheat on each other. Marrying somebody doesn't make everything better."

"I think you're the only woman I ever met who makes any sense." He looked at her as he took a long drag on his cigarette. Maybe Enzo was right. Maybe she wasn't as nice as she seemed. Maybe she was tougher than he suspected, or maybe it was all an act. He couldn't be sure, but he wanted to find out. He wanted to know everything about her.

"You know what I think?" She arched a brow, looking into his glossy eyes. "I think you've had too much to drink."

At this, he broke into a wide smile. Scarlett stared for a moment too long before breaking her gaze away. Her eyes landed on a black-and-white portrait of a couple. She walked towards it and picked it up. "These your parents?"

"They are."

Scarlett pointed to the old image of Francesco's father. "You look just like him."

"I know. *Papà*. His name was Gennaro."

"And your mother?"

Francesco stood and walked over to Scarlett, taking the portrait in his hands. Nostalgia fell over him like a heavy springtime rain. "Pia. She was famous in our neighborhood for her homemade bread. I know they make Italy look all glamorous in the movies, but there's a lot of poverty in Naples. My mother would save money by making everything herself. Bread and pasta were the staples, and the cheapest to make. She knew how to stretch the yeast to make as many loaves of bread as possible. She would spend hours in the kitchen kneading dough and cutting different types of pastas.

When we were kids, me and Enzo would go around the neighborhood and bring food to our neighbors. Everybody loved her for it. Not just because the food was free, but because it was good, too."

"Sounds like your mother is a pretty amazing woman."

"She was," Francesco said with a certain sadness. "But she wouldn't admit to it. She was humble. Shy, almost." He set the frame down and instead of studying the picture of those who had passed, he studied the woman in front of him who was very much alive.

"Both your parents passed?"

"*Mamma* first. She had diabetes and never took care of it. *Papà* had a bad heart from a young age, and he couldn't handle losing her. He died of a broken heart a year later. This was a few years ago. Enzo and I wanted to bring them here to live with us, but they weren't interested in leaving home. They never got to see our place."

"I'm sorry."

"Everybody should have parents like I did. They would've died for me and Enz."

"You're lucky." Scarlett's eyes fell to the picture frame and glossed over. "My mother will choose a martini over me any day."

"You'll make your own family."

"How do you mean?"

"You've got us. And we're all a bit nuts, but everybody here has a good heart. We're there for each other. You're a part of that now too."

"I appreciate it, Fran. Everything. You opening up your home to me, I can't even begin to thank you."

"You don't have to." He went back to the sofa and fell back into the plush cushions.

"Why'd you ask me about marriage?"

Francesco ran his hands down his long thighs. "This woman I was seeing. Lisa. We were together about a month, but tonight, she brought up marrying me."

Scarlett crossed her arms in front of her chest. "And?"

"And it freaked me out."

"Can I tell you something? It freaks me out too."

Scarlett bade him a good night, and he closed his eyes. In no time, he fell asleep, dreaming of nothing but Scarlett in a white dress.

It didn't freak him out in the least.

TWENTY-ONE

ATLANTIC CITY, NEW JERSEY
SUMMER, 1985

Atlantic City was only a couple of hours from Manhattan but driving there with Enzo felt like an adventure. He had proposed the trip to Scarlett a week prior and made mention of having to attend a business meeting. Though New Jersey wasn't high up on her list of destinations to visit, the prospect of spending a few days with Enzo outside of the city sounded like paradise. The early summer air had grown a tinge warmer, so they rolled down the windows and let the breeze kiss their faces as they glided down the Garden State Parkway. As they drove, Enzo sang along to Italian music. She preferred the moody, jazzy sounds of the tracks from the sixties and seventies over the modern pop tunes, and Enzo appeased her taste in music with a Fred Buscaglione tape. The language that used to feel so foreign to her now felt familiar, and whenever Enzo spoke Italian to her, it made her fall even harder for him. Everything about him was sweeping, whisking her away. They chain-smoked cigarettes until they turned onto the Atlantic City Expressway. It felt as if they were driving away from real life, away from all their responsibilities and the people who held them to them.

Scarlett had never been to a place as glamorous as the Tropicana Hotel. They pulled into the bustling valet lane where people poured out of their cars and into the casino doors. As soon as Enzo put the car in park, a swoon of attendants and bellhops surrounded the car and unloaded their bags from the trunk. Enzo handed out rounds of twenty-dollar bills to each attendant as if he were giving out candy. He put his hand on the small of Scarlett's back and led them to the door where a doorman swiftly opened it for them, greeting Enzo by name.

Scarlett admired the lobby of the hotel. Overhead, long stretches of glittering lights blinked, and she could already hear the chimes and songs of the slot machines. They arrived at the counter, bypassing the long line of other casino-goers, and checked in.

"Mr. Valenti," the woman at the front desk greeted him. She was already pulling out room keys, as though she'd been expecting him. "You're in room 714. You'll use the elevator bank in the north tower. Mrs. Valenti," the woman said and turned to Scarlett, "here's a brochure about our spa services if you'd like to visit during your stay."

Scarlett took the brochure with shaking hands as she repeated "*Mrs. Valenti*" over and over again in her head. Enzo took the keys and swiftly moved them away from the counter towards the escalators.

"How does everybody know your name?" Scarlett asked as they ascended towards the casino floor. As they rose, the colorful lights of the slot machines came into her view and the air rang with cheers of the lucky daytime gamblers.

"That's some good customer service, isn't it?"

Scarlett marveled at the sheer size of their hotel room that wasn't a room at all but a suite, as was Enzo's typical practice. She passed through the expansive living room complete with a full bar, the floor-to-ceiling windows overlooking the pool, and the huge bedroom with a plush king bed and a dozen white pillows. She could hardly take in all the grandeur.

"Sweetheart," Enzo called for her from the bedroom. He opened up his suitcase and pulled out a suit.

"Yes?"

"I've got to head to my meeting. I'll be gone for a couple of hours." He held up two suits, one navy blue, the other pinstripe black. "Which one?"

"The pinstripe one definitely means business," she said as she leaned against the doorframe.

"We think alike."

"We do." She smiled as he pulled his wife beater tank overhead and began redressing into his suit. She watched him, noting how being with Enzo, like this, felt so comfortable.

"What do you think?" He stood back and let her drink him in in all his handsomeness.

"If I tell you what I really think, that head of yours is going to get so big it might pop."

"Tell me anyway." He adjusted his tie as he leaned in to kiss her. "What are you gonna do? You wanna go to the spa?"

She shrugged. "I don't know."

"What am I saying?" He shook his head and pulled out his wallet. "What woman doesn't? Here." He handed her a wad of cash. "I know how you women like to get all dolled up. When I get back, we'll go down to the casino with my friends. You ever play roulette?"

She shook her head.

"Tonight, you'll learn. Best game there is." He spritzed his musky cologne around his neck and checked his reflection, satisfied with himself.

"You look perfect," she said.

He went over to her and wrapped her in his arms, planting a big kiss on her full lips. When they broke apart, he beamed. "I'll see you in a bit."

With Enzo out the door, Scarlett fished out the spa brochure from her bag. She did a quick count of the cash Enzo had handed her. Her eyes went wide at the thousand bucks he'd so casually handed off to her. As she dialed the extension to the spa and sank into the plush pillows on the bed, she reveled in the feeling that this thing of theirs wasn't too complicated at all. In fact, it was panning out to be quite fun.

ENZO'S CHEST ROSE AND fell at a rapid pace as he stood in the elevator. His eyes fell to the illuminated number eleven on the panel as he willed the elevator to move faster. Smoothing down his sport coat, he checked his watch for the umpteenth time. He would be right on time for his meeting, just like he wanted it to be. John, Michael, and Angelo weren't the type of men to keep waiting. Enzo hated that his nerves were getting the best of him, but jitters had taken over his body and his mouth had gone dry. The meeting would determine his future, if he had one at all, with John and his crew. Their agreement had been going on for the better of two months, and it was time to collect his cut. He promised himself a tall glass of whiskey or three as the elevator doors opened.

If Enzo thought his hotel suite was impressive, it had nothing on the one he now found himself in. Crystal chandeliers hung in every room and not only did they have a full bar, but a full staff to work it, too.

"Enzo," John called, waving him over to the sitting area, "what are you drinking?"

"Whiskey neat. Make it a double," Enzo said to the in-room butler.

"Have a seat." Angelo handed Enzo a cigar which he promptly lit with a match. There were a few other men scattered about the room, but

Enzo didn't recognize any of them, nor did anyone make introductions. This meeting? It wasn't about friendship; it was about cash.

"Enzo, how you doing?" Michael joined them. On the glass coffee table, he set down a gray duffel bag.

Enzo swallowed. Everything went silent.

John pointed to the bag. "Open it, kid."

Enzo hesitated at first, but he obeyed and stood, smoothing down his pants. He leaned over the coffee table and unzipped the bag, feeling everyone's eyes on him. And then, he went breathless at the sight of hundreds of thousands of dollars of cold hard cash, neatly bound and wrapped. "The hell is this?"

"You did good, kid. You did good." John stood and patted Enzo on the back.

"This is for me?" Enzo tried but failed to keep his voice cool.

"You earned it," Angelo said with a nod. "That's your cut."

"What the hell?" Enzo laughed; his disbelief apparent.

"We're happy with the way things are going," John explained. "You've earned everyone's trust like we knew you would. We'll up your share to forty percent, but besides that, we welcome you into the family."

Enzo wasn't high, but he felt like he was. He didn't know how much cash was in the bag, nor did he care. He was in; that was all that mattered. As long as he was in, he was invincible. In his eyes, he had finally made it.

Enzo kept glancing down at the duffel bag to make sure it was really there in his hands. He couldn't wait to get back to the room to do a slow, satisfying count. He walked through the casino and suddenly everything felt fresh to him again, like maybe there could be more for him than schmoozing people at his restaurant every night and going home to a wife he didn't love. Maybe he could have it all. Maybe he didn't have to look up anymore. Maybe he had reached the top of the world.

He passed by the shops just past the casino floor when one in particular caught his eye. Fur coats and fine diamonds were on display in the window. He stopped, scanning over the items. He had to get something for her. For the way she had revived him, it was the least he could do to repay her.

———～———

SCARLETT FELT LIKE SHE finally *looked* the part of being Enzo's girl. She caught sight of her reflection in the mirror on her way back to their suite; her cheeks were flushed with a glowing shade of pink, her eyelids had been swiped with denim-blue shadow, her lips painted berry, and a shiny lacquer of red polish topped her almond-shaped fingernails. As she made her way through the smoke-filled casino, she could feel the stares on her, but instead of wanting to hide, she felt proud of the way she looked.

Back in the room, she found Enzo lying down, his feet elevated on the arm of the couch as he puffed away on a cigar. He had since taken off his sport coat and tie and his shirt was halfway unbuttoned. He looked relaxed, but when he saw Scarlett, he sat upright.

"Look at you," he said as he scanned her over. "Wow."

"Do you like it?" She fluffed her full blonde mane.

He stood and went towards her, dropping his cigar in the ashtray on the coffee table. He took her in by her waist and kissed her, slow and long before pressing his lips against her neck.

"I got you something," he murmured.

"What?"

"Come here." He held her hand, leading the way to the bedroom. Two cherry-red shopping bags sat on the bed. "Those are for you."

"Both of them?" She turned back to look at him as she walked towards the bed.

"Yeah," he said with a laugh.

Scarlett sat on the edge of the bed and peeled the tissue paper from the top of the bag. Enzo watched on, clearly pleased with this showering of gifts. She felt like she was in a frenzy with red and white tissue paper flying all over the place like confetti. Finally, she uncovered the first gift. She fished out a huge white fur coat, the weight of it surprising her. It was the most glamorous thing she had ever run her fingers over.

"Enzo," she gasped, standing up and holding the coat before her. She took in the details, the fine, pointed spokes of fur that blended together to make a thick coating of pure luxury.

"You like it? It's mink."

"It's the most beautiful thing I've ever seen! It's so soft." She wrapped herself in the coat as fast as she could get her arms in the sleeves and walked over to the mirror. Studying her reflection, she barely recognized the glamorous woman staring back at her as she ran her fingers down the front of the coat, soaking in Enzo's affections. She had never imagined she'd look so rich. In this coat, she was Scarlett the woman, no longer Scarlett a girl. In Enzo's eyes, she deserved this. She deserved the world.

"Open the other one," Enzo said.

Scarlett didn't bother with taking her time anymore. She tore open the tissue paper and underneath it all she found a square velvet box. She opened it, only to reveal a necklace of dazzling marquis diamonds and a matching pair of earrings.

"Enzo!" Her head shot up out. "Oh my God. You got me diamonds?"

"I thought they looked like you."

Scarlett went back to the mirror and poked the earrings through her earlobes, tilting her head to the side so the diamonds caught in the light overhead. Enzo went behind her and fastened the necklace around her neck, letting his hands linger on her shoulders as she took everything in. The fur, the diamonds, the affections, Scarlett was in a whirlwind, one she couldn't quite believe was real. Things like this didn't happen to people like Scarlett; that was what she had always believed. But as she turned around to him, taking his face in her hands, it all became real again. The way they looked at each other with a fire in their eyes, it was as if they were silently thanking each other for breaking their hearts wide open and letting each other in. She began to cover him in kisses.

"I don't know how I'm gonna thank you for all this," she said in between kisses.

Enzo moved slow and deliberate. He peeled the coat off her, letting it fall to the ground. Their eye contact was unshakeable as he took off everything else she was wearing, until she had nothing on but the diamonds. "Yes you do."

CHAPTER

TWENTY-TWO

Enzo had never known such a perfect day. He had a quarter million dollars sitting in a duffel bag in the closet, the best woman he'd ever had hanging on his arm, and he would finish the day off with one of his favorite pastimes in the world: a game of roulette.

They strutted into the casino liked they owned the place to the soundtrack of slot machines and cheers from the craps tables. There were other glamorous-looking people throughout the casino: women clad in fishnet stockings and flashy jewelry that caught the light from the chandeliers overhead; men draped in suits made of fine fabric – they were probably high rollers like himself. But Enzo felt like a star among them. He could already feel a flush of excitement running through his veins as he led the way into the high-limit room. Scarlett looked up at the massive crystal chandelier overhead, the dim light casting a golden glow on her face.

"Fellas," Enzo said as he approached the roulette table. Michael, John, and Angelo had already gotten a head start on the action. "This is Scarlett." He moved her forward with his hand on the small of her back. He was proud she was his.

"Nice to meet you all," she said, evoking the grace and elegance of a woman beyond her years as she kissed them all on the cheek. They drew her into the center of the group with Enzo by her side.

A cocktail waitress materialized behind them, clad in a purple dress and a beverage tray on her arm. "Drinks?"

"Whiskey neat for me. Vodka tonic for my lady," Enzo ordered, but his eyes never left the roulette table before him. He pulled out a wad of cash from his sport coat, peeling off a stack of hundreds. "Give me nickels. I want the red chips." Enzo threw down the cash as the dealer began to count. "I'm superstitious," he told Scarlett.

The mirrored turret spun in a constant, even pace, reflecting the numbers as it turned. Enzo traded a few thousand dollars for stacks of red chips. The dealer slid them across the table until they reached Enzo. Immediately, he peeled off a few and fiddled with them in one hand.

"Place your bets," the dealer instructed.

And with that, Enzo went into his zone. His vision became tunneled, seeing nothing but the neat rows of numbers in front of him. He placed chips all over the board from top to bottom as if he had the thing memorized. Who was he kidding? He *did* have the board memorized.

"Vodka tonic, whiskey neat," the cocktail waitress said as she handed the drinks to Scarlett.

"Here you go, sweetheart." Enzo looked over his shoulder to hand the waitress a few chips. "Those are nickels."

"Oh, thank you, Mr. Valenti."

"She knows your name too," Scarlett said as Enzo put his arm around her waist.

The dealer waved his hand over the entirety of the table. "No more bets."

Everyone's attention moved to the spinning wheel, watching to see where the little white ball would drop. It was only the first spin, but Enzo's heart was already pumping, adrenaline coursing through his veins. It was like a high in and of itself, waiting to see if his instincts were right, waiting to see if he was the lucky one.

"Ten, black, even," the dealer said as he placed a silver pin on number ten where Enzo had one lonely chip placed.

"It's a push bet," Enzo reasoned, pulling out a cigarette and lighting it as the dealer slid him two uneven stacks for his small win. "Always bet the same numbers, that's the trick," Enzo explained to Scarlett as he immediately launched into placing more bets. His eyes darted all over the table, making sure he had all his usual numbers covered. He placed a tall stack on his lucky number seventeen.

It was a rush as they went through the same routine, over and over again. The placing of the bets, the wave of the hand, no more bets, waiting for the ball to spin and spin until it fell, far away from lucky number seventeen. Enzo's pulse raced quicker with each spin. He drained his glass and asked Scarlett to order him another drink. After a few more spins, he was out of chips. *Shit*, he thought. He couldn't let himself look like a fool in front of not only Scarlett, but his friends, now colleagues, too. They would think he was reckless. They might not trust him anymore.

"Nickels," Enzo commanded as he threw down another two grand. He could feel it. Seventeen was going to hit. It was only a game of odds, wasn't it? At some point over the course of the night, seventeen would have to come out. He just had to keep playing until it did. He didn't care how much it cost him.

"Hey, come on, it's okay, Enz," Michael said in an effort to calm him down, but Enzo wasn't listening. He had already started placing more bets.

Enzo could feel Scarlett's questioning gaze on him as he continued to gamble, his tall stacks of chips dwindling with each bet, his drinks draining every few hands. He became engrossed, so much so that no other thoughts entered his mind. His heart hammered against his chest as he got down to his last two stacks. He felt hot all over as he backed away from the table.

"Put those on seventeen," Enzo told Scarlett as he walked away.

She approached the table quickly, so to place the bet before the dealer waved his hand. She took the two stacks and layered them neatly on top of seventeen. Enzo turned his back to the table. Everything fell silent, save for the sound of the ball falling.

"Seventeen, black, odd," the dealer announced.

"Yes!" Scarlett cheered.

Enzo turned around. Only when he walked up to the wheel to see the little white ball in the socket of seventeen did he let himself smile wide. All of his friends and even some gamblers from nearby tables let out a cheer.

"My lucky charm." Enzo kissed Scarlett on the cheek. "Almost had a heart attack thanks to you," he said to the dealer. "Give me the purple chips." Enzo lit his last cigarette and took a final swig of his whiskey. By now, he had lost track – of time, of how many drinks he had, of how much money he gambled. All that mattered was that he had won.

"It's your lucky night," the dealer said as he paid Enzo his winnings.

"It's *your* lucky night," Enzo tossed back. "If you didn't hit my number, I was gonna have to give you a beating. Know what I'm saying?"

"Alright, Enz. Take it easy. Go be with your lady," John said, turning Enzo away from the table.

Scarlett took hold of his arm, leading him away from the high-limit room, away from the sweeping allure of gambling. Enzo was on a high. He was right, as he usually was.

Luck, as it turned out, could in fact change. You just had to believe it would.

———

EVEN BACK IN THE room, they were still riding on the rush of adrenaline. As soon as Enzo closed the door behind him, he covered Scarlett in kisses and began undressing her like he needed, craved her. But Scarlett was amused by him. She had never seen him so intoxicated, so out of control. She would have been surprised if he remembered anything in the morning.

"Enzo." She giggled as she grabbed his face. "Enzo, you're drunk!"

"Yeah? And you're not?" He stumbled as he took off his sport coat and threw his tie to the ground.

"Not as drunk as you. I can still walk straight." She strutted past him before kicking off her pumps.

"You little showoff, you." Enzo took her by her waist. "All confident with those diamonds around your neck, are you now?"

"Mm hmm. And I helped you win roulette. How much did you win anyway?"

"A lot of fucking money. Let's have some champagne to celebrate."

"Enzo." She ran after him, though he was already behind the bar, pulling out a bottle of champagne. "Enzo, honey, you've had enough to drink."

Enzo popped the bottle of champagne. "I don't care. I want to celebrate. With you."

"You always celebrate like this when you win a game of roulette?"

"We're not celebrating my gambling, sweetheart."

"Then what is it?"

Enzo handed Scarlett a glass. He traced the length of her jawline with his thumb. Then, he headed towards the closet and returned with a duffel bag.

"You ever see this much cash in your life?" Enzo opened the bag to reveal stacks and stacks of neatly bound cash.

"What the hell is this? Where did you get all of that?" Scarlett retreated. There were many things Scarlett didn't know, but she knew enough to know that having this much cash didn't come from any business. It came from dirty business.

"What? You think I'm just selling pasta out of my place?" Enzo smirked.

Scarlett searched his face as her mind reeled, trying to put the pieces together. The cash, the supposed business trip they were on, none of it had made any sense from the start. "What's really going on here, Enzo?"

"You know what they say about gambling? *The house always wins.* So you know what I did?" Enzo pulled out a wad of hundreds. "I became the house."

As much as she hated to admit it, she had to. Not only had Helen been right, but her mother had been too. Between the cash and the men Enzo surrounded himself with, Enzo's true character was unfolding in front of Scarlett as if Lana and Helen had written a script. "Is that supposed to impress me? That you're some wannabe gangster?"

He dropped his bag. "Excuse me?"

He tried to reach for her, but all the adrenaline and booze had worn off as she dodged him. Suddenly, she felt completely sober as she walked away from him.

"Scar, honey, where are you going?"

"You know, when you invited me on this trip, I knew it wasn't *business.* Your business is in the city. And yet you lied to me. Again."

"It is business. It's *my* business," he yelled, trying to defend himself.

"Yeah, well, I'm with you so now it's *my* business. I can't keep making excuses for the way you keep things from me, Enzo."

"My own wife doesn't even know."

"I can't believe you just said that to me."

He walked up to her, and she could feel his whiskey-laced breath on her skin. "What else do you wanna know? Hmm? I'll tell you anything."

They stared at each other, heated and intense. Her chest heaved up and down, her breath shallow, her heart pounding. Did she know this man she had shared her heart with at all? "What's the real reason everybody in this casino knows your name?"

Enzo maintained their eye contact. "I like to gamble. A lot."

"Evidently."

"Anything else you wanna know?"

"What do you want with me when you have a wife at home? Honestly, Enzo."

"You don't know nothing about marriage." He rubbed his forehead and shook his head. "That came out wrong. But you don't know what it's like, Scar. When you get married, you don't think things are gonna change. You don't think feelings are gonna change. Claudia don't love me anymore, Scar. She hates how much time I spend at the restaurant. She wants me home every night at the same time, eating the same food. Do you know what that feels like? Knowing I gotta go home to that for the rest of my life? Do you know what that's like for a man like me? It's a death sentence."

The room spun around her, and not from the alcohol. *The rest of my life.* Enzo didn't see Scarlett as his future at all. Was she only a temporary fix for his problems? For the way he felt, or didn't feel, about his wife? Would she ever be anything other than his secret? Then, she remembered what he had said about his children. His *three little critters.*

"The kids, right? That's why you gotta deal with this for the rest of your life?"

"I would die for my kids. You know that."

"So that's it? You're gonna keep doing this until you die? You know, you seemed like you had it all when I met you. But you don't seem that happy."

"I'm not."

"Well gambling all your money away isn't gonna fix it, Enzo. I don't understand you. You have so much." Scarlett's eyes fell to Enzo's bag of cash. "And you're risking it all for *what*?"

Enzo dropped his gaze to his hands. "Remember how I told you I came from nothing?" He looked back up at her. "Sometimes, even with everything I have, I still feel like I am nothing. Like I've got so much to prove. And then a guy like John comes around and makes me an offer that makes me feel like I'm *everything*. That's why, Scar. 'Cause that feeling is worth more than anything I've got."

Scarlett licked a salty tear from her top lip. She knew how Enzo felt because she was doing the same thing. Risking everything she had – her reputation, her self-respect, all priceless intangibles – for the value Enzo gave her. "Yeah. I know what you mean."

"You seemed so tough when I met you. You remember?" he asked.

"Yeah," she said, crossing her arms.

"Why?"

"Because," she started, taking a shallow breath. Despite clenching her jaw to stop the hot tears from pouring out, they did anyway. "Because I think if I act tough, no one can hurt me."

"But you know that's not true," he said, cupping her face.

Scarlett pushed Enzo's hand away. "Are you going to hurt me?"

"I don't think that's the kind of thing someone plans on doing."

"Lie to me, Enzo. Tell me you won't."

Enzo put his arms around her, enveloping her, but she felt like her body was nothing more than a vacant shell. He hadn't lifted a finger nor uttered a word, and yet, cracks had started to form.

TWENTY-THREE

LITTLE ITALY, NEW YORK

SUMMER, 1985

Francesco couldn't remember the last time he had taken a proper vacation. It might have been in '78, when he went back home to Naples to visit family, though traveling home wasn't truly what he considered to be a vacation. Or, it might have been '80, when he took a solo trip to Malibu. Had there been a time in between? He couldn't remember. All the years looked the same to him, which was why he resented his brother even more.

Enzo jetted off on his gambling trips without warning, without having to answer to anyone. He would disappear for days at a time, and rather than explain himself, it was everyone else's job to accept that this was the way Enzo lived. It wasn't that Francesco wanted to go off and gamble away his hard-earned money, but it wouldn't have been so bad to get a change of scenery every once in a while. It might have even done him some good.

Francesco climbed the steps, two by two. He still had a bout of energy left in him, as he usually did at the end of a long shift. He could still feel the rushing pace of dinner service, and his skin was still warm from the heat of the stoves. As he got closer to the apartment, he heard a voice. Was that music? He opened the door and was greeted by the sound of one of his old Diana Ross records blaring through his place. He looked around, wondering what the hell was going on. Scarlett had been gone for a few days, and he wasn't sure exactly when she would be back. Though he knew it was none of his business, he had his suspicions that she was with Enzo. Where else would she be? Enzo was a man of opportunity. If he had the chance to take her away for a few days, he would surely take advantage of it. As Scarlett came into view, wearing nothing but a pair of shorts and a bra, holding a mink coat in her hands, Francesco had his answers about her whereabouts.

"Scarlett?" he called out over the music.

Scarlett shrieked and dropped the coat to the ground where it resembled a dead animal. Francesco retreated into the living room where he lowered the volume on the record player. His breath had left him as he caught sight of her again, seeing her almost bare. She had her back against the wall and her eyes closed. Breathing heavily, she covered her ample chest with her hands. "Shit," she muttered as she retrieved a sweatshirt from the closet and tugged it overhead as fast as humanly possible.

"I didn't mean to scare you," Francesco said. He found her back in the hallway once she was redressed, though laughter brimmed just beneath the surface of his smile. "But I have to admit, that was kind of funny."

"Maybe for you it was. You could have, I don't know, let out a warning call," she said, still flustered by his intrusion.

"A warning call?"

"Yes. Something like that." She smoothed her frizzy hair back, trying to compose herself.

"Maybe you would have heard me, but the music was blasting."

"I like my music loud."

"Obviously."

"Well, anyways," she said, waving her hand through the air in an attempt to end the debacle as fast as it began.

"It's good to have you back. It was quiet around here without you," Francesco said as he retreated to his room, leaving the door cracked. He peeled off his chef's jacket and looped his arms through a freshly washed T-shirt and went back into the hallway. "You should hang your coat up." His eyes fell to the white mink on the ground. He knew right away it was Enzo's doing. His older brother had a taste for the finer things in life. He wondered how it made Scarlett feel, to be on the receiving end of something like that. "Something that expensive doesn't belong on the floor, you know."

"I was hanging it up until you walked in and scared the crap out of me." She swiped the coat from the floor and tucked it into the closet, sliding the door shut. She faced him again and put her hands on her hips. "You're not going to ask me where I've been?"

"Nope. None of my business."

She tossed her arms up. "Okay then."

"Brichi's Fine Accessories." Francesco read the name of the store printed on the cherry-red shopping bags. "You know that's the best store in Atlantic City, right?"

"You're slick, you know that?"

"Sometimes."

"This might come as a surprise, Fran, but I don't frequent Atlantic City."

"Win any money?"

"I don't gamble."

"What do you do then, Scarlett?" He crossed his arms and leaned his head against the doorframe, a spiral curl flopping in front of his eyes. He didn't bother to brush it away.

"That, Francesco, is none of your business," she said, appearing pleased with herself. She picked up the shopping bags and retreated to her room.

He could hear her rustling through her bags. It was apparent that neither one of them could sleep. Surely, Scarlett was thinking about Enzo. But him? All he kept wondering was why he felt so happy that Scarlett was home.

ENZO FELT LIKE HE hadn't been home in months, and he had forgotten what it was like to spend the day at home with his family. But when he returned from Atlantic City, Claudia had insisted. He sat at the head of his kitchen table, reading the paper, ignoring everything going on around him. His youngest daughter cried from another room, and he could hear meatballs frying on the stove, but he tuned it all out. He was tired. The ups and downs of the weekend had sucked the life right out of him.

Claudia Valenti was never a beauty, but when he'd met her a decade ago, she had something else to offer him: a business. Her parents owned a bustling restaurant in Little Italy, and upon marrying Claudia, Enzo took it over. Three years later, he had enough money to buy the building next to it, and Valenti's Ristorante was born. In the beginning, Claudia liked to spend time with him there. She would do up her hair that was not yet flecked with gray and she would dress in tight clothes that clung to her body, the body Enzo knew she so longed for again. But now, self-conscious of her stretch marks and tired eyes, she didn't bother herself with going to the restaurant anymore. Besides, Enzo didn't want her there anyway. The restaurant was his place. Their home? That was hers.

She turned each meatball, one by one, the hot oil spraying everywhere and decorating the stove. Enzo knew she would clean the mess later. She always did.

"Enz, can you go check on the kids? Maria's been crying for five minutes," she pleaded with him, but he didn't so much as look up. "Enzo?"

"Yeah," he said, flipping the page of the paper. "Give me minute."

"Not in a minute, Enzo. Now!" She slapped her wooden spoon against the countertop.

"Hey!" Enzo stood in one swift motion, keenly aware of the rage in his wife's voice. "Lower your voice!"

"Me? You want me to lower my voice? I'll lower my voice when you tell me where the hell you were this weekend." She walked towards him, pointing with her wooden spoon that dripped with hot oil.

"You wanna question me?"

"Oh, I have a million questions and you're gonna answer them."

"It was business," he yelled.

"Bullshit," she yelled back.

"I'm your husband and you don't believe me?"

"You call yourself a husband?" she cried. "You call yourself a father? Our son is always asking where you are, and your daughters barely even recognize you when you bother to come home. You're always down at that damn restaurant with tramps."

"I do what I have to do to keep a roof over our heads, so don't you talk to me about my restaurant."

Claudia couldn't take his excuses anymore. Enzo knew it. He was running out of ways around the inevitable truth: he would either have to step it up, or he would have to step out for good. He sighed as he watched her lean against the counter, her shoulders shaking up and down as she cried. He could feel it. The guilt bled into every crevice of his heart. He stood behind her and wrapped his arms around her waist. It felt foreign to him; he hadn't done it in so long.

"I've given you a home. Three beautiful children who you barely *know*. I've given you my life, Enzo."

"Claudia," he said, closing his eyes. When was the last time he had uttered her name out of love rather than disdain? "What do you want, hmm?"

"End it, Enzo. Whoever she is, just end it. I can't take this anymore."

Enzo's heart dropped to his stomach. How could he quit Scarlett? He was as addicted to her as he was to the gambling, to the whiskey, to doing things that nearly killed him. But he couldn't leave his family. He wasn't that type of man. He couldn't let his kids grow up without a father. He couldn't let Claudia do it all on her own. "Okay."

Claudia faced him. Enzo's chest felt heavy with the burden of his sins as he looked her in the eye, holding her face in his hands as he wiped away her tears.

"Look," he said, his voice nearly breaking, "why don't you come down to the restaurant? Like old times. Get all dolled up. I'll invite the neighbors and we'll have dinner just the four of us. What do you say?"

He could see it on her face, that sad glimmer of hope. "Yeah. Okay."

"Okay." He drew her in and kissed the top of her head, but his eyes glazed over. Though he never considered the consequences of his actions, that didn't matter. What mattered was, he didn't have a choice. He had to face them.

TWENTY-FOUR

LITTLE ITALY, NEW YORK
SUMMER, 1985

Shit." Fausto stormed through the dining room. "Shit, shit, shit." Scarlett exchanged a quick glance with Julie. "What the hell is wrong with him?" she said under her breath. The staff was preparing the restaurant for dinner service and thus far, everything seemed to be routine. Scarlett had yet to see Fausto flustered until now.

Before Julie could answer, Francesco and Fausto joined the girls by the bar. "Would someone like to kill Antonio for me? I'll pay a hefty rate," Fausto said.

"Calm down, would you?" Francesco said while his eyes scanned the dining room.

"Antonio decided to go and get food poisoning today," Fausto explained. Scarlett had never paid much attention to the head bartender,

Antonio. He didn't have a big personality, but he ran an efficient bar. "On a Friday night. Does he think I was born yesterday? I'm from Queens, for Christ's sake."

Scarlett thought of a solution, but she hesitated. Though she had never made head bartender at her mother's bar, Scarlett knew the fundamentals of the craft. They were in a pinch and Scarlett wanted to help, but she could hear her mother's words as if Lana were right there, whispering in her ear. *You're not good enough.* Determination to prove her mother wrong rose until it boiled over.

"Um, hello. I know how to bartend," Scarlett said. Julie, Fausto, and Francesco looked at her as if she had just broken out in fluent Italian. Her cheeks burned as she scolded herself for such a suggestion. She wasn't cut out for a bar like Valenti's. "I mean, you know, I'm no Antonio, but I know how to mix drinks if you need help tonight. That's all."

Fausto jerked his head to the side. "Go mix a Manhattan."

Scarlett found her post behind the bar, the familiar feeling of being on stage returning. She took a deep breath to orient herself and scanned over the choices of bottles and barware. Though she hadn't mixed a drink in months, muscle memory kicked in. She picked up a shaker, scooped in some ice, and measured out the whiskey, vermouth, and a few dashes of bitters. Francesco, Fausto, and Julie watched as if they each had a mental stopwatch in their heads.

"Neat or on the rocks?" Scarlett asked.

"Neat," Francesco said.

Scarlett topped off the drink with a twisted orange peel and a toothpick of maraschino cherries. Satisfied with her work, she slid the drink across the bar. Francesco reached for it first. He maintained a straight face as he took a sip, deciphering the notes and flavors, and passed the drink down to Julie, who winced at the whiskey. Finally, after taking a sip, Fausto's blue eyes lifted to meet Scarlett's.

Doubt seeped into Scarlett's pores. *He's gonna say it's lousy.* She had worked at a dive bar where most people either walked in already drunk, or only cared about getting bombed as fast as they could. What did she know about crafting balanced cocktails?

"It's good," Fausto said.

Though she didn't quite believe him, her mood brightened. "Yeah?"

Fausto looked to Francesco. "What do you think, Fran?"

"You fill in for Antonio tonight," Francesco said. "But listen, if you get overwhelmed, you let Fausto know. We'll pull someone off the floor to work as barback. Good?"

Flattered and proud of herself all the same, Scarlett nodded. Though the rest of the night would be a series of hurdles, she had overcome the biggest one. "Sounds good."

"You're going to kill it," Julie said once Fausto and Francesco were out of earshot. "Not to mention you're also going to rake in a ton of cash. They never have female bartenders. This is your chance."

Scarlett remembered Enzo's long-ago words. *This is a man's business.* She would show him that it sure as hell wasn't.

———

But Scarlett's excitement over showing off her skills in front of Enzo dimmed with each passing minute. She had been busy behind the bar for the past hour, and there was still no sign of him. Strange, she thought. It was Friday night. A weekend without Enzo was like a year without Christmas. Impossible.

Distracted by wondering about Enzo's whereabouts, Scarlett moved to the end of the bar to greet her latest customers, a pair of couples. The ladies ordered Long Island iced teas, the men, gin and tonics. She whipped up the four drinks with speed and accuracy and placed them on coasters.

"Can we also see a menu?" one of the men asked, his wife holding onto his arm. She was dressed stylishly and despite her air of maturity, the woman looked as if her greatest worry was wondering what she was going to wear and how she would style her strawberry-blonde hair.

"You sure can." Scarlett retrieved four menus underneath the bar and handed them out. "Have you ever dined with us before?"

"Plenty of times," the other woman chimed in. "Our daughters are in kindergarten with little Antonella. It's a shame Claudia couldn't join us tonight."

"When your husband offers to take you on a surprise date, you go. She hates leaving the kids with a sitter," the strawberry-blonde said as she shook her head, making her disapproval known. "But I told her, a sitter is crucial to keeping the spice in a marriage alive. Look at us!"

The two women laughed, and they were so distracted by their own conversations of spicing up marriages that they thankfully didn't so much as give Scarlett a second glance. Scarlett felt like the woman had reached into her chest and ripped her heart out. Enzo wasn't there because he was with Claudia, something Scarlett didn't quite believe. *This* was Enzo's life. This electrifying place of fine food and glamour and energy. But Enzo, Scarlett considered, had a life at home with Claudia, one they didn't discuss because neither of them wanted to. Scarlett was tempted to take the woman's cocktail and drink it all herself. She knew it wasn't easy being someone's mistress. Tonight, it was excruciating.

Stepping away from the scene, Scarlett tried to center herself. This was her stage. This was her chance. She had a life outside of Enzo, didn't she?

Fueled by the mental image Scarlett had of Enzo and Claudia out on a romantic date while she became stained with whiskey and gin, Scarlett made her choice. She would make her future with each customer and each drink she mixed. This was her ticket to more. Making their regulars smile, wowing the first-time diners, and working with speed to maintain the pace of the restaurant. Scarlett would show Enzo. She would show everyone who she was and what she was capable of when in the spotlight.

Two hours later, her bar was standing room only. Made up of mostly men clad in suits and shiny loafers, they didn't mind having to wait a few extra minutes for their drinks or if their entrées took longer than usual to come out. Scarlett was a hamster trapped in her own wheel as she moved about the physical confinements of the bar, running from one end to the other to retrieve bottles, re-rack them, pull down glasses, and pick out garnishes. She felt energized, her focus returned. Being among the people was where she shined. That was where Enzo and Scarlett were the most similar of all.

"Where the hell have they been hiding you?" a customer Scarlett recognized asked as she mixed his amaretto sour. He was a regular, one whom Scarlett hadn't had much interaction with prior to this exchange.

"Bussing tables. You believe that?"

"What a waste. What's your name, sweetheart?"

"Scarlett. You?"

"I'm Tony. I own a restaurant down in Florida. Delray Beach. You ever want to come work for me during our busy season, you have a job waiting for you."

Scarlett didn't have time to react. Enzo appeared behind him and put his hands on Tony's shoulders. "You trying to poach my best employee?"

Tony turned around. "Hey, Enzo. Look at you, you handsome son of a bitch."

Scarlett caught Enzo's eye. How had he gotten away from his date with Claudia? Had he gone at all? With them in conversation, Scarlett turned around, but not fully.

She caught Francesco at the end of the bar watching her. Their eyes met and they exchanged a smile. He was electric, that smile of his, that took over every inch of his face. Scarlett tried to look away but couldn't. She wondered what he thought of her and her work tonight. He held her gaze and shook his head, his curls dancing around his head like a crown.

Finally, tossing a bar rag over his shoulder, he turned away, leaving Scarlett feeling nothing but pride.

Pride, and a flutter of attraction that she promptly swallowed down with a shot of vodka.

—⁓—

"GOT TIME FOR ONE more?" Enzo asked as he took a seat at the bar.

In the midst of cleaning the now-closed bar, Scarlett leaned a mop against the wall. "Whiskey neat?"

Enzo nodded. "Whiskey neat."

Scarlett pulled down a rocks glass and poured him his drink. She leaned her arms on the freshly cleaned marble, not caring if she had to wipe it down another hundred times. She needed to talk to him. Though nerves churned in her stomach, she put on a display of confidence. "How was your date?"

"My what?"

"Your date. With Claudia."

"Are you guessing—"

"One of the mothers of Antonella's classmates was in tonight. She says that a babysitter is a *necessity* to keeping the spice alive in a marriage," Scarlett said, aware of the sarcastic edge to her voice.

Enzo paused before letting out a scoff. "She was giving me a hard time, alright? I'm never home, you know that. What was I supposed to do? I called to check on things, and Fausto told me you were behind the bar tonight. I had to see you. After Claudia nearly killed me with her hair dryer for cancelling, I came here."

Scarlett knew it had to be some sort of bad karma to feel a happy glow at hearing he'd chosen to watch her work over spending an evening with his wife. "A hair dryer? Interesting choice of weapon."

"There she is." Francesco slapped the bar as he approached them. He looked at Enzo. "I think we have a new bartender."

"No, no, no," Scarlett protested. "This was only for tonight. Just me filling in."

Enzo tilted his head back and downed the rest of his drink. "Tell me why the hell we should keep wasting you away as a busser when you can bartend like this."

"Because I don't want to bartend," Scarlett said as she wiped down the counter where she'd been leaning. "I've done this before. I don't want to do it again."

Francesco walked backwards, looking at Scarlett and Scarlett alone. "You eat tonight?"

"No," she said, untying her apron.

"Come up. I'm going to cook."

"Oh." Scarlett suddenly felt the oddness of their dynamic in front of Enzo. "I'll be right up."

Enzo looked at Scarlett. "Looks like I'm not the only one who has a date tonight," he said without a trace of a smile. *Jealousy,* on full display.

"I didn't eat tonight, Enzo. That's it. You know how your brother is." When Scarlett came out from behind the bar, Enzo rushed to stand in front of her. "What?"

"You know you're mine, right?" he asked as he cupped her face and kissed her as if he were claiming Scarlett as his own. "I don't like to share."

"I'm an only child. Neither do I."

TWENTY-FIVE

LITTLE ITALY, NEW YORK
SUMMER, 1985

Scarlett would have thought the best part about living with Francesco was the fact that it was rent free, or that she had no commute at all, but the real perk about living with him was his cooking. He liked to use the small kitchenette in the apartment as his test kitchen. He usually worked late into the night, well past the time Scarlett had already fallen asleep, but he always saved her the leftovers for the next day. But tonight, it was not yet midnight and she could already smell something delicious brewing.

In her bedroom, Scarlett added her tips to a shoebox where she kept her cash. She did a quick count, adding the night's earnings to the bundles she had neatly organized. Four grand in the shoebox, plus her money in the bank. She felt secure knowing she had a nice savings growing.

She closed her box and tucked it away before heading into the kitchen. Francesco had his boombox on the kitchen table and he was humming along to some opera music. Though his record collection was eclectic, it seemed his taste was, in truth, limited to these strange melodies that Scarlett didn't understand. At the counter, Francesco sliced a loaf of fresh Italian bread, and he had a sauce simmering on the stove. Scarlett inhaled. The scent of heaven.

"I hope you're making enough for two."

"You want to eat? You gotta earn it. Come give me a hand," Francesco said, still slicing as he looked over at her.

"I can guarantee you I will be of no help," she said as she joined him near the stove. "The most gourmet thing I've ever made is boxed macaroni and cheese."

"That's a sin," he said with a laugh, dusting his hands off on his apron. "Luckily, I don't need you to cook. Here." He handed her a wooden spoon. "All I need you to do is stir."

"I think I can manage." She took the spoon from him and dunked it into the red sauce. "What are you making?"

"*Mozzarella in carrozza,*" he told her as he whisked some eggs together. "You know what that means?"

Scarlett shook her head.

"In a carriage. Mozzarella in a carriage." He cut even slices of mozzarella, placing each one between two slices of bread.

"Looks to me like you're just making a grilled cheese."

"I'm going to make you eat those words." He glanced up at her as he continued to work.

In another bowl, he mixed breadcrumbs, fresh parsley, and of course, more cheese. He dipped each sandwich in the eggs first, then the breadcrumbs. Scarlett examined his every move. She found it fascinating to watch him cook, like watching an artist at work. When he worked with food, he was consumed, his attention solely on the creation he was making with his own two hands. Once he had coated all of the sandwiches, he reached down to a cabinet and pulled out a frying pan.

"Hand me the olive oil?" he asked.

Scarlett handed him the big tin can sitting by the windowsill. He poured enough olive oil to sink a ship and turned the gas stove ablaze. "What's that for?"

"Now," he said and picked up one of the sandwiches with his bare hands, "now we fry." Once the oil reached the proper temperature, he dropped each sandwich in as the olive oil bubbled and a sizzling sound filled the kitchen. As soon as the sandwiches each turned a golden color, he flipped them. "Go sit. These will be done in a second."

"I didn't really help you."

"I didn't really need your help. I just didn't want you to get bored watching me cook."

"I could never get bored watching you cook. Let me at least set the table." Scarlett went on her tiptoes to open the cabinets, but she came up short. She wasn't sure why she found it surprising that Francesco didn't have a set of matching dishes. The apartment was, after all, his bachelor pad until she'd crashed it. She opened another cabinet where she found four mismatched plates. She grabbed two and set them out on the table with a fork and knife.

"Wine?" she asked.

"Come on now, what kind of question is that?"

She laughed. "You're right." From the fridge, she grabbed a bottle of Pinot Grigio. Even though it was his favorite and not hers, it would do.

"Let's do red tonight," he said.

"Aren't you full of surprises."

She put the wine back in the fridge and instead she found a bottle of Chianti on the counter. She expertly uncorked it and poured two generous servings. Finally, they met at the table. Francesco had piled his creations onto a plate. The *mozzarella in carrozza* were fried to a perfect golden color. He set down a bowl of marinara sauce and sat across from Scarlett.

"Let's eat," he said.

They each took a diagonal cut piece of the *mozzarella in carrozza* and she cut a small bite. The crust was crispy and flavorful, but the cheese inside was gooey and stringy. She followed Francesco's lead and submerged her piece in the sauce before eating it. She closed her eyes, savoring the warm, comforting meal. The fact that Francesco was able to whip those kinds of flavors up in a matter of minutes in this tiny kitchen, Scarlett couldn't deny his talent. No one could.

"This is ridiculous," she said with her mouth full as she cut off another piece. "Seriously ridiculous."

"I know. It's one of my favorite guilty pleasures."

"How many guilty pleasures do you have?"

"An undisclosed amount." He laughed, taking a swig of wine to wash everything down.

"How come you don't make this at the restaurant? I feel like people would go crazy over this."

"Enzo doesn't like it. Says it's too rustic for our clientele."

"But you're the chef," she said. "Don't you get to decide what's on the menu?"

"You would think, right?" His gaze fell to his plate. "But Enzo's the boss."

"I thought you were co-owner."

"Oh, I am. But my brother is the boss." He shrugged, as though to say, *It is what it is.*

"You *Napoletans* have some weird ways. You know that?" Their eyes met. "What about all the other stuff you make up here late at night?"

"It's more of a hobby," he said, grabbing another piece with his fork and putting it on his plate. "This is where I get to experiment and test out new ideas, or sometimes, like tonight, make old dishes like we had back home in Naples. But downstairs, I have to stick to the script."

"You ever get tired of cooking the same stuff over and over again?"

"I do. That's why I come up here after sweating my ass off over the stove for eight hours and cook some more."

"It's your art."

"Yeah, it is. But what you do is art, too. All of us, at the restaurant. It's all performance." He paused to take a few bites. "So, speaking of Enzo, I've been talking to him about you."

Scarlett thought she might choke. She clutched onto her glass of wine. "What about?"

He stopped himself short of laughing, but she still detected a look of amusement on his face. "About making you a waitress."

"You want to promote me?" Her eyes went wide as her hand flew to her chest. It had only been a few months, but Francesco's offer told her everything she needed to know. This belief she was starting to have in herself, the seed Enzo had planted in her head about dreaming big – it wasn't a dream at all. It was a destination, and she was finally on the right road.

"Yeah," he said with a nod. "I think it's time. And not just because of tonight."

"Oh my God. Francesco, thank you. Are you… are you sure?"

"You put in the work, and you learned fast. Some people are in this business for years and never get it down pat. But it seems like it comes naturally to you."

"You have no idea how much that means to me. Especially coming from you."

"I'll have you shadow Julie. You'll memorize the menu, and you already know about mixed drinks from your bartending days, so it's perfect."

"It is." She leaned back in her chair and raised her glass to him. "Thank you. For the promotion, and the food. It was so good."

"Beats grilled cheese, right?"

"I take those words back."

"Thought you would."

"I'll clean up." She stood, reaching for the now-empty dishes.

"Leave it," he said. "We'll get it in the morning."

"It's no problem."

He pointed up. "You ever go up to the rooftop?"

"No."

"Wanna come have a smoke with me?"

"Oh, um, uh, yeah. Sure," she said, stumbling over her words. She set the plates down and traded them for her glass of wine that Francesco had since refilled.

They went out on the fire escape in the back of the apartment and climbed their way up to the rooftop. Rusty pipes of all different widths and heights were scattered around, but it was peaceful up there. New York felt quiet and still in the dark of the night. Streetlights and neon signs from below glowed. Francesco lit a cigarette and handed it to her, then lit one for himself.

"It's nice up here," she said, looking up at the sky. Out of the corner of her eye, she could feel him watching her, but then he turned his gaze up, too. He leaned against the wall, digging one hand into his pocket. She closed her eyes, letting the warm breeze wash over her.

"It is."

"You've been home more than usual," Scarlett said as she opened her eyes once more and took a sip of her wine.

"I'm not seeing that girl Lisa anymore."

"Haven't replaced her yet?"

"Not yet." He laughed, but he seemed embarrassed.

"How come you're not married like Enzo?" she blurted out, not even sure where the question came from. But Francesco wasn't deterred in the least. He paused, considering his answer.

"Because I'm terrified I won't be any good at it. It's hard to find someone who understands what I do. I don't just cook because it's my job. I cook because I have to. It's my gift."

"It sure is."

"But a business like this, it's almost impossible to have a family. I see Enzo. I see Claudia. Neither one of them are very happy." His forehead wrinkled. "Sorry. I shouldn't be putting my brother's business out there like that."

"Your secret is safe with me," she assured him. She would just add it to the list of other Valenti brother secrets she was carrying around. She went next to Francesco and they faced downtown, leaning their elbows against the top of the wall.

"And what about you?" he asked.

She kept her gaze forward, out at the city. "What about me, Fran?"

"How come nobody's snatched you up yet?"

She looked at him. She knew he knew about her and Enzo. He had to. Like Enzo had said once before, Francesco wasn't blind. And yet, Francesco danced around it, time and time again. "I," she started, trying to think of the right thing to say, "am un-snatchable."

"Is that so?" Francesco asked, his lips curved into a smirk.

"Yeah, it is," Scarlett said, laughter dancing in her throat.

"Well alright then. Maybe that's my problem too." He clinked his glass to hers and faced the city once more. "Maybe we're just un-snatchable."

───

FRANCESCO HELD A PEN in his hand, hovering it over a blank sheet of paper. Around him, the sous chefs were busy de-boning delicate fillets of sea bass, pounding veal and chicken until they were paper thin, and stirring sauces of all different variations. Everything going on around him was a derivative of his direction, his imagination, his creations. And yet, he still didn't feel like he had any control. The blank sheet of paper before him was his place to let his creativity run free: the specials. But he couldn't fully let his star shine. He had to dim his light to meet the confinements of Enzo's expectations.

His attention snapped away when Scarlett walked into the kitchen with a tray tucked under her arm. Her gaze fell to the blank piece of paper.

"You writing a book?" she asked.

"The specials." He let out a frustrated sigh as he set the pen down. He was fresh out of ideas anyway. Maybe he would run the same dishes as last week. What was the difference? Would anyone even notice?

"Ah," she said with a nod. "You know, I know I don't know much about food, but I think you should run the *carrozza* tonight. See how it goes." She shrugged, like her suggestion was casual.

"Enzo wouldn't be too happy about that."

"This is *your* kitchen."

"It doesn't feel like it."

"Blame me. But once he sees how good it sells, he won't be able to be mad."

Scarlett walked away, but in her absence, gears started to shift. He dared to put his pen to the blank page. With each letter, his pulse quickened. The juices were flowing. Ideas flooded his mind. He would run the *carrozza*, and some of other dishes like *impepata di cozze, rigatoni vongole e fiori di zucca,* and spaghetti *alla nerano,* recipes he only dared to make in his own kitchen. What would Enzo do about it? What was the worst that could possibly happen? And why, after all these years behind the line, was he now only able to dare to do this? Did Scarlett have that much power over him?

A new energy washed over him as he got to work, explaining each dish to the line of sous chefs. A smile took over his face, seemingly out of nowhere. But were the origins really unknown? Maybe Scarlett wasn't the source. Maybe she had a way of motivating him, of activating the gifts and talents and ideas that were already inside of him.

Maybe she was the push he needed to stand up to Enzo and take control of the one thing that was totally and completely his: the kitchen.

Or maybe there was just something about her, some invisible thread that connected them that he wasn't sure how or when or why it existed in the first place.

ENZO SURVEYED THE DINING room. He clutched onto his crystal rocks glass full of whiskey, but he didn't busy himself with sipping on it. He couldn't. He had to regain control of his restaurant. Though every seat was filled, and the flow of the evening was running at an impressive pace, things felt wildly off kilter each time he saw an unfamiliar dish being carried from the kitchen to the dining room. Foreign scents of seafood and zucchini and lemons filled the air.

He burst through the stainless-steel doors to the kitchen and his eyes adjusted to the florescent lights overhead — a stark contrast to the dimly lit crystal chandeliers in the dining room. The kitchen was mayhem and though it was his name on the sign out front, this was the one place in the restaurant where Enzo felt he didn't belong. He spotted Francesco behind the line, pausing amid the rush to wipe the sweat on his face with a bar rag.

"I need four *carrozza* on fire," Scarlett said to the line as she expertly pulled a tray from the service station and began examining the hot plates in the window that were ready to be run to the dining room.

Enzo snapped out of his trance and turned to her. He snatched the tickets from her hands and scanned them over. *Carrozza. Impepata di cozze. Fiori di zucca. Nerano.* A fresh well of rage surged in him. Who had approved this? He looked up and found his younger brother's eyes.

"Who did the specials tonight?" Enzo asked, holding up Scarlett's tickets.

Francesco's shoulders rose and fell. "Me."

"Have you lost your mind? What are we running, a pizza joint? *Carrozza*? Why would you do something like this?"

Enzo looked expectantly at Francesco, but Francesco didn't answer him. Instead, Scarlett inserted herself and snatched her tickets back from him.

"Because it's fucking *good*," she said before backing out of the kitchen.

In her absence, Enzo felt like he could unleash. "You wanna explain yourself, kid?"

Francesco opened his arms wide to the fast-paced chaos going on around him. "I can't really do that right now."

"Don't do it again. You hear me?"

Francesco turned his back to him and reached up, pulling down a clean frying pan from the hanger. "I hear you," he tossed over his shoulder, but his voice got lost in the impossibly loud, clanking song of the kitchen.

As Enzo headed out of the kitchen, Scarlett came back in. He glanced down at her and his eyes followed her every movement. He noticed her confidence, the way she was growing surer of herself.

Maybe, Enzo considered, it wasn't Francesco he needed to unleash on. Maybe it was Scarlett. Maybe Francesco was right all along. She wasn't nice. She was smart, smarter than he ever gave her credit for, and all he had done was help her realize it.

Scarlett's body radiated with fatigue. Though she had been working at Valenti's for the better of three months now, being a waitress proved to be a different type of work: manual labor with the addition of emotions. Passion came into play when she had to make dish recommendations to her tables. Personality was her greatest asset when it came to connecting with people, ensuring she was equal parts hospitable, attentive, and professional. After closing out her last table, she snuck out back for a cigarette before she had to tend to her closing tasks. She leaned her back against the wall and closed her eyes, feeling as though she were melting into the bricks.

"Can I talk to you?"

Enzo's voice filled the alleyway. His footsteps grew closer. When she opened her eyes, he stood in front of her. She drew on her cigarette and exhaled a long cloud of smoke. Her feelings towards him were twofold. Since returning from Atlantic City, they had barely spent any time together one-on-one. Perhaps it was because she now knew too much and Enzo had become evasive, or maybe she was partly to blame. Though she missed him, maybe by avoiding him, she was protecting herself.

"Talk," she said.

"What the hell was that about tonight? You making me look like a *strunzo* in front of Fran?"

She rolled her eyes. What was he talking about? All she did was encourage Francesco to do the very thing he was paid to do. The very thing he was *born* to do. To cook. And to cook the things his heart desired to make. In her eyes, she was doing the right thing to help him. Then she wondered why she even cared to help him at all. "I did not," she dismissed him.

"Yes you did," he said, his eyes full of intensity.

"He told me how you won't let him put what he wants on the menu. I walked in tonight when he was trying to write the specials, and I told him to run the *carrozza,* just to see how it went."

"So all of a sudden you're an expert on Italian cuisine?"

"No, but I know enough to know that if your brother's the chef, you should let him write the menu."

Enzo pointed her. "Stay out of my business."

She threw her cigarette to the ground, growing just as angry as him. "Don't tell me what to do."

"How much time do you spend with him anyway?"

"What's it to you?" She crossed her arms and leaned into one hip. Despite themselves, they moved closer to each other until she inhaled his ever-familiar scent and felt the heat of his body.

"Are you blind? Or can you see like everybody else that he's wanted you since the minute you walked into my restaurant?"

Scarlett let out a sarcastic laugh. Even if that were true, didn't Enzo have faith in anyone? "You must not trust me. Or your brother."

"I don't like what you did tonight."

"Too bad, Enz." She walked away, her hips sashaying side to side.

"Where are you going?"

"Home to your brother," she said, her words drenched in sarcasm.

Before she reached the door, he caught up with her and reached for her arm. At his touch, their flush of anger turned into a heat of attraction. Irresistible. They moved back until she was pressed against the wall and their lips met in that ever-addictive way they had with each other.

"You drive me nuts." He buried his face in her neck. "You gonna make it up to me?"

She held onto the nape of his neck and leaned her head against the wall, surrendering. "I hate you."

"You love me."

TWENTY-SIX

LITTLE ITALY, NEW YORK

SUMMER, 1985

"*Bucatini all'Amatriciana*," Julie said. She had become Scarlett's latest mentor, teaching her the proper pronunciation of each dish, explaining the way they were prepared, and what the ingredients were. Waitressing would come with its own set of challenges for Scarlett to overcome, but she was an eternal student. She would study as hard as she had to. "*Guanciale* is the main ingredient in this dish. Say it."

"*Guanciale*," Scarlett repeated, though her accent didn't sound as refined as Julie's. "But what is it?"

"The cheeks of a pig."

"*Cheeks?*"

"Don't look so freaked out. It's delicious. It's a classic Roman dish."

Francesco emerged from the kitchen with three hot plates on his arms.

He set them down on the table. Part of Scarlett's curriculum was to taste every dish on the menu and know the ingredients they were comprised of. This, she had no complaints about.

"You ready to eat?" Francesco asked. He handed them forks.

"Always," Scarlett said. She lifted her fork, ready to dig in, but he stopped her.

"You have to learn first. Tell us the names of these dishes," he said.

She studied them. Though she knew the names in English, she had to know them in Italian. "*Spaghetti vongole*," Scarlett said, referring to the plate of spaghetti with clams.

"Good." Francesco put his hands on his hips. "Next?"

She moved her eyes to the next dish, a bowl of pasta topped with dark, heavy meats stewed with onions. Her mind blanked. "I know it starts with a G. Right?"

"Think of the five families," Julie said.

Scarlett snapped her fingers. "Genovese. Pasta *alla Genovese.*"

"Ziti. That's Ziti pasta. But yes, Genovese sauce," Francesco said. "Last?"

The next dish was all too familiar, a layered dish of eggplants and red sauce in a small skillet. "That's eggplant parm."

"You can't call it eggplant parm." Julie nudged Scarlett's shoulder. "*Melanzana alla parmigiana*," she said. "Say it."

Scarlett tried to repeat after her, though her "R"s didn't roll in the same exotic way as Julie's.

"Come on. You're Italian," Francesco encouraged Scarlett.

"Only half. And I don't speak the language," Scarlett said in her defense.

"Another thing. Stop saying you're only *half* Italian. That's the only half that counts, as far as I'm concerned," Julie said. "Come on. Practice with me."

While she attempted to teach Scarlett to roll her "R"s, Francesco walked away, laughing and shaking his head.

"He's gone," Scarlett said under her breath. "Does that mean we can eat now?"

"Hurry up. If there's one thing this business will teach you, it's how to eat fast. Giovanna's already got people at the door," Julie said as they lowered their heads to their plates and began to dig in.

A half-hour later, Scarlett had tables. They were easing her into the job, giving her smaller sections than the seasoned waiters. Still, she settled into the groove of the evening, moving about the dining room with expertise and retreating to the kitchen when necessary. But as she stood on the service side of the line, firing main courses for one of her tables, Julie stormed in and grabbed Scarlett's sleeve, pulling her off to the side.

"What's the matter with you?" Scarlett asked.

"We need to switch sections," Julie said.

"Why?"

"Enzo's here."

"Yeah. And?"

"With Claudia."

Scarlett looked around for Fausto, though he was nowhere to be found. "Are you and Fausto trying to prank me? Because that's not funny."

"I'm not trying to be funny, Scar. They're here, together, and they're in your section."

Scarlett felt like someone had struck her with a match. Enzo wouldn't do this to her. He cared about her; he had told her himself. He cared too much to hurt her like this in the one place that was safe and sacred to her. Her eyes remained locked with Julie's. Scarlett felt every urge to unravel, but she tightened the buttons to her soul and stood up straight. Enzo might have thought her toughness was an act, but as Scarlett pictured Enzo and the image she had conjured up of Claudia in the dining room, she went on autopilot. Scarlett had become exactly who she was when her mother had told her she was going to live with Dustin. Tough. Not because she'd wanted to be, but because she had to be. Because if she didn't put up a strong front, she might crumble completely.

"Let's just switch sections," Julie said again, shaking Scarlett out of her thoughts.

"No. No way."

"What? Why?"

"Because," Scarlett said and retied her apron tight around her waist, "he wants to make me feel like shit? I'm gonna make him feel like shit right back." She jutted her chin out in defiance as she turned on her heel and walked out of the kitchen.

The dining room bustled with loud music and even louder chatter as people dressed in flashy outfits poured through the front doors. She spotted Enzo from a mile away. When it came to Enzo, she would know him anywhere. He wore the same pinstripe suit he'd worn in Atlantic City and he sucked on his cigarette as though it were his source of oxygen. His eyes darted around the room and Scarlett wondered if he was looking for her. From where she stood, Scarlett could see the back of who she assumed to be Claudia. Her hair was black and flecked with faint traces of gray.

Scarlett walked towards Enzo's table as her vision tunneled. Her heart raced so fast she nearly felt faint, but she put on a smile as she finally faced the man she loved and his wife.

"Hi," Scarlett said as she surveyed the table. Enzo and Claudia sat with another couple around the same age as them. "I'm Scarlett. I'll be taking care of you all this evening. Can I get you started with some drinks?"

"I'll have a cosmopolitan," Claudia said. Scarlett got as good a look at her as she could without staring. She was probably ten or so years older than Scarlett, but she looked like she could be Lana's age. Her hair was fastened in a half-up, half-down style, and her face was framed with big dangling earrings made of geometrical crystals. Her eyes were dark like

Enzo's, and the hollows underneath were traced with a tinge of blue. She wasn't pretty, but she wasn't unattractive either. She looked tired.

"I'll do the same," said the other woman at the table. Scarlett jotted down their order as her husband ordered a gin and tonic.

"Great." Finally, Scarlett's eyes dared to find Enzo's. Everything fell away as she stared into him, as it always did when they were together, but not in a good way. She felt like she was staring into a glimpse of her life, as if all her times with Enzo were replaying in her head like a movie. Except it wasn't a movie. Here and now, Scarlett looked at the man she loved with her whole heart, and he was sitting next to the woman to whom he belonged. Strange, to be faced with something that only lived in her imagination. "Your usual?" she asked, her arched brow drawing a stark contrast to her weak voice that was etched with hurt.

"Yeah." He gave her a slight nod, not daring to peel his eyes away from her. He swallowed hard and Scarlett could see his Adam's apple bob up and down in his throat. Out of the corner of her eye, she spotted Claudia reach for Enzo's hand, placing it on top as her fingers curled into his, like they were two becoming one.

Scarlett blinked a few times, bringing herself back into reality. "Great," she said, her mouth bone dry. "I'll get those right out for you."

Scarlett tried to take a deep breath as she walked away, but it wouldn't come. It was one thing to wonder about Claudia, to hear Enzo and other people talk about her. But to see her in real life? In the flesh? How could Scarlett even begin to explain how awful she felt? How stupid, how ashamed was? To think a man like Enzo could love her when he had Claudia? He didn't just have a wife. Scarlett had mistaken Enzo for her home when he was already home to someone else. She had been nothing but a fool the last few months. The whole time, she had been angry with Enzo for keeping things from her, for lying to her when the entire time, she had been lying to herself. She had been dreaming of the day Enzo would love her with reckless abandon, for the day when he would tell her she was all he needed. But seeing Claudia, Scarlett knew the day would never come. His life with Claudia was as certain as how sure Scarlett was that he'd be three whiskies neat deep by the time his entrées were fired.

She pushed open the kitchen doors and found Julie behind the line, scanning over some tickets with Francesco.

"Is it too late to take you up on that offer?" Scarlett asked.

"Of course not. Give me your tickets." Julie extended her hand through the window.

"Here. He's at table fifty-six. I took their drink order."

Julie took the tickets from Scarlett, her eyes filled with nothing but sympathy.

"I owe you," Scarlett said.

"Hang in there, Scar."

Scarlett would try her hardest to hang in there. She would try everything to keep up that strong façade for as long as she could. She loved Enzo. But no matter what he told her, no matter what lies he tried to convince her were truth, she couldn't have him.

CHAPTER

TWENTY-SEVEN

LITTLE ITALY, NEW YORK
SUMMER, 1985

Francesco didn't need to ask who was at table fifty-six. The minute he took in the look of absolute disappointment on Scarlett's face, he knew it could only be one person in all of New York. His brother. As he worked through the night, enveloped in the blazing heat of the kitchen, he couldn't escape the image of her face. He felt sorry for Scarlett, and angry with Enzo. He had tried to warn him from day one, but as it always went, Enzo never listened to Francesco. And Scarlett, she wasn't just nice. There was a side to Scarlett that was damaged, broken, even. She had already lost so much. If Enzo gave a damn about her, why would he hurt her in an irreparable way?

As Francesco closed up the kitchen and began to restock for the next day, he wished he didn't care. He wished he could tune out Enzo's life the way Enzo tuned out other people's feelings. But he couldn't. He pushed open the door to the pantry closet with force where he found Enzo, who was hunched over a shelf laying out a line of coke.

"Jesus," Enzo snapped. "Ever heard of knocking? Almost gave me a heart attack."

"If anything's gonna give you a heart attack, it's the shit you do. Not me."

"What did you just say?"

"You heard me," Francesco said as he picked up cans of tomatoes. "It's either gonna be the coke or having your wife and your girlfriend in the same room at the same time."

Enzo defiantly snorted the line, maintaining eye contact with his brother. "So you came in here to lecture me? Huh? You think I need advice from you?"

"Yeah, actually. What the hell are you doing, Enz?"

"It's none of your damn business. How about that?" Enzo approached his brother. They locked eyes, the air heavy with a pent-up rage that had been brimming for years. Enzo pushed the cans out of Francesco's arms and latched onto his shoulders, ramming him against a wall of shelves. Though Francesco had the advantage of height, Enzo had the advantage of his bravado. Before either of them knew what was happening, they started taking jabs and swings at each other. Enzo held Francesco by his collar. "You got a problem with me?"

"Yeah. You're a real asshole."

"Yeah? You jealous? Because she's young and hot and she wants me instead of you? Don't think I'm a fool," Enzo said, panting out of breath. "I see the way you look at her."

Francesco's frustration surged as he swung at Enzo, making contact with his ribs. "Shut the hell up. I'm gonna kick your ass."

They beat each other until they had gotten it all out, and by the end of it, the pair of brothers were hunched over, struggling to catch their breath. Francesco felt something trickling down his face. When he wiped his brow, blood covered his fingertips.

"Nice. Real nice," Francesco said. He found a bar rag and wiped his hand. "Listen to me. I've never been jealous of you. In fact, I think the way you live is kind of disgusting."

"Oh really? Last time I checked you're the one who has a different broad in his bed every week."

"At least I'm not cheating on anyone. I always keep my mouth shut, don't I? But what you're doing is wrong. You have a wife, and she's a decent girl. You're messing with both of them and neither one of them deserve it. If you're so miserable at home, then leave. But you can't keep doing this, Enz."

They stood, silent, hands on their hips, trying to slow their breath. With each passing moment, Francesco hoped he was getting through to his brother. They shared the same blood. Sometimes, Francesco felt like he was an extension of Enzo. They had to, on some level, share the same creeds.

"Enzo? The hell?" Francesco said.

"You're right."

"I'm right?"

Enzo's eyes darted around the room. "Yeah."

"So you're gonna end it?"

Enzo collected himself, smoothing down his pants and adjusting his belt. He rubbed his nose as he finally came to. "They day I listen to you is the day I die."

Whatever hope Francesco had taken hold of, it left as fast as it came. For so long, in so many situations, Francesco had tried to save his brother. But the further Francesco got away from Enzo, the more he thought that maybe the problem was that Enzo didn't want to be saved at all.

SCARLETT COULDN'T FAKE IT for one more minute. Alone, she grabbed a pack of cigarettes and a lighter and went out into the back alleyway, closing the door behind her. She lit it up, her eyes glazing over as she stared into the flame. Finally, she let it all out. Her mother, Dustin, Helen, Enzo, Claudia, it all came out of her with such force, it scared her. She couldn't control the way she cried, the way her shoulders shook, the way she could barely catch her breath. All her life, she'd never understood why Lana turned to alcohol to numb the way she felt from how life had disappointed her. But now she understood it completely. The woman she'd never wanted to be like, Scarlett had become.

Though she didn't want to believe he would, Enzo had hurt her. And the worst part was, he'd done it with ease, like it required no effort at all.

Scarlett looked up when the door snapped open, but she relaxed again when she saw Fausto and Julie bringing her a tall glass of vodka.

"I thought you could use this," Julie said, extending the glass to her. "It's the expensive kind that all the big shots drink. I can't even pronounce the name of it."

"Oh, Jules." Scarlett forced a smile and took a long gulp that burned her throat and sent a shiver through her body. She didn't care how much the clear liquid cost; the cheap stuff tasted better.

"Come here, sweetheart," Fausto said. He sat down on the ground and drew her into the crook of his shoulder, hugging her close. "Let it out."

She sobbed into his shoulder as Julie joined them, wrapping her arms around them. If nothing else, Scarlett was still thankful to Valenti's for giving her the two very best friends in the world, Fausto and Julie. Unlike Helen, they weren't trying to fill the void Lana left, nor did they live to such a standard that Scarlett couldn't reach. She had fallen further and further down the wrong path, but her friends were there to catch her.

"An affair," Scarlett wailed as they pulled apart. "I'm having an affair." She smoothed her hair back and she could feel her eyes going wide. She felt like she was spiraling, like she had just realized then and there exactly what she had been doing for the last few months. How had she gotten here? Who had she become? "God, what am I doing?"

"If it makes you feel any better, you're a million times prettier than her," Julie said.

"And I hate to say it, but I think he has real feelings for you, Scar," Fausto added.

"No, no." Julie waved her index finger. "The only person that ego maniac loves is himself. No offense."

"Thanks, bitch," Scarlett joked.

"Okay, so what are you gonna do about what he did to you tonight? I know you. You're not gonna let him live this down," Julie said.

"What did he do, though?" Scarlett asked, hands folded in her lap. "He came to the restaurant he owns to have dinner with his wife."

"He hurt you," Fausto said. "That's what he did."

"I deserved it."

"No, you didn't."

"What has he told you about Claudia anyway?" Julie asked.

"He described his marriage as a death sentence," Scarlett said, recalling their conversation in Atlantic City.

"That's romantic," Julie snorted.

"So he led you to believe he wanted out. That he wanted something with you," Fausto concluded.

"That's what I thought. I thought, one day he would realize how much he wanted to be with me…" she trailed off. "I feel so stupid. I can't believe I thought I could handle being with a guy like Enzo."

"Maybe it's him who can't handle you."

As Scarlett sipped on the contents of the crystal rocks glass in her hand, the door opened again and this time, Francesco and Enzo emerged. All eyes landed on Francesco, whose brow was dripping in blood. He casually wiped it away.

"What the hell happened to you?" Julie asked as she and Fausto closed in on him.

Scarlett remained planted where she was. Enzo moved towards her, but she scooted until her back was against the wall. She couldn't look at him the same, let alone talk to him after seeing him for what he was: someone else's husband.

"Why you crying?" Enzo said as he crouched down in front of her.

"Give me a break, Enzo." She looked away, but Enzo turned her face back to him.

"I want to see you tomorrow."

"No."

"Scarlett, please," he begged.

"Do you know what you did to me tonight?"

"I want to make it up to you."

"That's the thing, Enzo. There is no making it up to me."

"Scarlett, I need you. You know that."

She took a drag on her cigarette and stared at him. She didn't say anything at all because what was there to say? He needed her, but what did she need? What did she want?

"I'll come by tomorrow," Enzo told her before backing away. He then bade farewell to everyone, but no one said goodnight back.

———

SCARLETT HEARD WEIRD NOISES coming from Francesco's bedroom as she made her way up the stairs. She paused, hoping she wasn't walking in on him and one of his girlfriends. But as she got closer, she made sense of what she was hearing. Francesco was in pain.

"Francesco," she said as she knocked on his door. "You okay?"

Francesco opened the door. "My eye's swelling." His right eye had doubled in size and was almost closed, and a bruise had started to form.

"Oh my God. Let me get you some ice."

Scarlett went to the kitchen where she filled a bag with ice. When she returned, Francesco was sitting on the edge of his bed, wiping the cut with a wet rag.

"What happened to you anyway?" she asked, holding the ice over his eye.

"My brother. We got into a fight," he said, exhaling in relief as the ice hit his skin. "That feels good."

Scarlett stepped back, ice bag in hand. "Wait what?"

"Ice," he said, pointing to his eye. "And yes. We beat the shit out of each other."

"Over what?"

"He's an asshole."

"And you just discovered that tonight?"

"Oh no. I've known my whole life. Tonight, I just had enough."

"He did something to bother you?"

"He always does something to bother me." Francesco opened his left eye and looked up at her. "You got any brothers or sisters?"

"Only child. And when I see brothers fighting like you two do, I'm kind of happy it's just me."

"God, I can't even imagine. It must be very peaceful."

"It's quiet."

"And what about you?" Francesco took the ice from her and leaned back onto the bed. "You were crying."

Scarlett didn't think he had even noticed her when he came outside. She thought about lying, about trying to continue hiding her relationship with Enzo from him. But she knew he already knew. Besides, the relationship was over as far as she was concerned. What was the point in hiding it any longer? "Your brother," she said while avoiding his eyes.

"What about him?"

"He's an asshole." She dared to make eye contact. She worried she might have offended him. Not only were they brothers, but she knew how seriously Italians took their bloodlines. But instead, he wore a wide, half-crooked grin.

"And you just realized that tonight?"

"Yeah." She shifted her weight from one foot to the other. "I think so."

"Well, I have known him my whole life, so I have a bit of an advantage."

"That is true."

"Thank you." He held up the ice. "I wish I could do something for you, but I don't think a bag of ice will fix what you've got going on."

"No, it definitely won't."

"He's an asshole, but he's got a good heart," Francesco said, stopping her short of turning around and heading to her room. "You're gonna be fine."

She took Francesco in. With his face so open and honest, she felt like his words weren't mere words. They were a promise. If she held onto them tight enough, maybe they would be true. Maybe she would be fine.

"I hope you feel better," Scarlett said.

"I hope you do too."

She backed away, closing his door behind her. A cut to the brow? That would heal in a few weeks. But a broken heart? There was no telling when it would heal, or if it would at all.

CHAPTER

TWENTY-EIGHT

LITTLE ITALY, NEW YORK

SUMMER, 1985

Scarlett didn't have to wonder who was knocking on her door. When she opened it and Enzo filled the frame, in her gut and in her heart, she knew it would be for the last time. Not so much because she wanted it to be, but because it had to be.

"Come here," Enzo said as he reached for her and closed the door behind him. "I'm sorry, Scar. You don't know how sorry I am."

Though she had tried to numb herself, her tears wet his shirt as he drew her into him and kissed the top of her head. "I asked you not to hurt me, Enz." She looked up at him. "Why? Just tell me why. Is it something I did?"

"No. God, not at all, Scar. Claudia knew, okay? She knew I was seeing somebody else. What was I supposed to do, you know? I had to try and at least pretend to, I don't know…" he trailed off. "I don't know what I was trying to do. All I know is I want to make it up to you."

"You can't."

"Come on, sweetheart. Tell me what I have to do. I'll buy you anything you want. Take you any place you want to see. I'll do anything."

"Enzo," she said, her voice as unsteady as she felt. Her body shook with nerves as she felt him take a lock of her hair and twist it around his finger. She knew he probably expected her to melt. To forgive him. There was a part of her that wanted to. But she couldn't. Every time she thought about letting him back into her heart again, she replayed the images in her head of him and Claudia together even though the very thought of it felt like a knife was piercing her heart.

He pulled apart from her and met her gaze. "What?"

She knew she had to do it. She knew exactly what she had to say; she had been rehearsing it in her head since last night. But looking into his eyes, it was harder than she'd ever imagined it would be. She didn't just see Enzo. She saw every moment she'd shared with him, the ones in secret and the ones on full display. She saw how being with him had changed her, and she was scared of who she would become without him. "Enzo," she said, her voice no louder than a whisper, "I can't do this anymore."

"Do what?"

"This. The affair."

"Is that what you think this is?"

"What else do you call it?"

All traces of his sweet tenderness were gone. She thought he might turn around and leave right then and there.

"I'm trying to talk to you," she demanded, trying once more to gain his attention.

"I don't want to talk about it."

"You don't have a choice."

Enzo shot his cuffs and straightened his tie. "Fine. Fine! Let's talk about it. What do you have to say?"

"I have never felt so small — and that's saying a lot — as when you came into that restaurant with your wife," she said with her finger pointed at him. "I can't keep coming in second. I can't keep being your secret, Enzo. I won't do it."

"You knew what you were getting yourself into."

"Well now I want out."

"You can say that all you want. You and I both know how you feel about me, sweetheart," he said with a twinge of sarcasm. "You want to end what we got just so you can come running back to me?"

"I won't. There's only one way you can make it up to me. It's me," she paused, feeling breathless, "or her." Her heart pounded against her chest as Enzo's face clouded with anger. As soon as the proposition left her lips, she knew she had set herself up for quite possibly her biggest disappointment yet. And all the same, it was what she wanted. A definitive choice. Black-and-white. Her, or Claudia.

Scarlett had always been second best to everyone in her life. Enzo had been the one who'd made her believe she deserved to be in first place. That she was worth more. Now, he would pay the price of his actions.

"Choose?" he yelled. "She's my *wife*. Those are our kids. If you don't understand that then I don't know what to tell you, Scarlett. You want me to give everything up just because you're a pretty face to keep me entertained while I'm bored at work? You think that's worth giving my family up over?" Enzo's eyes looked crazed. "This is not worth all this," he said under his breath as if he were talking himself off a ledge. "Not worth it."

"What's not worth it?"

"Scar, I'm leaving now."

"Tell me," she yelled. She grabbed his arm and turned him back to face her. All she wanted to know was if he had the nerve to say what he was thinking to her face. "Say it, Enz. Say it to my face."

"Scarlett, I mean it. Stop it."

"Enzo—"

"You! You're not worth it, alright? You're not worth all of *this*. This isn't what I signed up for. This was supposed to be fun, and it's not fun anymore." His lips thinned as his chest moved up and down at a rapid pace. "You can keep your job as long as you like, but you and me, we're done."

Scarlett's heart broke, not in two, but into hundreds of tiny, shattered pieces. How cruel it was to be shown the world, only to return home to a cardboard box.

To know what it was to feel loved. To mean nothing to someone you'd given everything.

As she watched him walk away, she knew there would be pieces of him that she would always miss. Traces that she would long, ache for. She would look for him in everyone she met. She would lie awake at night and miss him and wonder if he was somewhere out there thinking of her, too. *What if.* Would he run down the endless list? Would he conjure up images in his head of the life they could've had together as she would?

As with any first love, her fire for him would never truly die. Her well of love for him would never truly run out. Though her heart was broken, no matter who she loved afterwards, he would always hold some of the pieces, right in the palm of his hand; in the very depths of him, she would always belong to him somehow. And the pieces he did share with her, the ones she had to grapple and fight for, she would hold onto them and carry them with her in the fabric of who she was. That's what love is, even when it's gone.

It wasn't until she heard the door to the apartment close behind him that she let out a cry, one like she had never let out before. She let herself release it all out without fear of anyone hearing her or judging her. It was just her, like it had always been. She was all she had left. All it took was a few sharp, biting words out of his mouth and he had her convinced she meant nothing. A few words, and she was broken. And yet, in those same words, she was set aflame – low and flickering, but one that would grow to be blazingly furious. She would show him that she was, in fact, everything. By the time he would realize it, it would be far too late.

For there is nothing more dangerous than a woman with someone to prove wrong.

<hr />

WHEN LANA HAD HANDED her Dustin's business card, Scarlett wasn't sure if she would look at it again. Yet, she had kept it safe, almost like she was carrying around a tangible piece of hope. Now, she dug around in her nightstand looking for it. It was tattered and worn; the edges crinkled. She tightened her robe around her and leaned back into her pillows, studying the card between her fingers, the numbers written across it. She could call Lana, and what? Tell her mother she had been right? That she'd made a mistake? That she was no different, no better than her? And then what would happen? Scarlett didn't want to go live on Long Island. Despite how hard and cold New York felt to her tonight, the city was her home. Her job at Valenti's was the one thing that was all hers. She had earned it, and it was pure good. She couldn't lose it, no matter how hard it would be to cross paths with Enzo every day.

But maybe it wasn't saving she wanted from Lana. Maybe Scarlett simply needed some motherly advice. Maybe Scarlett wanted to know how her mother felt when she got her heart broken, on multiple occasions, and how she got over it. But Scarlett knew she was kidding herself. Lana had never been there for her. Lana never gave her what she needed.

In the bathroom, Scarlett splashed some cold water on her face, running her wet hands through her hair, all the way to the ends. The very hair that Enzo used to run his fingers through, the strands he had twirled around his finger earlier. She hated that something that belonged solely to her made her think of him. From the medicine cabinet, she pulled out a pair of scissors. Gathering all of her hair into one thick bundle, she began to cut a jagged line, right above her shoulders. Golden wefts fell to the ground, quiet and gentle as a New York snow. She looked up and faced herself again, wondering why in the world she thought chopping off her hair would make her feel better.

"Scarlett?" Julie's voice came from the other side of Scarlett's bedroom door. "Scar? It's me. Can we come in?"

Setting the scissors down, Scarlett ran to answer the door. Julie and Fausto took a breath, going still at the sight of Scarlett's altered appearance.

"What the hell happened to your hair?" Julie asked.

"Delivery, Julie. Delivery. Okay, this looks manageable," Fausto said, examining Scarlett.

"No, it doesn't."

They closed in on Scarlett, grasping the short, jagged pieces of her hair. "You want to tell us what happened?"

"It's over, me and Enzo," Scarlett explained.

Fausto drew her into one of the warmest, safest hugs she had ever known. Julie wrapped her arms around her too and squeezed her tight.

"Alright, listen, this is a sweet moment and all, but we're already running late," Julie said. "If we want to get a good view of the fireworks, we have to leave soon."

"Fireworks?" Scarlett's eyes opened wider as they fell to Julie's *USA* tank top and Fausto's American flag T-shirt. They had planned weeks ago to watch the Fourth of July fireworks display from Pier 26. "Guys, I'm sorry. I can't go out tonight. I won't be any fun. But I want you two to go and have a great time."

"Oh, no, no, no," Julie said. She leaned into one hip. "You think I'm going to let you sit up here all night and pine over Enzo? No shot in hell."

Fausto pressed his lips together and pointed at Julie. "If I were you, I'd listen to her."

Julie moved further into Scarlett's bedroom. "Get me a dryer and some hairspray. Come on. Chop, chop." Julie clapped her hands together.

Under the sink, Scarlett retrieved Julie's requested tools and handed them over. "Work your magic."

CHAPTER

TWENTY-NINE

Francesco was on his third whiskey, drinking straight out of a plastic cup. He was grateful for the night off. He didn't much care about the fireworks, but he was glad to be outside in the warm summer breeze instead of the wall of smoldering heat he was accustomed to. His curls blew in all different directions as he weaved his way through the crowd, alone. At home, he had a phonebook filled with names and numbers; women who would've been readily available had he bothered to call and invite one of them to join him. He had decided against it. Francesco was coming to terms with the fact that being in the presence of someone who made him feel alone was worse than actually being alone.

He was in search of a familiar face, but everyone blurred together. Everyone except for one. Though she was petite and short, he would be able to pick her out of a crowd anywhere. Even from afar, she looked different, not that he could pinpoint how or why. Seeing Fausto and Julie by her side, he made his way to them.

"Francesco," Scarlett called out his name.

"Hey," Francesco said as he joined their trio.

Fausto patted him on the shoulder. "You look lost, boss."

"Whiskey will do that to you," Francesco said, raising his plastic cup. His cheeks went red. His staff rarely saw him outside of the restaurant, save for Scarlett. What would they think of him down at the pier by himself while everyone around him was celebrating with friends?

"Well, come on," Julie said. "We can't let you drink alone. Fireworks should be starting any minute now."

A blanket of dark sky covered Manhattan as they made their way closer to the Hudson, though it never felt dark in the city. The lights from the skyscrapers along the West Side glistened off the river. Music blasted through the air as the fireworks show began, waking Francesco out of his whiskey-induced daze. A hush fell over the crowd as the dynamite was lit and the first fireworks exploded in the sky. Glittering colors illuminated their faces as they reveled in the show. Francesco looked over at Scarlett. She was gazing up at the sky, her eyes filled with awe at taking in something bigger than herself, something so booming, loud enough to wake her out of her own dilemmas and quandaries. The fireworks were going off, one after the other in sync with the music, the big booms sending an electric wave of excitement throughout the crowd.

Their eyes found each other. He had to admire Scarlett. He knew she was in pain, the kind of pain that couldn't be fixed with a pill, a drug, or a drink. And yet, she was here, out, giving life another chance. And God, he wanted to give life a second chance, too. He wanted more than hot stoves and the success, which his brother took all the credit for anyway. Something of his own; something his heart truly desired. He knew it looked like he had it all, but inside, there was a gaping hole in his heart. And the more he looked at her, he started to believe the hole in his heart was shaped like Scarlett.

Francesco put his hand on Scarlett's shoulder. It was rough and calloused and covered in burn scars, and it enveloped her shoulder completely. She turned to him, quick, then slow. All at once she faced him as though she could feel it too. He dropped his cup of whiskey to the ground and put his arms around her waist, moving her along to the music. He tried to sing but he messed up all of the lyrics, making her laugh which was its own special melody. Everything fell away, like the only thing in existence was the woman in his arms, the woman who slept every night in the room next to him, the one he dreamed of knocking on her door and telling her how he felt about her.

But he soon realized it wouldn't be so cut and dry. A simple confession wouldn't suffice. Could anything ever be that simple? Her eyes that had been glowing began to dim. They stopped moving. Everything became plain and obvious to him. She didn't have to say it, but Scarlett's heart still was in Enzo's hands. He backed away from her, disappearing into the mass of faces in the crowd, left wondering if it always would be.

———

Francesco listened to the continuous booms of the fireworks from the rooftop. He had laid out a blanket, set out his boombox, and brought up a bottle of wine, though it remained untouched. For once, he didn't want to numb his feelings. Tonight, he would feel it all. He turned up the volume until Pavarotti's voice filled all of Mulberry Street. He lay flat on his back, looking up at the sky. The stars weren't visible; they never were in New York.

"You always listen to opera."

He heard her voice first, and then he turned his head. Scarlett stood there in her cutoff jean shorts and a cropped shirt, her torso peeking out.

"Want to join me?" he asked, returning his gaze upward.

"Sure," she said. She sat down cross-legged next to him, but soon after, she also lay on her back. "Why?"

"Why what?"

"Why opera? Don't you ever get tired of it? It seems so… serious."

Francesco thought about giving her the standard answer, that opera was beautiful. But instead, he chose to seize her interest, figuring it a way for her to get to know him better. "It makes you *feel*. Some arias are sad. Tragic, even. Others make you laugh. Some are just plain stunning, and you can't help but wonder how a *person* could create something so spectacular. When I was a kid, I was alone a lot. Everyone else in the family had their responsibilities, but I was the baby. I was kind of just *there*. Enzo was always out playing with the kids that were his age, and my parents worked. No one else in my family liked opera, but a neighbor of ours would lend me his records, one at a time. It was *my* thing.

Whenever the house felt too still or silent, I'd turn on the records. It was like a magic trick. As soon as those first few bars would play, I wasn't lonely anymore. I felt whatever it was the arias made me feel instead, and even when the music made me feel sad, that was still better than feeling lonely. It was like the opera was my friend. Might sound weird, but it's true. As long as I had the music, I was never alone." Francesco adjusted his arm underneath his head and swallowed. "Plus, not to mention, it's beautiful."

Scarlett took her time answering, as if she were soaking in these facts about him and storing them away. "I like this one."

"This one comes from an opera called *Turandot*. I listened to all the composers growing up, but Puccini was always my favorite. It's about a princess who will only marry a nobleman if he can solve three riddles, but if they try and fail, they'll be killed. A prince eventually does solve the riddles, but she still refuses to marry him."

"Why?"

"Because her heart is like ice. But when the prince kisses her, she *feels* for the first time. She knows it's love."

"So it has a happy ending."

"Happy, and sad. A slave girl was in love with the prince, but he breaks her heart when he goes after Turandot. The girl loved him so much that in the end, she killed herself."

Scarlett's mouth opened. "That's tragic."

"That's opera."

"I guess that's love, too," Scarlett said with a certain poignancy. "When you'd rather die than see the person you love with someone else."

"Or when you'd rather die than not be with the person you love."

"Maybe we should stop talking about dying and just listen to the music."

Francesco laughed. "Maybe you're right."

But Francesco was lost in his thoughts. He knew she had probably come to her own conclusion about the opera's meaning by making the connection to how she felt about seeing Enzo and Claudia together. Francesco knew the feeling all too well, too, having had to watch his own brother get to know Scarlett in the way he wished he could. Like the slave girl in the opera who fell for the prince after he merely smiled at her, Francesco's heart had been tugged at by Scarlett since the moment he met her. Would he have an ending no less tragic?

"Anyway, this aria is called 'Nessun Dorma,'" Francesco said as he hummed along to the tune. "*No one sleeps.*" He began to sing along, his voice glittering with vibrato. Unlike earlier, he knew every lyric to this angelic song.

When the song concluded, she looked over at him, her eyes misted over. "I had no idea you could sing like that."

"You never asked." He smiled at her, but when she loosened her hair from the clip she had it in, his brows knit. "What happened to all your hair?"

"I cut it off."

"Why?"

"Because," she said as she turned on her side, "remember how you said I couldn't fix my problem with ice? I tried chopping my hair off. And news flash, it didn't work."

Francesco didn't want to laugh, but when she started to giggle, her shoulders shaking as she fell back onto her back, he did, too. He could listen to her laugh all night.

"You okay?" he finally asked.

"I don't know. Does it get any better?"

"I wish I could tell you yes. I don't know, though. I wouldn't know."

"I guess that makes sense. Most men do the heart breaking. Not the other way around."

"I never broke anybody's heart on purpose."

"I'm not sure anyone does, you know? I don't know if anyone sets out to do that kind of thing on purpose. Would be kind of cruel if they did."

Francesco wished he could make it better for her. But he saw the way it was written on her face. Enzo had hurt her, deeply and totally. And Francesco wanted to kill Enzo for doing it. After he had warned him, begged him not to, Enzo had gone ahead and done it anyway. And for what? Did he realize the price Scarlett was paying for his ego trip? "You'll be fine," he finally said, for lack of better words.

"You keep saying that, but how do you know?"

"Because I saw you tonight," he said, daring to look her in the eyes. "I watched you. And even though I don't know everything, I know you've been through some shit. But you were there. You looked up at the sky like it was the most amazing thing you had ever seen. You know there's more out there for you."

"You could tell all of that just from looking at me?"

"Yeah." He looked back up at the sky. He wasn't sure if he should have said so much.

"You know what I could tell about you?"

"What?"

"You have everything, but to you, it doesn't mean anything. You were alone tonight, but I don't think you wanted to be alone."

He could feel Scarlett's stare on him as his jaw clenched. "All that," he said, finally looking over at her again, "just from looking at me?"

"You're a pretty easy book to understand."

"I hope that's a good thing."

She laughed. "It is."

Francesco felt like they were talking in code. "How do you know all this?"

"I'm young." Now it was Scarlett's turn to lie back down and search for the invisible stars. "But like you said, I've been through some shit. Play that song again, would you?"

He did. Of course he did. He would play her whatever song she wished for, over and over again until she grew tired of it. And after a while, as he watched her eyes flutter shut and her breathing calm, he couldn't help but marvel at how pretty she looked when she slept. He took her in his arms, careful not to wake her, and carried her back down to her bedroom. When she opened her eyes again, they were almost to her bedroom.

"I fell asleep."

"You did," he said. He placed her down on her bed. "Go back to sleep."

CHAPTER

THIRTY

HOBOKEN, NEW JERSEY

SUMMER, 1985

A few weeks later, Scarlett met Julie outside of Port Authority bright and early. Commuters zig-zagged in every direction as they purchased tickets and boarded a bus to Hoboken. They were off to Julie's sister-in-law's salon. Everything about the place, including Julie's sister-in-law Toni, was quintessential *Jersey girl*, from the freestyle music to the leopard-print cape snapped in place at the nape of Scarlett's neck. She pulled the banana clip out of Scarlett's hair and ran her fingers through it, shaking all the jagged pieces out.

"You think you can fix this?" Scarlett asked.

"She's a Jersey girl." Julie rolled her eyes, sinking into the empty seat next to Scarlett. "Of course she can."

"Get comfortable." Toni patted Scarlett's shoulders. Her nails were long and bright bubblegum pink, her eyeliner big and thick, her blue-black hair even bigger. She had a warmness about her that put Scarlett at ease. "We're going to be here for a while."

"I still can't believe you did this," Julie said to Scarlett. "I'm going to permanently remove those scissors from your apartment. You ever see heartbreak hair like this?" she asked Toni.

"Every girl does something to their hair after a heartbreak. It's the best way to say *screw you* without having to say it," Toni said.

Scarlett studied herself in the mirror, jagged ends and all. They were representative of how she felt. Broken. Like she was missing something. Though Toni would shape her golden hair in desperate need of resuscitation, Scarlett feared it would always remind her of what once was and what was lost. Though she had a natural aversion to change, change was exactly what she craved. "I want to color my hair," Scarlett said.

"Scarlett Marie," Julie said with wide eyes. "You already did something crazy. You don't need to go mental."

"That's not such a bad idea," Toni chimed in. "This blonde washes you out."

"It does," Scarlett agreed. She glanced up at Toni's dark locks and thought of her father. He was of typical Sicilian appearance – skin that remained tanned all year long, dark, wiry hair and eyes the same color. Scarlett examined herself in the mirror. Underneath the bleach she had used to try to look more like her mother, wasn't that who she truly was? She had worked hard to be this person she so evidently was not. Would returning to her roots require no effort at all? "Let's do jet black."

Toni bent down and laid a weft of her jet hair against Scarlett's. "Let's do it."

With her mouth hung open, Julie shook her head. "You're more insane than I thought."

Scarlett relaxed into her chair, wishing she could fast forward to see what she would look like. "There are worse things to be, Jules."

Toni drenched Scarlett's hair in color, and while they waited for it to develop, Julie went to the bodega and brought back the latest issues of *Cosmopolitan* and *People*. "So," Julie started as she tucked her legs underneath her, "last week, down at the pier, I saw you and Fran getting close. What was that about?"

"Nothing. We both had too much to drink, and I was a living, breathing female. That's about all it takes to catch his eye."

"Somebody is finally onto the Valenti brothers."

"I don't know. These last few days I've been thinking, what if I'm better off getting a job somewhere else and just starting over?"

Now that Scarlett had *real* experience under her belt, she had considered it, every time she stole a glance of Enzo at work, every time her heart gave a strange twist when she was around Francesco. What if she vanished from their lives completely? Would it give her the fresh start she imagined it would, or would the impact they already had on her chase her around?

"No, no, and no. I'm not going to let you."

"It's hard, you know? It's hard to see him all the time and pretend it didn't happen."

"It'll be harder if you *don't* see him. If you don't see how miserable and bored he is without you. You think the way you feel is going to disappear if you're not around him anymore?"

"No," Scarlett conceded. Scarlett knew that no matter where in the world she went, whether down the street or across the ocean, Enzo Valenti would always be on her mind in some capacity.

"So, there's your answer. We're stuck with you, and you're stuck with us."

Satisfied with the coloring process, Toni shampooed Scarlett's hair and brought her back to the chair. Swift with her scissors, Toni cut at different angles and positions, precise with her work as she made sure each strand fell perfectly into place. Scarlett closed her eyes as the heat of the dryer warmed her. Toni stood in front of Scarlett, making it impossible for Scarlett to catch a glimpse of herself in the mirror as she ran a big round brush through Scarlett's freshly colored locks.

"Can I see?" Scarlett asked the minute Toni turned off the dryer.

"Not yet. Nikki!" Toni yelled across the salon. "Come make the girl up, would you?"

Scarlett sat in the chair another half hour. Nikki, the salon's makeup artist, blended all types of foreign powders and creams on her porcelain skin. When Scarlett finally opened her eyes again, Julie, Toni, and Nikki surveyed her intently.

"Holy shit, Scar," Julie said.

When Scarlett met her reflection, she understood Julie's reaction. Scarlett's hair was an even shade of ink, and the fringy bangs covering her forehead made her brown eyes pop. Her eyebrows were filled in, sharp and angular, something Scarlett had never bothered to do before, and her lips were overdrawn ever so slightly to appear fuller. Scarlett wasn't a girl anymore. She was a woman, inside and out. A woman who was discovering who she was on her own; who she was born to be. She studied herself in the mirror. "I look like *me*," she said, more to herself than the women surrounding her.

Julie tugged Scarlett out of the chair. "Come on. It's time to go make Enzo wish he was never born."

SCARLETT AND JULIE SAUNTERED down Mulberry Street, taking in all the glances, nods, and whistles from the neighborhood men. After the salon, they passed by a boutique where Julie picked out an outfit for Scarlett: a leopard pencil skirt and an emerald silk blouse.

Instead of her work flats, Scarlett wore black pointed kitten heels. She felt glamorous, even if they were just going into work. "Don't you think everyone's going to wonder why I'm all dressed up? I'm going to have to go up and change anyway."

Julie held open the door to Valenti's. "So? It's about making an entrance." She motioned her arm for Scarlett to walk in.

"My Juliet," Fausto wore a sly grin as he took in Scarlett's new appearance, "you have truly outdone yourself." He twirled Scarlett around and put his hand on the small of her back. "You're going to be ruffling a lot of feathers tonight, my dear. Just get ready."

"Thanks, Faus," Scarlett said as Fausto drew her into a hug.

"Now come on girls. We're already late for the staff meeting."

The Valenti's staff were huddled in the main area of the dining room. Pre-shift meetings were customary on weekends, but the air held an unusual intensity. Francesco and Enzo stood, facing the entirety of the group.

"The governor doesn't like a lot of noise, so we're putting him at table sixty-eight, so he has some privacy," Francesco explained. "Try to keep your guests at bay. I don't want people going up and asking for autographs or photos, okay? Fausto will be taking care of him, of course, but should he need anything, I'm counting on all of you to help him. The service has to be perfect and well-tended. We all know from last time this guy's a demanding customer. Understood?" Francesco surveyed everyone as they gave him their undivided attention. That was, until Julie and Scarlett walked in the room. Francesco's eyes fell to her first; then everyone else turned around.

"Where the hell are you two coming from?" their fellow waitress, Mary, asked.

"Jersey," Julie said casually, finding a seat in the back. "Sorry we're late. Traffic in the tunnel was a nightmare."

"Nice of you to join us, ladies," Enzo said sternly. "Now, everyone—"

"You look amazing, Scarlett," Mary said to her, much to Scarlett's surprise. She turned back around in her seat and looked at Enzo. "Sorry, Enz. Now please, continue boring us with facts about governor what's-his-face."

The whole room stifled a laugh, but Enzo's face clouded with anger. It was evident that he didn't like the way Scarlett had stolen the spotlight from him.

Scarlett looked around the room until her eyes found Francesco again. He was already staring at her. As she felt the heat rising to her cheeks, she averted her gaze elsewhere, becoming keenly interested in the Florentine pattern of the carpet. Eye contact with Francesco felt forbidden, let alone being attracted to him.

Soon after the meeting concluded and the staff dispersed to prepare the restaurant for service, Scarlett headed towards the stairs to change into her uniform. She hated the idea of taking off her glorious new outfit, but she had a job to do, and a messy one at that.

"Scarlett," Francesco called after her. "Need to talk to you."

"Sure. What's up?"

"I need Fausto's full attention to be on the governor tonight. Do you think you could work the door?"

"Oh, yeah. Sure. I mean, I've watched him plenty enough to know how it works. I think I can manage," she said. She had never hosted, but she knew how important of a job it was. As the host, she would be the first point of contact when guests walked in, and the last face they saw when they left. And even better, it meant she got to keep her nice new outfit on.

"For sure," he said with a confident nod. "And you're already dressed the part. You look beautiful." He lifted his caramel eyes just above her face. "Your hair."

A hand instinctively flew to her freshly colored locks. "Thanks." Enzo had been the first man to tell her she was beautiful, but Francesco was the first who meant it beyond her looks. She didn't just look beautiful;

she *was* beautiful, body and soul. They broke apart when Enzo walked up to them, enveloping them with his presence.

"Fran," Enzo said with force, "got a problem with one of the ovens. Come fix it."

"Be right there," Francesco called after him, already nodding at Scarlett before dutifully making his way to the kitchen.

Francesco entered the kitchen without looking back, but Enzo remained in the doorway and gave Scarlett a onceover. Although she wished she didn't care, Scarlett couldn't help but wonder what he thought of her; she couldn't help but hope that his heart was being stabbed with regret until it bled with nothing but love for her.

CHAPTER

THIRTY-ONE

LITTLE ITALY, NEW YORK

SUMMER, 1985

After their VIP guest of the night had come and gone with great success, the staff relaxed into their usual rhythm. The dinner rush had concluded and most of the guests on the books had already been seated, save for a few late-night stragglers who were coming in after nine. Scarlett's feet ached in her heels, and she was itching for a cigarette, but at the door, there were no breaks.

She stood up straighter as a woman walked through the front doors, alone. The woman wore a dramatic, all-black ensemble and her hair was the same color as her clothes. She had tawny skin, and even though Scarlett greeted her with a smile, the woman wore a look of annoyance.

"Good evening, welcome to Valenti's. Do you have a reservation?" Scarlett greeted her.

"I'm here to see Fran," she said, putting her cigarette out on the ashtray on the host podium. "I'll be at the bar. Tell him I'm here."

"Oh." Scarlett stepped back. She was too taken aback by the woman's abruptness to focus on the pang of envy that hit her. "What was your name?"

"Tina," she scoffed, as if Scarlett should have already known.

It took all of Scarlett's will not to let out an eye roll or tell the woman off as she made her way to the kitchen. "Fran?" Scarlett yelled over the line. The door might have calmed down, but that meant the kitchen was in full swing. "A woman is here to see you. Tina? She's at the bar."

Francesco swayed a pan over the gas flames a few times before he responded. He wiped beads of sweat from his forehead with his arm. "Tell the bar staff to keep her drinking until I'm done so she loses track of time. If she asks how long I'll be, tell her twenty minutes."

"How long are you really gonna be?"

He glanced at the clock. "At least another hour and a half."

After Scarlett gave Francesco's message to the bartenders, she returned to the host podium. She sat the last few tables on the books, and then she stood there, not sure what to do with herself. Working the tables, there was no time to be bored. But up here, while she had slowed down, the dining room was bustling. She wished she was back there where she belonged instead of playing fill-in by herself. She felt like she was missing out on the action. She also hated the fact that this lull afforded her mind to lay dormant, giving room for thoughts. Lately, Scarlett didn't like to think. As if reading her mind, Fausto swooped by to check on her.

"How do you like it up here?" he asked.

"It's fun, but I think I like working the tables better."

"You like the hard work." He winked, his blue eyes sparkling. "You look good up here, kid. I wouldn't be surprised if they stick you up here with me every so often."

"Hey, you." Scarlett heard a sharp, angry voice. She turned around to find Tina holding an empty champagne glass. "I told you to tell Fran I'm here."

"Oh, Tina, I did tell him."

"Well, where the hell is he?"

"I'll go see if he's free now," Scarlett said as politely as she could. She turned back to Fausto for some sense of encouragement. He nodded her on.

As she swung open the kitchen doors and walked in, she crashed right into Mary. The salads Mary had on her tray crashed to the ground and pieces of romaine were scattered all around the kitchen floor. Mary wore a helping of Caesar dressing on her blouse.

"Nice, real nice," Mary yelled as she surveyed the mess around her. "Watch where you're going next time!"

"What the hell is going on here?" Francesco came out from behind the line. Scarlett didn't know why, but she sensed that wasn't a good thing.

"Are you just going to stand there? Clean it up! It's your fault," Mary said as she wiped her uniform with a bar rag.

"Somebody, anybody, clean it up! We don't have time for this. We have a restaurant to run," Francesco shouted.

"I'm sorry," Scarlett said, but the words barely came out of her mouth. She grabbed a broom and dustpan and began sweeping up the pieces of the broken plates and the salad. She bent down, pushing the contents into the dustpan, trying to hide how her eyes were wet with hot tears of embarrassment.

"What were you doing back here anyway?" Francesco asked. Scarlett's eyes traveled from the soles of his shoes to his face. Francesco stood over her with his hands on his hips. "The hosts don't usually come in the kitchen that much."

She dumped the contents of the dustpan into the trash can and returned the broom to the wall before looking at him. "I came back here to tell you that your girlfriend is out there bitching to me about how long she's been waiting for you," she said. But before she turned all the way around, she looked at him again. "And for the record, I'm a waitress, not a host."

SCARLETT NEVER REMEMBERED A shift upsetting like tonight. She peeled off her gorgeous new garments and tossed them aside for the dry cleaners. They weren't the kind of clothes to wear while sweeping up salads and broken plates, but she had done just that in them. After she took a long, steaming shower, she wrapped her body in a robe and her hair in a towel. She couldn't shake her bad mood. Between Mary, Tina, and the way Francesco had spoken to her, she couldn't pinpoint who upset her more. She decided she deserved a cigarette and a drink.

In the kitchen, she was sifting around for a bottle of wine when she heard the door to the apartment open. She assumed it was her one and only roommate, and she didn't bother to turn around. She wasn't in the mood to talk to him. His heavy footsteps broke the silence in the apartment until they came to a stop in the kitchen. She felt his stare on her back. Reluctantly, Scarlett turned around to find him staring straight at her.

"Hey," he said, his voice raspy and tired.

"Hi."

"Listen, I'm really sorry about earlier."

"You don't have to explain anything to me," she said, returning her attention to her wine.

"What if I want to?"

She stopped and glanced up at him, her unresponsiveness giving way for him to speak. He pulled out a chair at the small kitchen table for two. He sat with his legs open, leaning his elbows on his knees as he ran his fingers through his chestnut curls.

"You know, I work all night. And I drink more than I should. Women, they're supposed to be the one thing that'll make me forget about it all, make me happy. And then I meet a girl like Tina, and she's nuts. Makes me nuts."

"She's not for you."

"I know." He stopped and looked up at her. "How do you know?"

"She doesn't understand you, or what you do. And what you do – that's who you are."

"Exactly! Thank you. You get it!"

"I do." She poured herself a glass and took a sip. The more she looked at him, the harder she found it to stay mad at him. "You want some?"

"Why the hell not?" He sighed. "What's one more glass at this point?"

She set a tall glass of wine in front of him and took a seat across from him. They were quiet. She was still trying to shake off what had happened at work, and judging from the conflicted expression on his face and the apology written in his eyes, he was trying to process not only his evening with Tina, but how awful he felt for snapping at Scarlett.

"I'm not going to see her anymore," he finally said.

"Tina?"

"Mm hmm."

"Why not?"

"Shouldn't love make me happy? She doesn't make me happy."

"That – you and her – that wasn't love."

"How do you know what love is?"

Scarlett went quiet. How did she know? Because she'd lived it, for many months with Enzo. If there was one thing she had learned, it was that love sure as hell didn't equal happiness. Love, to her, was messy, sad, brutal. But how was she supposed to tell him that?

"I don't think I've ever really been in love." He looked out at nothing in particular and leaned back into his chair. "Have you? I mean, the real thing."

"Yeah. Wouldn't recommend it."

He laughed heartily at her ability to turn something so painful into something she could joke about. But soon, his head tilted to the side as he focused on her, the same way he did when he was working on a dish that required his full attention.

"Why are you looking at me like that?" she asked.

"You don't deserve what he did to you."

The way he looked at her, it almost made up for the way Enzo had treated her. In his own way, he was apologizing for Enzo. Maybe this wasn't the first time in his life he'd had to do that; she imagined it wasn't. Scarlett felt like it was a turning point. They had always danced around her relationship with Enzo. It felt monumental that Francesco had finally addressed it. What surprised her the most was that she didn't wish for the earth to open up and swallow her whole. There were no traces of embarrassment, just like in his eyes, there were no traces of judgement. She kept her gaze locked so intensely with his that nothing could break it. Under Enzo's gaze, she had always squirmed, always wanted to hide. But with Francesco, even if she wanted to hide, there was nowhere to go. He could see everything clearly. And she was fine to let him.

"I thought being with him would fix me," she started to explain, surprised at her own willingness to be totally honest. "I always tried to be perfect so my mother would stop drinking. I was the perfect student, always got good grades. I never gave her trouble about letting me to go to parties or out on dates. I thought if I was perfect, she'd choose having a relationship with me over a relationship with her martinis. Once I realized it wasn't working, somewhere along the way, I stopped. I stopped trying to be good enough. When I met Enzo, I tried to do the same thing. Tried to be great at my job. Didn't tell him about how messed up my home life was because I was afraid it would turn him off. Sometimes I wouldn't say what was really on my mind because I didn't want him to think I'm difficult.

"Enzo had so much to lose, you know? His whole family was at stake. I thought if he chose me over all of that…" she trailed off, trying to shake away the tears glistening on her face. She lifted her eyes to meet Francesco's. He was concentrated on her every word. "That's why it hurt so bad. Not because I loved him and I was sad it didn't work out. It was because I tried to be good enough, and I wasn't. Again."

Francesco leaned his arm on the table and opened his palm. "Why are you only telling me this now?"

Scarlett traced one of his burn scars with her finger. "I just want someone to understand why I did it. I knew it was wrong. You don't think I felt guilty? You don't think I hated what we were doing? Sometimes I can't believe I did what I did. But I needed something from him."

"And he didn't give it to you."

"No. He didn't. He couldn't."

"I feel like it's my fault," Francesco said. He finally broke their eye contact and leaned his elbows on the table.

"What? Why would you think that?"

"I talked to him the night we got into that fight. I told him what he was doing to you was wrong. That you didn't deserve to be humiliated in the middle of the restaurant while Claudia sipped on cosmopolitans. Not to mention she doesn't deserve him to be running around on her either, but that's another conversation. The whole thing, everything he was doing was messed up. And I'm the one who told him."

"All you did was tell him the truth." Scarlett was comforted, in a way, knowing Francesco had tried to protect her or defend her. It made her feel like maybe she wasn't alone after all. "Thank you."

"For what?"

"For talking to him. And for letting me stay here even after everything that happened between me and your brother. You didn't have to let me stay, but you did." Then, Scarlett remembered her promise. This living arrangement was temporary. She had wanted to pay rent. She pushed her chair out from the table and stood. "Be right back." In her bedroom, she sifted around her dresser until she found her shoebox of cash. She didn't know how much was fair, so she peeled off a stack of hundreds. She would let Francesco tell her what was owed. Back in the kitchen, she placed the cash on the table. "How much do I owe you?"

"What?"

"Rent." Scarlett blinked a few times. "I told you I would pay you rent, and I meant it."

Francesco slid the money back towards her. "And I meant it, when I told you no."

"Fran, I can't live here rent-free forever." Scarlett slid the cash towards him, though he stopped her, covering her hand with his.

"I like having you around."

"That's not the first time you've said that."

"It's not, is it?" Francesco smoothed his hair back, revealing his sharp widow's peak, which only further revealed his cheeks that were burning red.

"Why?" She tried to find his eyes, but he kept his focus on the ground.

"Why what?"

"Why do you want me to stay? I mean, it's not a problem between you and Enzo, is it?"

To her surprise, Francesco stood. He looked so tall, towering over her, like he was taking up all the space in their tiny kitchen. He took a big inhale and his broad shoulders visibly rose and fell. "I like you, Scarlett. That's the problem."

Francesco drained the last of his wine and set the glass down. His eyes never found her again, but she couldn't peel hers off of him. Scarlett watched his every movement, the way he drunkenly stumbled down to his bedroom, the way he ran his hand over his head like it would help him find the solutions to his problems. He liked her. And the only thing Scarlett could think of was that she liked him, too.

And that was, in fact, a very big problem.

CHAPTER

THIRTY-TWO

"Is everything as it should be?" Scarlett asked. The evening had been slow, by Valenti's standards, so she was able to give her undivided attention to her last few tables.

"We'll take a round of espressos for the table," said one of the guests at the table.

"Any dessert?" Scarlett asked, refolding a rumpled napkin into an artful triangle.

"Oh, how can we resist. Whatever you recommend. Enough for everybody."

"You got it," Scarlett said with a wink. At the espresso machine, she pulled down four demitasse cups and began to brew.

Francesco emerged from the kitchen and joined her. He leaned his hip against the counter. "Hi."

"What's up?" Grateful for the distraction, Scarlett focused her attention on her espresso making so she wouldn't have to look him in the eye. They hadn't seen much of each other since Francesco's confession, and it was clear they were avoiding each other.

"I was wondering if you had plans this weekend," Francesco said.

She narrowed her eyes at him as the espresso machine droned loudly and hot, brown liquid poured out. "How do you know when my birthday is?"

"Your birthday?"

"The fifth."

"It's also Labor Day."

"Oh." Scarlett blushed. "Right. No, no plans."

"I have a tradition. Every year, I rent a condo out in Montauk, just for a couple of days. Whoever wants to come is welcome. I wanted to invite you, and since I now know it's your birthday too," he said with a smile, "we can celebrate while we're there."

Montauk. Scarlett hadn't been in years, but her love for Long Island's furthest point rivaled how she felt about Manhattan. Even when her father was still alive, they were a family of little means, but he had always managed to take his girls to Montauk for one week each summer. How vividly she remembered turning the crest of Montauk Highway in the backseat of her father's Oldsmobile, the way that first view of the crisp blue ocean never ceased to amaze her. She had only returned once since her father's passing, though at just the mention of it, she could still see the white sand beach, rolling dunes, and smell the salty sea air.

"Who else is going?" she asked.

"Fausto and Julie are definitely in. A few other stragglers might join us as well. Who knows who will show up. Everyone deserves a break, you know?"

Scarlett pulled down an extra demitasse cup, feeling the heat of his eyes on her skin.

"You should come."

Scarlett thought it over as she loaded a silver tray with four espressos and handed the extra one to Francesco. "I'll come."

—~~—

"ALRIGHT, WE'RE IN MONTAUK now. Time to have a shot," Fausto said as he opened a bottle of Smirnoff. The four of them had laid out their beach towels all in a row, each one a different bright colored pattern. Francesco busied himself with setting up the radio, trying to move the antennae to just the right spot so they'd get a signal.

Scarlett put her hands on her hips when Fausto held out the bottle for her to take. "I just want to relax," she protested.

"Shot, now. It's your birthday, bitch," Julie commanded.

"Fine." Surrendering, Scarlett tilted her head back as Fausto poured the vodka down her throat. Her nose wrinkled as she swallowed. "It's way too hot for this."

"Take off your sundress and it won't be." Julie slipped out of her sarong, revealing a high-cut, metallic one piece.

"Fran, you're next." Fausto passed the bottle to Francesco.

Francesco took the shot with ease and slipped his tank top overhead, revealing a wide expanse of a tanned, defined chest with faint whispers of gold, curly hair. He lay back on his towel, smoothing his hair back and letting the sun kiss his face. Scarlett noticed the gold chain dangling around his neck with a small Italian horn at the base. It was identical to Enzo's, though Scarlett was pleased to realize that this was the first time she had thought of Enzo since she'd left Manhattan. She hadn't thought it would, but time was proving to be a friend, healing the wounds Enzo left behind and allowing Enzo to slip further from her mind with each passing week.

It was Scarlett's turn to undress and settle into the day. She tried to swallow but her throat still burned from the vodka. Her cheeks were hot as she lifted her sundress overhead, revealing her taut stomach and toned legs, both a result of her profession. She felt everyone's stare on her as she adjusted the waistband of her neon fuchsia bikini, though she tried to ignore it.

"Hey, Fran?" Julie said.

"Yeah?" he answered.

"Can you please fatten her up a bit so I don't have to be so jealous?" Julie shook her head and turned to Scarlett. "If I had your figure, I'd walk around naked all the time."

"Shut up." Scarlett laughed.

"Alright, it's hot as hell. I'm going in the ocean. Who's coming?" Fausto looked around.

"You guys go." Scarlett waved Julie and Fausto off as they trekked down the beach to the ocean. She laid down on her towel next to Francesco's and tilted her face towards the sky, her body sinking into every dip and grain of the sand.

"You want sunscreen?" Francesco asked, nodding towards Scarlett's pale skin.

"Nah." She hadn't been on a proper vacation in so long, she wanted to soak in all of the sun, even if it scorched her. "You?"

"I don't need it."

Scarlett knew he didn't spend much time outside, but his Neapolitan skin was a permanent tawny color. She looked over at him and took him in, doing her best not to stare. She had never seen him like this, relaxed, wearing nothing but a pair of shorts. Sure, they had been alone plenty of times in the apartment, but there was always a line they didn't cross.

Here, in the sand by the sea, there were no lines. Scarlett felt bare having him see her like this. She wondered if he felt the same way.

"So, how does it feel to be…" he paused, his brows furrowing. "How old are you today again?"

"The big two-four."

"God, what I wouldn't give." He groaned and his eyes went distant like he was already reminiscing about when he was Scarlett's age. She wondered what he was like back then. Was he different or was he always *him*?

"It's not that exciting to be my age."

"Wait until you're thirty like me. Then you'll understand."

"I'm sure I will."

"You seem older," he said, but caught himself immediately. "I don't mean it like that. You don't look old. I mean you act older. You're mature."

"It's okay. I knew what you meant."

"So, what do you wanna do tonight to celebrate?"

"This is good enough for me. I haven't been to the beach in, God, maybe eight years?"

"No way."

"My dad used to bring us out here, the same week, every summer. After he died, my mom tried to keep the tradition going the first summer without him. We took the Hampton jitney from the city and stayed at a motel for a few days, but it wasn't the same. I haven't been back since."

"I'm sorry." He rolled onto his side, taking her into his full view. She did the same, propping herself up one elbow. His muscles enveloped him, and as Scarlett further studied his appearance, she wished her mind wasn't so busy tossing around the idea of how she might like to wrap herself in his arms and rest her head on his chest. "Must be a special place to you."

"It feels pretty surreal to be back here, to be honest. You know what I used to think when I was a kid? I thought, *God, if I ever have a beach house out here, I'll know I've made it.*" New York City ran through her veins, but there was a version of Scarlett who imagined living in a place where the birds sang and flew freely, and the ocean roared in constant.

"Is that so?"

"Mm hmm. It was silly."

"I don't think so. I'm sure there are plenty of women out there who dream about having a beach house and a family to fill it with."

"Two kids, so they have each other to play in the sand with." Scarlett looked past him and scanned the crowded beach. It wasn't often she talked about her future like this with anyone, dreaming about what it might be like to have a family of her own someday. Having little to model it after, having her own family seemed like a far-off dream. Her cheeks burned with vulnerability. "I never had anybody to play in the sand with."

"Well, I think we should do something big tonight. I'll cook us a big dinner, and then we should do something crazy."

"Like?"

"Shoot off fireworks on the beach. Maybe even go out to a club. If you want."

"It sounds like that's what *you'd* like to do. We don't have to do anything big."

"We don't have to, but we should."

Scarlett shielded her eyes with her hand to get a good look at the mischievous grin on his face. His curls had gone absolutely wild from the humid, salty breeze.

"Surprise me. Deal?"

His eyes crinkled at the sides. "You got yourself a deal."

THIRTY-THREE

MONTAUK, NEW YORK

SUMMER, 1985

Francesco wanted to make the evening special for Scarlett. Though he was having a hard time expressing how he felt about her with his words, maybe he would have an easier time by showing her with the language he was fluent in: his food. He had spent the day next to her on the beach, worshiping the sun as her skin turned golden and his brown, content in their comfortable quiet. He wondered if she could feel his nerves around her, seeing her body in its full splendor, thinking how he might like to hold her in his arms. Though he had confessed he liked her, it had been weeks since, and they hadn't brought it up again. But her birthday? This was his chance. To prove to her that she could trust him; that he wasn't some carbon copy of his older brother. And although she hadn't given any indication that her feelings were reciprocal, the fact that she had agreed to spend her birthday with him said something.

While Julie, Fausto, and Scarlett were still out on the beach, Francesco carried in the last of his ingredients from the local market. He would make a feast of her favorites and pistachio cake for dessert, a nod to her Sicilian roots. Then, he would put on a firework show for her. He hoped that she would look at them the same way she did on the Fourth, her eyes full of wonder and hope.

"Hey boss," Fausto said as he came in from the deck and closed the door behind him. In a matter of hours, his blonde hair had gone lighter, and his skin was almost as deep as Francesco's. "You know, you deserve to relax more than we do."

"It's for her birthday," Francesco said as he got to work.

"We could've done takeout. You cook twenty-four seven."

"She deserves a nice home-cooked meal." Francesco put the debate to bed.

Fausto looked over at Francesco as he grabbed a bottle of water out of the fridge. "You need some help?"

"Not with the food, but you think you could run an errand for me?"

"Of course."

Francesco grabbed his wallet off the counter and pulled out some cash. "I want the biggest fireworks they've got."

"You got it." Fausto tucked the cash into his pocket. "Need anything else while I'm out?"

"Candles, for the cake. Maybe some flowers? Get a nice bottle of wine, too. Red."

"Just one?" Fausto joked.

"As many as you think we'll need," Francesco corrected himself. "We've all got some pretty bad habits."

"The curse of working in restaurants. Alright, I'm out. See you in a bit."

"Thanks, Faus."

Francesco went into his zone as he cooked. It felt different, cooking a meal for someone specific, someone special, rather than a nameless face sitting in his restaurant. He laid out a platter of antipasti, delicately folding each piece of *mortadella* and *prosciutto* like works of origami. He layered thin slices of eggplant, sauce, and a blend of cheeses and popped it into the oven. Then, he stewed together her favorite pasta dish, *spaghetti alla nerano*, a simple sauce of zucchini and cheese that he only made in his own kitchen in the apartment, save for his one night of rebellion at Valenti's. For main course, he would prepare a seafood stew of mussels, clams, lobster and langoustines; he was proud that Scarlett's palate expansion was due to him. He had made these very dishes hundreds of times, yet tonight he poured all of himself into his food. His heart was in the very flavors and essences.

Like his friends, he was savoring his time away from the restaurant. Away from the grind, away from the mundane scenery, and truthfully, away from Enzo. But was he truly away from Enzo? Francesco knew how he felt about Scarlett. But where did Enzo fit into those feelings? How would Enzo react if something happened between them? The most frustrating thing of all to Francesco wasn't that he was having a hard time admitting to Scarlett, or to himself, how he felt about her; it was that, as he always did, he had to consider Enzo before he could make a move.

AN HOUR LATER, HE had plated his creations and set the table. Francesco lit as many candles as he could find and turned on the radio for some background music. The pistachio cake was setting in the fridge and the fireworks were outside in the sand, ready to go. The last ingredient was his guests at the table.

"You guys, dinner is ready," he yelled down the hall. He wasn't sure if it was how good the food smelled or his booming voice, but the three of them reached the dining room within seconds.

"Oh my *God*," Julie said with a gasp as she took in the scene. "How romantic does this look!"

"Beautiful," Fausto said as he squeezed Francesco's shoulder.

"Wow," Scarlett said. She took her time as she moved further into the room to take in the details. "You did all this?"

"Yeah," Francesco said, hands on his hips. He tried to hide his excitement, but he admired his own work.

"Everything is so beautiful, Fran."

"Sit," Francesco instructed. He put his hand on the small of her back, leading her to the table. "Come on, let's eat."

On Scarlett's place setting, she found a bouquet of white roses sprinkled with baby's breath. From her chair, she looked up at him with glossy eyes. "White roses are my favorite."

"Lucky guess," Francesco said with a wink. Scarlett ran her fingers over the delicate white roses and baby's breath. Francesco felt like his heart might pump out of his chest. Was it too much? Too forward to buy her flowers?

"Dig in, guys," Francesco said as he helped pass around plates. When he was a child, Francesco couldn't comprehend his mother's shyness. Why she blushed at a compliment or breezed past kind words. Tonight, he understood. Art was intimate. Through his food, Francesco could reveal concealed parts of himself, and watching his close friends consume his art was more intimidating than if they were food critics. What would his creations reveal?

Throughout the dinner chatter, Francesco stole glances at Scarlett. She looked overwhelmed, like she was trying to make sense of everything and what it meant. He wondered if anyone had ever done anything nice for her, for the sake of being kind and not because they wanted something from her.

"I would like to make a toast," Fausto said as he stood and raised his glass of Chianti. The table had been cleared and Francesco had set out dessert in front of Scarlett. "To *one of* my favorite girls." He winked at Julie and Scarlett. "May this next year bring you all the love and happiness you deserve. I think I speak for all of us when I say that you've been a great addition to our little crazy crew."

"Why are you crying?" Julie reached for Scarlett's arm.

"This is the nicest thing anyone's ever done for me." Scarlett's hands flew to her chest. "All of it. Thank you. You guys have no idea what all of this means to me."

"This is what us Italians do for the people we love," Fausto said.

"For our family." Julie squeezed Scarlett to her side.

Francesco raised his glass. "*Alla famiglia.*"

"Shall we sing? In three, two, one." Fausto conducted them in as they all sang "Happy Birthday" to Scarlett. Her golden skin glowed in the candlelight. Before she blew them out, she closed her eyes and her forehead creased. She didn't say a word, but everyone knew she had made a wish with all her heart. For what, they did not know. When she opened her eyes again, she looked at Francesco.

"Night's not over yet. I've got one more surprise," Francesco said after they had dessert.

"You did too much," Scarlett said as she stood and set her napkin on the table.

"Come on. It's outside." Francesco led the way out on to the beach where he had set up the fireworks. The beach was deserted and dark, the only light being cast from the condominium building and the bright moon overhead.

Scarlett paused when she saw the row of fireworks laid out in the sand. "I thought you were kidding about the fireworks."

"Dinner and a show? Aren't we getting the royal treatment tonight," Fausto teased as he elbowed Scarlett.

Francesco fished out a lighter from his pocket. "You guys wait back here. I'll go light them up."

Scarlett, Fausto and Julie sat next to each other in the sand as Francesco lit the first few firework shells, running away before they exploded into the sky. Their eyes traveled upward until they watched the explosions of red, blue, gold, and purple, marveling at the sheer size of them. Francesco felt a pang of satisfaction as he noticed the smile on her face, the amazement in her eyes, the way she laughed and cheered at each boom in the sky.

"And now, we run into the ocean." Fausto grabbed Scarlett's arm and tugged her up from the sand. They all ran into the ocean, fully clothed. "Happy birthday, Scarlett!"

Their laughter filled the air as Scarlett held onto Fausto's shoulders and Julie and Francesco treaded the water. The cold ocean sent shivers down his spine, but Francesco didn't care. He would've liked to stay there all night. Had he ever felt so free? He knew Scarlett felt the same way as she tilted her head back in the water and let the moonlight kiss her face.

"It's freezing," Julie said through her shivers. She swam to shore first.

"You coming?" Fausto held out his hand to Scarlett.

"I'm gonna stay," she said as she treaded the waves.

Francesco moved closer to her as they bobbed in the water. Though the sea was bone-chilling cold, he instantly warmed as he put his hands on Scarlett's waist and held her up. "You're freezing."

"I don't care. I'm not ready to go in yet. I'm having too much fun."

"Good."

"Francesco?"

"Yes?"

Scarlett pointed to the beach. "I think you forgot to light one."

"You should light it."

"I don't know how."

"I'll show you." Francesco helped her out of the water and back onto the sand, their clothes drenched and clinging to them. As Francesco searched in the dark for his lighter, out of the corner of his eye, he spotted Scarlett peeling off her shirt made of silver chainmail. She wore nothing but her bra and cutoff denim shorts. A wave of heat washed over him, despite the cold water dripping off his body. He followed suit, tugging his shirt overhead. "Come here. Once you light it, we have to run."

He stood behind her as she crouched down and lit the base of the canister. Before it could explode, he grabbed her hand as they ran into the ocean, high on adrenaline. They got deeper into the water as the dynamite exploded, but instead of looking up at the sky, she had her gaze fixed on him.

"What?" he asked.

"I don't know where to start. Thank you doesn't begin to cover it," she said, out of breath as she treaded the water. Francesco stood, his toes still touching the sand.

"Why don't we start by you coming here so your arms don't give out?" They shared a smile as she reached out and held onto his shoulders, her body snug against his. It fit there, like the only place she was made to belong was pressed against Francesco's chest. His breath went staccato as he held her, at the way he felt like he could never let her go. "You were saying?"

"This was the most amazing birthday. Ever. I wasn't expecting all of this."

"It was nothing."

"It was everything." She moved a curl out of his eyes and let her hand linger on his face. They could both feel it, some inexplicable connection drawing their faces closer and closer. As she tilted her head to the side, he pressed his lips against hers, hard and intense. She pulled him closer as she kissed him back, running her hand through his thick hair, wrapping her legs around his waist. He could hardly believe it was happening. He finally felt untethered, like life was giving him the second chance he so desperately wanted. He'd never known how bad he craved her until he had her on his lips. She was the most delicious thing he had ever tasted; a flavor he was sure he would become addicted to. In her kiss, he was home and everywhere all at once, the whole world wrapped up in one human body. She was everywhere he could ever want to go, and the one place he'd always want to return home to.

But, as sure as his feelings were, he could feel her hesitation. As with any broken heart, she would be careful with whom she entrusted it with next. It was too fragile to give it to someone on a whim, on a moonlit night of seawater and Smirnoff. Scarlett was scared. And when the fear took over her, her kisses slowed down and her hands fell to his shoulders. They pulled apart, panting out of breath.

"Francesco," she whispered, leaning her forehead against his.

"Yeah?" He tenderly stroked her back. His body vibrated with longing for her.

"I want to," she said, holding his face, her eyes pleading with him to understand, "but I don't think I'm ready yet."

He felt like his shoulders fell all the way to the ground, like he might let the waves wash over him and take him away. Life was a lot like a wave anyway. Some big, others small, some gentle, some calm. But with all of them, you never could know when or where they would crash, and who they would take down with it. In an instant, he felt like he had been knocked out, like he was tumbling along in a crashing wave, with no way of catching his breath.

"I get it. It's okay." He backed up, opening up the space between them.

"I'm sorry."

"Don't be."

"I am," she said, desperately tried to find his eyes again. "I don't deserve what you did for me tonight."

"That's the thing, Scarlett. You do. You just don't realize it."

"What about Enzo?" she whispered. "What will he think?"

"I don't really care," he scoffed.

"You don't mean that." To his surprise, her chest rose, and her eyes welled with tears. "You and I both know how Enzo is." She rested her hands on his shoulders, pleading with him to look at her again. When he did, she continued. "I wish I had seen you first."

"You see me now, don't you?"

They listened to the waves, calm and constant, welling up and crashing and drawing back again. "I can't ask you to wait for me."

"I will," he said without hesitation. "I'll wait as long as I have to. All you have to do is ask."

But she never did. They said nothing as they walked back into the house, chilled to the core. But Francesco's heart felt cold too. When would it be his turn? Why did things come to Enzo with ease, when everything for Francesco had to be a battle? And if this thing with Scarlett was, in fact, a battle, he would put up a fight. He had to. Whether she wanted it or not, she had his heart.

THIRTY-FOUR

UPPER WEST SIDE, NEW YORK

FALL, 1985

There was nothing quite like autumn in New York. Vacationers returned, tourism was back in full swing, and the city felt alive again, like its pulse had returned in full force as leaves of orange and red floated down to the sidewalks. Scarlett had settled into her routine, working six nights a week, sometimes picking up double shifts. It proved to be the best way to distract herself from her own mind.

She often thought of her mother, wondering what had become of Lana on Long Island, but more often than not, it was Helen whom Scarlett missed the most. There had been countless times over the summer when Scarlett had wanted to pick up the phone and call her, to fill her in on every aspect of her life, to hear her familiar voice again. After Francesco had kissed her, though Julie and Fausto had lent a listening ear, it was Helen's sound advice she'd truly wanted. But she also knew Helen didn't want to hear about any of it. Raised a Catholic, Scarlett knew it would take some sort of miracle for Helen to forgive her. As for her part, all Scarlett could do was try.

Early on a Saturday morning, Scarlett rode the subway to the Upper West Side, feeling like a foreigner as she walked the familiar route to Helen's apartment building. Though things were surely the same, Scarlett saw everything through a different lens. How many times had she walked these streets and taken her friendship with Helen for granted? She felt like a stranger passing through as she rode the elevator and pressed her index finger against the doorbell.

Scarlett heard rustling before the door opened. At the sight of Helen's fiery orange ringlets, tears sprang to Scarlett's eyes and her heart ached with a homesickness she didn't know she had. Scarlett gave her friend a onceover as if she hadn't seen her in years, taking in Helen's stylish jeans and blouse, the headband tied in her hair, and the round diamond ring glistening on her left hand.

Helen, on the other hand, went still. "Scarlett?"

Scarlett took a deep breath, preparing for rejection, praying for acceptance. "Can we talk?"

After Helen's mother brewed a pot of coffee, they found their usual spot on Helen's balcony and closed the slider door behind them. They sat in silence, sipping their coffees and watching the cars zip by below, but finally, Scarlett worked up the courage to speak.

"You were right," Scarlett said, looking down at the city below her. "As usual. And I didn't come here to vent about what happened or tell you all the details, because I know you don't want to hear them. But you were right, and I just wanted to say I'm sorry. You were the only one who was ever there for me, and I was terrible to you." Scarlett finally looked Helen in the eye. "I only pushed you away because I didn't want to hear what you were saying, even though it was the truth."

Helen scooted to the edge of her seat. "I never wanted to be right, Scar. I just didn't want to see you get hurt."

"Well, I did." Scarlett laughed through her tears, but her eyes that held a new sadness told a different story. "I think deep down, I knew everything you said was true, but I didn't want it to be. I was hoping I'd be able to prove you wrong." Scarlett swiped away a rolling tear. "You weren't the person I was supposed to be proving wrong. You're one of the only people that's ever really cared about me, and I've been keeping myself distracted with work and my other friends all this time, but I regret the things I said to you, Helen."

Helen gave a tight smile. "I know you didn't mean them. I was never mad at you, you know. I was confused. The Scarlett I knew? She would kick some guy's ass for lying."

"Used to be that way. I guess I just got swept off my feet. Enzo was that kind of guy." Scarlett took a deep breath. "I don't know if you've missed me as much as I've missed you—"

"Of course I have, Scar. You're my best friend."

"Are?"

"Still are. Even when we weren't talking this summer, when I would make new friends at work, or when Andrew would introduce me to friends of his, I always told them about you. It's been us for as long as I can remember."

"We've been through everything together."

"And we still will." Helen looked down at her engagement ring. "When I got engaged, you were the first person I thought of. We came back to the apartment after and had champagne with my parents, but all I wanted to do was call you."

"I should've been there for that," Scarlett said with regret, knowing that no matter how they moved forward, they would never get to relive such a special occasion. "But we can make up for it. We can still celebrate."

"I want you to meet him soon."

"I'd love that."

"I owe you an apology too," Helen said.

"Helen, you don't."

"I do. I don't know if you've ever needed me more than when you came to my apartment that day, all your stuff in bags with no place to go. I pushed you away when I should've been there for you, and I think in a way, I was trying to protect myself."

"From what?"

"Your life was changing. You had changed. I know this might sound silly, but I've always looked up to you, Scar. I still remember when we were kids. I was this nerdy kid who wore huge, thick glasses and loved math class for crying out loud. And you were always the pretty one. I couldn't believe you wanted to be friends with me," Helen confessed. "When you got the new job and Enzo started to whisk you away, it was kind of what I always imagined would happen. I always thought you'd have guys chasing you from every which way. I was afraid I was going to lose you to him, to your new life, so I pushed you away before you could leave me."

"Even if I *did* have men chasing me from every which way," Scarlett said, reaching for Helen's arm, "no one could ever take your place. Trust me, I tried. I've made new friends. But none of them are you."

Helen lifted her chin and gave Scarlett a smile. "I'm glad to hear that." They laughed, their earlier awkwardness dissipating at once. "So where in the world did you end up living then?"

"Above Valenti's," Scarlett explained. "I live with Francesco. Not as a couple or anything, but he had a spare room and I was in a pinch, so..." she trailed off.

"So you *do* have men chasing you from every which way."

"Only men from Mulberry Street."

"Do you like him?"

Scarlett took a deep breath. "There's something different about him, Helen, and I can't explain what it is. And don't worry, he's not married."

Helen gave a meek laugh. "We're already off to a good start."

"The only thing he's ever said is that he likes me. But it's the things he does for me, and the way I feel around him. When I'm with him, I feel like *me*."

"So what's the hold up?"

"I'm scared," Scarlett admitted. "I'm scared of getting hurt again, and I don't know if time will fix me or if I'll always feel this way, but I'm too scared to let him in even though I want to." The confession of wanting to let her relationship with Francesco blossom was news as much to herself as it was to Helen. Butterflies danced in her stomach.

"You want my advice?"

"More than anything. You have no idea how much I've missed your advice."

"I think you should go for it," Helen said. "And don't wait around until you think you're ready, because I don't think anyone's ever *ready* to hand their heart over to someone else. You think I wasn't scared to give Andrew my heart? But I trust him. And from what you're telling me, the look on your face, I think you trust this guy too."

"He's never given me a reason not to," Scarlett considered.

"See? You didn't need my advice. You had the answers in here all along." Helen poked Scarlett's forehead. "Now seeing how things turned out, I wonder what would've happened if I didn't react like the way I did."

"It's done now." Scarlett waved off the idea. "And who knows? Maybe this was how everything was supposed to happen."

"Very philosophical of you," Helen pointed out.

"I did think it would take a miracle for you and me to make up."

"A miracle, hm? Wait here." Helen opened the sliding door and went inside. When she returned, she had a pair of wooden rosary beads in her hand. "I know you probably haven't said the rosary since we left Our Lady of Pompeii, but all those Italians you're working with have got to be Catholic like me. Take them." Helen folded the beads into Scarlett's hands. "They've brought me everything good in my life. Maybe they can do the same for you."

Scarlett examined the beads in her hands, running her thumb along the cross. They would never leave her possession. "I hope so."

"Come inside. My parents will be so happy to see you. They always ask about you."

"I'd like that." Scarlett stood up. "Thanks."

"Hey, speaking of parents, did Lana ever come back?" Helen paused at the door.

"I haven't heard from her since the day she left. But it'll be okay," Scarlett assured her. "It'll all work out."

"It will. All it takes is a little bit of faith. Trust me."

"You're not going to call me delusional?"

Helen put her arm around Scarlett's shoulder. "I don't think you're delusional at all. I'd prefer to call it optimism."

THIRTY-FIVE

LITTLE ITALY, NEW YORK

FALL, 1985

"**S**an Gennaro is the patron saint of Naples," Francesco explained as he and Scarlett walked the impossibly crowded streets of Little Italy. The Feast of San Gennaro was an annual tradition in the neighborhood, though during the times Scarlett had attended in the past, she had always focused more on the fried street food and live music than the history of the festival.

"That was your father's name," Scarlett said, remembering.

"I swear, I think every single family in Naples has a Gennaro. It's like it's a law or something." They kept walking until they reached a tented booth where the statue of San Gennaro stood on display with red satin ribbons pinned with money just beneath it. Francesco reached in his back pocket and pulled out two twenty-dollar bills. "Here," he said, handing one to Scarlett. "Pin it to the ribbon and say a prayer."

"You have to pay to pray?" Scarlett joked, making Francesco laugh.

"When you put it that way, this does seem like a strange tradition."

Scarlett leaned forward, jostling her way through some of the other reverent prayers and pinned her money to one of the ribbons. She fell to the kneeler below and clasped her hands together. Though she found it difficult to concentrate with all the chatter and laughter and music around her, she closed her eyes. She prayed to San Gennaro, for faith, not in the spirits above her, but in herself. That no matter what outcomes and heartbreaks lay before her, she'd trust she could get through them. When she opened her eyes, Francesco was kneeling next to her, though she did not disturb his moment of prayer.

They wandered down Mulberry as Dean Martin's "Non Dimenticar" floated through the night air. Overhead, banners of green, white, and red were strung with lights, and on either side of the street, vendors were busy frying dough, serving various flavored cannoli and gelato, and selling items like jewelry and T-shirts. The neighborhood felt alive, with all the thousands of people crowded in the streets to celebrate Italian culture, or at least New York's variation of it. When they neared a booth selling Sicilian pizza, Scarlett's stomach growled.

"Want to grab a slice?" Scarlett asked.

Francesco stopped walking. He glanced over at the booth, filled with trays of the thick, square slices, then back at her. "You think *I'm* going to let you eat street food?"

She laughed. "It's a festival. That's what you're *supposed* to do."

"If you want pizza, we'll go back to the restaurant, and I'll make it for you."

"Come on. I bet you anything, if you try it, you'll like it."

"If you're wrong, you'll be the one making the pizza when we get back."

"And if I'm right?"

The sides of his mouth curved into a smile. "I'll have to think of a proper reward."

Francesco paid for their slice of pizza. After they moved away from the booth, he held it between them and they leaned in, their eyes locked as they each took a bite from either end. But as the flavors found Scarlett's taste buds, she understood why Francesco had been opposed to her suggestion. Once you become accustomed to the finer flavors in life, you can't go back. Scarlett grabbed the slice out of his hands and threw it into the nearest garbage can.

"Looks like I won the bet," he said, wiping the corners of his mouth that had curled into a devilish, satisfied smile.

"*I'm* the one who hated it, which means *you're* the one who's going to be doing the pizza making." Scarlett looped her arm through his. "Let's go."

<hr />

FRANCESCO FLIPPED THE LIGHTS on in the kitchen and went into the walk-in box to retrieve his ingredients. "You're getting off easy. The dough is already made." Francesco went back in to fetch a small pot of sauce, cheese, and fresh leaves of basil.

"Oh, no, no, no," Scarlett said, backing away.

"I'm going to teach you. It'll be fun."

"I don't find cooking *fun*."

"Punishment now, reward later."

She sighed in submission and put her hands on her hips. "So all I have to do is assemble it?"

"First, you have to roll out the dough."

Her sass on full display, one of her angular brows arched higher than the other. "If you don't help me, we're going to starve."

Amusement danced in his eyes. Leaned against the wall with his big arms folded up in front of him, he pushed himself upright. "Fine." At the counter, he grabbed a fistful of flour and dispersed it directly onto the stainless-steel surface. "Put the dough on here."

Scarlett plopped the dough down in the center of the flour.

"Now, cover your hands in flour."

Francesco went behind Scarlett. His body was snug against hers, and she could feel every curve of his muscular being. For a chef, hell, for anyone, he was in great shape. Scarlett hoped he couldn't feel how fast her heart was racing, how shallow her breath had become at being this close to him. He put his hands over hers and guided them as they began to roll the dough out into a thin, circular crust.

"You got it. More flour, so it doesn't stick."

Scarlett grabbed another fistful of flour, shaking some over the dough, but then playfulness crept up in her as she turned around and tossed the flour right at Francesco's face. She stifled a giggle.

"You. Did. Not," he said, wiping his face with his palm.

"I did."

His smile spread, his eyes sparkling like champagne. He moved sveltely around the kitchen, trying to catch her off-guard as he surveyed the contents of the dessert station. "You like cannoli?"

"Yeah, why?"

"Good. Here." He swiped some of the cannoli cream across her face.

"You didn't!" She gasped, laughing with her whole heart. "Oh, it's on."

"You started it."

"You have an unfair advantage. You know where everything is."

He opened his arms wide. "It's all yours."

She stared at him, her eyes narrowing as she sauntered over to the dessert station. She did a quick survey and decided on some rum cake. "Do you like rum?" She turned around fast and smeared a dollop of the dessert across his lips. He licked them.

"My favorite," he said, his eyes defiant. "You've got something here." He looked at her lips and in a flash, he made a stripe of Nutella across her face.

"Not Nutella!" She scrammed around, looking for a bar rag to wipe her face. She rushed to the mound of flour and grabbed another fistful, tossing it at him. Their back-and-forth became quicker and quicker until the flavors of cannoli cream and cocoa-topped tiramisu blended into one on her lips and her cheeks hurt from laughing so hard. "Okay, truce. Truce! God, we made a mess." She surveyed the kitchen as they moved close together again. It was so quiet, Scarlett worried that Francesco could hear how heavily her heart was pounding.

"I don't care," he said, keeping his eyes on her as his smile began to fade.

His stare grew intense. With flushed cheeks, his jaw clenched and relaxed. Scarlett started to believe maybe he was as nervous as she was.

"I know something else you like," she said, her voice trembling.

"What's that?"

"Me."

His gaze fell as soon as she said it, but she wouldn't let him get away with it.

"You like me." Her voice grew stronger, bolder, with every passing moment.

"I already told you."

"Tell me again."

He finally looked at her again, his face wrought with uncertainty. "Why?"

She walked up to him, closer, until there was hardly any space at all between them. She brushed a curl off his tanned face and kept her hand there. "So I can tell you that I like you too."

"I like you, Scarlett," he said, trying to make sense of her, so she could savor every word.

"I like you too, Francesco." She wanted to say it with confidence, but her voice betrayed her. Wobbly. Terrified. What had she just done? She had told the truth. She didn't just like laughing with him and pretending to help him cook. She didn't just like listening to opera together or staring up at the non-existent stars with him. She liked every bit of him, the way he towered over her, the way his broad, muscular shoulders flexed every time he moved, the way his eyes looked like the most scrumptious caramel, the way she knew he wouldn't start this thing with her unless he thought it was real. The way she felt like *her* around him. She liked every bit of him. She wanted, craved every bit of him.

The air was charged with a nervous tension, neither one of them knowing what to do with the connection they had, but knowing it was time to do something about it. Finally, as if directed by fate, they moved in at the same time. Their kisses were sure and hungry, like they needed each other for survival. She held him as close as she could get him to her, wanting more. With their height difference, he lifted her up and sat her down on the counter, wrapping his arms around her. His lips never left her. He was the most delectable thing she had ever tasted. She couldn't consume him fast enough.

He broke away, panting. "Are you sure?"

"Do I not seem sure to you?" She laughed as he dropped his head and shook it, his curls dancing around his face. "I'm sure." She lifted his face to meet hers again. "Are you?"

Though he resumed kissing her, he stopped again. "I should probably take you out on a date first. Buy you flowers, the whole nine yards."

"You already bought me flowers, Fran, and I don't care about going on a date." She gripped the collar of his shirt and pulled him close. "I just want you."

His movements were slow, but he picked her up again. He carried her to the staircase where they attempted to make their way upstairs, but they kept falling against the steps, kissing each other, and shedding layers of clothing all the way until finally, out of breath and half dressed, they reached the apartment.

In his bedroom, she expected things to move quickly, but he slowed down the pace. He rolled on top of her, still in his jeans, and trailed her neck with kisses.

"What are you doing?" she finally asked, laughing as he covered every inch of her with his warm, full lips. She felt like everything was moving in slow motion.

He lay next to her and held her face. "I'm savoring you."

"What?"

"We don't have to rush," he whispered. "I don't have anywhere else to be. We have all night."

Scarlett was met with an instant realization. This was nothing like her times with Enzo, where everything was a rush, even their most intimate moments. Enzo always had somewhere to be or someone to go home to. But Francesco? She was all his and he was all hers. They had nothing but time.

And their time they took, until they gave each other everything except their skin and bones.

CHAPTER

THIRTY-SIX

LITTLE ITALY, NEW YORK

FALL, 1985

They woke up at the same exact time. Lying on their sides, they held each other. Francesco could hardly believe it was real, that Scarlett was in his bed, in his arms, and not in the room next to him. He felt as if he were floating on a cloud. He held her face and studied her like he was examining a precious gem. He would have waited forever for her, but God, he was glad she didn't make him.

"Why are you looking at me like that?" she asked, sleep still in her eyes.

"Like what?"

She shrugged. "Like I'm special or something."

"Because you are." He drew her into his chest as she wrapped her arms around him.

"It's just me, Fran," she mumbled, kissing his bare chest.

"You're not *just* anything."

She pushed herself up onto the pillow so they were eye to eye. "You know what's strange?"

"Tell me."

"This doesn't feel new, or weird, or crazy," she started, though she was met with Francesco's confused expression. She continued explaining. "It feels like we've always been like this, you know?"

"It does." He brushed her hair off her face. "Scarlett?"

"Hmm?"

"I don't know if it's too soon to ask you this."

"As me what?"

He took a deep breath. "What if I wanted it to be just you and me? Together?"

It took her a minute to process what he was saying, but when it all clicked, her eyes lit up. "Are you asking me if I'll be your girlfriend?"

"Yeah. But only, you know, if you're ready." He stroked her arms, afraid of what her answer might be.

"Ask me."

"Scarlett…" he rolled her on top of him, "will you be my girlfriend?"

Scarlett let his question sink in. Francesco felt like he was watching a thousand emotions cross her face. Confusion, excitement, fear, all at once.

"Yes," she said with a beaming smile. Would he ever grow tired of being the cause of her happiness? "You and me," she whispered into his ear.

Francesco knew that everything about being with Scarlett should have felt wrong, but he didn't see it that way. He didn't see her as his brother's former girlfriend, former mistress. In her, he saw the future he could never find in anyone else. He felt like the road of *what ifs* before them were more like *what would be's*. They could have something real together. In their ease with each other, they both felt safe, like they didn't have to hide or pretend to be people they weren't. He took her as she was and he loved her for all she was – all her flaws, her mistakes, her hurts. And despite it all, when he looked at her, those weren't the things he saw. He saw who she was underneath all of that, besides all of that. The parts of her that had yet to be unearthed, the woman she would become. His heart expanded as he rolled her over and buried his face in the crook of her neck. He fit there like it was a place made for him and him alone. When he looked up at her, he couldn't imagine anyone else in her place. He didn't want to. It was just him and Scarlett. Together.

At once, they were them, as if they'd always been.

———

EVERYTHING FELT DIFFERENT. FOR the first time in her life, Scarlett belonged to someone. Francesco had chosen her, and her alone, over everyone and everything else. As she descended the service steps from the apartment, she didn't care what work threw at her tonight. Knowing she was going home to Francesco, and not the bedroom next to his, filled her with anticipation. But, she had made Francesco promise they would keep their distance at work, for the time being. Funny, she thought, that even though Francesco wasn't married like Enzo, he was still forbidden. Francesco tried to insist they had nothing to hide, but Scarlett knew there was one person and one person alone they had to hide their relationship from for as long as they possibly could.

As she got closer to the kitchen, step by step, she heard Enzo's voice. She slowed her pace and placed one foot on each step until she reached the landing. From her vantage point, she could see the back of Enzo. He looked as he usually did, dressed in an expensive suit, shiny loafers, sporting big gold cuff links that peeked out from the sleeves of his jacket. Francesco stood in front of him, dressed in his whites.

"Size four," Enzo said as he paced, the sound of his footsteps creating an even rhythm. He held something made of white fabric. Scarlett squinted, trying to decipher what it was, and when he held it up, her hand flew to her mouth. He held up her blouse, the same one Francesco had unbuttoned and thrown to the ground on their way up to the apartment last night. "You know who wears a size four?"

"Who?" Francesco ran a palm over his face and folded his arms.

"Scarlett."

They were quiet for a while, but Scarlett held her breath as she waited in the wings. She hadn't expected Enzo to find out about them a few hours into their relationship. She hadn't expected him to find out like this, holding a garment of hers like it was a piece of criminal evidence.

"I know damn well you didn't sleep with her. I know my own brother wouldn't do that." Enzo looked expectantly at Francesco.

"Enz, come on," Francesco dismissed him.

Enzo threw her shirt to the ground. "You think you can make me look like an ass?" He grabbed Francesco by his collar and pulled in. Enzo's rage filled the entire kitchen. "You never have any respect for me, Fran, never! After everything I've done for you. You don't even have the decency to sneak around. I have to watch the two of you right in front of me. I have to see her clothes strewn about in *my* kitchen."

"Get off of me." Francesco tried to push Enzo away, but Enzo had a white-knuckle grip on him.

"Do you know how stupid you are? What do you think, huh? You think she understands you? That she likes you? That she loves you? Give me a break, Fran. She's using you to get back at me. Open your eyes."

"You're wrong!"

"I'm right! You'll stop seeing her. You hear me?"

"No, I won't."

"Yes, you will."

"I'm in love with her, Enz," Francesco rushed to say, sounding winded.

"What about me? What if I loved her?"

"You didn't love her. You loved the way she made you feel."

"What the hell is the difference?"

"It's a big difference. I love her, Enz."

Scarlett's eyes went wide, and her body began to shake. Francesco didn't just like her; he *loved* her. And it was the last way she'd ever expected to find out.

CHAPTER

THIRTY-SEVEN

Something other than Sinatra's voice and the aroma of Francesco's cuisine filled the air at Valenti's: the growing tension between Enzo, Scarlett, and Francesco. It enveloped Scarlett the entire evening, inescapable no matter where she went. Post-shift gossip sessions with Julie and Fausto were customary on more nights than not, but tonight, while they sipped on wine and sucked on cigarettes, they sat in silence as they listened to Enzo's angry voice coming from the bar.

"What the hell is wrong with him tonight?" Julie asked, staring at the scene.

"He is in rare form," Fausto agreed.

They both looked at Scarlett.

"What are you looking at me for?" Scarlett said.

"You know him better than us, my dear," Fausto pointed out.

"Used to," Scarlett said. "But I might have an idea of what's going on."

"Which is exactly why we're looking at *you*, bitch," Julie joked. "Spill."

They couldn't peel their eyes away from the bar. Enzo stood, waving his arms emphatically. Scarlett recognized one of the men from their trip to Atlantic City. Enzo spoke in Italian, so Scarlett couldn't make out what he was saying, but she didn't need to know another language to know Enzo wasn't happy. Thankfully, the other men didn't engage, and not long after they threw down some cash and headed out, leaving Enzo to stew in his rage.

"And again, I'll ask you." Julie looked at her again. "Spill."

"Francesco's in love with me," Scarlett said, keeping her gaze straight ahead.

"Oh my God." Fausto closed in on her, realizing she was in no way joking.

"Wait, *what?*" Julie said as she held her cigarette in one hand, her wine glass in the other.

"He said it. Today."

"He told you he's in love with you?" Julie asked.

"He didn't tell *me*. He told Enzo."

Julie and Fausto exchanged a look that Scarlett couldn't quite decipher, but the one thing she did know was that they weren't all too surprised. Before she knew it, they were all laughing.

"Holy shit," Julie said. "You did that. You made both of those nut jobs fall in love with you."

"Wait, wait, wait. Back up," Fausto instructed. "Start from the beginning."

Scarlett recounted the details of last night's events. "And then this morning, he made it official. He asked me to be his girlfriend. And I said yes." She tried to shrug it off, but it was of no use.

"You're in love with him too," Fausto said in his usual way of drawing conclusions.

"You're glowing," Julie marveled. "Like, literally glowing."

"He's amazing, but I'm worried. Enzo is furious. The craziest part is Fran doesn't seem to care what he thinks."

"I mean, I have to ask." Julie leaned in and lowered her voice. "Come on, was it a little weird?"

"No." Scarlett swatted her away, laughing. "He's nothing like his brother. It's just…" she paused, trying to find the right words. "I never felt like I could be myself around Enzo. I tried to be who I thought he would like or who he wanted me to be. But I feel so comfortable around Fran, and I think he feels the same way. It's crazy. He could have anyone, and I don't know what I did, or didn't do, to make him feel the way he feels about me."

"Sometimes, two people are just meant to be together." Fausto's face misted with a certain nostalgia. "I've known these Valenti boys a long time. I never once heard Francesco say he was in love."

"Never?"

"Not a once."

"So…" Julie looked at her. "When are you going to tell him that you're in love with him too?"

"I don't know. He doesn't know I overheard, and I don't know if he's ready to tell me yet."

"Everything will happen when it's supposed to," Fausto said in his ever-wise way. "If there's anything I've learned in my life, it's that." He got up and headed towards the bar.

"Where are you going?" Scarlett yelled after him.

"Champagne, darling. We're celebrating." Fausto came back with three crystal flutes and poured them each a glass.

"So you guys aren't going to judge me?"

"For what?" Julie asked, taking a glass from Fausto.

"You don't think I'm awful for being with Fran, right?"

"My darling, I think this is the precise opposite of *awful*." Fausto raised his glass to her. "A toast," Fausto said as they all raised their glasses, "to true love."

"I can't toast to that." Scarlett stepped back and put her hand on her chest. "We just started dating."

"Raise your damn glass," Julie insisted. "To my favorite crazy bitch."

"You're both crazy bitches," Fausto reminded them. "But you're my crazy bitches."

SCARLETT'S HEART RACED AGAINST Francesco's bare chest. They were lying on the sofa, an aria spinning from the record player, in their own comfortable quiet. She tugged on the sleeve of her sweatshirt and rested her hands under her cheek. She didn't want to start off their relationship by harboring secrets. If they were going to do this, they were going to do it right. She just had to tell him she knew he was in love with her.

"You okay?" she asked, looking up at him through her lashes. "You're so quiet tonight."

He glanced down at her and smiled. "I'm great. You?"

Scarlett pushed herself up so their faces rested next to each other. "I have to tell you something." She placed her palm on his chest and felt his own heart racing. "I want to be honest with you."

He swallowed. "Honest is good."

"Today, I was coming down the service steps to the kitchen, and I overheard you and Enzo talking."

Francesco froze. "What did you overhear?"

"I know he knows about us."

"Yeah. But I handled it."

"I heard the part where he said he thinks I'm using you to get back at him. You have to know that's not even remotely true, right?"

"Of course, I know that," Francesco said, adjusting his body and resting his arm behind his head. "We knew he'd have some sort of big reaction, and he did. But he'll get over it. I don't want you to worry, alright? I'm glad you told me, but he's my brother. Let me handle him."

"Right. Of course." Scarlett searched his face.

Francesco's cheeks began to burn red, extending all the way to his ears and his neck as an uncomfortable expression fell over his face. "That's not all you overheard, is it?"

"No, it's not."

Lying flat on his back, Francesco stiffened. "Go ahead. Just tell me."

Scarlett afforded him the luxury of not having to look her in the eye. "I heard the part where you told him that you're in love with me."

Francesco cringed as he wiped his face with his palm. "Scarlett, that's not how I wanted you to find out."

"I know that."

"And it's so soon, you probably think I'm crazy."

"I don't think you're crazy." Scarlett sat up so he was forced to look at her. "How about we do this? We forget about today, and you tell me when you're ready to."

"You already know now." He wore a look of angst. "You heard me say it."

"Fran," she reached for his hands and took them in hers, "it's okay. It's just me. I don't care if it's too soon or if it's not how I was supposed to find out." Finally, his eyes met hers. "You told me you've never been in love before."

"I haven't."

"So how do you know you are with me?"

Francesco rolled his body upright and sat cross-legged on the sofa. He took her hands in his and began. "I love coming home to you. Even before last night, when we weren't together, I loved coming home to you. I cook, Scar. I cook every night for hundreds of people, thousands of people a week. Nameless faces. It's a rush. I'm on a high when I leave that place; that's why I have to come up here and cook some more to calm myself down. I used to come up here and I would be all alone. It was nothing but silence. That's why I always have my music playing, to drown out the quiet. And then you came along. And I didn't *have* to come home to you every night. I *wanted* to. I wanted to come up here and cook for you and watch you, the way you savor every bite and the way you look like an angel when you fall asleep. I don't care if I'm downstairs behind the line or up on the rooftop drinking wine. When I look at you, I feel like I'm home."

Scarlett didn't know exactly what she had been expecting, but surely, whatever expectations she had, Francesco had exceeded them. A steady stream of tears fell from her eyes, though she didn't bother to wipe them away. She held onto his hands as though she would never let him go, and though she often shied away from her own vulnerability, around Francesco, there were no walls.

"I love that I don't have to try with you," Scarlett started. "I can say stupid things, and be silly, and laugh with you, and act like I'm a kid again. I can talk to you about anything, but we can also be quiet together, and I'm comfortable either way. I love that when you look at me, I know you don't see what I see in myself. You don't see what's wrong with me. The mistakes and the bad choices I made. You don't see all the ways other people have hurt me. All you see is me, and that's all I've ever wanted, Fran, is for someone to see me for who I really am."

"When I look at you, all I see are beautiful things." Francesco traced her jawline with his fingers. "That's what I want you to see in yourself too."

Scarlett smiled through her tears. She had spent so long trying to be beautiful in her mother's eyes, in her old environment, and when she'd failed, she had thought it a reflection on her and what she lacked. Instead, maybe she had been in the wrong arena. Maybe how Francesco saw her was how the world saw her. Maybe who she was in his eyes was who she truly was. "I don't know what I did right to deserve you."

"You didn't have to do anything. Neither did I. Everyone deserves to feel the way we do."

All her life, Scarlett wondered what love was like, and from the things she'd seen, she had worked hard to avoid it. But this kind of love? The kind that was pure and complete? She never thought she deserved it. She didn't think that people like her got to experience this kind of love. The things she experienced with Enzo were what she expected out of a relationship. The kind of rollercoaster that hurt like hell and made her question everything, the kind where she had to wonder if he even cared about her at all. But maybe she had to go through the darkness to appreciate the light that was Francesco. Though she would always carry a love for both brothers, she was beginning to learn that no two loves were the same. That was the scariest, most beautiful part about it.

"If you're ready, I'm ready," Francesco said.

"Ready."

Francesco took her face in his hands, a warmth in his eyes and a softness to his touch. "I'm in love with you, Scarlett. Since the moment I met you, I've been in love with you."

Scarlett didn't concern herself with wondering if things were moving too fast, or what people, particularly Enzo, would say or think. Instead, wrapped up in this man and the way he had opened her heart and her world, she pressed her lips against his and promised she'd always adore him. "I'm in love with you too, Francesco. I'm in love with everything about you."

CHAPTER

THIRTY-EIGHT

LITTLE ITALY, NEW YORK

FALL, 1985

It had been a several weeks of bliss with Francesco. They avoided Enzo as much as humanly possible and whenever they weren't downstairs at work, they were together. They took long walks through the city and Francesco liked to take her to the market with him to pick out fresh ingredients for the restaurant. Every moment of their lives became intertwined, like they had fallen into a perfect rhythm. Sometimes, Scarlett couldn't believe he was hers, that out of all the people they could've crossed paths with, they'd chosen each other. It was morning, and they had just woken up. Francesco stood at the stove making French toast while she read the paper. Even being with him like this in their comfortable routine, still wearing their pajamas, it was the best thing she had ever known.

"Extra syrup," he said as he placed a dish in front of her. She closed the paper and tilted her face up for him to kiss her.

"Thank you." She cut off a piece of her French toast. "So, are you excited for today?" It was a big day, not only for Francesco, but for Enzo too. The *New York Times* was interviewing them and reviewing Francesco's cooking. As if Valenti's wasn't busy enough, when the article was released, their reservations would be booked out at least three months in advance.

"I'm trying not to think about it," he said as he drizzled a light coat of syrup over his breakfast.

"Why?"

"I don't want to get too in my head. We've had write-ups before, but never the *Times*."

"You're amazing, Fran. They're going to love you."

"And if they don't?" He raised his brows at her.

"Then screw them. What do they know anyway?" They laughed, but she still noticed the tension in his face. "You still haven't talked to your brother, have you?"

"You mean not since he accused my girlfriend of using me as some sort of revenge scheme? No, I haven't."

"Fran, that was weeks ago. Are you sure you're okay? I'm worried about you."

"I'm fine. So, I was thinking," he said in between bites, desperate to change the subject, "I want to take you out tonight."

"Are you asking me out on a date?"

"Only if you'll say yes."

"Where are we going?"

"It's a surprise."

"I have to at least know what to wear."

"Must you always be so vain?"

"Absolutely," she said with a wink, taking a sip of her orange juice.

"A nice dress. Maybe some heels, I don't know. We'll leave here at seven."

"What's the occasion?"

"The occasion is, if I think about you wearing a nice pretty dress all day, I'm pretty sure the food will taste better when I cook for this reporter today."

"You got yourself a date." She stood up and covered his face in kisses. "I love you."

———

FRANCESCO SLIPPED INTO HIS zone. Though his pulse raced at an impressive pace, and his chest ached with nervousness, his gift for cooking kicked in on autopilot. In the heat of the gas stoves, he had frying pans and pots going over the flames, but his mind was elsewhere. He was happy with Scarlett. Happier than he ever remembered being. She filled him up in a way no other woman had ever been able to do, simply because he knew she was right for him in every conceivable way. Since he had been with her, he hadn't thought about or looked at another woman. And yet, he couldn't fully revel in his new relationship. As much resentment as he had towards Enzo, he had an equal amount of love for him. They were blood. Enzo was his only brother. And there they were, for the first time in their lives, not on speaking terms. Except today – today, they couldn't avoid each other. They would have to put on a united front for the reporter's sake, even if it was just a front.

"How you doing? The reporter should be here soon," Enzo said as he broke through the kitchen doors, startling Francesco out of his thoughts so much that Francesco burned himself on the edge of one of the pans.

"Jesus!" Francesco pulled his hand back. The side of his right palm was branded red. "Do you always have to barge in here like that?"

"Let me see," Enzo said. He reached for his brother's hand and examined it. "You in pain?"

"Feels like my hand might fall off." Francesco moved to the sink where he ran his hand under cool water. He needed his right hand to function properly if he wanted to sauté everything to perfection. "Can you watch this without messing it up? I have burn cream up in my apartment."

"I'll go."

"No. I'll go."

"Fran, you stay. I'll go. Where is it?"

"Kitchen. In the drawer next to the fridge," Francesco finally surrendered.

Francesco's eyes followed his brother until he was out of sight. And then he remembered Scarlett was in the apartment.

<hr>

ENZO TREKKED UP THE stairs, taking two at a time. He wouldn't admit how excited he was to anyone, especially not his brother, but he was riding high on the thought that the two of them had made it. Two immigrant kids from Naples, they would be featured in one of the most prestigious publications in the entire country. And they couldn't even enjoy it together, all because his brother had to go and fall in love with the one woman who was off limits.

He didn't expect to find Scarlett in the apartment, though he wasn't sure why. She lived there, after all, and thanks to him. But still, as familiar as she'd once been to him, now he felt an intense amount of disdain for her. Disdain, and lust. Even though she had done the unthinkable, in her presence he was constantly reminded of their chemistry that had intoxicated him for months on end.

"Fran burned himself," he said once he reached the top of the stairs. Scarlett jolted upright on the sofa, lowering the volume on the TV. "I came to get the burn cream."

She looked startled, maybe even a bit scared as she went into the kitchen. He followed her. "Is he okay?" she asked, rummaging through a drawer.

"He'll be fine. He's been burned before."

She avoided his eyes as she handed him the burn cream. "Well, there you go."

"You know, I just want you to know one thing, Scarlett."

She folded her arms and leaned against the doorframe. He could tell she was doing what she always did. Pretending to be tough. But he knew her. He knew that inside, she was trembling. "What's that?"

"In my life, my entire life, I never went a day without speaking to my brother. Not one day, and now it's been, what, two months? Maybe even longer? All because of you."

"Don't put this all on me." She stood up straighter, though she remained under his shadow. "Your brother chose me, so don't act like I did this."

"Oh, but you did do this, Scarlett. You could've had anybody in this city. And who did you choose? My only brother. You could've found another way to pay me back, to try and make me jealous, alright? I know I did you wrong. But this?"

"I know you might have a hard time believing this, Enzo, but this isn't about *you*."

Enzo leaned down so their noses nearly touched. "He's my *brother*, Scar. What do you think, he's better than me? He's not as sweet as you think he is. You forget he's been with every broad in this town? What do you think? You're the one that's gonna make him stop?" Judging from the way she fell silent, he knew he had gotten through to her. Hit her sore spot.

Her eyes scanned the kitchen, where remnants of their breakfast remained. "I am the one that's made him stop," she said, though her voice held no conviction.

Enzo tossed his head back with a sarcastic laugh. "You're still so naïve. It's a shame, really. You could have this city by the horns if you opened your eyes."

"Just, stop it, Enzo," Scarlett yelled, putting her hands up. "You know, I don't know why you even care. I meant nothing to you. I was just a pretty face to keep you distracted from how bored you are, remember?"

"You actually believed that?"

"It was the truth. You didn't love me."

"I didn't?" He shifted his weight from one foot to the other. "That's why I gave you a place to live, right? That's why I gave you a job? Because I didn't love you?"

"You did all of that because you wanted to sleep with me, not because you loved me, Enz. And now you're angry because you're not the big man in town anymore."

"I'm not, am I?"

"No. Your brother is."

"You think he's any different than me?" Enzo leaned forward so his face was level with Scarlett's. Jealousy spilled out of his pores. "You wanna find out who my brother really is? You go right ahead. Don't say I didn't warn you."

<hr />

"Here," Enzo said as he handed Francesco the cream.

"Thanks." Francesco studied his brother's sudden change of demeanor. They avoided each other's eyes. "Was Scarlett there?"

"Yep," Enzo said with a nod. "Scarlett was home. Make sure that shit's ready to go." Enzo pointed to the stoves. "It's almost time."

"Yeah. Be right out." Though Francesco wanted to know if Enzo and Scarlett had talked, he would have to wait until later to find out. For now, he had to focus.

Francesco struggled to keep his nerves at bay, let alone the building strain between him and Enzo, but as soon as Ken, the *Times* reporter, entered their restaurant, all bad blood between brothers was instantly forgotten. Enzo traded his anger for his signature charm.

"Ken, welcome. It's a pleasure to meet you," Enzo welcomed the reporter. Enzo stood tall and proud as he shook Ken's hand. "This is my younger brother, the famous chef. Francesco Valenti." Enzo put his hands on Francesco's shoulders and moved him forward. "Please, have a seat. Best table in the house. What can I get you to drink?"

"Water's fine for me," Ken said. Round, wire-rim glasses framed his eyes and faded jeans covered his long, lanky legs. From his worn and tattered messenger bag, he pulled out a legal notepad and a pen. He surveyed the restaurant around him, scribbling some notes.

"So, Francesco," Ken started, "acclaimed chef and restaurateur. Before I dive into the food, I'd like to get to know you and your story. Why don't we begin with how you got started in the industry?" Ken took hold of his pen, ready to take notes.

"Sure. I came to New York eight years ago. My brother had already been living here for a couple of years with his wife. He convinced me to come to the city and we opened this place together not long after I arrived."

"And you were a chef in Italy?"

"Started out as a fisherman, in a small seaside town near Naples. I learned to cook at home, from my *mamma*. It always came easy to me. I spent some time cooking in a commercial kitchen in a town called Positano, at a hotel restaurant. Real upscale place. I spent two summers doing that until I got the call from my brother." Francesco looked over at Enzo. "Enzo thought I'd be good in the kitchen, and once I started, it was like I'd been doing it my whole life. It comes naturally."

"So you owe much of your success to your brother, then? Sounds like he gave you your start here in New York."

Francesco swallowed hard. "He did."

"And what about your life now? Married? Kids?"

"I love my nieces and nephew."

Ken flipped his notepad to the next blank page. "Now, onto your cooking. It keeps a line out the door every weekend, and it's near impossible to get a reservation. What's the secret?"

"Even if I knew what the secret was, I wouldn't tell you," Francesco joked. "There is no secret. I love what I do. I have a good palate. That's not something you can learn in culinary school. I can smell a sauce and know if it's seasoned right or if it needs something added. I can taste something and know how to make it. I can't explain that. Every dish I make has to be perfect. I won't send out anything less."

"Well, I'm dying to taste perfection." Ken set down his pen. "Can we eat?"

Despite his burn, Francesco's confidence grew once he had retreated to the kitchen and gave everything one final sauté. He expertly plated each dish to the point of painstaking perfection. First were the fried peppers, *ziti Genovese* and spaghetti in a light lemon cream sauce, and finally, the decadent veal *osso bucco*. Once satisfied with his work, Francesco brought the dishes out to the dining room and placed everything in front of Ken.

"And now, now I'm gonna tell you a story with my food." Francesco stood back and surveyed the spread he had laid out on the table, like an artist admiring his own work.

Enzo and Francesco watched in anticipation as Ken took his first bite. Ken's face gave away nothing but when he went in for a second bite, Francesco tasted his first flavors of victory.

"Simple, but fantastic. God, these could be addictive," Ken said as he moved over to the pasta dishes. He picked up a heaping mound of pasta *Genovese* and took a bite, then another, and another, moving from one dish to the other, the only sounds between the three men were that of Ken's chewing. His gray eyes grew wide. "My God! This is why everyone comes here. This is what they're talking about. I've been in this business a long time. You boys, New York is lucky to have you."

Francesco did his best to conceal his pride and excitement, but nothing could stop the smile from growing on his face. He exchanged a glance with Enzo, who was working hard to suppress his own emotions. Francesco didn't see Enzo as he was now. He felt like they were kids again, like he was glancing over at his overly confident, brazen older brother who he couldn't wait to grow up and be like. He wouldn't dwell on how far they had drifted, how drastically things had changed.

"DID YOU SEE THE look on his face when he tasted the pasta?" Francesco said to Enzo, still reeling from Ken's praises. He lifted some freshly cooked ziti pasta out of the boiler and mixed it together with the leftover *Genovese* sauce before plating two dishes. One for him, one for Enzo. "It was great. I can't imagine what he's going to write about us. Here." Francesco held out the plate.

"I'm good," Enzo said.

"It's your favorite."

"I'm good. I'm going home."

"Enz, come on." Francesco felt disappointment sink deep within him. "Come on. I thought we could—"

"Thought we could what? Fran, what?" Enzo snapped.

"I don't know. What we did today—"

"We did our jobs, Fran. We did our jobs."

And with that, Enzo backed away, leaving nothing but the confused gaze of two brokenhearted brothers hanging in the air.

THIRTY-NINE

NEW YORK, NEW YORK

FALL, 1985

Though Enzo's words still rattled her, nothing would make Scarlett let Francesco down. If Francesco had been thinking about her wearing a nice dress all day, she would deliver on her promise. She wore the tightest, shortest dress she owned, the color of crimson and made of velvet with black lace accents. Her legs were clad in sheer black pantyhose and pointed stilettos, and she slid her arms into a blazer to complete her look. She slipped an extra tube of lipstick in her clutch before heading into the living room. All she needed was her date to come home. She smiled when she heard his voice and his heavy steps trekking up the stairs.

"Scar?" he called out.

"I'm in here." She stood up and smoothed down her dress.

"Wow," he exhaled when he took in her appearance. "You look beautiful."

"Come here." She kissed him. "How did it go?"

"It was great. They did the interview, took some pictures, and that was it."

Scarlett studied his expression, the way his forehead was lined with worry and how his voice was strained and tired. "But your food, Fran. How did he like your food?"

"He loved it. Really loved it, actually."

"So why don't you seem more excited?"

He remained quiet for a while and took a seat on the edge of the sofa. "You know, for a minute there, I thought Enzo was going to come around. Forget about what's going on and enjoy this moment with me. I wanted to sit down and have a meal to celebrate. And he wouldn't do it. You believe that? We came here from Italy, we poured our hearts, our lives into this place, and when the biggest paper in Manhattan comes to interview us, he won't sit down and have a lousy bowl of pasta with me to celebrate it."

"Because of me." Scarlett couldn't help the way her chest twisted with anxiety and guilt. She had tried to push out Enzo's words, but they were things she knew already to be true. It wasn't a question, but a fact. Had she not inserted herself in their lives, had she not let herself fall in love with Francesco, he would have been downstairs celebrating with Enzo.

"Scar, don't say that. My brother and I had our problems long before you came into the picture. Don't kid yourself."

"But if I weren't in the picture, you two would be downstairs together right now. This is all my fault. Enzo said so today, himself. He blames me for everything."

"It's not your fault." Francesco stood tall over Scarlett and began unbuttoning his chef coat. "Enzo has always gotten a say in my life. I want you in my picture, Scar. This isn't about him. For once, just for once, this isn't about what Enzo wants. This is about what I want, and what you want."

"Even if it means you fighting with him?"

"Yes," he said with definitiveness. He checked the gold watch on his wrist. "I'm going to shower. We'll leave in fifteen."

"Are you sure you still want to go out? We don't have to."

"You're the only thing I'm sure of."

True to his word, fifteen minutes later, Francesco stood in the hallway shrugging on his suit jacket. A fresh pang of attraction hit Scarlett as she took in his appearance, from his fine tailored suit to his leather loafers with a gold Gucci horse bit on each shoe. He had skipped the tie and instead wore the first few buttons of his shirt undone.

"You look like a movie star. Your suit," she said as she ran her hands along the fine fabric of the lapels. "I've never seen you in a suit before."

"You like it?"

"A lot." She pulled him close and stole a kiss before they left.

After a friend of Francesco's drove them uptown, they finally arrived at Rockefeller Center where they rode the elevator to the sixty-fifth floor. When the doors opened, her jaw dropped.

"You're bringing me to the Rainbow Room?" She tried to keep her voice low, but it still ebbed with excitement. The Rainbow Room was the type of place that Scarlett only read about in the papers. It was the stuff of legend.

"I am," he said proudly. In the dim light of the chandelier overhead, his eyes sparkled like the fine champagne they were about to drink.

"How did you even get us in here?" Scarlett held onto his arm as the glamorous hostess led them to their table.

"I'm a chef, and I know other chefs. A friend of mine works in the kitchen here and was able to pull a few strings to get us in."

Scarlett marveled at the glittering, sparkling chandelier in the center of the room that must have been made of thousands of multi-faceted crystals. Then, her eyes fell to the stage where later a band and singer would fill. Out the window was the most spectacular view she had ever seen. New York looked different from this vantage point. She felt like she could reach out and touch the Empire State Building. She felt like she could take all of New York right in her hands.

"I can't believe we're here."

"Aren't you glad I surprised you?"

"If all of your surprises are like this, keep them coming."

Francesco ordered a bottle of champagne. She entrusted her dinner order to him, too, and finally, they sat back and relaxed, taking hold of their heavy, crystal champagne flutes.

"Thank you for bringing me here."

"You were made for a place like this." He leaned in and kissed her cheek. "To you and me."

"You and me." She raised her glass. She swore even the champagne tasted better. It was crisp, rich, and bubbly, and it sent a thrill through her.

"I'm glad we came out." He looked around the room, taking in their opulent surroundings. "Sometimes I need to get away from the restaurant. I live in the city, but I never get to see it."

"I get it. That place has been your life for almost a decade."

"It's like I forget places like this exist. Wait until you see the entertainment, Scar. I always wanted to have entertainment at our place."

"So why haven't you tried it?"

"Enz says it's not who we are. He says we're a restaurant, not a club. We can't be both."

"And yet, this place is."

"I know."

"Can I ask you something?"

"Of course."

"How come you let Enzo get away with calling all of the shots?"

"It's just the way it is. I can't imagine it being any different. I know we're fighting right now, and I know he's a pain in the ass, but I still love working with him. Besides, we're good at different things. I love being in the kitchen, not out in the dining room schmoozing with people or bossing the staff around. I'd be no good making the big decisions."

"Do you actually believe that? Or is that just what Enzo wants you to believe?"

"Maybe a little bit of both," he finally said.

"Well I think if you wanted to, you could do your own thing."

"What makes you think that?"

"Because I can see outside of the box Enzo has put you in all your life," she said as she held his hand tenderly. "I just wish you could see you the way I see you."

Scarlett knew there was more to Francesco – more than the food, more than being locked away in the kitchen for hours. He was a dreamer. He had a vision inside of him, one that he couldn't realize because Enzo wanted to keep Francesco's visions where they were: inside of his head, never to be carried out. Francesco looked at her like he wanted to say something, but they broke apart as the waiter approached their table with the appetizers. Scarlett took mental notes, examining the service and the way everything was so uniformed – even their movements were alike.

Francesco picked up his fork. "Let's eat."

———·~·———

SCARLETT SWORE THEY HAD put something in the champagne. It was either that, or drinking expensive booze sixty-five floors above New York City made you feel like you were floating and flying high. After Francesco opened the back door to Valenti's and flicked on some of the dim chandeliers, they were drawn to each other. She had lost track of time, but the restaurant was dark, still, and empty. They stumbled back into the kitchen where Francesco picked her up and set her on top of the counter. She wrapped her legs around him and pulled him close until his mouth was on hers. He tasted like champagne and citrus cologne and all she wanted was more of him.

She wasn't sure how long it took for her to realize that Enzo was in the kitchen. Her worst nightmare, realized, as she spotted him out of the corner of her eye. Her heart dropped to her stomach as she jumped down from the counter and smoothed down her dress, but it was of no use. Enzo stared them down like they were hardcore criminals.

"Christ, Enzo, I told you, you gotta stop doing this to me. What are you still doing here?" Francesco pleaded with his brother.

Scarlett expected Enzo to sound off, to start yelling and flailing his arms in his usual way. But instead, Enzo laughed.

"Last time I checked, this was my restaurant." Enzo went closer to them, his voice low. He pointed at Francesco with his cigar. "Watch your tone with me."

"Look, I'm sorry." Francesco's hand flew to his chest, and he sounded out of breath. "I didn't think you'd still be here."

"Like that matters? Like you care about how I feel in all of this?"

"And how do you feel, Enz?"

"You really have to ask me that?"

While the pair of brothers stared each other down, Scarlett decided she had to get out of there. It wasn't her place to get in the middle of their fight. Besides, from what Francesco had told her about their relationship, she was starting to think their fight went much deeper than her relationship with the two brothers. She tried to slip past Enzo, but he stopped her.

"You're not going anywhere, sweetheart. You did this," Enzo said.

"Leave her out of this," Francesco yelled. "You and I both know she's not the problem. You are."

"Me?"

"Yeah, you." Francesco's eyes looked like they were lit on fire. "You go around and live your life the way you do, and you don't ever explain yourself. You keep me locked up in this kitchen because you're so afraid I might be better at something than you."

"She put this in your head." Enzo pointed at Scarlett but kept his eyes on his brother. "Are you that weak? You let a woman fill your head with crazy ideas?"

"I don't understand why you hate to see me happy. What is it, Enzo? What do you want from me?"

"I want you out." Enzo said it so quickly, Scarlett wasn't sure she heard him right. His voice was quiet and even, and worst of all, sure.

Her head whipped between them, trying to figure out what the hell had just happened. Her body shook with panic.

Enzo said it again, so it was clear. "I want you out."

"What?" Francesco could barely get the word out. Enzo might not have thrown hands, but Francesco looked like he had been punched in the gut.

"You, and her." Enzo pointed to Scarlett again. "Out."

"No." Francesco shook his head, but there was no strength behind his words. "You can't do that! This is my place too."

"I brought you here. I can tell you when to leave."

"You need me! You could never do what I do."

"There's a million guys just like you in this city." Enzo rocked on his heels. "A million guys who slave and sweat over these stoves. It's you who can't do what I do. The magic of this place," Enzo opened his arms, "that's all me."

Scarlett wanted to take Francesco in her arms. She wanted to do something, anything, to protect him. He might not have ever had his heart broken by a woman before, but she knew what she had witnessed.

Enzo had broken his brother's heart like he had broken hers. Enzo's face held no trace of remorse or uncertainty. Instead, he looked calm, like severing his relationship with his brother was something in the ordinary.

"So that's it?" Francesco tossed his arms up. "You're gonna let this come between us like this? After we built this place together?"

"I expect you two to be out by the morning." Enzo puffed on his cigar, letting out a trail of smoke as he backed away, glancing at Scarlett before he disappeared completely.

"Fran," she whispered. She felt like her heart had been cracked open as she watched him cry. He half-sat on the counter as he covered his face. She wrapped her arms around him and held him close as he cried into her chest. She knew how much Valenti's meant to her; she knew how much she loved it. She couldn't even begin to fathom what it meant to Francesco. And in an instant, it was all gone, and no matter what he said, she felt like she was the one responsible. She loved him, and yet, she was the one causing his life to unravel. "Fran, I'm so sorry."

"Maybe I can..." he looked up at her, trailing off. "Maybe I can talk to him tomorrow when he cools off."

She wiped his tears away with her thumbs. She didn't say anything because what was there to say? They knew once Enzo made his mind up about something, that was all there was to it. It was as permanent as cement.

"What do you think I should do, Scar?" He looked at her not only like he wanted her opinion, but like he needed it.

"I think we should do exactly what he wants us to do. I think we should go. And I think we should open our own place."

"Scarlett—"

"You're the reason there's a line out the door every weekend. You're the reason people can't get a reservation for weeks on end. You, Fran. The food you make with these hands." She squeezed his hands tight.

"It's not that easy. I've done this before. I've built the place from scratch. It's hard."

"I'm not saying it's going to be easy. And we're not starting from scratch. You've got a name in this town. They'll come, wherever you go."

He wouldn't meet her gaze. She couldn't blame him. She wasn't asking him to make an easy decision. She was asking him to make a life-altering, incredibly expensive decision.

"I don't know if I can do all of this on my own. I've never done anything without Enzo."

"You're not on your own." She held his face. Though he was in his thirties, with the expression he was wearing, he looked like a boy. "You've got me. And I know I haven't been doing this for too long, but you said it yourself. I'm good at it. I've got ten grand saved. If you want to do this with me, it's all yours."

CHAPTER

FORTY

LITTLE ITALY, NEW YORK

FALL, 1985

They checked into a hotel in SoHo. They had exchanged few words the entire day, spending most of the morning apart as they packed up their belongings and bade their friends farewell. Everything felt temporary, and yet, the feeling of having nowhere to go suffocated Scarlett. Would she ever know what it felt like to be settled? Francesco paced the length of the room. Her eyes moved like a pendulum as she hugged her knees to her chest.

"We could go get jobs," she offered. "Any restaurant would die to have you."

"No." He shook his head and stroked his chin with his fingers. "It's not that simple to walk into a kitchen. You don't know the dynamics. Chefs have big egos. They get territorial with new people."

Scarlett stayed quiet, deciding to let him come up with the next suggestion.

"You've got ten grand," he said.

"Yes." She sat up straighter. "You?"

Francesco picked at his cuticles. "A quarter mil."

"*Cash?*"

"Do you know how far that'll get us in this city?"

"Farther than my lousy ten grand."

"You got any credit?"

"No."

"Me neither. Everything's in Enzo's name."

"Doesn't he...I don't know...have to buy you out or something? You did own half the place, didn't you?"

"Not technically. Not legally. I only had sweat equity in the place." He sat down on the edge of the bed and looked at Scarlett.

An idea percolated in her head. "You have a proven track record."

"What do you mean?"

"You've worked every single day of your life for the last eight years. Everyone in lower Manhattan knows who you are. Isn't there someone you can think of that would give us a lease? A regular or something?"

He ran his hands up and down his thighs, quiet in his own thoughts. "There was this man who used to come in, a *paesan*. He owned a bunch of real estate, mainly here in SoHo. I only remember him because he had a funny name. Saverio."

"He liked your food?"

"Loved it."

"Do you remember where any of his buildings are? Any of the businesses?"

"One of the clothing shops. Custom suits. He invited me to come in and get fitted for one. Brunelli or Bernardi, something like that."

Scarlett stood and reached out her hand. "Get up."

"What?"

"Get up. We're going to find Saverio."

Tracking down Saverio proved to be a harder task than Scarlett had anticipated. The suit shop was closed, and the tenants of the neighboring businesses were tight-lipped. By the time they reached the diner on Houston Street, Francesco had grown so frustrated, he decided to wait outside. Scarlett walked up to the counter.

"Can I help you?" the waitress asked.

"Hi. I'm looking for a man named Saverio. Do you know if he owns this building?"

"Saverio Bernardi?"

Finally, a glimmer of hope. Scarlett suppressed a smile. How many Saverios could be lurking in SoHo? "Yes. That's him."

"He's got an office in Tribeca. I can give you the address." She pulled a pen and notepad out of her waist apron.

"That would be wonderful. Would you also be able to get him on the phone?"

The waitress glanced up at Scarlett. "Is there something I can help you with?"

"It's more of a Saverio thing," she explained. "Please?"

The waitress set down her pen and picked up the phone. "What's your name?"

"Scarlett Valenti," Scarlett lied. "Tell him my husband is Francesco Valenti. He's dined at our restaurant in Little Italy. We'd like to speak with him about a space for our new restaurant."

Scarlett retreated while she listened to the woman relay the message on the phone. *Scarlett Valenti? Husband?* Where did these lies come from and why did they slip out of her mouth so easily?

"He can see you at two," the waitress said as she slid the paper with the address on it across the counter.

Scarlett glanced at her watch. It was quarter to two. They would barely make it. She ran out of the diner and found Francesco smoking on the street corner. She grabbed his arm. "Come on. We have to go now."

"Did you rob the place?"

Scarlett held up the paper with the address. "I found him."

———

"The chef." Saverio pointed at Francesco with a warm smile as the couple walked into his office. "Didn't know you got married. Beautiful wife."

Scarlett pinched the back of Francesco's arm and hoped he knew that meant to *go with it*. She had forgotten to fill him in on her little lie, or maybe her omission had been on purpose.

"This is Scarlett," Francesco said, making the introduction.

"Thank you for seeing us at such short notice," Scarlett said, shaking his hand.

"Have a seat." Saverio motioned to the two chairs facing his desk. "So, what can I do for you?"

"My gir— wife and I are looking to open a new restaurant together. A completely different concept than Valenti's. We wanted to see if you had any vacant spaces," Francesco said.

"Where are you looking to open up shop?"

"Wherever you have available."

Saverio peeled off his round glasses and his eyes darted between the two of them. "Location is everything in the restaurant business. You're not scouring the city for the best spot?"

"That's the thing." Scarlett moved to the edge of her seat and rested her arm on the desk. "We're newlyweds, just starting out. We don't have any credit. All we have is our work history. You've been to Francesco's other restaurant. You've seen what a success it is."

Saverio's eyes moved to Francesco, then back to Scarlett. "You're in the business too?"

"She is," Francesco answered. "She's got years of experience."

"How long has Valenti's been open now?"

"Just shy of a decade. We're averaging about a million in revenue a year. This year looks like it'll be even better than last."

Scarlett side-eyed Francesco. *One million* dollars a year? Were those the kinds of figures they would be looking at if they had their own place?

"You're a damn good chef," Saverio said, leaning back into his chair. "I have a space zoned for a restaurant, but it's been vacant for a year. Awfully outdated and no one seems to want to put in the TLC it needs. If that won't do, I'm afraid I can't be of much help."

"If you give us the space, you'll eat for free for the rest of your life at our new place," Francesco joked, though Scarlett knew it wasn't a joke at all. Then, he started speaking in Italian. She didn't understand, but Francesco's words must've worked magic.

Saverio leaned in. "I can give you a lease, but you'll have to personally guarantee it."

"I don't care," Francesco said. "Just tell me where to sign."

CHAPTER

FORTY-ONE

LITTLE ITALY, NEW YORK
WINTER, 1985

Brick by brick. That was how it began. Saverio's description of the vacant restaurant had been generous, and the studio apartment directly above it where Francesco and Scarlett lived wasn't much better. It was a small space on the north end of Mulberry near Houston Street, and to stretch their funds as far as possible, they had done most of the demolition thus far themselves. Walls were bare, carpet torn up, and light fixtures had been removed, but they had only just begun.

The winter air was biting, but they were New Yorkers. No amount of snow or sleet or gray skies would stop them. Francesco had hired a construction crew to begin work in a few weeks' time, and the permit requests for the larger renovations had been filed. Tomorrow, they would pick out furnishings and fixtures. Tonight, though, Francesco was back where he belonged. The kitchen. The food, after all, would be the star.

As arias from *La Bohème* blared throughout the kitchen, he let his creativity have free rein, plating things in unusual ways, experimenting by combining ingredients he wouldn't ordinarily marry. Fennel and olives. Hazelnuts with mozzarella. He put new spins on classic dishes and served seafood *crudo*. His days as a fisherman came in handy, knowing which types of fish he could serve raw. The ones he couldn't, he crusted with things like pistachios and coffee grounds. The food wouldn't resemble anything else on Mulberry, which he knew would be a risk. But as of late, everything he was doing was one big risk.

Scarlett had set up a card table and two folding chairs in the bar area. Francesco walked in carrying three steaming plates on his arms. "There's more," he said, setting the last plate down. "I'll be right back."

"Who's going to eat all of this?" Scarlett called after him.

"We are," he tossed back, already back in the kitchen.

When he returned to the bar, Scarlett surveyed all the plates. "Tell me what everything is."

High on his own creativity, Francesco began his grand display. "Beef *carpaccio*." He gestured to one of the plates. Impressively thin slices of meat were artfully fanned out over the plate, topped with a swirl of olive oil, fennel, olives and capers. "This is *pesce crudo*. Raw fish."

"*Raw* fish?"

"It's safe, I promise. Then this one," he pointed, "is a caprese salad, but I've changed it up a bit. Tomato and mozzarella topped with crushed hazelnuts and truffle oil. That one is pistachio-crusted salmon."

Scarlett picked up one of the dishes. "Is this *black* pasta?"

"It's made from squid ink. I added in shrimp and a pesto sauce." His heart pounded as he awaited Scarlett's thoughts, though she remained quiet for some time. "Well?"

"I've never seen food like this before." She looked up at him, her forehead wrinkled. "It's almost too pretty to eat, Fran. It looks like art."

"Exactly. That's what I was going for."

From the bar, she grabbed her polaroid camera she had been using to document their renovation process. She snapped a few photos of the food, then one of Francesco, smiling as he held up one of his dishes. She set the polaroids out on the bar top to develop and sat down at their small card table. "Can I taste?"

Francesco glanced at her every other second as they tasted each dish. She seemed to like the pasta *nero* the best, going in for a second bite of the spaghetti and shrimp in pesto. After she had tried everything, he set down his fork and folded his hands over his dish. "Please say something."

Scarlett dabbed at the corners of her mouth and when she lifted the napkin away, Francesco let out an exhale of relief at her smile. "Fran," she said with a shake of her head, "this is unbelievable. People will never expect food like *this* to come out of Little Italy. It's different. It tastes as wonderful as it looks. And the flavors, they have..." she trailed off, for lack of vocabulary to describe food.

"Contrast?"

She snapped her fingers. "That's it. Contrast. The sweet fennel with the salty meat."

"That's the exact reaction I was hoping for," Francesco said, clasping his hands together. "I always wanted to create dishes that would surprise people. Things that no one would expect, especially here, in the neighborhood. Enzo stuck to the classics because they came with guarantees. *Carbonara* is from Rome. So is the *amatriciana*. They sold well. But they're not who I am."

"These are who you are," Scarlett said. "They're art and they're beautiful, and that's you. Though," she held up her index finger, "they're very modern. I didn't have you pegged as a modern man."

"I like that I still get to surprise you every once in a while."

"That makes two of us." Scarlett pressed her palms against the tabletop and stood. "It's my turn to surprise you." Scarlett walked over to a closet and came back, carrying three big frames. She flipped them around. "I called the Met."

Francesco's brows lifted an inch. "*You* called the Met?"

"I did, and I asked if they had any old promotional posters from the operas. I got all your favorites framed. *La Bohème. Turandot. Tosca,* and *Madame Butterfly.* I thought they'd look good in the dining room, and we'll put lights underneath, like little spotlights."

Francesco stood and examined the large gold frames. "You outdid yourself. But now I owe you a date to the Met so you can actually *see* one of these operas." He drew her to his side and kissed her. "I love them."

"And I've been doing some thinking, about the design." Scarlett began to pace the room. She spread her hands out and motioned to the wall behind the bar. "A mirror, those kinds with the fancy designs etched in them of animals. You know which ones I mean? And black marble for the bar top, but the one with white veins in it."

"Marquina," Francesco said, providing the name.

"Marquina," she repeated. "Velvet bar stools. Maybe emerald green? Or a dark red."

"Rich colors," Francesco remarked.

"And black carpet with a gold design. Better than tiles; easier on everyone's feet. Then, over the bar," Scarlett pointed, "little gold pendant lights and we'll keep them real dim. On the tables, we'll have miniature lights, so each table will feel intimate. And the ceiling," Scarlett looked up, "let's do those tin tiles with a fancy pattern. It'll reflect the light and keep it cozy. Oh, and back here, I think there's room for a stage, Fran. I know you've always wanted to have entertainment, and even if we have to sacrifice a few tables, I think it's worth it, don't you?"

Francesco went behind Scarlett, wrapping his arms around her waist, and rested his chin on her shoulder. "Know what I think?"

"Should I be scared to find out?" she teased.

"I think you were made to do this."

With proud smiles, they fell into laughter for lack of anything to say. How could they express how they felt about what they were about to embark on with mere words? Together, they stood in what was, imagining what would be, while Francesco held the woman he knew to be the other half of his heart.

"Hey, Fran," she said, breaking him out of his thoughts. "What are we gonna call this place?"

A singular word popped in his mind. "That's easy. *Amanti.*"

She looked up at him. "Which means?"

He picked her up in his arms and kissed her. "Lovers."

<hr />

"THE SIGN LOOKS GREAT," Scarlett said, rubbing her hands together as she closed the door behind her. Their neon sign had been branded to the front of their building, completing the exterior work. She peeled off her coat and draped it over a chair. Only when Francesco didn't respond did she look up, to find a trail of candles leading towards the back of the restaurant where a small stage had been built. "Fran," she called out. "Francesco?"

He came out from the kitchen, dressed in a pair of jeans and a crewneck sweater. His curls appeared to be freshly washed and his face glowed in the candlelight. "Hi."

"What's with the candles?" she asked, gesturing to the floor. But as the question left her lips, her heart fell and her hands began to tremble. "Francesco?"

"No more questions." He reached for her hands. "Now I'm about to ask you something, and I have a feeling you'll say yes, but before you do, I want to say a few things. I thought about taking you somewhere fancy to do this, or to one of the big landmarks, but then I thought, what better place to ask you to be my wife than the place where you and I are going to start our lives?"

"Francesco," she half-laughed, half-cried.

"I didn't ask yet." He maintained a smile, though his lips began to quiver. "I'm not perfect. I've never been a saint and I don't pretend to be one. I'm sure somewhere down the line, I'll disappoint you or make you angry. I never wanted to get married because I never thought I'd be any good at it, but I think I can do this, because all I want to do is make you happy." Her smile was so wide, he grabbed her cheek and squeezed it. "You and me make a good team, Scar, and I love you more than anything."

"God, I can't take it anymore." She jumped up and down. "Ask me."

He laughed as he fell to one knee. "Scarlett Marie Ciccone, will you marry me?"

Though her answer lay on the tip of her tongue, she soaked in the question, the expectant look on his face, the pear-shaped diamond ring on a gold band that stared back at her. She felt nothing but beloved. "Yes. A million times yes."

He gave her one of his lazy smiles that drove her wild as he slid the ring on her shaking finger, a perfect fit. Together, they admired it.

"Hey," she said, finding his eyes, "you were wrong about one thing. You could never disappoint me, Fran. No matter what."

"Promise?"

"Yeah. I promise."

FORTY-TWO

LITTLE ITALY, NEW YORK

WINTER, 1986

Two weeks had passed since Scarlett and Francesco had ordered the fixtures. Slabs of marble, lumber, pieces of mirror, and new barstools had been delivered already. Their funds were dwindling with each passing day, but it was all necessary. The quicker they renovated, the quicker they could open their doors and start bringing in some money. But they couldn't build without a crew. Scarlett had brewed several pots of coffee for the construction workers, but by eleven, they had gone ice cold. The crew was nowhere to be found.

"Call the office," Scarlett said to Francesco.

"I'm not calling again."

"They could answer this time."

"On the eleventh try?"

Scarlett let out a frustrated exhale. "Where's their office? Why don't I go over there myself?"

"Queens, and you're not going. We already paid them the deposit. They'll want the rest of their money."

"They got the deposit for not doing any work. No they won't."

"Scarlett," Francesco sighed.

"Where did you find these people again?"

"Through a friend. Ciro, who owns the cannoli place down the street."

Scarlett ran up the stairs and grabbed her purse. Francesco stopped her by the front door. "Where do you think you're going?"

"To talk to Ciro. He vouched for these guys. Maybe he can explain why they decided not to show up."

"No. That's not your place."

"This is my restaurant, isn't it?"

Their almost-argument was put on pause when the mail fell through the latch of the front door. Scarlett bent down and began sifting through. Bills. More bills. And, two envelopes from the City of New York.

"The permits," she said, holding out the letters.

Francesco slipped his thumb under the lip of the envelope and ripped it open. His eyes moved left to right as he scanned it over. Again, and again. By the fourth time, Scarlett tore it out of his hands. Her throat constricted as she read it. Their electrical permit had been *denied*. In black-and-white. Reaching for the second letter, she ripped the envelope open. She looked for the same word, and sure enough, she found it. The permit to build a second restroom was *denied*.

"This can't be right." Her head shot up and she looked at Francesco. "We must've filled something out wrong."

"Or." He reached for the papers and scanned them over again.

"Or what?"

"Or Enzo."

"*What?*"

He held up the letters. "Angelo Ruggerio. Recognize that name?"

"Enzo has a friend Angelo. I met him a few times."

"Not just a friend. He's half a gangster. Works for the city and has everybody in his pocket. Enzo must've paid him off to deny our permits."

"Did Enzo really think we wouldn't know it was him?"

"I think he wanted us to know it was him. He's stopping us. That's all he cares about."

Scarlett took the letters from Francesco and ripped them apart. "He's not stopping us. He's delaying us. Now I'm going to talk to Ciro, and you're going to find us sledgehammers so we can start the work ourselves."

Scarlett didn't give Francesco a chance to respond. She was out on Mulberry, and she was on a mission.

<hr />

As soon as Scarlett opened the door to Caffè Catania, scents of cinnamon, anise, and almond paste greeted her. She didn't know what Ciro looked like, but she knew an owner when she saw one. Walking in further, Scarlett found a man sitting in the corner near the glass cases filled with fresh pastries. He sat across from another man, but Scarlett didn't care if she was crashing a meeting or not. She needed to talk to him.

"You're Ciro," Scarlett said as a statement, not a question. He did a double take. She had his attention.

"I am," he said. "Who are you?"

Scarlett pulled a chair from one of the nearby tables and sat down at the head of Ciro's four-top. He looked like he had the urge to tell her off or give her some long lecture about respect, but Scarlett launched into talking before he could. "There's something I think you should know. You vouched for some contractors, and I hired them to renovate my restaurant. We gave them the deposit, and today, they didn't show. I don't think you want these kinds of people out there making you look bad or untrustworthy, do you?"

Ciro started laughing. "Who the hell are you?"

"You know who I am."

Realization fell over Ciro's face. Scarlett had been right. He knew exactly who she was and what she was talking about. "Listen, I'm not getting involved in anything, sweetheart. I made a recommendation, that was it."

"They took our money, and they didn't start the work yet."

Ciro stood up and pushed his chair back. "I don't get involved in family conflicts."

Scarlett stood too and stopped him from moving past her. "Family conflicts? I'm talking about contractors. What are you talking about?" Scarlett could almost see the stranger's thoughts. *Enzo.* Enzo was behind this, too. "Tell me," Scarlett said to him. "Tell me what you're talking about."

Ciro took one last look at her. "I don't think I need to."

SCARLETT WAS TOO ANGRY to be hungry. Francesco was in the kitchen, and the scents of olive oil and onions and tomatoes swirled in the air. The countertop was scattered with pieces of paper scribbled with the beginnings of their menu. Francesco had also answered Scarlett's earlier request. Two sledgehammers were leaned against the bar. She slicked her hair away from her face, and despite it being winter, she wore nothing but a tank top and biker shorts. With great effort, she heaved the sledgehammer behind her shoulders. It felt like it weighed more than her. Working up nerve and strength, she rammed it over her head and into the Formica bar top. It crashed like thunder. Shards of plastic and plaster went everywhere. She dragged the sledgehammer away from the initial landing spot to reveal a gaping hole.

One swing, and she was already out of breath. She did it again, landing it in another spot. Again, and again. She could barely breathe. Her chest had gone red, and veins budded out of her hands. Frustration fueled her; she wasn't physically strong enough for a job like this. In each spot she hit, she pictured Enzo.

"Shit, shit, shit." She rammed the hammer down. "Damn you, Enzo!"

"Hey." Francesco put his hand on hers to stop her.

She set the hammer down and stepped away from the counter. She wiped the sweat from her forehead, then put her hands on her hips and tried to catch her breath.

"What are you doing?" he asked.

"The work our crew was supposed to start today."

"Relax, will you? I handled it. I found another crew of contractors. They can start next week."

"But they already took our money."

"I don't care."

"You don't *care*?"

"Scarlett, we have bigger things to worry about. We can chase them down for the money after we open."

"Do you know why the contractors didn't show up today, Fran? You guessed it. Your one and only brother."

Francesco tossed his hands up like he had already been defeated.

"See? That's the problem. You give up too easily. The minute you knew he was behind those permits being denied, you should've gone and told him to stop messing with us."

"He's my family, Scarlett."

"Yeah, he's really treating you like family right now," Scarlett scoffed.

"Like you would know? You never had a real family, so don't tell me how I should handle my brother."

"You know, you're really something else." Fuming, Scarlett stormed off. Was Francesco, or anyone, for that matter, worth all of this? Would Enzo ever be satisfied, or would he continue to put up roadblocks until they fell flat on their faces and had nothing left? She had the urge to pick up and run away, but something stopped her. Enzo was behind not only the permits and the crew, but this fighting of theirs like they had never fought before. Scarlett went back into the bar where she found Francesco leaning against it, rubbing his chest. He was out of breath. "No," Scarlett said.

"I didn't mean to say that. I didn't mean it."

"This is what he wants."

"What?"

"He wants us to fight like this so we give up. On the restaurant, and on each other. We can't give him what he wants," Scarlett said with a renewed sense of determination. She wouldn't let Enzo win, not when it came to their restaurant, not when it came to her making it across the finish line with Francesco.

"I'm sorry."

"How sorry?" she asked. She lifted her shirt overhead.

"So, so very sorry," Francesco said, walking towards her.

"Show me how sorry you are."

He brushed the shards of plastic off with his arm in one motion and lifted her onto the counter. Scarlett didn't care if the sharp pieces dug into her thighs and cut her. She needed him to show her how hard he would fight for them as a couple and what they were trying to build together.

Though she went through the motions of their mad, messy kissing and their frantic need to apologize physically, her mind was elsewhere. Scarlett hated how Enzo was infiltrating every aspect of their lives, even something as sacred as their own intimacy. He was bleeding ink, stain-ing everything. They weren't free from his grip. Scarlett wasn't because Francesco didn't have it in him to stand up to Enzo.

If he wouldn't, Scarlett would.

FORTY-THREE

LITTLE ITALY, NEW YORK

WINTER, 1986

"June?" Francesco asked.

"Is that too soon?" Scarlett said as she wiped down the freshly installed Marquina bar.

"I'd marry you tomorrow if you'd let me, but I know you want the big white wedding."

Scarlett turned the radio down. "I never told you I want a big white wedding."

As Francesco took a breath to respond, they heard knocking at the front door. He moved around the bar and went to answer it.

"Who is it?" Scarlett yelled across the otherwise quiet room. When he didn't answer her, she came out from behind the bar. A bottomless pit of worry opened up in her belly when she saw Enzo, clad in a heavy trench coat and leather gloves. Enzo walked into their restaurant with the same air of authority he had at his. Francesco trailed behind him. "Fran, you didn't tell me Enzo was coming by," Scarlett said, hoping he would clue her in to what was going on.

"This is mine," Enzo said. He opened his arms wide, gesturing to the space, and then ran a hand along the marble bar top that had been installed a few days prior.

"What are you doing here, Enz?" Francesco finally asked.

"This place is mine."

"What the hell are you talking about?"

"You built it with *my* money. So, I think that makes it mine."

Francesco didn't say anything. His chest moved up and down, up and down. Scarlett walked closer to the two of them. It was half her restaurant, but she felt so small. "What do you mean *your* money? We renovated this place with *our* money."

Enzo let out a sarcastic laugh. He looked from Scarlett to Francesco. "Keeping secrets from your fiancé already, are you now?"

Her head whipped between the two of them as she wondered how Enzo even knew they were engaged. Francesco remained silent. "Fran," Scarlett said, grabbing his arm, "what is he talking about?"

"Do you know why I brought you here? To New York?" Enzo asked, his eyes squarely focused on his brother. When Francesco didn't respond, Enzo continued. "Because you're my brother. My only brother. My blood, Fran. I wanted you to have the best. And I've done everything I can to make sure you have it good here. Have I not?"

"You have," Francesco finally answered.

"Then can you imagine what it feels like to know that my own brother, who I've done everything for, my own blood stole from me?" Enzo moved a few steps closer so their eyes would've been level, if Enzo were as tall as Francesco. "You stole from me, Fran." Enzo pressed his index finger into Francesco's chest. "Did you think I wouldn't know? Did you think I wouldn't find out that I had a quarter mil missing?"

A quarter mil. The money was right where they could see it, every inch of their renovated restaurant. And it was Enzo's money. Scarlett broke out into a cold sweat. She'd known it was coming, hadn't she? That sooner or later, the other shoe would drop? That this romance with Francesco was too good to be true? The shoe had dropped, past the ground, into the earth, shaking her foundation to its very core.

"Alright, Enz. Let me explain," Francesco tried to reason with Enzo, but Enzo wasn't finished.

"Who the hell have you become, Fran? You steal from me? You betray me, and for what? For *what* Fran? For this? For her?"

"For my *wife*," Francesco yelled.

Enzo let out a bitter laugh. He grabbed Scarlett's left hand and studied the ring. "Yeah. What, did you spend too much money on this ring? Needed some extra cash? That's why you betrayed your only brother, isn't it?" Enzo didn't let go of Scarlett's hand. He looked her in the eyes. "And he didn't even tell you, did he? See what I told you, honey? Fran's not perfect. At least I'm honest about who I am and admit when I screw up. He's more dangerous than me. He's the one you have to worry about. I knew one day he'd show you his true colors, and I tried to warn you. But I'm the bad guy, right?"

Francesco pushed Scarlett and Enzo apart. He grabbed Enzo's shoulders and rammed him against the freshly painted wall. "That's enough. Do you hear me?"

But Enzo regained control and pinned Francesco against the wall. He reached into his pocket and Scarlett let out an audible gasp at the small gun in his hand. In one swift motion, Enzo had it held up to the side of

Francesco's head. "I've always protected you, Fran. I've always been there. But you're on your own now kid. This is how you want it? You can have it. You're not my brother anymore, you understand me?"

Without another word, only the sounds of scattered, jagged breathing, Enzo dropped the revolver to his side and left out the front door while Francesco slunk to the ground. He pressed his palm against his chest and rubbed circles, struggling to breathe. Under normal circumstances, Scarlett would have rushed to his side. Tended to him. Worried and tried to fix him. But instead, motionless, she looked down at him.

"You stole from him? Used *his* money to build our place instead of your own? And you thought you would get away with it?" Out of her peripheral vision, she caught sight of her own chest moving up and down at a rapid pace. "Were you ever going to tell me the truth?"

"Scarlett," he said, panting. "I knew if I didn't take the money, he would never give me what I was owed. The morning you and I left I went down to the office. I took what I thought was fair, not a dollar more."

"A quarter million dollars is fair?"

"I gave almost ten years of my life to that restaurant, Scar. *Ten years.* Whose side are you on?"

"I'm on my side, Fran. You know what I've been through. You know everything about me, and honestly, I can't believe you'd do this to me." Though she momentarily felt concerned for him, taking in the expression of pain on his face as he continued to rub his chest, her fear of getting hurt wouldn't allow her to let her guard down. She had wondered on multiple occasions why *her*. Why, out of every woman in New York who had eyes for Francesco, he had sought her out with such sureness. Was she that special? Was their connection that true and rare? Or was she merely a pawn in his rivalry with Enzo? "Why'd you do it? Was this all just some big plan to get back at your brother for everything he's done to you over the years? Or was it you trying to prove you'd be better at this whole restaurant thing than him?"

"It was none of those things. I did this for us."

"For you," she yelled. He stood and tried to come near her, but she put her arms out in front of her. "This is all for you. This restaurant, you being with me. Enzo told me—"

"You're really going to believe him over me? I'm your fiancé," Francesco reminded her. A sober, somber expression fell over his face. "You said I could never disappoint you. You promised."

"This is way beyond disappointment, Fran. You have me doubting absolutely everything."

Scarlett retreated to the apartment. She knew exactly where it was, tucked away with the last of her cash. Underneath the few bundles she had left was the business card her mother had handed her nearly a year ago. With her mother's track record, it would be a miracle if Lana and Dustin were still together, but she had to try. She needed to go home.

Whether she wanted to admit it or not, she needed her mother.

FORTY-FOUR

HELL'S KITCHEN, NEW YORK

WINTER, 1986

Scarlett's suspicions had been almost right. After spending the night at Helen's and trying Dustin's number countless times, despite the operator's cold voice telling her that the number was no longer in service, Scarlett wouldn't give up.

"If she's not there, just come back," Helen said. "I'll wait here until I hear from you."

Scarlett gave Helen a hug before heading out the door. "Thanks for everything. I know we used to say it more when we were kids, but I love you."

"Love you too." Helen gave her a reassuring smile. "You'll find her."

The bar looked like it had received a good cleaning. As Scarlett moved in further and her eyes adjusted to the dim light, Scarlett took note of how the old seats had been switched out to red leather barstools. She was surprised Lana would make such an investment. The bartender looked up at Scarlett. Scarlett knew turnover rates in the service industry were high, but seeing a man behind the bar threw Scarlett off kilter. What had happened to her mother's business practices in the last year?

"What can I get you?" the bartender asked.

"Nothing. I, um…" Scarlett dug her pockets into her oversized leather jacket. "I'm looking for a woman named Lana Ciccone."

"The old owner," he said with a nod.

"I'm sorry. Old owner?"

The bartender paused before launching into wiping down the countertop. "Sorry. *Former* owner. She's not old by any means."

"She sold the bar?" Scarlett asked, wishing he would get to the point.

"I'm sorry, who are you?"

"I'm her daughter." At this, the bartender's demeanor changed. "Do you know where she is?"

Left with nothing but an address, Scarlett took the subway to Union Square. She moved about the masses of people as if she were in a race, tuning out the sounds of pop music and chatter and taxi horns as she neared the building. She let out all the air left in her lungs when she reached a sober house.

After checking in at the reception desk, Scarlett was led to a communal sitting area where other people were visiting with family members. As soon as she spotted Lana and her mane of golden hair that was more unkempt than Scarlett had ever seen it, tears lodged behind her eyes. Lana was not yet fifty, but she looked frail. Dark half-moons hung underneath her eyes. She sat with her hands delicately folded in her lap. Scarlett sat next to her mother and wrapped her arms around her. She could feel all her mother's bones.

Being back in her mother's presence, the dam holding Scarlett's feelings in broke wide open. Lana let her cry, placing her hand on Scarlett's trembling body. Scarlett worried she was causing a scene, but she remembered everyone in there was going through the same thing. Lana stroked Scarlett's hair as she held her daughter, but Scarlett felt like she was the one holding her mother up.

"How long have you been in here?" Scarlett asked.

"Four months now," Lana said. "You believe that? I haven't had a sip of anything in *months*."

"What happened?"

"Things changed once I got to Long Island. Dustin was never around, always working. So what did I have to do all day, you know? I drank. I drank more than I ever did before. And he got sick of coming home to me drunk. So he brought me here."

"Why didn't you call me?"

"Look at me, Scar. Do you know what this feels like? To have my daughter see me like this?"

"I don't care. Maybe I could have…" she trailed off, because what could she have done? She couldn't stop her mother before; even Dustin didn't have that kind of influence over Lana.

"There was nothing you could do," Lana said, reading her daughter's mind. "You look different." Lana ran her hand over Scarlett's hair, which used to be the same color as hers but was now a blanket of silky black wefts. "You look more like daddy now."

"You haven't seen me in almost a year."

Lana looked different to her too, but Scarlett didn't tell her. It wasn't only that Lana looked different; Scarlett saw her differently. At one time, maybe Lana was like Scarlett. A young woman with dreams and hopes for a future bigger than her circumstances could afford. Maybe Lana had thought herself lucky, only to have to make do with the undesirable hand life had dealt her. Scarlett's resentment towards her mother had softened over their year apart, and instead, had been traded for remorse. If only Scarlett could have seen Lana as a woman rather than her mother, perhaps she would've made sense of her mother's choices in a different way.

"I thought you would've called sooner," Lana said.

"You left me, Mom. You left me." A surge of tears welled up in Scarlett again. "And there were so many times I needed you."

"I know that." Lana took Scarlett's hand in hers. "I'm sorry, Scarlett, baby. There's no excuse for the kind of mother I've been to you." Lana looked around the expansive room. "There's not much else to do here besides think. It's like prison." Lana rolled her eyes and gave the faintest of smiles, trying to lighten the mood. "Sometimes I lay awake at night, and I replay things in my head. The things I've said to you and the way I must've made you feel. I've been beating myself up about all of it."

"I don't want you to do that," Scarlett said, though she felt vindicated by the fact that her mother now saw her own actions through a clear lens.

"It's hard not to. Some people have a bunch of kids, but I only have one. And I made a pretty spectacular mess of motherhood." Lana's gaze fell to her lap.

Scarlett thought back to what her mother had revealed to her last year about the circumstances surrounding Scarlett's birth and her parents' marriage. Though forgiveness would take time and great effort, Scarlett wished to better understand Lana. Maybe Scarlett simply didn't know her, at least not underneath the veil of alcohol. Now, with it lifted, would she discover who her mother truly was? Would she be able to find peace with the way her mother had treated her?

"You did your best," Scarlett offered.

Lana looked at Scarlett, long and hard. "I don't know why you're giving me so much credit."

"Because I want us to be close, Mom. That's all I've ever wanted." Scarlett shifted in her seat and took her mother's hands in hers. "All I used to want was for you to be like Mrs. O'Connor, Helen's mom. I wanted you to wear aprons and make casseroles, and to help me pick out dresses for homecoming and prom. I wanted to talk to you about my high school crushes and get your opinions on how to act to get them to like me." Scarlett's smile began to fade. "And then I would look at you and want to say something, but I never did, because you always looked like you were in another world. Thinking and worrying about something or someone else. You would be right in front of me, Mom, and I would miss you. I tried so hard to be a good girl so I wouldn't feel like I was the thing that made you drink."

"You weren't." Lana smoothed back her hair. "My life didn't exactly turn out the way I had hoped it would, Scar. That was why I drank. I didn't know how to fix it or change things, and what scared me the most was thinking you'd end up feeling like me someday, because I couldn't give you anything better. I couldn't give you the perfect little family Helen has. I couldn't bring your father back. And no matter how hard I tried, I couldn't find a man good enough to help me raise you. So I gave in. It was easier to be a crappy mother than to want to be a good one and fail. And I'm sorry, baby doll. You deserved better than what I gave you."

"Can I ask you something?" Scarlett asked. When her mother nodded, she took a deep breath before continuing. "Before I left the bar, you told me you didn't think I was good enough to bartend, let alone to take over the bar. I just want to know why you think that of me."

Lana's lips thinned to form a straight line. "I was worse than you when I was young. Had stars in my eyes. My mother put me in a tap-dancing class when I was a kid, and I was convinced I would be on Broadway someday. I thought ambition was enough to make it out of where I came from, but then I found out it's not. I turned out to be this. A drunk who scraps for any attention she can get, even when it meant I had to steal it from you. I thought it would be better for you to have no expectations than to be disappointed by your life not living up to those expectations. I thought, in a way, I was helping you. Owning a business is tough, Scar, and doing it on your own is even tougher. I thought it would be easier for you to fall in love and have a family."

Scarlett looked up at her mother and felt like a child again. "I did fall in love," Scarlett said.

"You did?"

"Twice. And I think running the bar on my own would've been easier," she joked through her tears.

"What's wrong, baby? Why'd you come here today?"

"Somebody broke my heart. And then I fell in love again." Scarlett reached into her purse where she had been keeping her engagement ring in a small side pocket since she left Francesco. "He wants me to marry him, but I'm terrified. I don't know if I can trust him, and I don't think I can handle having my heart broken again."

"Do you love him?"

"More than I can even explain."

Lana drew in a deep breath. "Then I have some bad news, honey. Whether he leaves you or you leave him, your heart will be broken either way. Some people aren't replaceable."

Though it wasn't necessarily the advice Scarlett wanted, maybe they were the words she needed to hear. If she and Francesco were to part ways, the void he would leave would be immense no matter which way they parted.

"She's still in there," Lana said.

"Who?"

"The little girl I raised who wasn't afraid of anything. You just have to dust off all the shit that happened and find her again." Lana leaned her forehead against Scarlett's.

Scarlett's heart that had been so wrung with heartache finally released. When it did, love poured out.

"Look, why don't I try to do something and get you out of here?" Scarlett said.

"No, baby. No."

"No?"

"I need to be here. As awful as this place is, I need to get better. For both of us."

Scarlett didn't try to convince her mother otherwise. If Scarlett ever wanted a chance at a relationship of any kind with her mother, Lana needed help. Real help, not a temporary fix from a man. Scarlett dug in her purse and fished out an old receipt. She wrote down her address and phone number and gave it to Lana.

"Here's my number and my address. And some money." Scarlett handed over the little bit of cash she had on her. "If you need anything, you can call me."

"Why are you being so nice to me?"

"Because I want you to get better, too. Probably more than you do."

"I'm trying," Lana said as they stood.

"When can I see you again?" Scarlett asked, her voice filled with a child-like hope.

Lana couldn't say anything because like Scarlett, she appeared overwhelmed. "I love you, baby girl."

"When?"

"I'll call you. I promise."

<hr>

SCARLETT'S HEELS CLACKED AGAINST the tile floors of The Church of the Most Precious Blood as she walked down the center aisle, the sound reverberating off the impossibly high vaulted ceilings. She passed by the archways and pews, until she reached the altar and lit a candle. Most of the candles were already lit, the flames flickering at all different heights and paces. She thought of how each flame represented a worry, a request, a concern just like hers. A woman like her, with the way she had been living for the last year, it was the last place she expected herself to end up. But something drew her there. Maybe that was the mystery of church – it welcomed both sinners and saints in tandem.

Scarlett adjusted the black lace mantilla on her head so it wouldn't fall from her silky hair. The heavy scent of incense enveloped her, as did a sense of peace she could not fathom. Everything in her life was up in the air. Nothing for certain. And yet, a calmness washed over her as she collapsed onto the kneeler in front of the Blessed Virgin Mary. She placed her hand on the statue's feet and looked up into the Virgin's blue eyes. Though the statue itself was inanimate, Scarlett began to speak as if it were living and breathing.

"I know I've been doing everything wrong," Scarlett started. "All out of order. I fell in love with Enzo first, when I shouldn't have fallen in love with him at all. And I think you're probably supposed to get married before you move in and open a business with someone, but I did that out of order too. And now I don't know what's going to happen."

Scarlett felt as if the cracks on her heart were fresh and raw. Streams poured out from her eyes as her grip tightened around the statue's base. "I know how I feel about him. I didn't think I'd ever love someone the way I love him. I didn't want to, but I'm not sure you have a choice when it comes to falling in love with someone. I think maybe it just happens." Scarlett closed her eyes. "I don't know if I can trust him. I don't know if this whole thing is one big lie. On his end, at least. I don't want to believe it is." Scarlett opened her eyes again and looked up. "But if he can steal from his own brother and lie to me about it, what else is he capable of? If Enzo wouldn't have come over last night and did what he did, would Fran have ever told me the truth?" She let her question hang in the silence, though that silence was broken by footsteps. They approached and she turned to find a priest.

He pointed to the statue. "They can't talk back, you know."

Scarlett let out a smirk. "Kind of makes you wonder what the point of talking to them is, doesn't it?"

He approached Scarlett as she stood and smoothed down her skirt. "The statues can't speak to us. But the saints can. God can."

"How?"

"Be still. Be quiet enough to hear their voices. If we want answers to our questions, we have to take the time to listen."

CHAPTER

FORTY-FIVE

LITTLE ITALY, NEW YORK

WINTER, 1986

Enzo felt like he was going blind as he stroked his chin and paced back and forth. The colors and numbers and spades of the deck of cards fanned out before him all blended into one. Tonight's poker game had been going on for the better of three hours, and as the wee hours of the night pressed into morning, he wondered how he could remain awake another minute. When he played poker, adrenaline was his source of energy. Watching other people play the game sucked the life out of him. But he didn't have a choice; as long as these games continued under his roof, they would remain under his supervision.

The games had continued to be a success, though the initial excitement Enzo had felt over his arrangement with his friends, now colleagues, had faded. Ironic, he thought, that the bar to which he measured his success was constantly in motion. Constantly moving into more dangerous territory. He had agreed to host these games. What would come next? Would he ever draw a line, or did Enzo hold no pen to draw such lines? Though he had tossed out his moral compass long ago, would it ever find him again? He almost dozed off as soon as he sank into a chair in the corner, but when two of the players stood and began to yell, Enzo woke from his half-slumber.

"Hey," Enzo called out as he made his way over to the pair of men. "We don't tolerate this around here, you understand me?" He moved them apart, though the men were still clearly fuming. "What's the matter? What happened?"

"He's counting cards," one of the men said.

"Listen," Enzo said, pointing to his own chest. "You want my opinion? It's getting late, and we're all getting stupid. Why don't we call it a night?"

"Stupid?" the man repeated. Silence fell over the room.

Enzo's heart thrashed around in his chest. Perhaps *he* was the stupid one, for entrusting the safety of his business to these men he knew nothing of. He hated how in this moment where he needed clarity, he thought of his brother. How disappointed Francesco would be in him. How *right* his younger yet wiser brother had been. Enzo took a breath, ready to provide a calm, measured speech, but the words never left his mouth. There was knocking at the back door.

Enzo's deep eyes widened, the whites visible all around the irises. Operating on nerves alone, he began to move towards the door. "Get the cash off the table," he told the men in Italian. He didn't bother to look back and make sure they had done as they were told. He trusted them, on some level, didn't he?

With trembling hands, Enzo opened the door. His heart rate sped up to double time when four police officers barged their way in past Enzo. Enzo's eyes followed them, landing on the table where hundred-dollar bills were fanned out. Enzo made eye contact with the man who had started the fight. A mole. Someone somewhere had set Enzo up, and he had been too blind to see it, too naïve to believe it would happen to him. He couldn't fathom the scene before him was real until he felt the cold metal of handcuffs on his wrists behind him.

Enzo craned his neck around to the police officer. "What are you doing?"

"Lorenzo Michael Valenti," the officer said, "you're under arrest."

～～

NIGHTS ARE TORTURE WHEN sleep won't find you. Without the warmth of Scarlett's body in his bed, Francesco could not find rest. The sun had not yet risen, but Francesco didn't know what to do with himself. After changing into a pair of sweats and a T-shirt, he stumbled down to the main level of the restaurant where he brewed himself an espresso and popped his *Madame Butterfly* cassette into the stereo system before making his way into the kitchen.

Though the menu had been written, from appetizers to desserts to a list of after-dinner drinks, today, cooking wouldn't be work. Though the ingredients typically needed him to forge them together to make something beautiful, today, Francesco would let the grains of arborio rice and leaves of herbs guide him. Today, he hoped his art would heal him.

As he began to slice leaves of basil into thin green ribbons, he felt like he was on his own little island, isolated from the life he once knew with no foreseeable way back. To him, it didn't seem like there would be a ship coming to rescue him or bring him back to safety. Enzo had severed their relationship, permanently, and Scarlett had fled the scene. Could he blame her? Though he found it hard to believe that Scarlett, *his* Scarlett, would doubt him or his feelings towards her, he considered things through her lens. She had been hurt by his own flesh and blood. It was not so ridiculous that she might be searching for similarities among the brothers' differences.

Even though Francesco could find rationale in the way she felt, he couldn't understand the way things had panned out. Enzo had gotten his way, as he usually did. If Enzo couldn't have Scarlett, no one could. Enzo had set the wedge between Scarlett and Francesco and hammered it until it separated them completely. Had Francesco no strength to force the wedge out?

At the root of all Francesco's anger, though, lived a well of sadness. Scarlett had filled his life in the way he always wished a woman could. She had given him the home his heart always longed for. What would his life look like without her? Would it be nothing but pits and valleys and voids?

Francesco stopped chopping and set down his knife. He dusted the remnants of basil off his hands and moved to the back door where he heard yelling. The voice grew louder until Francesco swung the metal door to the alleyway open. "Fausto?"

Fausto's breath was visible in the air and his face was drawn with concern. "You have got to get a doorbell."

"What's up?"

Fausto caught his breath and his blue eyes looked as cold as stone. "Your brother's been arrested."

FRANCESCO HAD NEVER STEPPED foot inside of a jail before. He never imagined he would have to. He had exactly thirty thousand dollars left from the sum he had stolen, and he had all of said cash bundled tightly in a brown paper bag, stuffed into the pocket of his leather bomber jacket. With his hands stuffed into his pockets, fingers curled tightly around the money, his breath billowed in the dry air as he crossed the street. Despite the winter sun beating down, the building looked cold and mean on both the exterior and interior. He walked into the Manhattan Detention

Complex looking lost. When he spotted a correctional officer behind a desk, he went up to her.

"Can I help you?" the woman asked. She was burly and strong, probably stronger than Francesco.

"I'm here to bail out my brother."

"Name?"

"Lorenzo Michael Valenti."

Francesco waited as the woman flipped through a rolodex of index cards. "He's been booked. Still waiting on the arraignment."

"I'll wait."

"You might be here a while."

Francesco took a seat in one of the plastic chairs along the wall. "I'll wait."

And wait he did. He sat there in the plastic chair by the front doors, but as people walked in and out seemingly at all times, his eyes glossed over into nothingness. How had his brother taken so many wrong turns to end up in this place? How had Francesco not been strong enough to stop Enzo? Even though he knew it was Enzo's choices that had led him here, Francesco felt partly responsible.

Enzo had spent his life protecting Francesco; he'd thought it his role as the older brother. Francesco had never tried to protect Enzo because he didn't think Enzo needed protecting. But like him, Enzo was a man too. A man made of flesh and blood and clouded judgement. If they ever got past their differences, Francesco decided he wanted to be there for Enzo in ways he never was before.

Brotherhood was a bond, a knot so tight that even when they seemed close to unraveling completely, all it took was one tug to bring them back together. That was, at least, how Francesco saw it.

"Do you take cash?" Francesco asked as he pulled the bag out.

"Come on now, what kind of question is that?" the cashier joked through the glass divider between them.

Without hesitation, Francesco placed twenty-five thousand dollars on the counter and slid the bundles through the metal dip under the glass. His eyes lost focus as the woman undid the bundles and slid the bills into a money counting machine. Perhaps this was what he deserved for having stolen the money from Enzo in the first place. It was being repaid to Enzo, even if it was being used to pay for his sins.

Under a dark night sky, Francesco stood outside as the bitter air chilled him to the bone. He didn't care. He didn't want to spend a minute longer in that building than he had to. He waited for Enzo outside until he finally saw him jog down the steps, smoothing down his tie. They looked at each other in silence. It had been so long since they'd had a conversation that wasn't filled with animosity. Francesco was starting to forget what it was like before, when he and his brother were actually friends. The thought of it made his heart ache.

"How'd you know?" Enzo asked.

"Fausto came by this morning. I've been waiting in there all day." Francesco rocked on his heels. "What'd they get you for?"

Enzo averted his gaze, and the wind blew his jet hair around, one of the few times Francesco had seen his brother's hair unkempt. "They busted the game last night. Some rat was in on it. Left cash on the table so they'd have a reason to arrest me. I'm sure this will turn into something bigger once they do some more digging." Enzo blinked as the wind picked up and pierced his eyes. "Nothing I can't handle."

"Did it have anything to do with the money I—"

"No," Enzo said, cutting him off as he finally met his brother's gaze again. "The money you took was from the games. But I couldn't exactly tell them my kid brother took it, so I replenished it myself, out of my own account. Who knows. Maybe somebody set me up, or maybe I pissed somebody off so bad, they had it out for me. You don't get to the top without making enemies."

Francesco narrowed his gaze at Enzo, in wonderment more than anything else. Were their worlds so polar opposite that what Francesco considered to be the bottom, Enzo considered the top? "Right. Who knows." Worry bubbled in his chest, that Enzo had veered so far off track, he might never turn around and see that he had taken a wrong turn. Reaching in his pocket, now slimmer than before, he pulled out his keychain and freed one of the keys from the ring. "If you ever need me, or need a place to crash, or whatever it is, my place is yours."

Enzo stared at the key before taking it and slipping it into his pocket. "Damn right it is."

FORTY-SIX

UPPER WEST SIDE, NEW YORK

WINTER, 1986

Quiet is hard to find when you're actively searching for it. Though the air was still, save for the occasional taxi honking in the distance or siren wailing, Scarlett's mind was loud. She did some mental math, even though it wasn't her forte. It had been exactly forty-two hours since she'd left Francesco. Left him, their restaurant, and the future they were in the process of building together. The life she had only dared to dream of was just within her reach, and yet, she was willingly letting it slip through her fingers. Maybe her mother's words ran deeper than she thought. They had sewn themselves into the fabric of her makeup. Maybe she was letting this all slide away from her because she simply didn't believe she was worthy of the things that were just down the pike.

Quiet. She needed to listen.

She had shared her concerns with the saints above and asked the questions she wasn't sure anyone had the answers to. But *someone* had to respond to her inquiries. She took an inhale through her nose and exhaled through her lips. She didn't know exactly whose voice she should be listening for, or if she would hear anything at all. Instead, she felt a pressing on her chest.

Go.

Her eyes opened wide, adjusting to the darkness around her. Could she trust whatever pressing she felt? Was it her own instinct or was it some higher being guiding her?

Go.

She felt it again and by some sixth sense, she knew it would be the last time she would receive her answer. She sat up and shook Helen awake. "Helen?"

"Yeah?" Helen said through squinted eyes and messy hair.

"I have to go," Scarlett whispered, even though Helen was awake.

"Where?"

"I have to go home." Scarlett got out of the bed and slipped her feet into socks.

"Now? What time is it?"

"It doesn't matter. Go back to sleep, and I'll call you in the morning." After gathering her things, on the way out, she kissed the top of Helen's head.

"Hey," Helen called after her. "You think this is going to work out?"

"I'm delusional, Helen. Of course, I do."

Scarlett checked the time on her watch and decided to treat herself to a taxi. In the backseat of the cab, she tuned out Madonna's voice ringing from the radio and instead, focused her mind on what she would say to Francesco once she arrived. She would first ask him to tell her the truth. The whole truth, leaving nothing out. If they were going to work things out, they needed a solid foundation to build their lives on, and in her eyes, truth equaled solidity. Then, she would tell him how she truly felt about him. That even though he had disappointed her, not a moment passed where her love for him faltered. Where she questioned if her feelings were genuine. Because don't we always know truth when we see it? When we hear it and feel it in our bones? Scarlett knew that all she felt for Francesco, above all else, was love. All they needed to do was rebuild their trust in each other, and if they both were willing to, it could be done.

But once Scarlett had pushed her key into the knob and unlocked the door, raced up to the apartment, and paused only briefly to catch her breath, her mind was rendered blank when she saw Francesco again. When she took in how shell-shocked and gaunt he looked, how tired and weary. Her chest felt tight and heavy all the same, her breath weak and shallow as she wrung her fingers.

"Hi," she managed to get out.

Francesco sat on the edge of the sofa, his elbows resting on the tops of his thighs, a cigarette between his fingers. He lifted his eyes to hers, gave her a nod, before glancing back down at the ground.

"W-what have you been up to?"

Francesco let out a humorless laugh and looked at her again. "Nothing. I haven't been up to anything."

Scarlett moved around the coffee table and planted herself next to him on the couch. She caught sight of the staggering number of cigarette butts in the ashtray before finding his eyes. Tears pressed against her own as the tip of her nose stung with heat. She did her best to remember the things she had wanted to say to him, but no words would come. "I had this whole speech planned, but I can't remember any of it."

Francesco looked at her, long and hard, before leaning in. "You're here."

"Yeah, I am." She slid her hand into his, her previous suspicions about his true intentions melting away.

"I think that says a whole lot." Together, they searched for words that could not be spoken aloud. Hidden meanings in glances and breaths and expressions. Maybe they had their own language that didn't involve words at all. "We don't have to talk about anything tonight," he whispered. "Alright?"

Francesco stood and helped her up, their eye contact unwavering. Hands intertwined, he led her to their kitchenette. As he gathered the first few ingredients, she didn't bother to ask what he would make. Scarlett recognized the pieces necessary to craft one of their favorite guilty pleasures. *Mozzarella in carrozza.* Without a word, only faint swells and lulls of opera in the background, he stood behind her and taught her every step of the process. The assembling, the breading, the frying, all of it. She never got her hands dirty when he cooked, but tonight, she was all in. As they laid each piece in the hot oil, she was completely absorbed in the moment. Francesco's arms around her, cooking together, getting her hands in the food right along with him, understanding this piece of himself – this was her happiness.

She turned the burner off after he pulled the last piece out of the frying pan. Funny, she thought, that they had cooked together despite neither of them seeming to be hungry. She held his face and turned him towards her, drawing him closer until his arms wrapped around her and he held her tight against his body. She studied his face, tracing his cheeks with her thumbs. Where was the truth? The answers to her many questions?

He kissed her like he was hungry for her until they stumbled back into the bedroom. It felt like the very beginning, like the first time they had kissed. Back when she wasn't thinking about how being with Francesco would change his relationship with Enzo, back when they didn't have any cares in the world except for realizing how much they wanted each other. She knew they had nothing figured out. The only thing they were sure of was their love for each other that seemed to triumph over every obstacle that had been put in their path. Everything else fell away as he rolled on top of her and pulled her shirt overhead. He was moving fast, but she stopped him.

"I want you to savor me," she said, pressing her index finger against his lips. "And I want to savor you."

THOUGH JUST MERE HOURS ago had been a bubble of oblivion, as morning broke and soft beams of sunlight peeked through the sheer curtains, Scarlett knew they couldn't run from reality any longer. Daylight had arrived, and so had their time to talk about all the things they had pushed aside the night before. Wide awake, Scarlett stared at the ceiling as she ran her fingers through his curls while he remained asleep on her chest. Finally, as if a gift, her thoughts returned. Trust. Truth. These were the things they had to discuss before they could get back to business as usual.

He started to stir, but he didn't look up at her. She heard him breathing heavily. She could feel his chest rapidly rising and falling against her. Why wasn't he saying anything? She turned him over and he grabbed his chest. He looked up at her, but he didn't say anything. He couldn't. He gasped for air. Panic coursed through her body and her ears began to ring as she watched his own pain take him over. *No,* she thought. *Please, no.* She had noticed the times here and there when Francesco would rub his chest or appear short-winded, but each time she asked, he brushed her off. Now, as beads of sweat formed on his forehead and his tawny skin went white, she cursed herself for not pushing the subject further. She thought her own body might betray her and go faint too, but she couldn't. She had to save him.

"Fran," she yelled out his name, holding onto his shoulders. "Francesco!"

She jumped out of bed, reached for the phone and with shaking hands, dialed 9-1-1. Everything was a blur as she told the operator what was happening and gave them their address. Her own breath caught in her throat as she watched him clutch onto his chest and try as hard as he could to get air into his lungs. The worst part about it all, there wasn't a thing she could do to help him, to make the pain go away.

"Fran," she climbed back into bed, "you're gonna be okay. I'm right here." Frantic and clammy, her tears fell onto him and wet his shirt. "You're gonna be okay," she yelled again because she thought if she said it enough, maybe it would be true.

As she waited for the paramedics for what felt like forever, she called Enzo to tell him she was fairly certain his brother was having a heart attack. Then she reached over to her nightstand and pulled out the wooden rosary beads Helen had given her. She wrapped them around Francesco's hands and moved her face close to his. "Please don't leave me."

<hr />

SHE FOLLOWED THE PARAMEDICS outside, keeping her eyes on Francesco. He lay flat on a stretcher. His eyes fluttered closed, but she could still see the rise and fall of his chest. A sea of neighbors filled the streets and sidewalks as they opened the back of the ambulance and lifted Francesco in. She looked around, like she was expecting someone, anyone to help her or tell her what comes next.

Enzo's Cadillac sped down the street and came to a sudden halt as he pulled up to the curb. She had never been so happy to see him.

"Get in the car," he yelled out the window.

They followed the ambulance closely. Bright, blinding lights lit their path as she settled into the thick air between her and Enzo. All she could think about was what Francesco was feeling, thinking, as he lay there under the cold florescent lights.

"What happened?" Enzo finally broke the silence.

"As soon as he woke up, he was breathing real heavy. Then he was holding onto his chest like he was in so much pain," she wailed. She was unraveling. "And there was nothing I could do to make it go away. I don't understand. He was fine last night. He's always been fine; he's still young. He's never been sick before."

"*Minchia,* Scarlett." Enzo shook his head. "The kid lives hard. He's been smoking since he was thirteen. Used to drink like a fish. I don't know about now. I don't know."

She stared out the window. She didn't say a word, because nothing either of them said would make anything better.

"Stop crying, would you?" Enzo looked at her. "Listen to me, you wanna be his wife? You better toughen up. In our business, in our town, you gotta be tough."

"You don't think I've been *tough* through everything that's gone on this last year?"

"You and I both know it's nothing but a front." He pointed at her. "You have to be strong for him. You have to take care of him. You hear me? He's my only brother."

"I know."

"Promise me."

"I promise," she yelled. She tried to will herself to stop crying, but she couldn't.

"What is it?"

"You remember when you first met me? You asked me if I had anybody I'd die for?"

"Yeah."

"It's him." Her voice broke as the colored lights of the ambulance blurred into a haze of red. "It's him. I'd die for him, and the worst part is, he doesn't even know it."

Enzo ran his hand along his angular jaw, his muscles clenching and releasing. "So tell him, Scar. As long as he's still breathing by the time we get there, you tell him."

CHAPTER

FORTY-SEVEN

NEW YORK, NEW YORK

WINTER, 1986

A big, glaring sign read *no smoking*, but Enzo continued to defiantly puff away on a cigarette. Scarlett needed one too. She needed something, anything to numb the way she felt, but the last thing she wanted was to get kicked out of the hospital. They had taken Francesco back into the emergency room as soon as the ambulance pulled into New York Presbyterian. She and Enzo had been sitting in the crowded waiting room ever since. It felt like it had been an eternity since the morning, but Scarlett knew the look on Francesco's face while he was struggling to breathe would be forever etched in her memory.

"Sir," a nurse said as she approached them, "we've already asked you once. Please put out your cigarette or we're going to have to ask you to leave."

"Un-fucking-believable." Enzo stared the nurse down as he dropped his cigarette into a plastic cup of water.

"Is he okay?" Scarlett asked.

"On the mend. Come with me."

Francesco looked older than his thirty years. His skin, normally a golden bronze, had gone pale. His broad body was swallowed up by the hospital gown. As soon as she entered the room, she went to his side and took his hands in hers. She could tell he wanted to say something to her, but the doctor turned around and began speaking.

"What we've found so far from the EKG is that he's had a mild heart attack. We're going to be doing multiple rounds of bloodwork over the next twelve to twenty-four hours, as well as a CT scan. Once we have a more complete diagnosis, we'll determine the damage done and the course of treatment, or the possibility of any surgeries necessary," the doctor said, flipping through a manilla folder.

"He's so young to have these kinds of problems," Scarlett said.

"Many factors can cause these types of issues," the doctor explained. "Stress, poor diet, smoking, family history of heart problems, the list goes on. Moving forward, we'll do some more regular monitoring and get him on some medication. As for lifestyle changes, you'll need to add in some regular exercise, improve your diet, and absolutely no more smoking. I'll provide you with paperwork; it'll explain everything you can do to mitigate the risk of another heart attack."

"Okay," Scarlett said, though she had a hard time accepting the cold, hard facts the doctor provided.

"I'll be back in about an hour. We'll do another bout of bloodwork this afternoon, and if you need a nurse, just press this button." The doctor pointed to a call button near the bed before disappearing.

"Francesco," she whimpered as soon as they were alone. It all leapt out of her, the fear, the angst, all the worry. He was patient with her as she lay beside him and held him as closely as she could without disturbing the tubes and monitors connected to him. "We're going to do everything the doctor says."

Francesco was quiet before he answered. "Last night, when you came back, what did you want to talk about?"

"It's not important. I don't even remember."

"It is important." Francesco shifted to get a better look at her. "Just because this happened doesn't mean all our problems disappeared all of a sudden."

"We don't have any problems, Fran. I love you, and I don't want to lose you. But there is something I need to tell you, and I wish I would've told you sooner." Scarlett held his face, her fingers grazing the scruff on his chin. "Enzo once told me he would die for you. You know? That's how much he loves you. That's real love, when you find somebody you'd die for. You're that person for me, Fran. I never thought I'd love someone like that. I never wanted to. But all I want to do right now is take your pain and make it mine. That's how much I love you, and I'm so sorry I let you think otherwise." She leaned down and kissed his cheeks, letting her lips linger on his skin. "I can't imagine my life without you. You're everything to me."

Scarlett waited for his response. She thought this would ease him. That his worried expression would fall, and his shoulders would relax, and his smile and the glint in his eyes would return. None of her expectations panned out. Instead, his lips formed a thin line and his furrowed brows only deepened. "I can't do this to you."

"Do what?"

"I know you love me, Scar. And you have no idea how much I love you. But I can't expect you to marry me when I'm like this. I'm sick. I got my *Papà*'s heart. I don't want you to marry me when I don't know how long I'm gonna be around."

"I don't care if you're sick. I'd rather have you sick than not at all."

"Scarlett, you're twenty-four years old. You have a life to live. I don't want you to spend it taking care of me."

"I want to spend it taking care of you. I want to spend my life with you, even if you're sick. And we'll get you better."

"You don't know that. I don't know if they can fix me. I knew something was wrong. Been having chest pains for the last two years. I didn't want to face it. But me dealing with it is one thing. I don't want to put this on you."

Scarlett backed up to create space between them. "What are you saying, Francesco?"

Francesco's eyes searched her face before he looked away, out the door into nothingness. "I need some time alone, Scar. I need to think about everything."

"Fran, we can get through this."

"You can." He looked her squarely in the eyes. "I don't know if I can. My whole life, I did whatever Enzo wanted me to do. These last few months, I've been doing the same thing, but I replaced Enzo with you. And I don't resent you or regret it, Scar, but I need to think about what *I* want. What's best for me. And it's not because I don't care about you. It's the other way around. I care about you too much to marry you and promise you that I'll be with you for life, only for my own to be cut short."

"That might not be the case. We don't know what the future holds."

"Exactly. We don't know."

To camouflage her tears, so as not to burden Francesco any more than he already was, she stood and turned to find her purse. "If you want me to leave, I will."

"I do," he said without hesitation. The irony was not lost on her, as she rushed out of the hospital, her vision blurred by her tears, that those were the precise words he was to utter at the altar.

CHAPTER

FORTY-EIGHT

NEW YORK, NEW YORK

WINTER, 1986

Three days had passed with no contact. Since they had met, this was the longest Scarlett had gone without seeing or talking to Francesco. She looked around their almost-done restaurant and felt a sense of hopelessness. What would be the point of finishing the work now? Would they have to co-exist as professionals, but go about their personal lives separately? Maybe she would deem her small savings lost and let Francesco have the restaurant to himself, should he still want it. She didn't know if she could bear to see Francesco on a regular basis and not remain in love with him.

Seated on the floor of the dining room to be, she drew a bottle of vodka to her lips. She had done this many times before with Julie and Fausto, though tonight, the clear liquid tasted dangerous. When would she stop doing the things she knew she should not do?

She jumped up when she heard a noise coming from the front door. Grunting, followed by sounds of the lock being opened. She had no other weapon than the bottle in her hand, so she waited, heart thudding, breath jagged and staccato. She dropped her arm that had been poised to take action. "Enzo?"

"*Gesu Christo mio*," Enzo yelled as he jumped back. They stared at each other as they steadied their breath, though their matched expressions of simultaneous confusion and surprise remained. "What the hell are you doing here?"

"Me? What are *you* doing here? And how do you have a key to my place?"

Enzo locked the door behind him and shrugged off his coat, laying it over the back of a bar stool. "Fran gave it to me," he said, his tone making it clear that he wouldn't be offering up further explanation. "Why aren't you at the hospital?"

Scarlett's dark brows shot up like two rockets. She adjusted the headband in her hair and pulled the elastic waistband of her sweatpants up to her waistline. "He didn't tell you?"

"Tell me what?"

Scarlett sighed as she moved from the entryway into the bar, the bottle dangling from her fingertips. "I did what you told me to do. What I *wanted* to do. I told him I would die for him." Now behind the bar, she racked the bottle and instead, plucked out a half-empty bottle of whiskey and slid it to Enzo. "And he asked me to leave. Said he needed some time alone. He's not sure he wants to marry me anymore."

Palms resting on the bar top, Enzo let out a dry laugh. "You being serious?"

Scarlett nodded as she rested her elbows on the bar and cradled her chin in her hands.

"Kid finally got everything he wanted. A woman who loves him so much she can't even see straight, and a place to call his own. And what does he do?" Enzo unscrewed the top from the whiskey bottle. "Throws it all away."

"I don't know," Scarlett said. "I've been thinking about it. *Constantly.* I'm sure he's shaken up from what happened to him, but he never wanted to get married before. Maybe he changed his mind, and this is his way out."

Enzo cocked a brow at Scarlett. "You're thinking too much."

Scarlett shook herself out of her thoughts. "I'm sorry, can you please tell me what you're doing here? I don't think you answered my question."

Enzo took a sip of whiskey and exhaled through his stiff jaw. "Did Fran tell you I got arrested a few days ago?" Scarlett's mouth fell open, but Enzo continued before she could say anything. "Right. Well, I did, and then I've been fooling around with this broad that came in the restaurant a few weeks ago, and, anyways…" Enzo trailed off and looked into Scarlett's eyes. "Claudia kicked me out. Guess she finally had enough."

Scarlett swallowed her mix of emotions. Guilt. Worry. Relief. Jealousy. All the familiars when it came to Enzo. "She did?"

Enzo slid onto a barstool. "Asked me for a divorce. Told me she was going to take the kids with her wherever she went." Enzo picked at the corner of the label on the whiskey bottle. "I can't even blame her. Got no way to defend myself. Even if I promise to change, she and I both know I won't. Maybe this is what happens when you marry somebody for all the wrong reasons. I guess I really am a bad guy." He looked at Scarlett again, his momentary expression of guilt evaporated. "Fran told me I could crash here if I needed to, and since your two best friends decided to move into your old apartment the minute you and Fran were gone, I came here. Does that answer your question?"

After everything Enzo had put her and Francesco through in the last few months, Scarlett was taken aback by the pang of affection that hit her in the chest. She studied Enzo's face like a student reads a textbook. "Do you know what everyone says about you? Including your brother? That underneath everything you do that none of us understand, you have a good heart."

Enzo laughed, though his eyes appeared sad. "That's what they used to say?"

"I don't know what it is about you, Enzo. You've put your brother and me through hell these last few months, and before that, you completely broke my heart." Scarlett blinked a few times, letting her words hit him where they needed to. "But I couldn't hate you even if I tried."

"You tried to hate me?"

"I seriously didn't like you. For a long time. And some of the things you do are *so* maddening. But I still don't think you're a bad guy. And I don't know why."

Enzo's gaze hardened. "Because you understand me. Funny, isn't it? If Claudia had asked me for a divorce a year ago, we might not be sitting here right now. Things might've turned out different."

"They wouldn't have. Because I don't think I do understand you, Enzo." Scarlett leaned her arms on the bar again, so she and Enzo were eye to eye. "You kicking us out with no warning, blocking our permits, putting ideas in my head that Fran is someone he's not, I don't understand any of that."

"You don't?" Enzo asked. When Scarlett, wide-eyed and curious, shook her head, he leaned in. "When I left *Napoli,* my *mamma* was hysterical. Not because I was leaving; I wasn't her favorite. She knew one day Fran would follow me. Before I left, I made a promise to her. Not that I'd make sure Fran was successful, or that he'd have a great life, or that he'd be happy. I promised my mother that I would protect her son.

"You know I'd die for my brother, but that doesn't mean I want to," Enzo said. "As soon as he met you, Scar, I knew it was different. I would see the way he would look at you when he didn't think I was watching. I know I hurt you. Bad." Enzo slid his hand across the marble until his fingertips grazed Scarlett's. "And it was only natural that I question your inten-tions with my brother. You trying to make me regret letting you go was one thing. But my brother getting his heart broken in the process, I couldn't let it happen." Enzo sat up straight again and let out an exhale. "So I tested you. Cut off your source of income first. Nothing rips a couple apart like money problems. Then you two stuck it out. Followed each other to your new place. I blocked your permits. Paid your crew to not show up. Told you to your face that my brother stole a quarter million dollars from me.

"And guess what? You're still here. None of it worked. I wanted to make sure you really love him." Enzo ran his tongue across his bottom lip and began to nod. "And I guess you really do."

Gears shifted in Scarlett's mind as she started to see Enzo from a different perspective. Though she had her fair share of frustrations and resentments towards him, perhaps she never understood him in a true sense. Had she known the obstacles he placed in her way were done from a place of love rather than his ego, maybe she would've reacted entirely different. "You could've just asked me. We could've avoided all of this." Scarlett waved her hand through the air. "But why would you chase me when you knew your brother liked me first?"

Nostalgia clouded Enzo's eyes. "Because you used to look at me the way Fran looked at you." Remembering seized them. "I knew you were sort of nuts about me. I was sort of nuts about you too. Sometimes I think I still am."

"Still are?"

"I'm free now," he whispered. His face looked boyish with un-merited hope.

A new lens fell over Scarlett's eyes. Pity. Scarlett knew his offer was empty. Even in his darkest hour, Enzo couldn't lose. "You don't like to fold, do you? You like to bluff all the way to the end."

"Spoken like a true poker player."

Though she laughed with him, a poignancy hit Scarlett in the deepest places as she fell back down to reality. She had endured all of this, and what did she have to show for it? Her eyes traveled the length of the bar, and though she could envision it filled with glamorous people, laughing, drinking, talking, it felt like nothing more than a silly figment of her imagination. Here, she had the chance she had craved for so long. The spotlight she wanted to shine on her had been lit; all she had to do was step into center stage. What if she took this chance and failed? It would be easier not to try, though wouldn't there always be a part of her that wondered? "I don't know what to do, Enz. I was so close. *We* were so close."

"To what?"

"To everything I ever wanted. Marrying your brother, running the restaurant with him, having a place to call our own. Not to mention, proving my mother wrong. And you know what's funny, Enzo? All of that, and I still feel like *me*. Like the girl you met a year ago. I guess my mother was right. I'm not cut out to be the boss of anything. Maybe it's easier this way, you know? I won't try, and I won't have to be disappointed when I fail."

"You're talking crazy, Scar—"

"I can't do it, Enz," she yelled. "I can't run this place without him."

"Who said you have to run it? All you have to do is get it ready to open."

Scarlett's mind flooded with her running to-do list. Get the menus printed. Finish purchasing kitchen equipment and glassware and linens. Hire staff, both front and back of house. Not to mention training said staff. A monumental undertaking. "You think I can get this place ready to open? Alone?"

"Sure I do." Enzo looked at Scarlett through his dark, fringy lashes. "But it doesn't matter what I think. It matters what *you* think."

She scoffed. Scarlett knew she had the tangible, physical skills necessary to operate a restaurant. But did she have the guts? The nerve, to prove to herself, her mother, the Valenti brothers, and all of New York that she had earned her rightful place as the owner? At once, she understood why her mother hadn't made a better attempt at motherhood. When you dream of doing something, the potential to fail seems far more realistic than success. But she knew how much her mother regretted her choices. Scarlett didn't want to live with regret. She didn't want *what ifs* to haunt her for the rest of her days. Maybe success lived on the other side of fear. "Think bigger, right?"

"Nah. Think smarter." He cupped her cheek with his hand before backing away.

"Hey, Enzo," Scarlett called after him.

He turned his heel. "Yeah?"

With hands dug into her pockets, Scarlett shrugged. "I know you must be going through a lot with Claudia, and the kids. I don't know what's going to happen between me and your brother, but if you ever need me, I'm here."

Enzo's face softened as he approached Scarlett. He wrapped his arm around her shoulders and kissed her forehead. "That's very Italian of you."

"I hate to admit this," Scarlett said, creating space between them, "but you taught me a lot about being Italian."

"How about that?" Enzo walked away, this time, for good. "You got a couch upstairs?"

Scarlett was so engrossed in the moment, she had almost forgotten Enzo would be staying the night. As he disappeared into the next room and she heard his footsteps getting further away, she yelled after him. "There are extra blankets in the hall closet. The heat only goes up to seventy-one." Then, she muttered under her breath, "Make yourself at home, Enzo."

CHAPTER

FORTY-NINE

LITTLE ITALY, NEW YORK

WINTER, 1986

"You can have her," Enzo said to Scarlett. He put his hand on the small of Julie's back and moved her forward.

"You're trading me like a baseball player," Julie sassed back, arching a brow at Enzo before reaching Scarlett.

"What about Fausto?" Scarlett asked, though she knew it was a big request.

"What about me?" Fausto said, joining their trio, but Enzo put his arm out and blocked Fausto from moving in any further.

"Until the doors to my place are permanently closed, he's mine," Enzo answered.

"Who knew you were so possessive?" Fausto teased.

"But," Enzo raised his index finger, "I'll compromise. He can help you get things running while I get back to my place, alright?"

"Fair enough." Scarlett grabbed Fausto's arm and tugged him towards her. "Thank you for your generosity, Enzo."

With hands on his hips, Enzo studied the three of them. "You three get to work. I'm going to check on Fran."

Scarlett trailed behind him as Enzo reached the front door. "Will you tell him I asked for him? Or call me from the hospital? Just, something. I miss him and I hate not knowing what's going on."

Enzo put his hands on Scarlett's shoulders. "He asked for space."

"Right," she said as he retreated. "Right. Well, thanks again for sharing them with me."

With Enzo out the door, Fausto went behind the bar, brewed three espressos, and tuned the radio to Z100. On the counter, Julie spread out three catalogs.

"They have a whole catalog for table linens?" Scarlett said as she flipped through the glossy pages.

Julie read the less-than-thrilled expression on Scarlett's face and laughed. "Pretend you're shopping for clothes." She moved another catalog in front of Scarlett. "This one is for glassware, and the other one is for staff uniforms."

"Speaking of staff," Fausto said as he turned around. "I invited a few people over. They should be here by one."

"One thing you should know about Fausto," Julie chimed in as she leaned her head against Scarlett's shoulder, "his version of few is our version of many."

Scarlett took a deep breath in and out, attempting to shake off how overwhelmed she felt, and gave her friends a smile. "Shall we pick out some bar rags?"

An hour later, they were making headway. Scarlett found herself to be incredibly decisive when it came to the restaurant, knowing by instinct what to choose. As their ashtray filled with cigarette butts and the radio grew louder, things were being ticked off her list one by one. Fausto called in her orders to the various vendors, Julie helped make a list for the bar stock, and Scarlett did a rough estimate on how many frying pans and sets of tongs she needed to purchase. By the time their first *guest* walked in the door, Scarlett felt like she had made more progress in the last few hours than she had in the last few months.

"Santino," Fausto said warmly as he walked with open arms to greet the lanky Italian man covered in tattoos standing in the entryway. "Come on in. Meet Scarlett, the owner. Scarlett, this is Santino, your very talented new sous chef."

Scarlett exchanged a worried expression as she extended her arm with hesitancy to greet Santino. As Santino moved in further to get to know the space, Scarlett huddled next to Fausto. "I don't think I should hire anyone for the kitchen, do you? I mean, isn't that Fran's thing?"

Fausto inhaled. "I hate to bring up his circumstance, but I don't think he's in that frame of mind right now, honey. I think you need to take the reins on this one."

"What if they don't get along? Fran mentioned something about chefs and egos."

Fausto's head fell back in laughter. "Are you not yet used to Italian men and their egos?" This made Scarlett join in his laughter. "Look, he knows he's not the man in charge. He's here to support Francesco, whenever he returns."

"Thanks." Scarlett squeezed Fausto's hand and made a stop behind the bar before approaching Santino again. In front of him, she fanned out the polaroids she had taken of Francesco's dishes and the menu he had written by hand. "I don't have any of his recipe cards. I don't think he even *has* recipe cards for these dishes. But do you think you can work off this?"

Santino's greenish blue eyes scanned the length of the page, then the photos. "I'll take this with me to the market, gather all the ingredients, and when I come back, we'll see. Good?"

Scarlett had to work hard to understand his accent which was heavier and more punctuated than Francesco and Enzo's, but she nodded. "That's perfect. Thank you."

By the time Scarlett returned to the entryway, she heard a cacophony of chatter coming from the dining room. She turned the corner to see what the noise was all about. About ten or so people filled the small space. When Fausto spotted her through the crowd, he put two fingers in his mouth and whistled, causing everyone to fall quiet.

"Everyone," he said, splitting the crowd in two as he joined Scarlett, "meet your new boss. This is Scarlett, the owner."

The more Fausto referred to her as the owner, the more it felt real. Determination roared inside her chest like a lion. She was going to do this, if not to prove her mother or Enzo wrong, if not to show Francesco how much she loved him, but for herself. For the girl she once was who dreamt of a life beyond the parameters of her Manhattan neighborhood, for the girl she was not so long ago who didn't believe she deserved anything of the likes of which now was before her, for the parts of her that still doubted whether or not she was good enough to accomplish something of this scale. No, it wouldn't be easy. Sleep would become a thing of the past and worry would become a constant. But wouldn't it be worth it? This lifelong underdog joining the ranks of those who came before her?

"Fausto," Scarlett whispered with a smile still planted on her face, "where did all these people come from?"

"Fifteen years in the business, and people run when I call. They've all got some sort of experience, but they'll need to learn how you want things done here at your place."

"Let me guess. You're going to train them the way you trained me?"

"Absolutely not." Fausto squeezed Scarlett's shoulders. "You are."

Scarlett froze as Fausto walked away, leaving all twenty eyeballs in the room glued squarely on her. She shook off whatever doubt was trying to climb its way up telling her that these seasoned professionals had nothing to learn from *her*. Instead, she made her way over to a table stacked with dishes. "Hi everyone. As Fausto said, I'm Scarlett. I'm going to want to get to know all your names by heart, but that'll take time. I hope you'll be patient with me." Her shoulders relaxed at their polite laughter. "Amanti isn't going to be like any other restaurant on Mulberry. We're current. Maybe even ahead of our time. Our food is designed to be extremely modern. Fresh spins on old classics. Unexpected flavors that contrast one another. As for the service, we'll want it to have the same feel. Warm and inviting, but elegant and sophisticated. Fine dining, but to a higher standard. But we have to start with the basics." Scarlett picked up a bowl and winked at Fausto, who watched from the entryway. At once, she stepped into the spotlight of her own stage as if it were the precise spot she had been destined for. "Meet your archnemesis. The bowl."

CHAPTER

FIFTY

"Come on, Fran," Enzo complained. "You can't keep hiding away like this. You had *surgery* and you didn't tell a soul? What if something went wrong?"

"Nothing did," Francesco protested. "It was a stent, not open heart."

Enzo exhaled through his nose and pursed his lips. "We've gotta get you out of here."

Francesco glared up at Enzo. "You think I want to be in here?"

"Yeah, I do." Enzo studied his younger brother. Gaunt, pale, thinning out, the hospital seemed to be sucking the life out of him. What more would this cold, sterile building take of his once so vibrant sibling? "Are you scared to get married? Be honest with me."

Francesco scoffed and looked out into the distance before glancing up at Enzo again. "Yes. You happy now? There you have it."

Enzo sank down to the edge of the hospital bed. "Why? Is it her?"

"It's not her. But it is, too. When we got engaged, I told her I would probably disappoint her, and she told me I never could. And then I did, when she found out I stole from you, and she left. Ran away and didn't tell me where she was going. I'm going to do something else somewhere down the line to disappoint her. What if she does it again?"

"She came back, didn't she?"

"This time."

"Fran—"

"And it's your fault too." Francesco cut him off. "You hated being married."

"You're not me, Fran. And besides, you asked Scarlett to marry you because you love her. I proposed to Claudia because her parents owned a beautiful corner building."

"You're a real piece of shit."

"I'm trying to have a nice moment with you, alright? Don't ruin it. You don't think I know what I am?"

Francesco softened. "How you holding up with everything?"

Enzo focused on the speckled pattern of the floor tiles. "It is what it is. The case, Claudia, the kids. I'm more worried about you than anything."

"And I'm worried about you. You don't look like yourself."

"Then what do I look like?"

"Like you actually regret some of the things you did."

"I do. Ever since the arrest, hell, even before that, I've been replaying everything in my head. What if I had been a better husband? What if I would've listened to you more often? Maybe I wouldn't feel like I've lost everything."

"You're gonna be fine. And you didn't lose everything. You've still got me."

"Even though I've been an asshole to you for the last eight years?"

"You've been an asshole for *more* than eight years, Enz. But you know what? I wouldn't change a damn thing about you."

Enzo rolled his eyes and calmed his irritation, which his younger brother always knew how to stir up. "Do you miss her? Since you've been in here and you haven't talked to her, do you still think about her?"

Francesco licked his lips and rested his head back on the pillow. "All the time. Constantly."

"Constantly," Enzo repeated. "That's the same word she used. She's thinking about you constantly too."

"You talked to her about me?"

"I put her through every test I could think of, and she passed every single one of them. She loves you, kid. She *believes* in you. And you need to accept it. You've got it all, Fran. The woman, the restaurant, the talent, and someday, you'll have the kids to complete the picture. Don't throw it away. I mean it. Don't be like me, because you'll regret it."

Though he hesitated, Francesco couldn't hide his curiosity. "What has she been doing?"

"She's working hard to make you happy."

"What does that mean?"

"You'll see."

"What the hell?"

Enzo bent down and kissed the top of his brother's head. "If they don't release you tomorrow, I'll make a few calls."

"Discharge, not release. I'm not in jail."

Enzo laughed as he patted Francesco's cheek, though an aching loneliness filled his chest. Staring down his nose at his brother, confined to a plastic bed, Enzo felt like a child again. He wished there was someone stronger than him. Someone to guide him or to take charge every once in a while. Enzo was afraid, a feeling he thought himself immune to. Afraid that he had wasted precious time. Scared that he had been the cause of his brother's heart attack. Terrified that he might lose the one person he loved more than anyone else. Tears pressed against the back of his eyes, though he wouldn't let them fall. "*Mamma* and *Papà* are gone, but I know they'd be ashamed of how I treated you. *I'm* ashamed of how I treated you. I wasted all that time not speaking to you over *what?* My pride? And I almost made you lose the love of your life." Enzo looked down at his loafers. A tear fell from his eyes and landed on the shiny patent leather. "We're all we've got, kid. You have to get better, you hear me?"

"You know what's funny? All this time, you thought Scarlett was the one tearing us apart. But I think you and I were already further apart than we realized."

Enzo gave a smile. "You saying you think in some weird, twisted way, she brought us back together?"

Francesco appeared to be fighting his own emotion. He squeezed Enzo's hand. "Look at us, Enz. Look at us now."

Enzo ruffled his brother's hair before exiting the hospital, trying to shake off the heavy feeling in his chest. He loosened the scarf around his neck. Winter was about to break, and spring was on the horizon. He let himself into a phone booth and dialed a number he now knew by heart.

"Fausto?" Enzo said into the receiver, though he had a hard time deciphering whose voice it was. Scarlett and Julie were singing along, badly, to George Michael's "Careless Whisper." "Let me talk to Scar, please," he said, louder this time.

A few moments later, after some rustling and the radio being turned down, Scarlett's voice filled Enzo's ear. "How is he?"

"He had surgery last night. Nothing major, but he's doing fine."

"Did you tell him I asked for him?"

"He misses you. He's thinking about you as much as you're thinking about him." Enzo smiled, able to picture Scarlett's hopeful, happy face. "I'm hoping he gets out of there tomorrow."

"Tomorrow?" Scarlett went quiet. "Do you think he'll come home? Here?"

Enzo took a deep breath and looked around the glittering city around him, full of hopes and dreams and second chances. "If I have any say in the matter, he will. And let's not forget, Scar. He's got no place else to go."

CHAPTER

FIFTY-ONE

LITTLE ITALY, NEW YORK

WINTER, 1986

It surprised Scarlett how calm she felt speaking to her staff, which, in the last two days, had grown by ten more people. She also felt at ease giving instructions, though this was her first go at any form of leadership. Maybe, she thought, this had been her destination all along, and it simply took her longer than most to find her path. Or maybe, she was just distracting herself with her newfound career to avoid thinking about the fact that her estranged fiancé could walk through the doors at any given moment.

Enzo had called more than two hours ago giving her the news that Francesco was being discharged. She had zipped around the apartment, fluffing pillows, changing the sheets, and placing his *Turandot* record in the player, tuning it to the lowest volume setting so it would be playing when he walked in. The television had been tuned to NBC so that, judging from the time on her watch, by the time he got home, *Cheers* would be on. She hoped he would settle right back into their apartment and feel as at home there as she did.

"Scarlett," one of the newest hires, Mateo, said as he found Scarlett in the dining room. His arms were full of what appeared to be books and magazines. "The printing company dropped off samples of different menus. Julie asked me to give them to you."

Scarlett took the stack from him, eager to scan over the different options. Would this be yet another major decision she made without Francesco?

"If you need anything else, I'll be at the bar," Mateo said. He was one of the more seasoned employees, and Fausto had recommended that Mateo should lead the bar. As usual, Scarlett trusted her friend's instinct.

"Thanks, Mateo," Scarlett said. Arms still full, she turned her attention to the front-of-house staff who were deep in concentration, practicing their setup of the dining tables. Scarlett scanned them over, looking for any details that needed her attention. She bent down and whispered to one of the younger girls, "That's perfect." The girl, Kelly, or was it Katie – Scarlett was still working on the names – smiled back in appreciation. Her head on a swivel, Scarlett continued to glance over her employees' shoulders. She bent down and tapped one of the boys on the back. "A little tip," Scarlett started. "Kneel down on the ground, that way you can tell if everything is aligned. Obviously, we won't do that when we have guests in the dining room, but pre and post-service, we will."

"You got it," he said, already kneeling down.

Satisfied, Scarlett made her way down the center aisle, though her footsteps came to a full stop when she saw the face she would forever look for in a crowded room. Her hands went clammy, and she almost lost her grip on the menus.

"Francesco," she said as she rushed towards him. She tuned out everything going on around her and though she was filled at the sight of him, a sadness grabbed her heart when she saw how lost he looked. How pale his skin had gone and how, after even just a little more than a week away from his own kitchen, he seemed to have lost so much weight. Still, she dropped the menus to the ground and threw her arms around his shoulders. "You came back," she said, more to herself than him.

He put his hands on her waist, making space between them as he scanned the restaurant. How strange it must've felt to him to see the place he left vacant now filled with life and action and the beginnings of something great. Scarlett exchanged a glance with Enzo as Francesco watched the staff. Enzo gave her an encouraging wink.

Francesco turned on his heel. "What is all this?"

With a smile, Scarlett took a deep breath, her shoulders rising and falling. "I made us a restaurant." Scarlett felt as if she were looking into a mirror. They both began to cry through their laughter, shoulders bobbing up and down as Francesco took her in his arms and kissed the sides and tops of her head. Finally, he found her lips.

"Why would you ask me to do this with you when you could've done it all by yourself?"

She grazed his face with her fingers. She felt like the rope which tied their hearts together was tugging them closer together. "Because I do need you."

Evidently feeling like the third wheel, Enzo bowed out. "I'll be at the bar. Drinking. Heavily."

Scarlett laughed as she watched him walk away, though she turned her attention to Francesco. "I didn't think I could do this all on my own, but I had to try. I was worried you wouldn't come back, but I thought if you did, I wanted you to see that we made the right decision. That we can do this."

Francesco leaned his forehead against hers. "You *know* me."

Scarlett understood what he meant. It wasn't just that they clicked or had amazing chemistry. Scarlett knew the most complex parts of him without him having to explain those pieces of himself. She understood him, whole and complete. She knew, deep down, he had pushed her away out of love. In denying himself happiness, he was putting hers first. But she also knew that since he had returned, he must've believed he was healthy enough to have a future with her. "I do know you. And I know you're going to be just fine. And we're going to open this restaurant together, and get married, have a couple of babies, and laugh and cry and kiss and scream at each other until we're old and wrinkly. And I'll love every second of it."

"You know how you said you'd die for me? I'd die for you, too."

Tears flooded her eyes until all his features blurred together. "Don't. Please don't."

He kissed her forehead. Together, as he drew her to his side, they turned their attention to the staff, buzzing and busy as if the restaurant were already open. He squeezed her. "Thank you, Scarlett."

"For what?"

Looking down his Italian nose, his eyes lit up like two candles. "For loving me even though my heart is broken."

"I could thank you for the same thing." She rested her head against his chest, in the precise spot where his heart beat. She listened, grateful for the even rhythm. "All of our hearts are broken, Fran. Just in different ways."

FIFTY-TWO

LITTLE ITALY, NEW YORK
SPRING, 1986

Francesco had a gift besides cooking. He could sleep through almost anything. It was the eleventh of April, and in a matter of hours, Amanti would open its doors to the public for the very first time. And Francesco was sleeping.

Scarlett didn't want to disturb him. He would be the one slaving over a hot stove all night. Although everything had been prepared to the point of perfection, she didn't have Francesco's gift. She got out of bed, careful not to wake him, and showered and dressed in a hurry. She wanted to get a head start on things.

The kitchen staff would arrive by noon to get everything prepared for dinner service. With Francesco writing such a big menu complete with dishes that required the precision and steady hand of a surgeon, the prep work would be critical to a smooth night in the kitchen. The bar was fully stocked and organized, the bottles chilled. They had ordered plenty of linens, and every surface, piece of flatware, and glass had been polished until it sparkled.

She walked through the restaurant in the still and quiet of the morning, memorizing the space and making mental notes. She noted the best tables, the most intimate ones, the ones with the best view, and the ones at the center of the hustle and bustle. The evening would be like a production, a well-rehearsed play, yet one that had no script. They could prepare all they wanted, but the night before them was unpredictable. The unknown of what was yet to come consumed her mind. This vacant building that was filled with physical representations of the art inside of them felt like a gift. A stage, on which they would shine.

A while later, Francesco jogged down the stairs. "Hi, honey." He wore a set of whites and an apron knotted around his hips.

"Hi." Still in joggers and a pair of sneakers, she went on her tiptoes to kiss him. "How are you feeling?"

He gave her a dazzling smile. "Better than ever."

"You promise?"

"I promise." He held her face and covered it in kisses. "I'm going to prep. You going to get ready soon?"

"Right now. You nervous?"

"Nah. Tonight is gonna be perfect."

"And if it isn't?"

"It will be. Trust me."

Scarlett took her time getting ready, reveling in the anticipation building inside of her. She wouldn't believe it was really happening until guests walked through the doors and the dining rooms were filled. She had always imagined partaking in the responsibility of ownership by herself, on a smaller scale. Never did she dream of having two dining rooms and a bar that she could call her own.

Not only did she have her restaurant, but she had someone whom she could trust with her whole heart. Someone who gave her days meaning and her soul new life. Someone who was home to her as much as New York was. She would make sure their place was a success not only for herself, but for him too. Their work was who they were, and the two of them combined only made them a stronger force. She knew what kind of things could go wrong over the course of the night, but she tried to push those thoughts out of her head. What she had to focus on was proving herself to Francesco, to New York City, to everyone who walked through their doors, and most importantly, to herself.

After she finished applying her makeup and styling her hair into a French twist, freshly dyed bangs framing her dark eyes, she slipped into her dress. Made of black velvet with a deep sweetheart neckline, the dress was comprised of long puff sleeves that were tapered at the wrists, a skirt that grazed the tops of her thighs, and a bodice encrusted with little crystal stars that gave her the glamour she craved for the night ahead. Though she was confident her feet would be numb by the time the evening was over, she wore heels anyway. It was the most important day of her life, save for her wedding day, and she had to look the part.

She would make the magic, and Francesco would make the food. Their life together would be built on the combination of both.

—⁓—

THE ENTIRE STAFF CONVENED in the main dining room on the first floor. The energy had changed. The restaurant no longer felt like an empty space, a blank slate, or a restaurant to be. It buzzed with the excitement not too dissimilar from that of a crowd waiting for a Broadway show to start. It felt like magic, the very magic that she and Francesco had craved but worried they didn't possess. Scarlett peeked out the frosted window-panes of the front door and saw all of the people lined up. They had invited every conceivable friend, acquaintance, and Francesco's few contacts in the press. She tried to press her face against the glass to see how far down the block the line went, but Francesco pulled her away by her waist.

"You look so, so beautiful," he said with a radiant smile.

She surveyed him in his crisp, new white chef jacket embroidered with his name in gold and put her arms around his shoulders. "So do you."

Francesco turned to face the staff. "Alright, everyone. Bring it in. We're about to open these doors for the very first time. We've got one shot at making a good first impression. Scarlett and I have trained you as best as we can. Now it's your turn to show us what we're made of at this restaurant." His speech was met with cheers and applause from their staff that, in time, Scarlett was sure would become like family.

"And whatever you need," Scarlett chimed in, looking out at their expectant faces, "you can come to me. We want tonight to go as smoothly as possible."

"Alright everyone, places!" Francesco clapped his hands as everyone dispersed to their stations, bracing for the night to come. And then, as he turned to her, everything else fell away. They were calm, tuning out the fact that their lives were about to change in a matter of minutes. They stared into each other's eyes like they were having a silent conversation with each other.

"No matter what happens tonight," he said softly, "I just want you to know how happy I am that I'm doing this with you."

"I am too."

"It's six," Mateo yelled from the entryway. "I'm unlocking."

"I love you." Francesco kissed her again.

"I love you more, Fran." She squeezed his hands before letting them go. Those hands would be busy tonight, creating their future with each dish that he plated. She watched him as he jogged back to the kitchen, his unruly hair bouncing with each step.

"Are we ready boss?" Mateo asked her.

"We're ready."

———

SCARLETT'S CHEEKS HURT FROM smiling so much. They had been open for all of two hours, but she had already welcomed almost two hundred people through their doors. She personally welcomed and sat each of them, filling both the upstairs and main dining rooms to capacity. The air held the delicious aroma of Francesco's creations as their waiters transported dishes from the kitchen to the tables. Cocktails flowed and bottles of champagne were opened, everyone clapping each time that delicious *pop* sound erupted. Tonight, everyone was celebrating.

She had wondered if working at her own place would resemble her days at Valenti's, but immediately, she noticed the difference. Everything she learned there had helped, but what she was doing tonight was already in her. An innate gift. The way she talked to people, the way she welcomed them into their place, how she made each person feel important – this was her magic. As she took in the sights of people savoring food and sipping on fine wine, the rise and fall of laughter and dinner talk, the glances of admiration and the nods of respect, she let the success of the night, the feeling it gave her, heal her wounds. It was only one night. The very beginning. But no matter the valleys that lay ahead, tonight, she stood tall on this mountain peak.

Francesco emerged from the kitchen as if he were walking on a cloud. Red, glowing cheeks, wild curly hair, a bright, toothy smile. No words needed to be exchanged, for they were so interconnected, one was not complete without the other. Thoughts were interchangeable. Scarlett reached for his hand and led him to the dining room, where, as one, they walked down the center aisle in between the tables filled with their first customers. The foundation of what was to come.

He, the man in white with his name in gold, the chef; she, the lady in black, dripping in crystals, the owner, and soon-to-be, the wife.

FIFTY-THREE

LITTLE ITALY, NEW YORK
SPRING, 1986

Scarlett spotted a figure with a mane of blonde hair sitting at her kitchen table as she walked back into the apartment after tending to wedding errands. Before she even saw her face, Scarlett knew it was her mother. "Mom?"

Lana turned around to look at her; then Francesco came into view. He was cooking for her.

"What are you doing here?" Scarlett asked as she reached the kitchen and set her bags down.

Lana stood. "I told you I'd call you." Lana hugged Scarlett, but Scarlett was in such shock that her arms remained dangling at her side.

"You were out, and I answered the phone. I invited her over,"

Francesco explained. He kissed Scarlett's forehead as he plated two dishes of pasta. "Sit."

"Why do you look so surprised?" Lana asked.

"Because I am." Scarlett blinked a few times. "I hoped you'd call, but I didn't know if you would."

"I'm going to let you two ladies talk." Francesco set the plates before them and stepped back. "I'll be downstairs if you need me." He gave Scarlett a reassuring smile before heading out the door.

"He's wonderful," Lana said. "He's so attentive to you."

"He is. I'm sorry." Scarlett shook her head, trying to be in the moment. "I wasn't expecting to see you here."

"Baby," Lana said, reaching for her hand, "I know I've disappointed you in the past, more times than I'd like to count. And I can't erase how awful things used to be between us."

"I know that."

"Now that I'm not drinking anymore, I can't tell you how much I regret everything, Scarlett," she cried, trying to catch her breath. "I just want another chance at this. At us. I don't want to let you down anymore, and I want to be there for you." Lana let out a meek smile, her eyes filled with hope. "I want to get to know you. Who you *really* are."

Scarlett squeezed her hand. "I want that too."

Scarlett had seen Lana cry so many times before, but never over her only daughter. It was always over a disappointment, a heartbreak, or from the sheer cause of drinking too much. But never, never over hurting Scarlett. Seeing her like this, Scarlett felt like the walls around her heart were crashing down. The tough façade she had put up had finally fallen away, and she felt like Lana was truly sincere. The cynic in her wanted to believe that things between her and Lana would never truly be normal, but Scarlett didn't know what it was. Things felt different. Lana wasn't there because she had to be; she was there because she wanted to be.

"You're going to be a great wife," Lana started. "And one day, you're going to be the best, best mother." She squeezed her eyes shut but the tears continued to fall out of them. "You're going to give your babies everything I didn't give you."

"Mom, please." Scarlett's mind had wandered to the idea of becoming a mother herself many times with the wedding getting closer. How could it not cross her mind? Every time she thought about being a mother, she thought about how she wanted to do things differently. How she wanted to be there for her babies, every step of the way. She wanted to be the one to wipe away every tear, to ease every concern, to nurture and to teach. She had never wanted to be anything like Lana, but seeing her in this new light, maybe Scarlett never got to experience the real her. Maybe Lana had another side to her altogether, one that Scarlett would get to know with time. Maybe they could start from scratch.

"He told me you're getting married next week," Lana said.

"We are." Though her throat tightened, Scarlett was determined to get the words out. "I'd like you to come, Mom."

"I'll come as long as you're sure you want me there."

"I want you there. I'm positive."

"Okay." Lana's eyes filled with a joy that Scarlett had never seen before. "My little girl is getting married. Isn't that crazy?"

They shared a laugh before Scarlett picked up her fork. "Our pasta is getting cold. Eat. He makes the best food you'll ever taste."

<hr/>

THE CHURCH OF THE Most Precious Blood was bustling. The lanterns over the archways were illuminated in a warm light, and bows made of tulle were wrapped around each of the pews. A satin runner lined the aisle and had been covered in white rose petals. The procession had begun, and no matter how many deep breaths she took or how many Hail Marys she said in her head, Scarlett couldn't calm her nerves. She trailed her fingers along the delicate lace of her wedding gown, embroidered with small crystals and pearls. In her dress, complete with a full skirt and long lace sleeves, and her head adorned with a sparkling crystal tiara, Scarlett felt like a princess. None of it felt real, and yet, she had never felt so alive, so present in her own body. She clutched onto her bouquet that was strung with the rosary beads Helen had given her as Fausto went next to her. He wore a dapper black tuxedo and his white shirt looked crisp against his tanned skin. She could hear the opening bars of her favorite, angelic song, "Nessun Dorma," beginning to play in the sanctuary. Fausto, who was giving her away, lifted the veil over her head until it covered her face.

"Watch my makeup," she warned him as the veil kissed the tip of her nose. "I want to look perfect when Fran sees me."

"You do." He smiled as he looped his arm in hers. "You ready?"

"Let's go," she said with confidence, despite every inch of her body trembling. The doors opened, and their small group of family and friends rose to watch the bride.

Though her veil and her tears blurred her vision, she took everything in. Lana sat in the first pew, her face a mix of emotions as she watched her daughter emerge down the aisle. Helen and Julie stood on the left side of the altar wearing matching lilac dresses. To the right were Enzo and Francesco. Once her eyes found Francesco, she saw nothing else. Even from a distance, she could see his golden eyes brim with tears, his features wrought with awe and joy. Her breath caught in her throat as she studied him in his ivory tuxedo jacket and the way his curls were slicked back in a way he had never styled them before. For however fast her heart was racing before, it pounded like a drum, low and steady. It was as if she were seeing Francesco for the very first time. She was struck by him, by how much love her heart held for him. She no longer cared about her appearance. She let each teardrop fall in its own nature, each one filled with a different emotion, ones she couldn't even explain.

When she reached him at the ornate dome-shaped altar, her nerves calmed. Francesco lifted the veil from her face and draped it behind her. It was so intimate, like no one was watching.

"You look like an angel." He gave her a crooked, genuine smile as his voice broke. "You're perfect."

"So are you."

The priest commenced the ceremony as they followed each prompt as they had rehearsed the night before. Rarely did they take their eyes off each other, as though they were speaking solely via eye contact. She felt so connected, so in tune with him. She hadn't considered how marriage might change their relationship or their way with each other; their lives were already so intertwined. But as they exchanged vows, staring into each other's eyes like they were seeing every inch of their souls, everything felt different. Out of all the places her life could have taken her, out of all the people she could have met, she was so glad everything brought her right here, to this moment. She was so glad it was him.

Once they were pronounced husband and wife, Francesco took her face in his hands and pulled her towards him as he kissed her with such excitement that it nearly knocked her off her feet. She kept him close, unable to wipe the smiles from their faces. Nothing would ever compare to this day. She was sure of it.

The bars of "Nessun Dorma" resumed with more energy now. They emerged down the aisle hand in hand, as one. They looked at each other amid all the cheers and applause like they were savoring the moment, savoring the fact that they were husband and wife. They were one, this day, an ending and a beginning all the same.

Outside, their guests threw rice into the air. It looked like tiny stars were trickling down onto them. She felt like things were moving in slow motion as she laughed and smiled and committed every last detail to memory. It was pure joy, this day. Even though she knew their life wouldn't be perfect, because nothing ever was, she would always think back and remember their wedding day – the day her life truly began. As they walked down the steps of the church, Francesco raised a fist in the air like a runner who had won a race, looking down ever so humbly as if to say *vincerò*. Victory.

Tramontate, stelle!
All'alba vincerò!
Vincerò, vincerò!

FIFTY-FOUR

LITTLE ITALY, NEW YORK

"I never wanted to believe my husband got his father's bad heart, but he did," Scarlett explained. They were well into their second bottle of wine, and despite her tolerance, it was getting to her. All of it. The wine, the lights, the cameras, the reliving her past, the moments that she would have liked to forget completely and the ones she would give anything to experience again. "The restaurant industry is tougher than most people understand. For a long while, he was putting in eighty hours a week, and working on the line is probably the hardest job there is. He had two heart attacks during our marriage. Mild ones. Until the last one. Four years ago." Tears rushed to Scarlett's heavily made-up eyes. "Like everyone else, we had our ups and downs, but we were on an *up*. It felt like the beginning all over again, and then I woke up one morning, and he was gone. He died in my arms."

She looked down at her wrist, at all the bracelets and jewels her Francesco had picked out for her with such care. A pang of sadness hit her. Out of all her losses, he was the greatest. It hit her at the strangest times that he wasn't really there anymore. The big occasions – birthdays, holidays, and graduations – but more often than not, it was the little moments that got to her the most. It was when she went into the kitchen in her restaurant, and she no longer found him behind the line. When she wanted to sit down at the table and tell him about her day. When she went home every night to a silent house, when she climbed into bed, and he wasn't there to wrap his arms around her. That was when she missed him the most, so bad that her heart physically ached.

Lucia watched Scarlett intently, though she didn't dare interrupt. By now, the words were flowing from Scarlett's mouth like a river.

"And now," Scarlett said with a heavy sigh, "now, this is all I have left of him. This *legendary* place we created together. I know to some, it might seem like some old, outdated restaurant. But this place means everything to me. Sometimes I look around, and it's like I see everything with a new appreciation. One different decision back then, and we wouldn't be sitting here right now."

"It's not just a restaurant," Lucia said. She shifted so that she was on the edge of the sofa. "That's what's so magical about places like yours. They're so much bigger than just a place to get something to eat. Legendary restaurants have history. Meaning. Something personal." Lucia's chest rose and fell before she leaned in. "I know I don't know you very well, but from what I can tell, you sharing this with me wasn't easy. I want to know why you decided to do this."

Scarlett rested her elbows on the tops of her knees, interlacing her fingers together. "The restaurant hasn't been doing so well these last few years. I don't know if it's that I can't keep up with the new, trendy restaurants, or if I don't want to. I'm not naïve to the fact that *change* and I aren't exactly the best of friends."

Scarlett gave a smile, though it faded. "I always use the excuse that it's for the kids. That's why I want to keep this place going, so I can pass it down to them. But the truth is, I don't think I'll ever be ready to let it go. I don't know what I'd do with myself or my life without it. And I don't think it's just because I lost my husband, or because I love what I do. This place made me who I am. And Enzo was right. Even when we have it all, there's that piece of ourselves that still feels like we're nothing. Sometimes I look in the mirror and I feel like I'm that same kid from Hell's Kitchen who knew she wasn't like the rest. Who felt so small and insignificant." A melancholy expression took over her otherwise beautiful face. "And then I look around. And I know I'm not *nothing*. Here, in this building, this restaurant, I'm everything."

Lucia crossed one leg over the other and adjusted the tablet on her lap. "I think some might argue that you're *everything* outside of this restaurant too. Many women look up to you, Scarlett. Myself included, even more so now that I know the whole story."

Scarlett raised her index finger. "That was only the *beginning* of the story."

Lucia laughed. "Do I need to make a part two of this documentary?"

Scarlett nodded, the last twenty-five years replaying in her mind like a movie reel. Maybe she had to retrace her steps in order to start anew. "You just might."

<hr />

AFTER LUCIA AND HER crew had gone for the night, dressed in a satin nightrobe, Scarlett wandered the main level of her Greenwich Village townhome, following the trail of moonlight on the white marble floor. On the wall closest to the fireplace hung a black-and-white portrait from

Scarlett and Francesco's wedding day. She reached up and ran her hands along the photograph.

"Thank you for sending her to me tonight. I think her film is going to help our restaurant," she said to the photo of her late husband. "I promise, I'm gonna keep our place going. I won't let us down." Though tears streamed down Scarlett's now makeup-free face, hope filled every crevice of her body. Because even though her husband wasn't here on this earth, he was always in her heart, and no matter what happened, he always would be. Love transcended both time and death. The strongest warrior, love could survive the toughest battles. She stepped away, her fingertips only grazing the glass of the frame. "I did it once. I'll do it again." And finally, she let go. "You and me," she whispered.

She could feel it, in her heart, in her soul, in every fiber of her being, that somewhere up above, Francesco was saying it back. *You and me, and me and you.*

ACKNOWLEDGEMENTS

As the great Giacomo Puccini once said, "The music of this opera (*Madame Butterfly*) was dictated to me by God. I was merely instrumental in getting it on paper and communicating it to the public." No, I am not equating this book to the likes of *Madame Butterfly*, but I often feel like a mere channel of stories that come from elsewhere. I would first and foremost like to thank God, for giving me the gift of storytelling, for bestowing this story on me, and for giving me the courage to share it with the world. He could have made me anything. I am so grateful He made me a writer.

My dear friend and business partner, Leigh Esposito, thank you for interacting with me on Instagram, to which we credit our chance meeting. Thank you for your infinite support, wisdom, Sicilian sisterhood, and for believing in my book from day one. I am grateful to be on this journey with you.

To my many editors and beta readers—Claire Strombeck, Carmen Catena-Lewis, Rosanna Chiofalo, Graham Schofield, and others—thank you for reading early drafts and giving me your insight. This book would not be what it is today without your help in shaping it.

I always say my characters come to me as they are, and I'd like to thank mine. Scarlett, you glamorous, gritty, Madonna-loving girl, I have loved seeing life through your lens these last seven years. I wrote the story of you discovering your value as a woman, and all the while, here in the real world, writing your story helped me discover mine. I wish you were real so we could be best friends. My dear Enzo, I don't know what it is about you, but I've always had a soft spot for you no matter what kind of trouble you got yourself into or mayhem you caused. Call me crazy, but I think you're quite endearing. Thank you for all the laughs. Francesco, out of anyone I've ever written, you feel the most alive. Where I see other characters in broad strokes, I can see your face clear as day. I wish we could attend the opera together and laugh about how every woman who has read this novel is most definitely madly in love with you. On that fateful evening in March of 2016 when I began writing the first draft of this book, the three of you stepped into my brain and took up what feels like permanent residence. Thank you for choosing me to be the scribe of your stories. Thank you for being my closest friends. Thank you for helping me discover my purpose. Thank you for making my dream come true.

To my many social media followers who have become my online family, thank you for your constant love and support, and for every view, like, save, share, and comment. I love our Sweet Paisana community!

To my beautiful aunts, my amazing uncles, and my countless cousins, I am so blessed to be a part of our big, beautiful family. I love each and every one of you.

To my grandmother, Carmela, our bond has been special since I was born, and I cherish my every moment spent with you. Thank you for being such a wonderful teacher, storyteller, nurturer, listener, and for filling my life with so much love. I can still hear you singing "That's How Much I Love You" to me in the car on the way home from school. More than I could ever explain, grandma—that's how much *I* love *you*.

To my mother, Liz, thank you for supporting and encouraging every dream I have had since I was a little girl, no matter how outlandish they may have seemed. You've always made me believe that I can achieve anything, and you never let me give up on this book even when I wanted to. Thank you for all of your strength, love, encouragement, laughter, and for being my best friend. I love you more than words, and I am so blessed to call you *mom*.

To the twenty-one-year-old I was when I started writing this, you did it, sweet girl. Thank you for opening up your laptop that night. Thank you for not shying away from the daunting task of writing a first draft. Thank you for never giving up. To future me, I can't wait to see what you'll write next (although I *think* I have an idea of what's coming) and where our words will take us.

And finally, to you, my dear reader. Thank you for reading these words and this story, all of which came right from my heart. May you always know that you are enough, just as you are.

Dearest Reader,

If you've made it this far, you must have found my life as interesting to read about as I found to live it. I suppose if my life didn't have some sort of peculiar element, I wouldn't have had a book written about me, am I right?

Now, I know it's not usually customary for characters to write directly to their readers, but *hello*, you know about some of the most intimate moments of my life. I'm a private person by nature, and I've just entrusted you with some of the darkest secrets of my past, some of which my own children no nothing about. I think that makes us friends, don't you?

What you've just read is a snapshot into where and how my life began. But allow me to let you in on a little secret about life: it's full of beginnings (and endings too, but I'm going for a positive tone here, so let's just focus on the beginnings). Life opened up for me the minute I stepped foot in Valenti's. The line of before and after was drawn when I married my husband. Life started all over, or as I like to say, it *truly* started, when I gave birth to my son Emilio. My world was turned right side up when I had my daughter Pia (and some days, she turns my world upside down. My daughter is a bit of a menace, but don't tell her I said that).

(No, I don't have a favorite child. What kind of Italian mother would I be if I did?)

When my beloved husband passed away four years ago, that was a beginning too. A new phase of life rolled out in front of me, and truth be told, I'm still working on navigating these new roads filled with bumps and blind spots and broken pieces. I'm not sure being a widow suits me, but then again, I'm not sure it suits anyone.

This story is only the first beginning. A lot of life has happened in the last twenty-five years, and if I have it my way, I plan on sharing those ups and downs, beginnings and endings, and you guessed it, more secrets. In the words of my brother-in-law Enzo, I'm no saint. I made costly mistakes and I've done things that no one else in this world knows about. But soon, you will. I just have to get Sarah to write my damn story. Don't you worry, my friend. I haven't left her alone since the minute I stepped into her brain seven years ago. I don't plan on starting now.

I will leave you with this, my friend. As a twenty-something year old, falling in love and discovering who I really was all at the same time, I felt many things. Excitement. Anticipation. Hope. Heartbreak. Disappointment. Some more hope. But above all else was *love*. Falling in and out of it, learning that love isn't a feeling at all. It's a series of

choices. To choose someone over and over again, day in, day out, is the truest form of love of all. To put someone else's happiness above your own; to be willing to *die* for the one you've chosen over all the rest. To find home in someone else's soul. I know how fortunate I am to have experienced love in this way.

I hope through reading my story, you feel love too. I hope you know that you deserve it. I hope that you'll wait for the kind of love that hunts you down no matter how hard you try to run; that gets into the deepest crevices of your heart; that ruins you because you know no other love will compare. Wait for the love that feels like light.

After all, what is life without love?

All my love, always,

Scarlett

Follow Scarlett's adventures on TikTok
@scarlettmarievalenti

ABOUT THE AUTHOR

SARAH ARCURI IS AN author, screenwriter, and lifestyle influencer who is beloved by her six-figure social media following. Like many of her characters, Sarah has a southern Italian heritage which serves as a large source of inspiration for her works. She began writing her debut novel, *The Owner & The Wife*, while living in Baltimore's Little Italy and working at neighborhood restaurants. Sarah graduated *summa cum laude* from the University of Maryland with a B.A. in Communications Studies. Her screenplays have placed in national competitions. When she is not writing, she can be found filming cooking and lifestyle videos for Instagram and TikTok, playing golf, or lounging on the sunny beaches of Florida where she resides.

@thesweetpaisana